THE
LOYALIST
WITCH

THE LOYALIST WITCH

Thieftaker: Fall 1770

D.B. JACKSON

LORE
SEEKERS
PRESS

THE LOYALIST WITCH: Theiftaker, Fall 1770

ISBN 978-1-62268-159-4

First Print Edition: November, 2021.

Individual novellas also available in e-book form:
THE WITCH'S STORM, ISBN 978-1-62268-156-3
THE CLOUD PRISON, ISBN 978-1-62268-157-0
THE ADAMS GAMBIT, ISBN 978-1-62268-158-7

Cover illustration by Chris McGrath.

Map reproduction courtesy of the Norman B. Leventhal Map Center at the Boston
Public Library.

Lore Seekers Press is an imprint of Bella Rosa Books.
Lore Seekers Press and logo are trademarks of Bella Rosa Books.

10   9   8   7   6   5   4   3   2   1

Dedications

THE WITCH'S STORM

For Nancy,
Again,
Always.

THE CLOUD PRISON

For the storytellers,
past, present, and future.
We are, all of us, part of a
long and noble endeavor.

THE ADAMS GAMBIT

For Alex and Erin,
With love, and with admiration for who you've become.

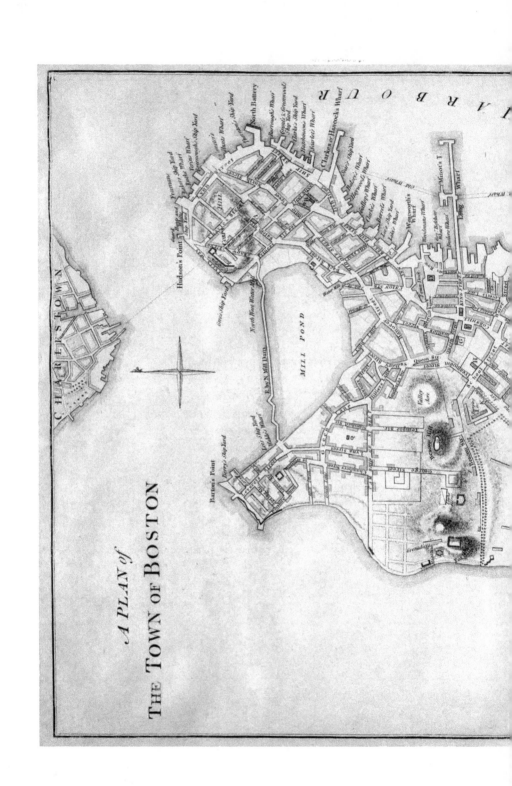

A PLAN of
THE TOWN of BOSTON

References to the Town.

A Christ Church
B Old North Meeting
C Anabaptise Meeting
D Faneuil Hall
E Town Hall
F Old Meeting
G Prison & Court House
H Kings Chapel
I Work House
K Granary Public
L Province House (General Gage)
M Old South Meeting (the Riding House)
N Trinity Church
O New South Meeting
P Friends Meeting
Q West Meeting

Scale of Yards.

Part I

THE WITCH'S STORM

I

Boston, Province of Massachusetts Bay, 16 October 1770

Ethan Kaille, former thieftaker, newly married bar hand, knelt on the well-worn wooden floor, setting the joint of a table leg. The *Dowsing Rod*, the tavern on Sudbury Street that belonged to his wife, Kannice Lester—and now to him as well—would be full in another hour, and this table, creaky and unbalanced, had been giving him fits since early afternoon. At last, he thought he had it fixed. He needed only to secure this last leg.

As he set the joint, a surge of magick through the tavern floor drove him to his feet. His hammer clattered on the wooden planks and the unsecured limb gave way once more. The sting of the spell tingled in Ethan's legs and feet.

"Ethan?"

Kannice regarded him from the bar, concern in her periwinkle blue eyes.

"I'm all right," he said, stooping to retrieve the hammer. "Someone cast a spell. A strong one."

"Janna?"

Tarijanna Windcatcher was, to his knowledge, the most powerful conjurer in Boston, and certainly the person most likely to be casting at any hour, day or night.

"Probably, yes."

He frowned as he spoke. The casting had seemed to come not from the Neck, at Boston's southern extreme, where Janna had her own tavern, but from somewhere close—the center of the city. Cornhill perhaps.

"You're humoring me."

Ethan met her gaze again. A wry smile curved her lips.

He grinned in turn. "A little bit." He walked to the bar, set down the hammer, and braced his arms on the worn wood. "The conjuring was too close to have come from Janna's place."

"Who else could it have been?"

"I don't know. That's what bothers me. There may be a new speller in the city."

She swiped a hand at a wisp of auburn hair that had fallen across her brow. "Whenever you speak of new conjurers, I get nervous."

"And why is that?"

"You have to ask?"

He didn't. Almost invariably the conjurers who arrived in Boston sought to do harm to the cause of liberty, or to innocents, or to Ethan himself. And on each occasion, it fell to him to thwart their dark ambitions.

"Maybe this one will be different," he said. "Maybe this speller, whoever he is, comes with saintly objectives and a pure heart."

She eyed him with such skepticism he could only laugh.

"Is that table fit to be used?" she asked.

"Almost." He returned to it and resumed his work. The buzzing in his legs had faded, but the remembered power of the casting continued to trouble him. He couldn't usually discern the intent of spells unless they were directed at him. For all he knew, this one had healed a wound or rescued a child from some dire fate.

He didn't think so, though. Like Kannice, he expected the worst.

Ethan completed his repairs and retreated into the kitchen as the tavern began to fill with its usual patrons. He crossed to the tavern's rear door and peered out at the alley behind. Leaden clouds darkened the sky, and a cold wind whipped through the streets and byways, carrying smoke from surrounding chimneys and the sour stench of fish and mud from the harbor shore. Not so long ago, he might have taken to the lanes in search of information about that spell and whoever had cast it. But he wasn't a thieftaker any more. At least not by profession. He was a bar hand. He belonged here, in the *Dowsing Rod*.

Not in front though, and not behind the bar. Kannice would assign him tasks later, as the crowd swelled. For now, he preferred to remain out of sight.

Marrying Kannice had brought him a certain legitimacy among her clientele. Most who frequented the *Dowser* no longer looked upon him with contempt as once they had. Many still considered him a ne'er-do-well, an unrepentant mutineer, but now that he was Kannice's husband, they did their best to hide their opinion. Kannice possessed a sharp tongue, and wasn't above banning men of even the most prodigious appetites and thirsts from her establishment if they gave offense. Most weren't willing to risk losing access to her fine stews and chowders.

To be fair, some of her regulars truly liked Ethan. Many though, still cast anxious glances his way when they thought he and Kannice weren't watching. They would claim to have forgiven him for his role in the *Ruby Blade* mutiny, but they remained afraid of him. Rumors of his "witchery" persisted, fed by the odd occurrences that had dogged him over the years.

Easier then to remain in hiding until Kannice and Kelf needed his help. Of course, for a time no one was more leery of him than the barman himself. Kelf knew beyond doubt that Ethan could cast, had seen him use spells to save Kannice's life the night of the bloody massacre on King Street. In the days immediately following, Ethan had thought their friendship damaged beyond all hope of repair. But the big man surprised him. Within a few weeks, he had made peace with the idea that Ethan was a "witch." Every now and then Ethan caught Kelf looking at him strangely, as if the barman thought to catch Ethan in the act of magicking. For the most part, though, their rapport had returned to how it was before that terrible night.

Ethan ate a bowl of stew—venison tonight; savory and rich and as delicious as Kannice's other concoctions—and filled a tankard with the Kent pale ale he preferred. Laughter reached him from the tavern's great room, along with an incomprehensible din of shouted conversations. But Ethan kept alert for additional pulses of magick, both dreading another spell and eager to try again to sense the conjurer's intent.

No spell came. He finished his stew and his ale, resisting the temptation to take more of either, and he returned to that open doorway, shivering in the wind, staring out as darkness gathered.

The truth was, he felt more than a little lost. He'd been a thieftaker for close to ten years. It was the only profession open to him when he returned from the prison plantation in the Caribbean, a convicted mutineer, disgraced, penniless. His thieftaking inquiries gave him more than a livelihood; they gave him an identity, a purpose. Giving them up had proven more difficult than he could admit to anyone. He missed tracking rum-dabbers and rooks and nappers. He missed casting spells. He even missed being hounded by Sephira Pryce and her toughs.

Kannice would think him insane if she knew.

"It's cold."

He turned. She stood in the middle of the kitchen, her cheeks flushed, her gleaming hair tied in a loose bun. She was lovely and brilliant and she loved him. He had no business lamenting the loss of a trade that nearly cost him his life day after day. He was fortunate beyond reckoning.

"It is." He reached for the door handle. "I can close this."

"No." She joined him on the threshold and took his hand. Her fingers were warm, smooth. "What are you doing?"

Being a fool. "Looking for conjurers, hoping the author of that spell will wander into this byway and cast again for my benefit."

A wind gust rattled the fence across the way from the *Dowser*. Kannice crossed her arms.

Ethan closed the door, pulled her close, and kissed her brow. She gazed up at him, worry creasing her brow.

"Are you all right?"

"I'm fine."

She narrowed her eyes.

"I promise."

"Well, all right then. We could use some help, if you don't mind."

He forced the creases from his brow, the tight lines from around his mouth. "Of course."

Her frown deepened, but he gestured for her to lead him out to the tavern, and fell in behind her.

The *Dowser* was more crowded than usual. The cold, harbinger of another harsh Boston winter, had driven people to seek comfort in Kannice's stew and the warmth of the tavern's stone hearth. For an hour or more, Ethan carried bowls, tankards, and rounds of bread to tables throughout the great room, until his bad leg ached and sweat ran down his face.

He caught snatches of conversation as he worked. Much of it was nonsense, but here and there men and a few women spoke in hushed tones of the trial set to commence in another week. At long last, the British soldiers accused of the shootings on King Street were to be held to account—not just their captain, Thomas Preston, but also the grenadiers: Messieurs White, Wemms, McCauley, Hartigan, Kilroy, Warren, Carrol, and Montgomery.

Ethan kept his thoughts to himself, but his stomach turned a slow, uncomfortable somersault. He'd been there that night, a stone's throw from the Town House. Yes, to his horror the soldiers fired their weapons into the crowd. Four died before sunrise, and a fifth was dead within ten days. And many others were wounded, including his friend, Devren Jervis, who lost an arm. But Preston and his men were goaded by the mob and, more to the point, were under the influence of dark magick. Ethan's magick, turned to malign purpose by Nate Ramsey, his sworn enemy. Ramsey was long since dead—Ethan had seen to that—and yet the consequences of his evil still plagued their city.

The throng in the *Dowsing Rod* lingered later than usual, only clearing out when Kannice announced deep into the night that she was weary, and sore of foot, and done serving them stew and ales. This was met with groans and good-natured grousing. Soon after, people began to file out into the night.

A few remained, however, including a cluster of men at a table at the back of the tavern. These included Tom Langer, long a regular in the tavern, who was well into his cups. Kannice watched him and his companions from the bar, her expression slowly curdling.

"They're doing no harm," Kelf told her, gathering another pile of empty bowls to carry into the kitchen.

"I'm not so sure."

Kannice's misgivings proved well-founded. Within a few moments, Tom was on his feet pounding the table with his fist to the approval of the others.

"I think they don't never intend to bring those men to trial! Preston, and the rest." As if anyone could be uncertain as to who he meant. "There's been delays and delays and delays. More than half a year past and still we haven't had justice done.

"Who knows what it'll be this time? They've got a hundred excuses, and they all lead to the same place. No trial! No justice! No punishment for them what deserves punishin'!"

"He's not wrong," Kelf said quietly, returning to the bar.

"Actually he is," Ethan said. "I was there, remember?"

The barman's face colored. He did remember. All of it. The attack on Kannice, Ethan's magick, and what Ethan later told him of the conjurings Ramsey had done to bring about the shootings.

Kannice stepped out from behind the bar. "Sit down, Tom. Or better yet, go home. It's late."

"We're just talkin', Kannice. There's no harm in that."

"There is when you're a fool who's spent too many hours drinking down my ale." She smiled to soften the words.

He cringed, even as he chuckled.

"Go home, all of you. I can't go to sleep until you do, and I'm tired."

Tom's companions stood, chairs scraping on the wood floor, and they shuffled toward the door, shrugging on overcoats and pulling on Monmouth caps.

Before they reached the entrance, however, the door swung open, revealing three figures in dark capes and tricorn hats. They entered, and the individual in front, who also carried a brass-tipped cane, reached to take off his hat.

"We're cl—" The word died on Kannice's lips.

The man had removed his tricorn and held it now in quaking hands, candlelight shining in dark blue eyes, his gray, plaited hair tousled by the wind.

To Ethan's surprise, it was Tom who found his tongue first.

"Mister Adams. Sir. This is . . ." He sketched a small bow. "This is an honor, sir. I wonder if . . . if you might allow a humble admirer to buy you an ale."

Samuel Adams' two companions removed their hats in turn, and Ethan recognized one, a tall, handsome man with dark eyes, as Doctor Joseph Warren. The other man was young, slight, and no taller than Adams. He was handsome as well, but his eyes were crossed, giving him a slightly odd aspect.

Kannice and Kelf spared not a glance for the other two men, but gaped at Adams, every bit as awestruck as Tom and the others.

"You're kind, friend," Adams said, laying a hand on Tom's shoulder. "And on another night I would gladly accept your generous offer. Tonight, though, I have business of an urgent nature that allows me no time for such pleasant pursuits."

"Business?" Tom said. "Here? At the *Dowser*?"

"Aye. With your friend there." He motioned in Ethan's direction with the cane. "Mister Kaille."

II

The way Tom and his friends stared at Ethan, one would have thought Adams had declared him the newly crowned king of England.

"Please make yourself at home, Mister Adams," Kannice said stepping past the patriot and his fellows to lead them to a table by the hearth. "We still have a bit of stew and bread, and more than enough ale for all of you."

"Thank you, but that won't be necessary, Missus . . ."

"Kaille," she said. "Kannice Kaille."

Adams faced Ethan. "Why, Mister Kaille. I had no idea. Congratulations to you both."

"Thank you, sir."

Adams, Warren, and the third gentleman arranged themselves around the table, the two younger men leaving the chair closest to the hearth for Adams. Ethan joined them, taking the empty seat across from Warren.

"Doctor Warren, it's good to see you again."

"And you Mister Kaille."

"This is Josiah Quincy," Adams said, indicating the young man with an open hand. "Josiah, may I introduce Ethan Kaille, thieftaker?"

"Josiah Quincy, *Junior*," Quincy corrected with a grin. "Father would insist." To Ethan, he said, "A pleasure, sir." He proffered a slender hand, his grip stronger than Ethan expected.

"An honor to meet you," Ethan said, and meant it. Quincy had a well-earned reputation as a passionate and eloquent advocate for the cause of liberty. "But I fear it's my turn to correct you, Mister Adams. I was a thieftaker, but I've retired from that profession. I'm a simple bar hand now."

Adams appeared to sag. "I'm sorry to hear that."

"He can still work for you," Kannice said from behind Ethan.

Ethan glanced back at her. She widened her eyes pointedly before facing Adams again. "He works here at the *Dowsing Rod*, but he retains all the skills he employed as a thieftaker. I'm sure he can help you."

Ethan turned back to Adams and gave a small shrug. "It seems my services are available."

If Adams found Ethan and Kannice's exchange amusing he kept it to himself. Instead, he dipped his chin with grim resolve. "I'm glad, because I believe this is a matter uniquely suited to your talents."

Magick. Ethan's thoughts returned to the spell he'd sensed earlier.

"Out you go, lads," Kannice said to Tom Langer and the rest. "No more gawking."

"G'night, Mister Adams." Tom peered over Kannice's head and raised a hand. His friends waved.

"Yes, good night," Adams called. "Be well, gentlemen, and thank you for your support of our great cause."

Kannice ushered them out into the night, and locked the door when they were gone. Then she joined Kelf behind the bar. There, she began to wipe down the wood, though she confined her efforts to that part of the bar nearest their table.

"How can I help you?" Ethan asked, his gaze flicking to each of the men. Warren regarded him somberly, but held his tongue. Ethan guessed that he deferred to Adams. Quincy, on the other hand, shifted in his chair, seeming eager to speak.

"Go ahead, Josiah."

The young man faced Ethan. "You are aware, I'm sure, of the trial set to begin next week."

"I am." A memory stirred, something Ethan should have recalled earlier. "You're helping John Adams with the defense, aren't you?"

"I am. And my brother, Samuel, is leading the prosecution."

Ethan straightened. "Isn't that a little odd?"

"It gets odder. He is a loyalist. I am decidedly not. And yet he seeks to condemn the King's men while I advocate for their lives."

Ethan had never heard of such an arrangement. "What kind of trial will these men have?"

"An uncommonly fair one, I believe," Adams said. "Which is what we have wanted from the start."

Ethan didn't respond.

"You know better than to doubt me, Mister Kaille. You will remember speaking to me mere days after the shootings. At the time, I had already urged John to take on the defense of the soldiers. These men must have a fair trial, not only because their lives are at stake—though that is reason enough—but because the world watches us. This is a test of what sort of nation we would be."

"And the possibility of an acquittal—"

"An acquittal is quite beside the point. The question ought not to be whether these men fired their weapons or whether they were provoked by the mob, or even whether Captain Preston ordered them to shoot. Of course they fired their weapons. And of course they were provoked. You told me yourself that all of them—the soldiers and the mob—were under the malevolent influence of a . . . a conjurer, as you call your kind. Isn't that right?"

"Aye, sir."

Adams opened his hands. "Well in that case, these men are both innocent and guilty. Any verdict will be wrong, and any verdict will be justified. Which is why we cannot be distracted from the larger import of what is about to take place in the Queen Street courthouse. British tactics themselves are on trial. The deaths of Crispus Attucks, Patrick Carr, and the others are not the fault of Preston or his men, but rather of King George III and his Parliament. One might argue that convicting these soldiers would absolve the Crown of blame, which I certainly don't want. And before you ask," he added, "Thomas Hutchinson is even more frightened of an acquittal than I am. And he's also terrified of a conviction. Any result, he fears, will bring renewed violence, which is why he seeks to put off for as long as possible this day of reckoning."

Even before the occupation and the King Street shootings turned Ethan to the Patriot cause, he had been impressed with Adams' intellect. To this day, he didn't always agree with the man's tactics, and was discomfited by the single-mindedness with which he pursued his political aims. He couldn't deny, though, that every conversation he had with Adams forced him to alter his view the world.

Throughout Boston, supporters of the Sons of Liberty spoke of nothing but the trial. And all of them, as far as Ethan could tell, including Kannice, Diver, Tom Langer, and others here in the *Dowser*, desperately hoped for a conviction. They would have been shocked to hear that Adams didn't. Ethan doubted that any of them except Kannice would have appreciated and understood the subtlety of the man's reasoning.

"This is all well and interesting," Warren said, his smooth baritone drawing their gazes. "But it's not why we came."

Adams sat back, his mouth twisting with displeasure. Ethan thought he would have enjoyed passing the night in conversation about the trial and provincial politics. "No," he said instead, "it's not."

"Mister Quincy indicated that you came to speak of the trial."

"And we did," young Quincy said. "But not the merits of either case. We're here, Mister Kaille, because the trial itself is in danger."

"In danger from . . ."

Quincy darted a glance to Adams, who nodded encouragement. Turning his odd gaze back to Ethan, he said, "I don't know how to speak of it other than to call it witchery."

Ethan inhaled slowly, not wanting to snap at the man. *It's not witchery.* "Someone used a conjuring?"

"Aye, a . . . a conjuring."

"Can you describe what the spell did?"

"It snapped the axle of a carriage that bore my brother's partner in prosecution, Mister Paine."

Robert Treat Paine was another prominent Whig here in the city. Some in the Patriot cause, alarmed by Samuel Quincy's appointment as chief prosecutor of the soldiers, had insisted that Paine be added to the prosecutorial team to ensure a vigorous pursuit of the soldiers' conviction.

"Was he hurt?"

"Thank goodness, no. Shaken, but uninjured. Still, in light of the rest of what's happened, we felt we had no choice but to engage your services."

Ethan frowned and looked at the other two men. "There have been other attacks?"

"Only threats," Adams said.

Warren shook his head. "Not only."

"A minor incident, Joseph."

"Perhaps we should allow Mister Kaille to judge how minor."

The incident in question turned out to be an act of vandalism at the home of Samuel Quincy. Two windows had been broken, and a threat had been smeared in mud on the side of the man's house. "Prosecute the King's men," it said, "or protect your family. You cannot do both."

According to Warren, Samuel Quincy and Robert Treat Paine had received other threats as well, all of them in the form of anonymous missives left at their homes in the wee hours of the night, all of them coming within the last fortnight. No one had seen the person or persons who left them, just as no one saw the vandal. The written threats, several of which Josiah produced from within his coat, were vague, scrawled in a spidery hand, written in complete and cogent sentences, though marred by smudges of ink. Each hinted at economic hardship or physical harm should the lawyers follow through on their intention to advocate on behalf of Preston and his men.

The three watched Ethan as he studied the messages, as if they expected him to cast a spell. And the truth was, he wanted to. He had no reason to believe these messages had been created or delivered with spells, but it was possible, especially if those issuing the threats had used conjurings for other purposes. He didn't wish to cast in front of these men, however, or in front of Kelf. Their friendship had healed since the night of the shootings, but the barman still did not approve of Ethan's abilities.

"Well?" Warren asked after some time. "What do you make of those?"

"The same as you probably do," Ethan said, handing them back to Quincy. "They strike me as no more or less than what they appear to be. Threats: menacing, but unimaginative."

"And is there magick attached to them in some way?"

"I don't know. I would have to cast to be certain."

"Why don't you then?"

Ethan hesitated, discomfited by the doctor's intense scrutiny.

"I would suggest we leave the missives with Mister Kaille," Adams said, seeming to sense Ethan's unease, "and he can ply his craft later. In the meantime, we should show him the carriage."

"Tonight?"

"Well, yes. It will have to be moved by tomorrow."

Ethan leaned forward, pulse quickening. "The carriage was attacked this evening?"

"Yes, just a short while ago."

The spell he sensed. "Where?"

"It's not far," Adams said. "It happened on Cornhill, near the Old Brick Meeting House."

Exactly where he'd thought.

"Aye, all right," Ethan said, standing.

The others pushed back from the table and began to pull on their coats.

"Thank you, Missus Kaille," Adams said, reclaiming his cane. "And to you, good sir," he added with a nod for Kelf.

Kannice dipped a curtsy, something Ethan wasn't sure he had ever seen her do. "It was an honor, Mister Adams."

"The honor was ours, dear lady. I'm afraid, however, that we must borrow your husband for a short while. I hope you will forgive us."

She looked to Ethan; he stepped closer to her.

"You remember the spell I felt earlier?" he whispered.

"Yes, of—" Understanding sharpened her gaze. "You mean that's what they came to discuss?"

"So it would seem. I'll tell you more when I get back."

Warren led them out into the cold. The sky had darkened to a hard, starless black, but if anything the wind had stiffened. Ethan pulled his coat tighter, anchored his tricorn with one hand, and limped alongside the others. Warren forged a grim path down Sudbury Street toward the heart of the city. The wind buffeted their backs—a small mercy—pushing them along toward Cornhill. As they walked, Ethan plucked shriveled leaves from the trees they passed, doing his best to keep his harvest concealed. He anticipated that he would need to cast at least one spell when they reached the carriage, and he didn't wish to cut himself if he didn't have to.

As they turned onto Queen Street, Ethan did this for the third or fourth time.

"What do you intend to use them for?" Quincy asked.

Ethan eyed him sidelong, earning a disarming smile. He hadn't been as stealthy as he'd hoped.

"I'm not sure I can explain."

"It has to do with your magicking?"

"He doesn't like to speak of such things, Josiah," Adams said from ahead of them. "I'd imagine he fears being hanged or burned for a witch." He glanced back, eyes dancing.

"I do, yes." To Quincy, Ethan said, "Spells require . . . fuel, for lack of a better word. Something that has been alive. Most times we use blood, but in a public setting that isn't always practicable. Leaves or bark or grass can work instead."

"Even such leaves as these? Old, stubbornly clinging to branches long after their brethren have fallen?"

"For the most demanding conjurings I prefer fresh greens, but for tonight's purposes, I believe these will do."

They walked by the courthouse and turned onto Cornhill Street, their footsteps echoing off the façade of the Town House, with its gable and familiar clock. Ethan's bad leg had begun to ache, the hitch in his stride growing more pronounced with every step.

"What did you do to yourself?" Quincy asked. Ethan wondered if he was always so inquisitive.

"It's an old wound," he said, purposefully vague. The man already knew him for a conjurer. He wasn't ready to reveal that he was an ex-convict.

"Over there," Adams said, pointing.

Just past the stolid bulk of the Old Brick, and before the graceful spire of the South Meeting House, stood a black carriage, its front supported by wheels, its hind portion resting crookedly on the cobblestone. One of its rear wheels had rolled free and lay in the center of the lane. The other was still attached to the broken axle and angled inward. The horses had been released from their harnesses and taken away. A few onlookers gawked at the carriage, though from a distance.

"You'll need to send them away," Ethan said to Adams, his voice barely carrying over the sound of their steps.

"Of course."

In the darkness, touched only by candlelight leaking from a few windows, the carriage resembled the carcass of some great beast. Ethan wanted to look more closely, but he waited until Adams and the others had cleared the lane. Then he crawled under the carriage and using a single leaf, summoned a dim glow to his palm.

Holding his hand near to the ruined axle, he examined the break. It looked natural. He saw no sign that the wood had been weakened with any sort of blade.

Using two more leaves, he cast again. "*Revela magiam ex foliis evocatam.*"

Reveal magick, conjured from leaves. Power snarled in the stone beneath him, an answer of a kind to the conjuring he'd felt earlier. The ghostly figure of an ancient knight materialized beside him, russet eyes gleaming beneath the carriage: his spectral guide, whom he called Uncle Reg, after his mother's waspish brother. Ethan eyed the ghost, but Reg kept his gaze fixed on the axle.

A tinted glow appeared on the wood, faint at first, but brighter by the moment. It was red, the color of fine wine: deep and rich. Whoever had cast the spell wielded deep magick—as potent as Ethan's, if not more so.

"Can you tell when the spell was cast?" he asked Reg.

The ghost gave a tentative nod.

"I felt something this evening, around dusk. Could it have been cast then?"

Reg answered with a more confident dip of his chin.

"Can you tell where it came from?"

A shake of the glowing head.

There were other spells he could try, one that might tell him what the conjurer had used to fuel this casting, and another—a finding spell—that could tell him where this man was now. But the first wouldn't shed much light on the matter, and the second would alert this person to Ethan's interest in finding him, which would be counterproductive. He did cast a spell to conceal that red magick, begrudging the thrum of power that accompanied his casting. The conjurer would sense it, just as Ethan had sensed the earlier spell, but there was nothing to be done. He couldn't leave the carriage glowing in that way without drawing attention to himself and this incident.

He tucked his last two leaves into a pocket and crawled out from beneath the carriage. Uncle Reg followed him, invisible to all who weren't conjurers as well.

"What did you find?" Warren asked. The three patriots gathered around him.

"I've confirmed your suspicions. It was magick that broke the axle."

"Damn," Adams said, rapping the butt of his cane on the street. "I would have preferred we were wrong. You're certain?"

"I'm afraid so. All spells leave a residue. And using a spell of my own, I was able to make that residue visible."

"As color!" Quincy said, his voice rising. "I saw it coming from under the carriage! It was red, isn't that right?"

"Yes, sir."

"Does that color mean anything to you?"

Ethan shook his head. "Not really. Every conjurer's power looks different. Mine is similar to this, but more russet than burgundy. If I knew the conjurer, I might recognize the hue. But as it is . . ." He shrugged.

"Does the conjurer wear this color? I see nothing on you, but I don't have your gift."

"No, sir. But knowing his color should allow me to trace other spells, future spells, back to this person."

Quincy's brow furrowed. "I see." Ethan had the impression the young man had expected more from his magick.

"Is there more you need to see?" Adams asked him.

Ethan crossed to the wheel lying in the lane and squatted beside it, scrutinizing the broken stub of axle still attached. He assumed a revealing spell on this would show the same red magick.

"I don't believe there is, sir," he said to Adams, straightening. "I would like to speak with Mister Paine, though."

"We can arrange that for tomorrow. In the meantime, the Sons of Liberty wish to engage your services."

"To what end? I'm a thieftaker. Or I was. I recovered stolen goods and was paid a fee for their return. In this case—"

"In this case," Warren broke in, "attorneys for the province are being menaced, their lives may be at stake. None of us is equipped to protect them. You are, simply by dint of your magicking abilities. We require your help."

"This trial must go on, Mister Kaille," Adams said, his tone more gentle than Warren's. "Surely you understand that. As I said before, the world watches us. If we cannot even try these men fairly, honorably, how are we to assume our place among civilized nations?"

"If it's the pay you're worried about—"

"It's not," Ethan said, his tone hardening as he rounded on Warren.

"Have done, Joseph."

"I meant no offense," the doctor said. "Truly. You have skills we require. You *should* be paid, and we have the means to do so."

"I don't question your means—as individuals or as an entity. But I wouldn't know how to gauge my success or failure. This isn't like recovering a stolen watch."

"That part seems easiest to me," Warren said. "When you find this conjurer, when he is placed in gaol for his offenses, you will have succeeded."

"The problem, Doctor, is that conjurers can't be placed in gaol. There isn't a prison on this continent that would hold the person who cast this spell."

At that, the three patriots shared glances, consternation flickering in Warren's features, frustration in Adams'. Alone among them, Quincy appeared to enjoy the intrigue.

"How then do we stop him?" Warren asked.

"I don't know." He stared at the broken wheel again, thoughts churning. He didn't want this job; he didn't like where it was certain to lead him. But he couldn't refuse them. *Whenever you speak of new conjurers, I get nervous,* Kannice had said earlier this evening. So did he, and this was why.

"I'll work on your behalf," he said, and was humbled by the relief he read on all of their faces.

"And how will we pay you?" Warren asked.

"We'll worry about that once I've dealt with this speller."

He didn't give voice to the thought that followed. *Provided I survive.*

III

Upon Ethan's arrival back at the *Dowser*, Kannice led him up to their room and proceeded to question him about every moment he spent with Samuel Adams. Most times, she wasn't easily impressed, and she and Ethan had been together long enough that he no longer felt the need to try. But nothing he'd ever done had impressed her more than having the great man himself come to her tavern looking for him. She kept them both up for almost two hours talking about the night's events.

In the morning, when Ethan told her that he needed to head into the lanes to investigate the attack on Robert Treat Paine, Kannice all but pushed him out the door. Whatever lingering concerns she harbored about him returning to his life as a thieftaker, she was more than willing to set them aside if it meant another encounter with Samuel Adams.

Ethan made his way first to the home of Mister Paine, where he and Adams had arranged to meet. Paine lived in a stately brick structure on the corner of Milk Street and Long Lane. The house was two stories high, with a broad gambrel roof and gardens that stretched far back along the lane.

Dark clouds still blanketed the sky, and the wind blew unabated, although the air had warmed somewhat with the arrival of morning. Cows lowed in nearby d'Acosta's pasture and crows scudded overhead, appearing helpless before the gale. The smells of chimney smoke and harbor brine lay heavy over the city.

A young red-haired servant admitted Ethan to the mansion and led him to a room overlooking the gardens. Adams and Paine awaited him there. Adams kept his seat, but Paine stood to greet him, extending a firm hand and offering a word of welcome, his voice deep.

He stood several inches taller than Ethan, with a mane of dark hair that he wore swept back from a steep brow. He was handsome, though with a severe aspect, and carried himself stiffly, his coat and cravat perfectly tailored and immaculate.

A second servant, older than the woman who had admitted Ethan to the mansion, entered the room carrying a platter that bore a teapot, cups, and saucers. As she placed these on a low table, Ethan sat, taking in his surroundings. The furnishings and art were tasteful and tidy, the housekeeping as fastidious as the man himself.

"Samuel tells me that you have some experience in taming the more savage elements of Boston's streets," Paine said after a brief silence. "He says you've agreed to track down those who have been harassing me these past weeks. I'm grateful."

"I'll do all that I can, sir."

"He indicated as well that you would have questions for me."

"I do. I'd like to begin with the unfortunate incident involving your carriage. Can you tell me if you saw anyone or anything unusual in the moments just before the axle broke?"

He answered with a small shrug, the gesture appearing odd on such a formidable man. "I saw nothing. I was on my way back here from the courthouse. I was . . . looking at papers, my thoughts occupied by my work. The disabling of the carriage caught me entirely unprepared."

"What about the other incidents?"

"Missives scribbled on parchment and thrown at my home. Acts of cowardice. I saw no one, heard nothing. Just as the perpetrators intended."

Ethan had expected as much. "Have you noticed unfamiliar faces in the street outside your office or at the courthouse?"

Paine shook his head. "Not that I recall. The courthouse and gaol occupy the same structure, so it won't surprise you to hear that I see more than my fair share of miscreants on a daily basis. The person or persons harrying Samuel and me—Samuel Quincy, that is—I expect they would blend in with the sort of men I see whenever I visit Queen Street.

"The fact is—and I know Samuel will chide me for saying so—the rabble in Boston's streets, even those who flock to our cause, are not the sort of men I would want to treat with on a regular basis. Moreover, there is very little to separate those who clamor for liberty from those who cling to the Crown. They are all of them brutes."

"Robert . . ."

Paine glanced at Adams before sharing a knowing look with Ethan. "I told you he would object."

"Do you have a theory then?" Ethan asked. "An idea of who might be leaving these messages?"

"Loyalists, obviously. Enemies of liberty who know that Preston and his men are doomed to be convicted and therefore seek to avoid a trial entirely."

Ethan certainly agreed this was the most obvious explanation. He wasn't sure, however, that this made it the most convincing.

"Well, thank you, Mister Paine," Ethan said, standing. "I don't wish to take up more of your time."

Paine levered himself out of his chair. "Not at all. I'm grateful to you for coming, and for helping us." He paused, casting an uncertain look at Adams. "Do you intend to . . . to guard our home, or the office?"

"No, sir, that's not—"

"Mister Kaille's talents are more investigative than martial," Adams said. "With some luck, he'll help us locate the people responsible."

"Yes, of course." Paine kept his tone bright, but Ethan sensed his disappointment. First Josiah Quincy and now this man. If he wasn't careful, he would gain a reputation for failing to meet expectations.

Paine saw Ethan and Adams to the door and bid them farewell. The two headed back toward Cornhill in silence. Ethan tried to think of other reasons someone might attempt to disrupt the prosecution of the soldiers, and as they turned onto Marlborough Street, he drew breath to ask Adams if he could think of any. At that moment, though, another surge of magick hummed in the cobblestones. He halted, swaying, trying to discern its origin. Like the first spell the night before, it hadn't come from far off. He thought it had been cast north of where he stood. The center of the city, again.

"What is it?" Adams asked, looking back at him.

"Yesterday, before you came to the *Dowsing Rod*, I felt a conjuring, probably the one we now know struck Mister Paine's carriage. I've just felt another spell." He pointed northward. "From that direction."

Adams peered that way before facing Ethan again. "Shall we investigate, then?"

"Do you have powers I don't know about, sir?"

Adams grinned. "Hardly, but I do enjoy a mystery."

They hurried on, only slowing when they had reached the market at Faneuil Hall in the busiest part of the city. There, his leg aching, Ethan halted and turned a circle. Adams watched him. All around them, men and women went about their business as if nothing had happened. Because, of course, nothing had as far as they were concerned. Ethan searched for a spectral guide like Reg, or for anyone who appeared as interested as he in the reactions of others. He saw neither.

Instead, he spotted something most unexpected. Sephira Pryce walked toward them, chatting amiably with an attractive well-dressed man, her arm hooked through his. So absorbed was she in their conversation that she didn't notice Ethan or Samuel Adams until Nap, one of the two toughs walking ahead of her and her companion, said something over his shoulder.

At this she slowed, ice-blue eyes scanning the lane until they alit on Ethan and Adams. Her lips curved.

She looked as lovely as ever, black curls flowing over her shoulders, a royal blue cape draped around her. She wore black breeches and leather boots. Ethan was certain she carried weapons—at least a blade or two—but she appeared the very essence of feminine charm and beauty, her chin tapered, her cheekbones high, her steps feline and fluid.

The man on her arm was nearly a match for her. His eyes were bright green, his chin square, his cheeks dimpling with a roguish grin in response to something she said. He was taller than she, lean, but also graceful. He wore a red cape and tricorn hat over what Ethan took for a green silk ditto suit.

The toughs with them had dressed with far less care, but they looked as dangerous as always: Nap, wiry and watchful; Gordon, homely and as huge as a seventy-gun ship of the line.

"Do you know the man with Sephira Pryce?" Ethan asked, marking their approach.

"I do." Adams said this with such venom, Ethan turned his way. "His name is Francis Lamb. He's the newest addition to the Customs Board."

"I see." Ethan thought of his brother-in-law, Geoffrey Brower, who was also a customs man, as well as a buffoon.

"Don't let that fool you, Mister Kaille," Adams went on, his voice low. "I know what people think of the customs men. I, myself, hold them in low regard. Lamb is different: canny, subtle. I wouldn't be surprised to learn that he's a spy for the Crown. Or worse. Don't underestimate him."

"Could he be our culprit?"

"Possibly, though these attacks strike me as too blatant for such a man." Adams glanced at him. "But I believe that's a question we've hired you to answer."

Ethan had no time to reply.

"Ethan!"

Only Sephira Pryce could fill his mere name with so much derision. He resisted the impulse to wince. Instead, he removed his tricorn. Adams did the same.

"Sephira, how unexpected."

"I was thinking the same thing. Weren't you put out to pasture?" Before he could answer, she turned to her companion. "This is Ethan Kaille, my dear. He was once—and is now apparently again—a thieftaker of limited skill and extraordinary unimportance. He fancied himself a rival to me, but, of course, never has been."

Both Adams and Lamb eyed the two of them, Adams with something approaching alarm, Lamb with faint amusement.

"How long did it take, Ethan?" Sephira went on. "I told you back when first you spoke of leaving the lanes that the arrangement wouldn't last. That was . . . what? March? And here it is October, and already you've proven me right."

He didn't attempt to argue the point. He *was* back in the lanes, and he couldn't bring himself to say, *Kannice gave her permission.* He knew what she would do with that tidbit.

"How have you been, Sephira?" he asked. "You look unchanged."

"How kind."

"Not really, no."

Her face and neck flushed, the smile ossifying. She cast a self-conscious peek at her companion. While she still recovered, he extended a hand to Lamb.

"Ethan Kaille."

"Francis Lamb. It's a pleasure to meet you."

"And you. I assume you're acquainted with Samuel Adams."

Lamb's grin rimed over and he didn't offer his hand. "Samuel."

"Good morning, Francis, Miss Pryce."

They stood thus for perhaps five seconds, tense, silent, currents of hostility flowing in all directions.

Sephira opened her mouth, probably to make some excuse and move on. Ethan wasn't ready to allow that.

"How long have you been with the Customs Board, Mister Lamb?"

"Not long. I only arrived in Boston in August. I was appointed to the board about a month ago."

"I see. And what do you think of our city?"

His gaze flicked toward Adams. "Like so many colonial cities, she reminds me of a girl just finding her way to womanhood. She is pretty enough, but she requires refinement and a firm hand, lest lack of discipline compromise her virtue."

"A flawed analogy if ever there was one," Adams said. "But I would expect as much: Servants of the crown have long confused liberty with licentiousness."

"You deny that one leads to the other?"

"I do. You compare the citizens of this fair city to children coming into adulthood. Very well, let us extend the metaphor. As with children of even the most mild disposition and pure intention, the more you seek to control them, the tighter the restrictions you place upon them, the more they will seek to rebel. Liberty, I would remind you, is the natural condition of mankind. Every limitation placed upon it is an affront to God's will."

Lamb took a half step forward, clearly intent on continuing their argument. Sephira, though, tugged on the arm she still held.

"Francis, darling, I'm bored. The weather is dreary enough. Let's not spoil what has been a lovely morning with more talk of politics."

It appeared to take some effort, but Lamb reined himself in. "Of course. Forgive me. We should continue our walk."

"We started at Copp's Hill and have been through all the loveliest lanes of the North End," Sephira explained. "Now we're on our way to Beacon Hill, and then the South End. By the end of the day, Francis will know the city as well as I do."

A thousand quips sprang to mind, none of them generous, but Ethan bit them all back. Nothing would come of baiting her further.

"That sounds very pleasant, Sephira. I hope you both enjoy the rest of your adventure."

She narrowed her eyes, likely sifting through his words for some sign of mockery. Finding none only deepened her frown. They said their farewells and moved on, leaving Ethan and Adams to stare after them.

"A despicable man," Adams said.

"Well, he's found his perfect match."

"Yes, you seem to dislike her as much as I detest him."

"I have cause," Ethan muttered, scanning the lane again. "As I'm sure you do."

"Indeed." Adams surveyed the street too. "It sounds, though, as if they've been together for the entire morning. If he conjured, he did so with Miss Pryce watching."

They resumed their search of the city, walking first to the waterfront near Long Wharf. From there, they headed up King Street toward the Town House, both of them growing pensive as they approached the site of the shootings. Ethan thought of Diver, whom he saw with far less frequency since that terrible night. His friend had grown sober and responsible, devoting himself to Deborah Crane, to whom he was now engaged, and his work as a shop clerk. But he had also lost much of the exuberance and spirit that Ethan had admired since they first met, when Diver was still a boy and Ethan an idealistic sailor seeking work in the New World. He understood—Diver's grievous wound might have broken lesser men—but still it saddened him. He missed his old friend.

They passed the Town House, crossed Cornhill, started up Queen Street. As they reached the courthouse, Adams mumbled, "Well, that's odd."

Ethan eyed him and then followed the line of his gaze. Across the street from the gaol entrance, Adams' cousin, John Adams, stood outside his law office, fists on his hips. He wore no coat, despite the wind, and his head was uncovered.

Adams quickened his pace and Ethan followed.

"What's happened, John?"

John Adams turned at the question, nearly overbalancing. He was shorter than his cousin, and rounder. Where Samuel remained somewhat dashing, notwithstanding the graying of his hair and the deeper lines in his face, John was odd in appearance, with a weak chin and heavy eyebrows.

"What are you doing here?" he asked Samuel. He slanted a glance Ethan's way. "Mister Kaille is it?"

"Yes, sir. I'm flattered you remember."

"John?" Samuel prompted.

"Well, it was most odd," John Adams said. "One moment, we were both working at our desks, and the next, one of the windows simply . . . well, exploded."

"Are you all right?"

"I'm fine. As I say, I was at my desk, in my office. But poor William—" To Ethan, he said, "William Tudor, my clerk."

"Yes, sir. I met Mister Tudor when I visited your office."

"Ah, indeed. In any case, William was showered with glass and suffered a number of small cuts. He was fortunate not to have worse. If one shard had struck an eye . . ." He shook his head.

"Do you have any idea what caused the glass to break?" Ethan asked, having an idea himself.

"I don't. We haven't found anything inside—no brick or stone or piece of metal. Perhaps someone with a hammer . . ."

Ethan met Samuel Adams' gaze.

"Would you mind if we looked around?" Samuel asked. "Mister Kaille is an investigator. He may notice things you and I would miss."

"Of course. I'd be most grateful."

John Adams led Ethan and Samuel into his law offices, which consisted of two rooms, a larger one out front, and a private office in back, where John had his desk, bookshelves, and papers. The window in question was about halfway back along a side wall, not far from William's desk.

John had not exaggerated. Glass lay everywhere, crunching under foot, glittering with candlelight on the desktop and shelves. Two small drops of blood stained the desk wood. Wind had blown papers onto the floor. The entire windowpane was gone, save for small uneven crescents in each corner, and a few nubs along the edge of the wood. Ethan saw no objects that might have been thrown through the window and, more to the point, he didn't believe any object could have done this sort of damage to the glass. He had a good deal of experience with such things, having investigated more house guttings than he cared to count. Certainly, a window could be broken this thoroughly, but not with a single blow. Or rather, not with one *physical* blow. Magick, however, could have done it. When opportunity allowed, he would check the window for the residue of a spell.

"Where is William now?" he asked John Adams, after orbiting the room two or three times.

"I sent him to Benjamin," the man said absently. After a moment, he faced Ethan. "Forgive me. Benjamin Church, a doctor and friend. He lives in the South End. I told William he was done for the day and sent him off."

Ethan knew Doctor Church, and had been to his home.

"The door between our offices was open when this happened," Adams went on. "I saw and heard most of what William did, and he told me the rest."

"Did he see anyone at the window?"

"No. That was the first question I asked. He saw no one."

"Have you had any threats, John?" Samuel asked. "You know that notes have been sent recently to Robert and Samuel."

"Yes, I'd heard." He brushed several fragments of glass off a stack of volumes. "I've received threats since March. You know this. All this time, there have been a few among those committed to the cause who see my defense of the soldiers as a betrayal. It is . . . unavoidable."

"What form do these threats take?" Ethan asked. "Are they missives? Comments made to you in person?"

"Both."

"Do you have still have the written ones?"

"I have the one I received this morning."

John retreated into his office, and another look passed between Ethan and Samuel. Concern etched lines in Adams' face.

John returned a moment later with a small piece of parchment. He held out it first to Samuel, who motioned him toward Ethan.

The message was written in blocky letters, as opposed to the uneven script of those sent to Samuel Quincy and Robert Paine. And yet, it resembled the others in the quality of the parchment, the color and consistency of the smudged ink, the tone of the threat itself.

"You are a traitor to the cause of Liberty," this one read. "And like all traitors, you shall pay for your crime with your life."

Ethan handed the missive to Samuel, who studied it by the light of another window before giving it back to his cousin.

Ethan asked Mister Adams a few more questions. This newest rash of threatening messages had started arriving within the past month. He hadn't seen anyone unusual lurking by his home or office, nor had he encountered any notable strangers in the course of his professional activities. To his knowledge, neither had his wife, Abigail, although he promised to check with her again about this. After some conversation, Samuel wrung from John a promise to share with them any future threats, and to contact them immediately if he or his family were subjected to more violent acts.

"This is all part of the work I do," John said. "The work both of us do," he added, appealing to Samuel. "I don't like being treated like a child."

"If I may, sir," Ethan said, "we're not treating you as a child, but rather as a man of import, a leader in our community. Because that's what you are. Any threat to you is a threat to all of us."

"You are kind, Mister Kaille. And you've a silver tongue. Have you considered a career in politics?"

Ethan laughed, which seemed to disconcert the man more than anything he had said. "I believe my wife would prefer I go back to thieftaking."

He and Samuel crossed to the door, intending to leave the office.

"Wait just a moment, please," John said before they could. He stared hard at Ethan, red spots high on his cheeks. "I have just remembered a detail from our first meeting, and a letter that you wrote, Samuel, by way of introduction for our friend here. Do you—" He broke off, shaking his head, his gaze returning to the empty window frame. "Do you suspect that supernatural forces are at work here? Back in March, you spoke of a conjurer influencing the soldiers and also the mob on King Street. Are similar powers interfering with this trial?"

"We believe so, sir. Before we leave here, I intend to determine if a conjuring was used to shatter the window."

"How would you do that?"

Ethan gazed back at him, saying nothing.

"Never mind. I don't wish to know. And I probably wouldn't understand." He rubbed his brow with a shaking hand. "Thank you, Mister Kaille. I'll admit that I am unnerved by all of this, but I feel better knowing you're helping us with this ugliness."

"I'm honored to be of service, sir."

Ethan left the Adamses to speak in private and walked around to the side of the building. Reaching the remains of the window, he bit down on the inside of his cheek, tasting blood. Checking the alley in both directions, he muttered the reveal magick spell. Power hummed in the lane, and Reg appeared beside him. Red glow—the same hue he had seen the night before on Mister Paine's carriage—flickered around the edge of the window, pale in the daylight, but unmistakable. He conjured a second time to hide the magick, and returned to Queen Street, where Samuel Adams waited for him.

"Well?"

"It was a spell, cast by the same conjurer. This person doesn't want the king's men going to trial, and is willing to harm attorneys from either side to make certain they don't."

"We must keep these lawyers safe, of course," Adams said, his voice low and taut. "But the trial cannot be put off again. It is essential—for the families of those who died, for the soldiers themselves, for Boston, for all the colonies—that we allow justice to run its proper course."

"I'll do everything in my power to find the conjurer and keep the attorneys safe. That's all I can promise you."

Adams took a breath and retreated a step. "Yes, of course. Forgive me." He rapped his cane on the street. "So, tell me where we're headed next."

Seeing the man was in earnest, Ethan resisted the urge to chuckle. "I think, sir, that you need to leave the thieftaking to me, at least for these next few hours."

Adams' face fell. "Well . . . Yes, of course. Again, forgive me."

"There's nothing to forgive. It has been my pleasure and honor to have you accompany me this morning. And without you, I would not have been able to speak with Mister Paine, or gain access to your cousin's office. But my next task is to locate the conjurer, and I don't think you should be with me when I do."

Adams paled and nodded his assent. They agreed to speak again within the next day, as soon as Ethan had more information to share, and they parted. Ethan returned to the *Dowsing Rod*, where Kannice and Kelf would be rushing to ready the kitchen for the midday crush of patrons.

He was just as glad to stay out of their way and out of Kannice's sight. She had all but pushed him out the door with Adams the previous night, but his inquiry was about to turn perilous. The moment Ethan cast his finding spell he would alert the conjurer to his pursuit. And at that point, he anticipated, this person would begin hunting him in turn.

Ethan went to the room upstairs that he and Kannice shared, and retrieved a pouch filled with mullein, a pungent and powerful magickal herb that fueled particularly strong warding spells. He also armed himself with a second blade, which he slipped into a sheath sewn into the calf of his boot. He left the room and descended the stairs, hoping to leave the *Dowser* without Kannice spotting him.

"When did you get back?"

She stood at the bar, her cheeks red, her hair loosely tied. Beautiful as ever.

"Not long ago. I'm on my way out again." He took a step toward the door.

She eyed him with suspicion. "You seem in a hurry."

He closed the distance between them, glancing toward the kitchen. He could hear Kelf chopping something. "The conjurer cast another spell, within the past hour," he said softly. "I want to find this person before he does more damage."

"Or she," Kannice said.

An interesting thought. "Aye, or she."

"Was someone hurt?"

"Yes. Not severely, but he was fortunate, as was Paine last night. Our luck won't hold forever."

"I shouldn't have gotten you into this."

"You didn't."

She raised an eyebrow.

"All you did was give me your blessing to do what I was inclined to do in the first place. This isn't your fault."

"Telling you to be careful has never done a bit of good, so I won't bother."

He grinned. "All right then."

She raised herself onto her toes and kissed him. "But be careful," she whispered.

Ethan left the tavern and set out for the heart of the city. As he walked, he pulled a few leaves of mullein from the pouch and cupped them in his hand, the acrid scent of the herb surrounding him like a cloud.

"*Tegimen ex verbasco evocatum*," he said under his breath. The leaves vanished. Ethan's spell trembled in the ground, announcing to the other speller that he had cast. Reg fell in step beside him, his glow muted. The warding settled over Ethan like a cloak.

When he reached Faneuil Hall, he eased into one of the small byways connecting Merchant's Row to the waterfront. There, he pulled his knife free, pushed up his sleeve, and cut himself. Reg watched him, avid, brighter here in the shadows.

"*Locus magi ex cruore evocatus.*"

A finding spell. Another rumble of power pulsed through the city. Another gauntlet thrown down. Magick spread from the alley, seeking in all directions. Within seconds, the spell snapped back: not a deflection or warding, but a response, the way the spell was supposed to work. A conjurer—*the* conjurer, he assumed—was close by. He might as well have been waiting for Ethan's finding spell.

And a moment later, magick buzzed in the street again, an answer to his casting. Power rushed toward him, like an ocean wave, and upon reaching him it lapped at his legs. Also a finding spell. Ethan sensed no hostility in the conjuring; it felt more like an invitation. South and slightly west. Maybe a block away.

He stepped out of the byway and started that way, stifling an urge to ward himself again.

He crossed the lower corner of Faneuil Square, followed Merchant's Row to King Street, and turned westward, past the Bunch of Grapes tavern. He hadn't taken more than a few steps when he paused and looked to his right. The British Coffee House. Since the occupation of 1768, when

British soldiers crowded the establishment, making it far less attractive to the Sons of Liberty and their supporters, this had become a haven for loyalists. Just a year before, James Otis, Samuel Adams' fiery colleague, was grievously wounded in a brawl within this building. Adams claimed to this day that Otis had been lured to the coffee house by loyalist merchants outraged by one of his many incendiary writings. Whatever the truth, the beating Otis received had rendered him even more mentally unstable than he had already been.

This was hostile ground for any supporter of liberty. And the conjurer was in there now; Ethan was certain of it.

Steeling himself, Ethan pushed through the door into a cacophony of voices and laughter, a haze of pipe smoke, and the inviting, bitter smell of roasting coffee. Glancing around, he spotted near the back of the room a woman sitting alone at a table. She wore a silk gown—burgundy, like the magick he had seen on the window and the axle—that accentuated the graceful curve of her slender neck, the contour of her shoulders. A white gem flashed at her throat. Her hair, fine and light brown, was wound into an elegant pile atop her head. And her eyes, brilliant green, were fixed upon Ethan.

Ethan took a single step toward her, only to be blocked by a man who could have been Kelf's older brother. He was huge, like Kannice's barman, his neck thick, his massive jaw set in a hard scowl.

"What do you want?" the man demanded.

"I'm . . . meeting a friend."

"Are you?"

"She's sitting over there."

The man turned, squinting in the direction Ethan had indicated. Ethan gazed past the behemoth in time to see the woman dip her chin once.

"All right then." The man sounded disappointed, as if beating a Whig senseless and tossing him bodily into the street would have been just the thing to improve his day. He shifted out of Ethan's way.

Ethan tipped his tricorn to the man, and walked to the woman's table. Others stared at him as he passed, little warmth in their expressions. He tried to ignore them.

Reaching her table, he removed his hat and sketched a small bow.

"You were looking for me," she said in a rich alto.

"And you for me."

"How delightful then that we've found each other. Won't you sit, Mister . . ."

"Kaille. Ethan Kaille. And you are?"

"Pleased to make your acquaintance."

Her eyes danced, and the corners of her mouth quirked upward. He sat in the chair opposite hers, his back to the door, which made the nape of his neck prickle.

From across the great room, she had been arresting. Sitting this close he saw that she was truly a beauty: olive complexion, sculpted features, a dimple in one cheek when she smiled. She couldn't have been more than twenty-five years old; her skin was flawless. Even her hands were captivating—slender, long-fingered, the simple turn of one when she spoke eloquent, expressive.

"You don't wish to share your name?" he asked.

"Not yet. Get yourself some coffee. This is the finest you'll find in Boston. Even better than the Crown offers."

She spoke with refinement, her accent of upper crust London.

Ethan stepped to the bar and ordered a coffee. He had to keep himself from laughing aloud when the barman told him the cost; one cup set him back as much as two ales in the *Dowser*. The coffee itself, though, smelled wonderful. He sipped it, found it as flavorful as it was aromatic. He returned to the table, resettled himself in his chair.

"Now will you tell me who you are?"

"Why did you cast that finding spell?"

"Why do you think I did?"

She thinned another smile, this one far less fetching than the first. "You will answer my questions, Mister Kaille, or our conversation, and your welcome in this establishment, will end."

He opened his hands, sipped his coffee again, and stood. "Very well. Good day."

He pivoted away from the table and walked to the coffee house entrance, expecting—hoping—that the woman would call him back. She still hadn't when he reached the door. Grasping the handle, he paused, waited. Finally he sighed, turned again and walked back to where she sat. She marked his approach with smug amusement, her gaze harder than before.

Ethan sat again, took another drink of coffee.

"A wise choice," she said, sounding like a school teacher speaking to a wayward boy. "Tell me why you were searching for me."

"Because I believe you're responsible for a spell that broke the axle on a carriage last night, and another that shattered a window this morning."

"So you use your magick to seek out mischievous conjurers."

"Mischievous? You're trying to harm men charged with conducting the trial."

"What trial?"

"Stop it!" he said, his voice rising.

Men at adjacent tables paused to look their way. If the woman minded, she showed no sign of it.

"You have a temper."

Ethan lifted his cup again, his hand steady.

She tapped a painted fingernail against the edge of her saucer. "If I wanted to harm those men, I would have. If I wanted to kill them, they would be dead. My aim was mischief."

"Your aim was intimidation."

Her eyes widened attractively. "Will you now tell me my own mind, Mister Kaille?"

"I will if you intend to keep lying."

As quickly as it came, her humor faded. "An ugly word."

He didn't respond, and her mien turned coy. "Really, do you expect me to believe that great men like Messieurs Paine and Adams—John Adams, that is—are so easily frightened?"

"You're a speller, just as I am. I shouldn't have to tell you that even the bravest man can be put off by magick. And you should know that you did harm someone. Mister Adams' clerk was wounded in your attack."

"His injuries were minor," she said. "A few cuts."

"He could have been blinded."

"He wasn't."

"What is your purpose here?" Ethan asked. "Who are you working for?"

"What is yours? A thieftaker usually only investigates robberies. So who hired you, and why?"

He sat straighter, regarding her anew. "I never said I was a thieftaker."

"No, you didn't. You also didn't tell me that you're now a simple tavern keeper, married to the widow, Kannice Lester, née Chapman. Nor that you come from Bristol, served in Her Majesty's navy aboard the *Stirling Castle*, faced court martial for your part in the *Ruby Blade* mutiny, and served fourteen years as a prison laborer on a sugar plantation in Barbados, where you lost half of your left foot." She canted her head. "I find it curious that a conjurer would allow himself to be imprisoned. Were you addled for all those years, or merely too frightened to cast?"

Ethan glared. The truth was, he had been ashamed—of his magick, of his failure to tell his betrothed at the time that he was a speller—and he eschewed casting for all those years as a form of penance. He didn't expect she would understand.

The woman smirked at what she saw in his expression and leaned closer to him. "I know that your father is Captain Ellis Kaille, that your mother, Sarah, is an accomplished speller, as is your sister, Susannah, who lives in Scotland. You have a second sister, Bett, married to Geoffrey Brower, a customs man. She doesn't conjure, and she doesn't like you very much. I know that you had a hand in the death of Peter Darrow back in '65. And I know that earlier this year you killed Nate Ramsey, for which every speller in the Colonies owes you their gratitude."

By now he could only gape. "Who are you?"

Another turn of an elegant hand. "That is largely up to you. I can be a valuable friend, or I can make your life an earthly hell. The choice is yours."

"Why have you come here? What do you care about the trial of Preston and his men?"

"I could ask the same of you. Not so very long ago, you considered yourself a loyalist, did you not?"

This woman—attractive, canny, too self-satisfied—had started to fray his nerves. She knew far too much about him, and he had yet to convince her to surrender so much as her name.

"Leave the matter to the Adams men and their allies, and stay out of my way. Go back to your wife and your tavern. You'll be safer there, and you'll have nothing more to fear from me."

"I don't fear you."

"Then you're a fool," she said, the words coming sharp and quick.

Ethan pushed back from the table. "I've had enough of this. You've yet to answer a single question. All you've done is mock me and make idle threats."

"Idle?" She laughed, harsh, venomous, the sound utterly at odds with everything else about her.

Magick roared in the wood floors and walls, the spell powerful enough to bring down the building. A server stepping past their table stumbled momentarily, but otherwise the men around them remained oblivious. A glowing red figure winked into view at her shoulder—a young girl dressed in an ornate gown, her eyes alight and unearthly.

Ethan still sensed the warding he had put in place before coming here. He had done nothing to remove or weaken it, and yet given the force with which her spell fell upon him, he might as well have been unprotected.

He couldn't move. He couldn't speak, or lift a finger. He certainly couldn't stand. Nor could he breathe. All he could do was sit and glare at her as he suffocated. No one in the coffee house would notice until he died. Even then, her spell might hold him in place, so that long after she exited the building and walked away, he would remain as he was.

As far as he could tell, she hadn't drawn blood. He hadn't seen her reach for any sort of herb. He couldn't imagine what source she had used to overmaster his warding with such ease.

"I don't make idle threats," she said and sipped from her cup.

Pressure built in Ethan's chest.

"I don't answer questions when I'm not inclined to do so. I mock you because you deserve mockery. You have some talent as a conjurer, or else you wouldn't have bested Ramsey. But you were fortunate to subdue Peter that night all those years ago, and I believe that's typical. You rely on luck as much as you do skill or intelligence. Neither will be enough against me."

He wanted to loosen his collar, to clutch at his burning chest. More than anything, he wanted to stand and flee this place, this woman. But her magick held him, as immutable as iron.

"You will end your inquiry. You will sever all contact with the Sons of Liberty, and you will refuse their entreaties and offers of more money. If you don't you will die. Your wife will die. Devren Jervis and his betrothed will die. Need I go on?"

He couldn't so much as shake his head. His vision swam, dark spots obscuring her face and the men around them.

"Moreover, when I release you, you will do nothing more than catch your breath. If you say anything about what I've done, if you threaten me or attempt to cast, I will destroy this building and everyone in it and walk away unscathed. Do you believe me, or will you dismiss this as another 'idle threat'?"

If he could have burned her to ash, he would have, and before this was over, if he survived this confrontation, he would. He promised this to himself. Today, though, he would do as she commanded. What choice did he have?

She allowed herself a soft laugh, seeming to read his acquiescence in his eyes.

The leaden weight of her spell lifted, and Ethan flopped forward, bracing himself on the table with both hands. He gulped at precious air, his eyes squeezed shut.

"Sit up," she said, her voice low, but whiplike.

He pushed himself up, staring daggers at her.

"I assume we understand each other."

Ethan clamped his jaw shut.

"I want an answer."

"I understand what you want of me."

She gave a small shake of her head. "That's not the same thing." As his silence stretched, she narrowed her gaze. In time, she stood. "Very well, Mister Kaille. A man's pride and all that. I'll give you until this time tomorrow to do as I say. After that, people you care about will start to die."

The woman brushed past him with a whisper of silk and exited the coffee house, leaving Ethan to recover his breath, slow his heart, and curse his weakness.

IV

When he felt steady enough, he left the coffee house. He didn't return to the *Dowser*. Not yet. Kannice would have questions he couldn't answer. Nor did he seek out Adams or any of the Sons of Liberty. He had no intention of abandoning them to this woman's magick, but he assumed she watched him even now, and he wasn't yet ready to act openly in defiance of her wishes.

She knew a good deal about his battle against Peter Darrow, an agent of the Crown who used a series of killing spells in an attempt to destroy the Sons of Liberty. More, she called the man "Peter." Had they been acquainted? He no longer doubted that she worked on behalf of the Tories.

No Tory wielded more power in Boston than Chief Justice and Lieutenant Governor Thomas Hutchinson, who had been acting governor since Francis Bernard was recalled to England the previous summer. Adams had said that Hutchinson sought to delay the trial further. Was this woman working for him? He thought he must be—the woman's spells would accomplish exactly what Hutchinson wanted.

In all of Ethan's many interactions with the lieutenant governor, however, Hutchinson had been consistent in his hostility toward magick of any sort. He mistrusted Ethan, had been fearful of Ramsey. He spoke often of the evils and perils of witchery. Would he cast his lot with this conjurer if it served his purposes?

He expected Adams, Warren, and their friends would answer in the affirmative—anything to achieve the Crown's aims, they would say. Ethan was less sure.

After a moment's thought, he started in the direction of the Town House, where Hutchinson had his chambers. He doubted Hutchinson would deign to speak with him, but Stephen Greenleaf, the sheriff of Suffolk County, also had an office in the Town House, and if Hutchinson worked with the young woman, Greenleaf would almost certainly know it.

He entered the building, climbed the wooden stairway to the second floor, and marched toward the governor's chamber. He passed an open door, and heard a deep, familiar voice call his name. Smiling to himself, he walked on.

"Kaille, you stop right there."

Ethan checked himself in mid-stride and turned. The sheriff stood in the corridor, feet planted, fists on his hips. He remained an imposing man: broad and tall, with a hawk-like nose and hard, pale eyes. Over the years, on occasion, he and Ethan had worked together—usually at times when Greenleaf needed Ethan's help with a matter relating to "witchery." For the most part, though, they were adversaries. Greenleaf had frequently stated his intention to see Ethan hanged for a witch. More than once, the sheriff had imprisoned him on charges that proved flimsy at best. When Ethan and Sephira worked at cross purposes—which is to say, all the time—Greenleaf invariably sided with her.

And yet, despite their considerable history, Ethan harbored a grudging respect for the man. As sheriff of Suffolk County, Greenleaf bore responsibility for keeping the peace throughout Boston and much of her hinterland. He had no officers under his command. He did administer the city's night watch, but most of the men who served in that capacity were unskilled and amoral. Greenleaf was neither. Under different circumstances—if Greenleaf didn't fear conjurers, and Ethan hadn't long ago made an enemy of Sephira—they might have been allies, even friends.

And if Ethan could conjure his arms into wings, he might fly.

"Good day, Sheriff."

Greenleaf scanned the corridor. "Are you here alone?"

"I am. I came to see Hutchinson."

"*Acting Governor* Hutchinson."

"Aye, that's the one."

The sheriff scowled. "You think you can just walk in here—a known witch, a mutineer, an ex-convict—and gain an audience with the most important man in the province?"

"That was the idea, yes. Would you like to accompany me? I believe you would be interested in what I wish to discuss with him."

"And what would that be?"

Ethan peered back at the door to Hutchinson's chamber, wanting Greenleaf to think him reluctant to give up on speaking with the lieutenant governor. He walked to where Greenleaf waited.

"In your chamber?"

The sheriff frowned again, but motioned him into the room, followed him inside, and demanded in a low voice, "What is all this, Kaille? I have no time for—"

"There's a new conjurer in the city."

Greenleaf studied him. "And you know of this witch how?"

"I've just come from speaking with her."

"Like drawn to like, eh? Maybe the two of you can hang together."

Ethan shook his head and crossed back toward the door. "Never mind, Sheriff. I'll speak with the lieutenant governor, and then you can explain to him why he first had to hear of this from me."

Greenleaf blocked his way. "No need for that. I didn't mean anything by it."

Ethan stared back at him.

"Who is she?"

"I don't know."

"I thought you said—"

"She wouldn't tell me her name, and she was powerful enough that I didn't dare push the matter too far."

That sobered the sheriff. He feared Ethan's powers, and he disapproved of magick in any form, but he also had a healthy respect for what he believed Ethan could do with a spell.

"What did you intend to tell Hutchinson?" Greenleaf asked, more subdued now.

"That she's responsible for magickal assaults on Robert Treat Paine and John Adams, that she's doing everything she can to disrupt the trial."

"You know this?"

"Aye."

Greenleaf just nodded. No more snide remarks about Ethan being a witch.

"Have you heard anything about her, or the attacks?" Ethan asked.

"Paine's carriage broke an axle last night, and someone shattered a window at the Adams office today . . ." Greenleaf trailed off, color draining from his face. "Are you saying—"

"She did those things."

"With her witchery?"

Ethan nodded, not bothering to correct him.

"Damn."

A thought came to him—recognition of connections he should have made sooner: two pairs of green eyes, two uncommonly attractive newcomers to the city.

"Are you familiar with a man named Francis Lamb?"

"O' course. He's a customs man—a recent appointment."

"Did he come to Boston alone?"

"I haven't the least idea. You believe he and this witch are connected in some way?"

"I have no real reason to think so, and yet they're both recent arrivals, they look a bit alike, and from what I can tell, they're both servants of the Crown."

Greenleaf bristled. "As am I, Kaille. As is the acting governor."

"I understand that. But I trust the two of you not to endanger the lives of the trial attorneys, particularly that of the man leading the defense of Captain Preston and his soldiers."

"You're not making sense. Why would a so-called 'servant of the Crown' do that? Either this woman has no loyalist ties at all, or you're wrong about her and her magick. Whichever is the case, I'll be damned if I'm going to take you into Hutchinson's chambers and allow you to make a fool of both of us."

"And just how would he do that?"

They both wheeled. Hutchinson stood in the doorway.

Ethan hadn't seen the lieutenant governor since just after the shootings on King Street. The intervening months hadn't been kind to the man. His face was pasty, his cheeks sunken. The skin beneath his large, dark eyes appeared almost bruised with fatigue. He was as tall as Greenleaf, but he held his narrow shoulders back, like a soldier standing at attention, which gave him a barrel-chested look.

"Sheriff?" he prompted.

"He has . . . some odd theories, Your Honor. About Mister Lamb and the upcoming trial."

"Indeed." Hutchinson turned to Ethan. "Would you elaborate, Mister Kaille?"

"Of course, sir. In the last day alone, there have been assaults of a . . . a magickal nature against both John Adams and Robert Paine."

"Magick," Hutchinson said with such disdain one would think the word itself turned his stomach.

"That's right."

"And what do these assaults have to do with Francis Lamb?"

"I don't know, sir. Perhaps nothing. But he is an agent of the Crown, and . . ." He paused, searching for the safest way to speak his mind. "And it is generally known that some who serve royal interests have sought to delay the proceedings."

"Is it?" the lieutenant governor said with a slight sneer.

"Yes, sir."

"Is that what Adams says?"

They had been speaking of John, but in this case Ethan knew Hutchinson meant Samuel. The two men were sworn enemies, their contempt for each other perfectly balanced.

"Do you deny it?"

"I reject the simplemindedness of it. Did I seek to delay the trial through the spring and summer? Of course I did. Any responsible leader would have. We needed time to cool the passions of last March. Surely you can see that."

"Yes, sir," Ethan said, and meant it. A trial in the immediate aftermath of the shootings would have been driven by rage and an unquenchable thirst for vengeance among the city's populace.

"If Adams truly wishes for a fair trial—" Hutchinson continued, "and I have my doubts as to his sincerity in that regard—he has to understand that these delays were necessary. Now, though, we must proceed with the trial. Just as a trial too soon would have thwarted justice, additional delay will only renew calls for violence."

"So you want the trial to go on?"

"I do. It is scheduled to begin early next week, and I have every expectation that it will. In fact, I am determined so."

"In that case, Your Honor, I believe you should know that there is a new conjurer in the city who is working at cross purposes with your desires in this matter. A woman, young, attractive, apparently wealthy and well-connected. And a loyalist."

"And it is this woman whom you believe to be connected to Lamb."

He offered it as a statement.

"That's right."

Hutchinson dipped his chin. "You may well be right, Mister Kaille."

"You know her?"

"I know of her. Mister Lamb, for whom, I will admit, I have little affection, brought with him to Boston a companion, a sister. According to the reports I have received, she fits the description that you offered, vague though it was."

"Thank you, sir. That's helpful."

Hutchinson gave a thin smile. "Of course." He started to turn, but then halted and eyed Ethan again. "Adams and Paine, were they hurt?"

"They escaped injury, sir, though a clerk in Mister Adams' office sustained a few cuts. You should know that Adams and Paine have received other threats, as have both brothers Quincy. This woman seems intent upon stopping the trial, though whether she does this with Mister Lamb's knowledge I can't yet say."

"Find out. Please. I can offer you five pounds."

"The province wishes to hire me?"

"Not the province, no. Me, personally."

That, he hadn't expected. "May I ask why?"

"You may ask," Hutchinson said with a haughtiness Ethan had seen in him many times before. "I choose not to answer."

"Yes, Your Honor."

The ensuing silence stretched for several moments.

"He is an ass," the lieutenant governor said, surprising Ethan again. "And I believe he covets my job. That's why. However bad you think me, he is infinitely worse. And he has the ear of Lord North and several prominent members of Parliament. You may not like me, Mister Kaille, and I may be the bane of Samuel Adams' existence. But I care deeply about this city and province. I'm doing all I can to prevent further bloodshed. Others, however, see additional violence as the cure for what ails us. Men like Lamb would like to see the colonies burn so that the king has no choice but to stamp the fires out."

"You're saying he wants a war?"

"He would call it an act of discipline, an imposition of order. The effect, though, would be much the same."

Ethan took a long breath.

"You'll find out what you can about him?"

"I will, sir. Thank you."

Hutchinson nodded again and left Greenleaf's office.

The sheriff considered him, grudging admiration in the glance. "So, now you're working for Samuel Adams *and* the lieutenant governor."

"Not the lieutenant governor. Thomas Hutchinson. There's a difference."

"I suppose there is."

Ethan took leave of the sheriff and returned to the lanes. Retreating to an alley, he pushed up his sleeve, cut his forearm, and whispered the Latin for a concealment spell. Power vibrated in the street, and magick poured over him like cool water. The woman—Miss Lamb?—would sense the casting, but unless she watched him conjure, she probably wouldn't know what Ethan had done with it. She wouldn't know he was concealed, and, more important, neither would her brother.

Sephira had said they were headed to Beacon Hill and then the South End. Ethan assumed they were not yet done with the former, so he struck out in that direction, following School Street past the Granary Burying Ground and across the edge of the Common. He turned onto Beacon Street and walked most of its length, until he could see and smell the waters of the Charles River. A young eagle, dark and huge, circled overhead. A flock of gulls kept their distance.

Ethan passed a couple of chaises and two men in suits on foot. He didn't see Sephira or Francis Lamb. Had they already finished with this part of the city and moved on to the South End? They would be harder to find there.

He started back along the lane, wondering if he should cut across the Common toward the waterfront. As he walked, though, he spotted four figures descending from the heights of Beacon Hill itself. The first pair, one massive and one the size of a normal man—had to be Gordon and Nap. Sephira and Lamb walked behind them.

Ethan needed only to wait at the base of the hill, concealed still by his spell. As they neared him, Ethan caught snatches of conversation. Mostly Sephira talked, telling Lamb about the city, and about her own renown within its boundaries. She kept a tight hold on his arm, but barely glanced his way. If she had, she might have noticed the rictus of boredom that had replaced his charming smile. Ethan had the impression that Lamb had long since tired of their walk through the city, and of Sephira herself.

Maybe Ethan should have enjoyed her humiliation, as she would have savored his, but he couldn't. He felt sorry for her. True, many who made their livings in the streets of Boston regarded her as royalty—the Empress of the South End, as most called her—but to a wealthy man from London, someone who was the confidant of statesmen and diplomats, she was a provincial. Nothing more.

Ethan followed them across Common and Marlborough Streets. He expected Sephira to take Lamb past her own home on Summer Street, but she didn't. Perhaps she realized that he would be less impressed with the structure than were people of Boston. As it was, he remarked with condescension on the cows in d'Acosta's pasture and the houses lining Milk Street, several of which were a match for hers. Sephira let his comments pass.

Beyond his observations about the livestock and homes, Lamb said little of interest. He didn't share his opinion of the trial or Boston politics. He was content, it seemed, to endure Sephira's boasts and feign interest in their flirtation.

Lamb walked with her as far as Fort Hill and the South Battery, but then took his leave. He thanked her for being "a most informative guide," and kissed her hand like the noble he was.

Sephira watched him walk off. Gordon and Nap stood a short distance away, studying her the way a sea captain watched storm clouds. Her expression darkened slowly, the good cheer she had put on for Lamb's benefit giving way to cold appraisal and—did Ethan imagine it?—discouragement.

"Come along," she said, turning on her heel and walking off toward her home.

Nap and Gordon followed her, their expressions guarded.

Ethan did not. He would never reveal to her that he had seen any of this.

Still, he did need to speak with her, and that meant going to her home. He waited until she and her toughs had followed Purchase Street around the base of the hill and beyond his seeing.

Once he was alone, he drew his knife and cut himself. "*Fini velamentum ex cruore evocatum.*"

Reg gleamed in the gray light and the concealment spell lifted. Ethan started back along the Battery, intending to walk up Milk Street and south on Marlborough—a longer path to Sephira's home than she had taken. He wanted to give her plenty of time to arrive and no reason to think that he had followed her.

After only a few steps another spell rumbled. A finding. Again. The tentacles of magick felt more menacing this time as they grabbed at his legs. The spell had to have been cast by Miss Lamb. And if she knew where he was, Francis would soon enough. Would he assume that Ethan had been tracking him?

He hesitated, unsure of where to go. He didn't want the young conjurer to find him so close to Sephira's house, or here on the Battery. Either would only raise more questions. Neither was he willing to retreat to

Cornhill or the bustling lanes of the South End—the finding spell had come from that direction.

In the end, he continued westward toward Marlborough Street, the main thoroughfare cutting through the city. It was the best of his bad options.

He angled northward as he walked, to put more distance between himself and Fort Hill, and so had just returned to the corner of Marlborough and School Street when a carriage rattled to a halt in front of him. A single passenger sat inside. She leaned forward and gazed out at him.

"Get in," the conjurer said.

Running struck him as futile, and he didn't dare start a magickal battle here in the bustling lane. With as much dignity as he could muster, he climbed into the carriage, taking a seat across from her.

"Miss Lamb, what a pleasure to see you again. I thought you had given me a day."

His use of her name didn't appear to bother her. She reached a hand out through the window in the door and tapped lightly on the roof of the carriage. It lurched forward, jostling them both.

"I was willing to wait a day so long as you didn't try to interfere in my affairs. Now, what were you doing along the waterfront?"

"Walking," he said. "Thinking about our conversation."

"You're a terrible liar. Answer my question. I won't ask a third time."

"Why would I lie—"

The casting whispered in the cloth and wood of the carriage, and the specter of that same burgundy little girl flashed into view in the seat beside the woman. Someone cried out from beyond the confines of the carriage.

Ethan's warding should have protected him still; he hadn't removed it. Then again, it hadn't done much to shield him from the conjuring with which she paralyzed him in the coffee house.

This spell was different, more vicious. It felt like a blade sliding into his cut, carving toward his heart. His body went rigid. He grabbed at his midsection, a hard gasp slipping between his lips.

"If you had spent any time at all thinking of our conversation," the woman said, "you would have known better than to anger me again."

Ethan struggled to breathe. Sweat ran over his face. Even the slightest motion—a short, sharp pull of air into his lungs—brought agony.

"I'm having trouble coming up with a reason to let you live. You clearly have no intention of heeding my warnings. I can only assume that you're lying to me now to conceal actions that would displease me. So why shouldn't I kill you?"

He looked down at his hands, saw they were crimson. This was no illusion. The blade might have been magickal, but the damage she had done to him was all too real. In another moment, he would be dead, and she would dump him out of her carriage.

Frange ex cruore evocatum.

Ethan recited the words within his mind, and didn't aim the breaking spell at her. Her wardings were bound to be proof against his attacks. He hoped the carriage was unprotected, and that she had not anticipated that he would use her own assault against her.

Wood snapped beneath them. The carriage rocked, tipped. The rear of the vehicle collapsed onto stone. The impact threw both of them against the side of the carriage.

Her composure slipped, long enough that Ethan managed to fling himself out of the carriage and onto the street.

Blood continued to flow from his wound and he cast again.

Ignis ex cruore evocatus.

Flame engulfed the carriage. The horses harnessed to it reared and the driver scrambled to get them free.

Ethan didn't remain to see if he succeeded or if the woman escaped the fire. He limped away at speed, arms wrapped around his gut. He did glance back once—a crowd had converged on the carriage, some helping the driver, others seeing to his passenger.

Ethan paused for an instant to get his bearings before making his choice. He knew of two surgeons in the city, both skilled, both with ties to the Sons of Liberty. He was closer to the home of Benjamin Church, so that was where he went—south and west to Winter Street. A gamble. He had some skill as a healer; he thought himself capable of mending a similar wound in another. But weakened by pain and blood loss, he didn't believe he could save himself. And if he didn't find Doctor Church at home, he would likely die before he reached the North End home of Joseph Warren.

Never had a walk of two or three city blocks felt so long. Every step jarred him, bringing another wave of torment. Blood soaked his shirt and breeches, his coat and the sleeves he pressed to the wound to keep from bleeding to death. At last, unwilling to risk another step, he paused to cast a healing spell, feeding the spell with the blood on his clothes, and maintaining the conjuring just long enough to stop the flow.

Reg gawked at him, his expression betraying genuine fear, which was hardly reassuring. Ethan would have preferred his usual mockery.

He staggered on, passing Winter and Summer Streets, certain that he would collapse before he reached the gabled house on the left.

He didn't. He approached the door, knocked once, leaned against the doorjamb. His vision swam, the landing on which he stood seeming to pitch like a sea-tossed ship. He started to fall as the door opened, landed on his side.

A woman screamed and then shouted a name. After that, darkness.

V

He woke in a bed, surrounded by the smells of spirit and soap and herbs, both bitter and sweet. A candle burned on a night table beside him. Otherwise the room was dark. No light entered around the lone window. Night, then. He assumed he was still in the house of Doctor Church.

With care, he laid a hand on his belly. A thick bandage covered the wound. Even through the wrap, his skin remained tender, though the sharp agony of earlier had been replaced by a dull, persistent throb.

A footstep creaked outside the room, and the door opened a crack. He looked that way.

"You're awake." A woman's voice. She pushed the door open wider and stepped in, carrying a second candle. She wore a robe, cinched at the waist. Her light brown hair was tied back in a long plait, and her pale eyes appeared luminous with the flame before her. "How are you feeling?"

"Better than I was, thank you. I'm Ethan Kaille."

"Yes, I know. Benjamin recognized you. I'm Hannah Church, Benjamin's wife."

"Thank you for welcoming me into your home. I'm sorry if I frightened you with my arrival."

"It's all right," she said, solemn and earnest. "Do you need anything? Tea, or watered wine?" She glanced back into the corridor. "Benjamin is sleeping. I'd prefer not to wake him, but if you need—"

"No, let him sleep. Some tea would be fine. Again, my thanks. Can you tell me—what is the time?"

"It's past midnight."

"Damn." He winced. "I beg your pardon. Yes, a bit of tea, and then I should really go. My wife—"

"Knows where you are."

He blinked. "She does?"

"She was here earlier. If we'd had room, we would have offered to let her stay."

"How did you know to find her?"

At that she surrendered a vague smile. "You have a good many friends in this city, Mister Kaille. While Benjamin saw to your wound, he had me send word to Reverend Pell at King's Chapel, and also to Samuel Adams. Between the two of them, they located your wife and told her what had happened. At least as much as we knew."

Ethan could imagine Kannice's reaction—a combination of desperate worry and slow-burning rage.

He lay back, fatigued from the mere exertion of carrying on a conversation. "I'm in your debt, Missus Church. Yours and the good doctor's."

Her brow creased. "I'll get your tea," she said, and left him.

Ethan closed his eyes, his thoughts returning to his encounter with the conjurer, Miss Lamb. Twice now, she had defeated his wardings without any obvious effort. One might have thought he hadn't cast a protection spell at all, so successful were her attacks on him. There had to be some secret to what she did. He thought he had an inkling, but his thoughts were clouded by lingering pain and fatigue and his worry for Kannice.

Hannah Church's return startled him awake once more. She set the tea on the table by the candle, and after asking if he needed anything else, left him, closing the door behind her. Ethan managed to take a few sips of his tea. Before long, though, he had fallen back into a deep slumber.

When next he woke, daylight shimmered at the edges of the window and Kannice sat beside his bed. Benjamin Church hovered nearby, watching him keenly.

"How are you feeling?" Kannice asked, her voice tight.

"I'm all right."

"All right," she repeated in a tone he knew too well.

"Yes."

"You were fortunate," Church said, taking hold of Ethan's wrist and checking his pulse. The doctor was tall, his shoulders stooped. He had deep set eyes, a strong nose and weak chin. He wore his hair powdered, in a long plait. "Whatever blade your assailant used came awfully close to several vital organs."

"Thank you for saving me, Doctor."

"You saved yourself, much as you did the first time you and I met. This time, though, I had to cut you open to make certain the damage to your vitals didn't require further attention."

Kannice paled at this.

"And?"

Church shrugged, released his wrist. "I should have known better. You're quite good at healing yourself."

"Would you leave us, Doctor?" Kannice asked, staring down at her hands.

Ethan almost asked the man to stay.

"Of course. Rest, Mister Kaille. You need time to heal." He stepped to the door. "You should know that I've called for the sheriff. I imagine he'll have questions about the source of your injuries."

Another conversation he dreaded. "Yes, Doctor. Thank you again."

Church stepped from the room and shut the door with care.

Kannice raised her gaze to his, blue eyes blazing. "What happened?"

"I'm so sorry, Kannice."

"That's—" She shook her head, tears flying from her face. "Just tell me. Was it Sephira, or one of her men?"

"No. It was the conjurer, the one Adams asked me to find. And she did it with magick. There was no blade."

"I should never have convinced you—"

"This was not your fault," he said. "I was warded. She shouldn't have been able to hurt me. Not like this. I don't understand. She has access to power that I can barely fathom. And I didn't even see what she used to power her conjurings. It almost . . ." He paused, thinking again of something that had occurred to him during the night. He had been too tired then to think it through. But now . . .

"Ethan?"

He raised a hand, silencing her.

The conjurer hadn't drawn blood with a blade. He hadn't noticed her biting the inside of her cheek. She carried no herbs that he saw. Both times she attacked him with magick, she appeared to do so without source or effort. Which should have been impossible. His thoughts snagged on a memory, a pair of them to be more precise.

In the coffee house, just as her spell fell upon him, stealing his ability to move or breathe, a man walking past their table stumbled. And later that same day, in the carriage, as her magickal blade ripped into him, someone outside the vehicle cried out.

Were these coincidences? Or was she somehow drawing upon other people for her magick? Not killing them, but stealing . . . something.

"Ethan?" Kannice said again.

"I'm sorry, I was just . . . Her magick is . . . odd. I can't figure out how she fuels her spells, but I believe it possible that whatever she uses as a source for her magick also explains how she's able to defeat my wardings with such ease."

"I don't understand."

He took her hand. "I know. That's all right. I didn't want to put you through this again—the worry, the fear. But I'm in it now. This woman is after me. I barely escaped her yesterday, and I'm sure she'll be coming for me again. She knows where I live. She knows about you, she knows that Diver and Deborah are my friends. None of you is safe so long as she lives. And as long as I'm here, Doctor Church and his wife are in peril."

She straightened and pulled her hand from his grasp, her gaze heating again. "No! You are not leaving that bed!"

"I have to. If something happens to Church—"

"And what about if something happens to you? Oh, wait. It already did!"

"You'd have me endanger their lives? Really?"

Kannice looked away, her jaw clenched. He could see that he'd convinced her; she knew he was right, which only made her angrier.

A knock at the door made them turn. The door swung open and Stephen Greenleaf entered the room, his tricorn in hand. He smelled of horse and wood smoke.

"Hope I'm not interrupting," he said in a way that made Ethan think he'd heard plenty before letting himself in.

"Good day, Sheriff," Ethan said, watching Kannice. She glared back at him, lips pressed thin.

"What happened, Kaille? Church says you were stabbed."

"I was, in a sense."

The man frowned. "What does that mean?"

"I was attacked with magick, by the woman we spoke of yesterday."

"Was Lamb with you? Did he have anything to do with this?"

"No."

Greenleaf exhaled, looked Ethan over, and spared a glance for Kannice. "Well, there's not much I can do then, is there?"

Kannice shot him a look that could have melted iron. "What? That's all? After all he's done for you?"

"Well, I—"

"He was nearly killed, Sheriff, in the very streets you've sworn to protect."

"Yes, but if she's—"

"And you can't even offer to guard him, to help him get home, where he belongs?"

Clever. Ethan hadn't thought to ask the man for protection. If Miss Lamb had ties to the Crown, she might be less inclined to attack while he was in the sheriff's company.

"Well, I . . . I suppose I could do that much."

"I should think." Kannice stood. "I'll inform the doctor of our intention to leave."

She stepped out of the room, leaving Ethan and Greenleaf alone.

"She's a formidable woman," the sheriff said, gazing after her.

"You have no idea." He considered again the nature of Miss Lamb's conjurings. "Have there been any reports of unusual injuries here in the city?"

"Well, you were stabbed."

"Aside from me."

Greenleaf scowled again and looked down at him. "I don't understand what you're asking."

"And I'm not sure I can express myself more clearly. Has anyone been hurt or killed in the past few days in a manner you can't explain?"

"No, I've heard of nothing like that. But a carriage caught fire yesterday in the middle of Marlborough Street. You wouldn't know anything about that, would you?"

Ethan didn't answer, his mind fixed instead on the first part of the sheriff's response. He had been so certain there would be something. Miss Lamb had to have been sourcing her conjurings in the lives of others. How else could she have defeated his wardings with such ease?

Kannice returned seconds later with the doctor in tow. Church didn't want Ethan leaving so soon. The wound, he said, needed time to heal; moving too soon could reopen the gash.

"You're safe here, Mister Kaille. The person who did this to you won't know from me or anyone else that you're in my home. Isn't that right, Sheriff?"

Ethan wondered if Greenleaf would ever lose the frown he'd worn almost from the moment of his arrival. He did nod, though. "I'll not tell a soul."

"The problem, Doctor, is that she need only cast a finding spell to know precisely where I am. And at that point, you and your wife will both be in gravest danger."

Greenleaf slanted a glance at Ethan. "A witch can find an individual? Just like that? Since when?"

Even now, the sheriff sought evidence to prove Ethan was a "witch."

"I told you yesterday that she possessed extraordinary powers."

This didn't appear to convince the man.

"I'm willing to take the risk," Church said. "You should remain in bed."

"I appreciate that, Doctor, but I'm *not* willing. If something happens to you, or to Missus Church, I'll blame myself. Besides, as you well know, this was no commonplace wound." Saying this, he flicked a quick gaze at Kannice.

"Come along, Sheriff," she said. "You and I should make preparations to take Ethan home. You have a chaise, yes?"

Greenleaf, shook his head. "No."

"Well, then, you need to get one, quickly!"

She took his hand, hers looking tiny next to his, and tugged him from the room.

Church waited until they heard the door to the house open and close before saying, "I don't like this."

"I understand, and I'm grateful for all you've done. But you know that I am . . . an unusual patient. If the wound opens, as you fear, I can mend it."

"Still—"

"What I can't do, at least not yet, is defeat the conjurer who did this to me. If she comes here, and she chooses to hurt or kill you or your wife, I'll be helpless to stop her. That is unacceptable to me."

"And if this woman finds you at your home, won't you be just as powerless, and won't that put your wife at risk."

"My life, my risk. And Kannice knew the danger when she married me. Putting the two of you in harm's way is different."

"Yes, all right." Church sighed the words. "If anything happens, though —if you do have to tend to the wound—I want to see you as soon as possible. Am I clear?"

"Yes, sir."

"Samuel told me why he hired you. The Sons of Liberty are grateful for your help. I know I speak for all my colleagues when I say that we never wished for you to be injured."

"I know that, sir. It's part of being a thieftaker, which is why Kannice was so pleased when I gave up the profession."

The house door opened, and moments later Kannice and the sheriff stood in the doorway to Ethan's room, Greenleaf looking pleased with himself. Kannice explained that he had located and pressed into their service a chaise that would carry them all back to the *Dowser*.

With help from the sheriff and doctor, Ethan made his way gingerly from the bedroom, out of the house, and into the carriage. Kannice sat beside him, Greenleaf across from the them. Church gave Ethan pouches of fragrant herbs from which to make a poultice: sorrel, burdock, and cowslip.

At the first shudder of motion, pain lanced Ethan's belly and he sucked a hard breath through gritted teeth. Kannice eyed him with concern. Even Greenleaf watched him, as if afraid he would have to sew Ethan back together.

The rest of their journey up Marlborough Street, and then over to Sudbury Street and the tavern, proved uneventful. Greenleaf went so far as to draw and grip his flintlock as they rode. Ethan could only guess that Hutchinson's interest in Ethan's inquiry had made the sheriff extra attentive; even so, it made him uncomfortable. He half expected Greenleaf to turn that pistol on him before they reached the tavern.

They rattled to a halt in front of the *Dowsing Rod*, eliciting another gasp from Ethan. Kannice hurried inside to get Kelf. Greenleaf and Ethan stayed where they were, gazes locked.

"She can find you because you're a speller, too, isn't that right?"

"Sheriff—"

"That's the only explanation that makes sense."

"The only one? That sounds like something only a conjurer would know. It makes me wonder about you."

Greenleaf chuffed a frustrated breath and glared out the chaise's window. "Just once I'd like an honest answer from you."

"And just once I'd like to feel that you weren't looking for an excuse to have me hanged."

The sheriff faced him again, glanced at his flintlock, and slipped it into his pocket. "That's fair, I suppose."

The admission shocked Ethan, and yet Greenleaf wasn't finished.

"The thing is, Kaille, I feel about this business much as the lieutenant governor does. I've lived here most of my life, and as much as I dislike Adams and his rabble, I wouldn't want to see another shooting like the one in March. Anything this witch does to roil the waters makes my life more difficult."

"So, for the time being, you have no interest in putting a rope around my neck."

The sheriff laughed. "For the time being."

"It's possible," Ethan said, "that she would have an easier time tracking and finding me than she would someone else."

"All right, then. You should have a care. And for the next few days, I'll see to it that men of the watch spend more time on Sudbury Street."

Kannice emerged from the tavern, Kelf lumbering behind her.

"We set a pallet downstairs in the back room off the kitchen. It's a bit cramped, but at least you won't have to navigate the stairway. Kelf and the sheriff can take you in."

"Aye, all right." Ethan regarded Greenleaf again. "Thank you, Sheriff."

"Don't mention it. To anyone."

Ethan grinned.

Between them, the barman and Greenleaf had no trouble helping Ethan into the tavern and to the pallet Kannice had arranged. Greenleaf left them, Kannice and Kelf went back to preparing the day's stew, and Ethan slept. When he woke next, late in the day, he felt much improved. He needed no help leaving the pallet and back room, and was hungry enough to eat two bowls of the fish chowder Kannice and Kelf had made. He offered to help them with the growing mob crowding the great room, but Kannice shooed him out of the way.

So it was that he had returned to the room off the kitchen when another spell shook the building to its foundations. No one else felt it, of course, but Ethan summoned Uncle Reg and confirmed that he hadn't imagined it.

"I thought it came from nearby," Ethan said to the specter. At Reg's nod, he asked, "The wharves?"

The ghost pressed his hands together as if in prayer and then pointed up.

"The North End. In the vicinity of the Meeting House?"

Reg shook his head.

"The Christ Church."

Yes.

"Do you know what kind of spell? What it did?"

No.

He wanted to leave immediately, and even considered slipping out of the tavern through the back entrance. Kannice wouldn't know he was gone until she came back to check on him, and on a night as busy as this one, that wouldn't be for hours. He could be gone and back by then.

He abandoned the idea after about three seconds. Kannice was worried enough without him vanishing into another stormy night. She deserved to know where he was going and why. He walked out into the great room, and, while Kannice was busy ladling stew, braved the stairs. He had to rest halfway to the top, but eventually reached the second floor corridor and the room he shared with Kannice. There he changed into fresh clothes and strapped on his blades.

Returning to the ground floor proved far easier, but Kannice waited for him at the bottom of the stairway, her gaze flinty.

"Heading out?" Her voice only just carried over the din in the tavern.

"I felt another spell."

"I don't care if you were invited to dinner with the king himself."

"That's hardly telling; you don't like the king."

He essayed a smile. She growled his name.

"This conjurer isn't going to wait for me to recover," he said, sobering. "The trial is approaching, and she is intent on stopping it. I can't let that happen."

"And if she attacks you again?"

"I'll find a way to protect myself."

"That's not very convincing."

"She's human, and a conjurer. She's subject to the laws of nature and magick just as I am. She may know more than I do right now, but she has to have a weakness. Ramsey did. Peter Darrow did. All of us do. I'll discover what it is and use it against her." He lifted a shoulder. "That's what I do."

He thought this would anger her more. It didn't. She put her arms around him and laid her head gently against his chest. "I know."

She looked up at him and kissed him, and they separated.

"I'll be back as soon as possible. You have my word."

He shrugged on his coat, grimacing at the anguish in his gut.

Kannice frowned. "You're mad."

"Aye, but you married me anyway, so what does that say about you?"

She slapped his arm. "Get going."

He left the tavern, stepping into the gale. The air had grown more temperate, though clouds still blanketed the sky. With his limp and knife wound, the walk into the North End was torment. By the time he came to the great spire and noble brick façade of the old Christ Church, he was sweating within his coat, his face damp and whipped raw by the wind.

Every step was like another magickal blade carving up through his leg and into his groin. He cursed the woman and her spells.

Men had gathered in a tight cluster at the church entrance, and Ethan continued along Salem Street in that direction as quickly as his injury would allow. Once on the church grounds he pushed his way past a few of the men, earning scowls and not caring in the least.

On the single stone step leading to the doorway, sat a man in a dark suit, his powdered wig askew, blood streaming over his face from a gash on his brow. He rubbed his temple with a shaking hand. Another man, Ethan saw, lay in the lane that intersected Salem Street. Several more people stood around this person. As Ethan watched, this second victim sat up, conscious it appeared, and not visibly hurt.

"What happened here?"

The first injured man raised his glance to Ethan's. He was younger than Ethan by several years and had dark eyes, a straight nose, and a cleft chin. In addition to the cut on his forehead, a bruise darkened high on his cheek.

"Who are you, sir?"

This was asked of Ethan by another man, a reverend, judging from his black robe and white clerical bands. He was older, with an unwelcoming aspect and a heavy wig of a style that hadn't been popular in Boston for many years. He hovered beside the hurt gentleman, protective, suspicious of Ethan.

"My name is Ethan Kaille, Reverend sir."

"Kaille?" the man on the step repeated. "I know that name. My brother spoke of you just a day or two ago."

"Your brother?"

"I am Samuel Quincy. I believe you are acquainted with Josiah."

The resemblance was vague at best, but he had no reason to doubt the man. "It's a pleasure to meet you, sir, though I regret the circumstance. Can you tell me what happened here?"

"Devilry!" the reverend said before Quincy could answer. "Wickedness! Unnatural occurrences that can only be the design of Satan!"

"It's all right, Mather," Quincy said. "*I'm* all right. Leave us for a moment, will you?"

"You're not all right. I've sent for a doctor. You're not to move from this spot." The reverend cast a warning glance Ethan's way, and sidled off a short distance.

"That's Mather Byles?" Ethan asked, watching the reverend.

"It is. I take it you've heard of him."

"I know him by reputation."

As his given name implied, Reverend Byles was a descendent of Increase and Cotton Mather. And like his forbearers, the latter in particular, he was among the most vocal of today's Boston clergy in calling for the burning of so-called "witches." He was also, Ethan gathered, a vocal loyalist. No doubt he disapproved of Josiah Quincy's writings and his connections to the Sons of Liberty. Then again, Ethan would have been surprised to learn that the Quincy brothers attended the same church.

"He's harmless enough."

Not to a conjurer. Ethan kept this thought to himself. "What happened, Mister Quincy. Who hurt you?"

"I don't know. I had just emerged from the church when I was struck by two objects—stones, I believe. One hit here." He pointed to the bruise on his cheek. "The other opened the wound you see on my brow."

"Did you seen anyone throw something or do anything else suspicious?"

Quincy leaned forward and peered toward the man sitting in the lane. "Well, that fellow there fell down around the time I was struck, so he might have been hit as well. Or maybe he threw the objects and then pretended to be hurt, though the direction isn't right. I thought the stones came from in front of the church."

"Do you remember seeing a woman nearby? Young, attractive?"

"No. No one like that."

"Have you been receiving messages, sir? Like those received by your brother and Messieurs Adams and Paine?"

Quincy's gaze slid away briefly. "Threats you mean?" he whispered. "Yes, I have. I hadn't put much stock in them, even after what happened to John and Robert. Foolish of me." He eyed the reverend. "Do you believe I was attacked with magick?" he asked, still in a whisper.

"Yes, sir, I do."

"And you . . . you have experience with such things?"

Ethan gave the slightest of nods.

"Then tell me what I should do, Mister Kaille. I don't like being frightened, or bullied."

"Do what you've been doing, sir. Prepare for the trial, keep your obligations to the province. This conjurer only wins if you surrender to her abuse."

"*Her* abuse?" Quincy repeated.

"Aye, sir."

"I see. Well, I thank you for your words of encouragement. I shall try to take them to heart."

"Very good, sir."

Footsteps behind Ethan drew the man's gaze. Ethan turned, and the figure walking his way checked himself in mid-stride.

"Mister Kaille."

"Doctor Church."

Church continued up the path, halting before Ethan and Quincy. "Samuel and I are old friends," he said.

Ethan didn't know how to respond. "Yes, sir. I know he'll be in good hands. I'll see to that other gentleman." To Quincy, he said, "Good evening, sir. I hope you recover swiftly from your injuries."

"Thank you."

Ethan started away, but hadn't gone far when Church called to him.

He faced the doctor again.

"I trust you're not exerting yourself overmuch."

"I'm doing what I have to, sir, and no more."

He continued past Reverend Byles and onto the street. The second man was on his feet now, though he looked dazed and unsteady. A few others still stood with him.

"Are you all right, friend?" Ethan asked, approaching the man.

He wore shabby clothes. His gray hair stood on end, and deep lines gave his face a cadaverous look. Even at this proximity, Ethan saw no obvious wounds on him.

"I suppose I'm all right," the man said, leery of Ethan. "Who are you?"

"I just happened by. I'm a thieftaker here in the city."

The man's expression brightened. "A thieftaker. Do ya know the Empress, then? Miss Pryce?"

Ethan managed not to laugh. "I do, yes. Can you tell me what happened? Did someone attack you?"

"Nothin' like that, no. I was walkin' by, on my way home from the shipyard. And as I pass the church, suddenly I feel funny. Like I've had one too many drams, if you know what I mean. Next thing I know, I'm lyin' in the street, and these coves are gathered 'round me like I died or somethin'."

A slow chill ran through Ethan's body. "Has anything like this ever happened to you before?"

"Nah. This was a first."

"And how do you feel now?"

The man scratched his head. "Well, I'm not sure. Odd, really, like I just woke up and can't clear my head."

Ethan had never considered that a conjurer might attempt what he suspected Miss Lamb was doing. He didn't even know if it was possible. But it did explain the man stumbling in the coffee house when she attacked him for the first time, and also the cry he heard just before she stabbed him with her magickal knife. And Janna Windcatcher, who knew more about conjuring than anyone in Boston, had told him more than once that a speller with the necessary knowledge and skill could do pretty much anything.

"I'm goin' t' be on my way then," the man said, after a short silence.

"Yes, all right," Ethan said, distracted by the dark direction his thoughts had taken. "Be well, friend."

Before the ship worker had gone far, Ethan strode after him. "One more question, if I may," he said, pulling abreast of the man. "How long have you worked in the shipyard?"

"Long time now," he said. "I apprenticed there as a lad, and have been working at full wage for nigh ten years."

Ethan almost stumbled. Even if the man started his apprenticeship late, say at sixteen or seventeen, that would make him only thirty-three or thirty-four now. He looked twenty years older than that.

"Well . . ." Ethan said. "Thank you."

The man frowned, clearly puzzled by their exchange, but walked on. Ethan halted in the lane and watched him go. His thoughts churned.

Blood spells were the most powerful conjurings he cast. He used herbs —mullein usually—for wardings, and betony for other forms of protection. And he sourced lesser castings in leaves or grass or sometimes bark. But for the most demanding spells, nothing worked better than blood.

Other conjurers, though, including some he had fought, some to whom he had very nearly succumbed, used killing spells. They took a life in order to bolster the potency of their conjurings. If a blood spell could shatter a window, a killing spell could bring down a house. No warding could stand up to such castings. On the other hand, killing spells invariably left behind a corpse, making them easy to trace.

What if this woman was doing something like a killing spell, but less obvious? What if she took some life for her spell, but not enough to kill? What if she had aged the ship worker twenty years in order to hurt Samuel Quincy? And what if she had done the same in the coffee house and carriage in order to harm Ethan? That would explain the unearthly strength of her attacks and the repeated failure of Ethan's wardings.

The question was, how could he combat a conjurer willing to commit such acts of barbarity in pursuit of her magick? He would not hurt others in order to defeat her. He had cast one such spell in his entire life—in desperation, and so that he could save another life, not his own. That spell, which killed a creature that didn't deserve to die, had haunted him ever since. He would not repeat the sin.

But failing that, how could he strengthen his own magick to match hers?

Another thought: Perhaps he was thinking about this backward. Maybe the answer wasn't to strengthen his spells, but rather to weaken hers. And he had an idea of how he might do that.

VI

He started away from the church, back toward the South End. Less than two streets south of Salem, just short of Middle Street on Love Lane, the finding spell hit him, coiling around his legs like a magickal vine and then retreating into the darkness.

Ethan spat a curse and quickened his pace, despite the aches in his leg and body. At his first opportunity, he headed east, toward the North End wharves. Which at this point in the evening, would, he hoped, be empty.

Seconds later, a second finding spell hit him, wrapping so firmly around his calves that he nearly fell.

He forged on, like a man wading through mud, and soon broke free of the conjuring.

He turned onto Fish Street—going north now, putting more distance between himself and the busier streets of Cornhill. As he followed Ship Street and then Lynn to the tip of the North End, he heard the rumble of carriage wheels on cobblestone. The air here was thick with brine and ship's tar, and the wind howled in the wood of hulking warehouses.

Ethan walked out onto one of the wharves, the longest he could find. At the end of it, he halted. He pushed up his sleeve, cut himself, and recited a warding spell. It rattled in the wood of the wharf. Reg shone beside him, grim-faced and watchful.

A carriage rolled to a stop at the base of the wharf and its door opened. There was no moon this night, and the street and waterfront were shrouded in shadow. He could barely see, but he knew this had to be Miss Lamb. She appeared to wear a pale gown and dark cape.

"Will you stay out there all night, Mister Kaille?" she called, a thread of laughter in her voice. "Do you fear me so?"

He did, but he also had a plan in mind.

He cut himself again and cast a variation on a fist spell, something he used often in fights. He aimed it not at her, but at the rump of one of the horses pulling her carriage. The animal reared. Ethan cut himself and magickally slapped the other horse. Both creatures surged forward and the carriage rattled away. The last Ethan saw of the vehicle, the driver was pulling on their reins calling for them to stop.

Miss Lamb stared after them. Ethan strode in her direction. Hearing his steps, she faced him.

"An odd tactic," she said.

"Not if I'm right about you."

He didn't wait for her reply, but cut himself again and said within his mind, *Ambure ex cruore evocatum.* Scald, conjured from blood.

It could have been a painful attack, but he felt certain she would be warded, despite her confidence. He was right. The spell didn't burn her, as it would have an unwarded victim. The impact of the casting against her wardings did knock her back, though, and it elicited a satisfying grunt.

She muttered something and her specter appeared beside her, small and deepest red. The conjuring hit him hard and brought renewed pain. But it didn't kill him. It didn't come close.

He continued to advance on her. "You're not as strong when you can't draw your magick from the people or creatures around you." He slashed at his forearm with his knife and cast as quickly. A fire spell.

It staggered her. She threw a conjuring back at him, but it broke against his warding, like a sea wave on rock. He gritted his teeth at the pain that came with the blow; he didn't break stride.

She retreated from him, searching over her shoulder for the carriage.

"Would you draw power from your driver or from the horses?" Ethan asked. "I can't decide which would be more cruel, and I'm wondering if you have any thoughts in this regard."

"Maybe I should take the power from you."

"I considered that. I don't think you can. You've threatened to kill me every time we've met, and yet you've never used me as the source for a spell. It would have been so easy. Except I ward myself, and while your enhanced spells can master my wardings, the act of casting can't. Isn't that right?"

"I can still match you conjuring for conjuring," she said, venom in the words.

"Aye, I'm sure you can. For a time at least. I've been a speller for as long as you've been alive, and I've learned plenty. I like my chances in an honest contest of magick."

He cut himself and cast again. This time he directed his magick not at her, but at the lane just in front of her. The spell thrummed and the cobblestones buckled. Miss Lamb stumbled and fell to her knees.

She gathered her petticoats and clambered to her feet.

"Despite what you have done to me, Miss Lamb, I have no desire to hurt you," Ethan said. "I was hired for one purpose: to end the harassment of John Adams, the Quincy brothers, and Robert Treat Paine. Promise me that you will cease your attacks on them, and you need not see me again."

The woman huffed a laugh. "I care nothing for your purpose, and have no intention of altering my own. And you should know that my name is not Lamb."

Ethan blinked. "You're not the sister of Francis Lamb?"

She said nothing, but canted her head. Ethan thought she was contemplating a reply. Too late, he realized she was listening for something. Carriage wheels.

He strode past her, carving blood from his arm and aiming another spell at her. She reeled. Ethan hastened his retreat, limping away at speed, the clatter of the carriage and the clop of horse hooves growing louder by the moment.

"You should run, Mister Kaille!" She called after him. "If only you could!"

Pain in his leg. Agony in his midriff. Yet, he could not move fast enough. Fleeing was folly, and he knew it. On the thought, he halted and spun. Another flash of his blade, another spell on his lips. "*Discuti ex cruore evocatum.*"

He directed the shatter spell not at her, but at the front left wheel of the carriage as it rolled toward her.

The rending of wood echoed off the warehouses. The carriage almost toppled onto its side, the driver struggling to rein the horses to a stop.

Ethan didn't watch more than that, but hurried on. A casting thundered in the street and he steeled himself, fearing what she sought to do to him now. Magick crashed into his back and he sprawled onto stone, scraping his hands and cheek, battering his already abused body. From this distance, though, her spell was too weak to best his warding.

He forced himself up and limped on. Behind him, the woman yowled in frustration.

Ethan turned at the next corner, eager now to make his way to the streets least likely to be crowded at this time of night. Anything to confound her.

He cut through the heart of the North End, and then Cornhill, breathing hard, every step knifing through him. He needed help, and he preferred to avoid Sephira if he could. He had built a friendship with Gaspar Mariz, a powerful conjurer who worked for Sephira. They had conjured together to defeat Nate Ramsey. Ethan hoped Mariz would help him again now.

He lived in a small flat on Shrimpton's Lane, not far from the Town Dock, but when Ethan reached the building, he found Mariz's windows dark. He knocked on the door, but to no avail. Left with no other choice, he continued on to Summer Street and Sephira Pryce's grand, white marble home.

One of her immense toughs, a man he didn't recognize, stood on her portico, arms crossed over his chest. As Ethan followed the cobblestone path from the street to her door, he stepped forward, arms dropping to his side.

"Easy," Ethan said, showing both hands. "I need a word with Mariz."

"Is she expecting you?"

He wanted to say that he had no desire to speak with Sephira, but he knew better. She would want to hear whatever Ethan said to Mariz.

"No. I'm Ethan K—"

"I know who you are." The man turned and entered the house, leaving Ethan in the gusty dark.

The door opened again moments later, and the same tough motioned him inside.

Ethan had visited Sephira's home several times before. It was luxurious, tastefully appointed with elegant furniture and artwork. Her study housed spectacular collections of firearms and blades from around the world. In short, it was far more than Sephira Pryce deserved.

She sat curled on a couch in her common room, wearing a black silk blouse and waistcoat embroidered in silver and purple. Her hair hung loose, candlelight glittered in her eyes. A cup of what Ethan assumed was Madeira wine rested on the low table before her.

Nap and Gordon stood nearby, their countenances no more welcoming than hers.

"It's late to be calling, Ethan."

"I know. Forgive me. I came to speak with Mariz."

"Casey told me as much. Why?"

He had prepared himself for this.

"I need help with a magickal matter. There's a new conjurer in Boston, and she is . . . formidable."

"And why should I care?"

"She seeks to prevent the trial of Preston and his men, to sow chaos and bring about more violence. At the very least, she's attempting to re-kindle the grievances of February and March."

Sephira leaned forward and picked up her cup. "That would be . . . un-fortunate. The last thing we need is another excuse for Adams and his friends to stir up trouble."

Sephira had long been a loyalist, and she knew Ethan had recently em-braced the Whig cause. He let the comment pass.

"Is this woman the reason you wound up at the home of Benjamin Church yesterday?"

He stared. "How did you know that?"

At this, she smiled. "Ethan, you have to ask? I know everything." She quirked an eyebrow, waiting for his reply.

"Aye, she's the reason. She came within a hair's breadth of killing me. A blade spell that nearly disemboweled me."

Sephira wrinkled her perfect nose. "More than I needed to know." She sipped her wine. "She sounds like someone I should meet."

"You might have already. I believe she's the sister of your friend."

She stilled. "What friend?"

The ice in her words warned him: He had strayed into dangerous wa-ters.

"Francis Lamb."

Sephira set her cup back on the table, and uncoiled, like a hunting cat. "Charlotte is a conjurer?"

"Charlotte," Ethan repeated.

"You said his sister, didn't you?"

"She hadn't told me her name, although she denied that her family name was Lamb."

"It's not. She is Charlotte Whitcomb." Sephira stood and retrieved a de-canter of wine. "Would you care for some?"

"Please."

She poured some wine into a cup and reached for a pitcher of water, looking a question his way over her shoulder.

"Just a splash."

"Lamb is a business acquaintance," she said, her back to him. "Nothing more."

He had the good sense not to mention her coquettish manner the day he saw them together. "My mistake."

"An honest one, I'm sure."

She turned, handed him the wine. Her cheeks had colored. He wasn't sure he had ever before seen her embarrassed.

"What do you know about the sister?"

"Not a lot. Francis is a good deal older than she. His father died, and the mother remarried. It would seem she wed a witch."

She said this to goad him. He didn't reply, which earned him a smirk.

"So, you need Mariz . . ."

"It's hard to explain."

"Try me," she said, in a way that told him he wouldn't get to speak with the conjurer otherwise.

Ethan told her what he had learned about Charlotte's magick and the sourcing of her spells. The more he talked the harder her expression grew.

"This is why I hate your kind," she said when he was done. "The insidiousness of it all. At least when I hurt someone, I use normal means—fists, firearms, blades. But you and your fellow witches . . ." She shook her head. After another sip of wine, though, she cast a look Nap's way. "Bring Mariz."

The ensuing minutes passed slowly and in taut silence. Ethan wandered the room, scrutinizing the art and the baubles on her tables and shelves. Gordon watched him. Sephira returned to her couch, adopting an attitude of indifference.

Nap returned eventually with Mariz a step behind him. Mariz was by far the slightest of Sephira's men. Lean, narrow-shouldered, with wheaten hair, a wispy beard and mustache, and golden-rimmed spectacles, he looked more like a bookseller than the hired tough of Boston's leading thieftaker. After two years as the man's rival and friend, though, Ethan knew him to be smart, resourceful, and an accomplished speller.

Mariz greeted Ethan with a nod before turning to Sephira. "*Senhora*," he said, his Portuguese accent coloring the word. "You sent for me."

"At Ethan's request. He wants your help with a conjurer." To Ethan, she said, "You will discuss this here, now. If the plan you develop meets with my approval, Mariz will help you. If not . . ." She lifted a shoulder, dark curls shining.

He didn't like her conditions—this was why he had hoped to find the man at his home—but Mariz worked for her, and Sephira had long been suspicious of Ethan and Mariz's friendship. She had only a rudimentary understanding of magick, and she probably feared that the bond between conjurers could prove stronger than Mariz's loyalty to her. She might have been right; Ethan truly didn't know.

With Sephira listening, he explained again his battles with Charlotte Whitcomb, her harassment of the trial lawyers, and the nature of her magickal attacks.

When he finished, Mariz said, "So, we would need to ward the people of this city. That way, she could not draw upon them for power."

"That's right. But it's not just the people."

Mariz frowned, but dipped his chin in agreement. "Quite right. Have you spoken of this with the African woman?"

Janna. "She's my next conversation. I wanted to ask for your help first."

"It sounds to me like this helps Samuel Adams more than anyone else," Sephira said. "You hadn't mentioned earlier that he hired you. I'm not sure I like this."

"Maybe it would interest you to know that Hutchinson has hired me as well. He doesn't like this business with Miss Whitcomb." *Nor does he like Francis Lamb.* This, he kept to himself.

She scowled. "Well, it certainly interests me in the coin you're earning. With all these men paying you, I would want a cut."

"Only two men are paying me, Sephira: Adams and Hutchinson. But by all means, I can offer you a third of what I'm earning."

"Why not half?"

"Because you're not the one who was gutted by a magickal blade."

That, of all things, made her laugh. "Fair enough."

"What would you like me to do, *senhora*?"

"Bring me the wine," she said, with a gesture at the decanter. He did as she instructed and waited as she refilled her cup. "What role do you believe Francis plays in all of this?"

Ethan opened his hands. "I've met the man once. You know him better than I. What do you think?"

She frowned.

"Are he and his sister close?"

"He speaks well of her. And often." She said this in a flat voice. Ethan thought he sensed a twinge of jealousy.

"May I ask, what was the nature of your business with him?"

Sephira sent a scalding glare his way. "No, you may not ask." She set her cup on the table, sloshing a drop over the rim, stood, and began to wander the room.

"I'm sorry I—"

She rounded on him, leveling a finger at his heart. "Don't!" After a moment, she lowered her hand. "The rest of you leave. Including you, Mariz. I'll have instructions for you soon enough."

Nap waited until she had looked away before glancing at Gordon and raising an eyebrow. He led the other toughs from the room, leaving Ethan and Sephira alone.

He waited, wary and uncomfortable. If she wanted to do him harm, she would have given the task to Nap and the others; he knew that. The truth was, though, he feared her intimacy as much as he did her fury. They had been mortal enemies for too long.

She regarded him and rolled her eyes. "Oh, good Lord, don't look so frightened. I'm not about to bare my soul to you." She waved a hand in the direction her toughs had gone. "There are just certain things I prefer they not hear."

"So I don't need my confessional stole?"

The corners of her mouth quirked. "Hardly." She plucked a bottle of dark spirit from the end table that had held the wine, filled a glass, and held it out to Ethan.

"No, thank you."

"You've asked me questions. You're going to drink with me."

He acquiesced with a small shrug and took the glass. She filled a second glass and raised it in salute. Ethan reciprocated. Sephira drained hers in a single gulp and gazed expectantly at Ethan. What choice did he have? He sniffed the glass. Rum. It smelled sweet, rich with molasses and spice. He downed it, the burn smooth and warming. She refilled both glasses.

"I misunderstood my relationship with Francis," Sephira said, resuming her orbit around the room. "He wanted information—about Boston's merchants and business owners, and, yes, her lawyers as well. I thought he was asking as a Customs man and loyalist. I assumed he wanted me to introduce him to our wealthiest Tories so that he might unite them and put an end, once and for always, to non-importation and other tactics used by Adams and his rabble. And I would have been happy to oblige. I also assumed . . . Well, let's just leave it at that: I assumed."

Ethan thought it best to avoid commenting on this last. "You no longer believe Lamb is interested in fighting Adams on the non-importation agreements?"

She didn't answer, but drank down her rum and eyed him until he did the same. Again, she filled both glasses.

"This is from Martinique, by the way," she said, holding up the bottle, "and worth more by far than whatever Adams and Hutchinson are paying you. So enjoy it."

"It's good rum," he said, and meant it.

"To answer your question, I don't believe Francis is your usual Customs man. I think it far more likely that he is a spy. His sister, too. And now that I know she's a conjurer, I'm even more convinced of this."

Samuel Adams had said much the same thing. She might have found this amusing. Or insulting. This, too, he kept to himself.

"I wouldn't think you'd object to the Crown sending a spy or two to Boston," he said. "His aims are your aims, aren't they?"

"I thought so, until you arrived." She paused before her hearth, and peered back at him, alluring as ever, and more thoughtful than he'd ever seen her. "This may surprise you, but I don't want another shooting, and I don't want Whigs and Tories fighting in the streets. Lest you forget, Boston has been my home for a good deal longer than it's been yours."

Hutchinson, Greenleaf, now Sephira. If someone had asked him only a day or two ago, he would have listed all three as enemies, even villains. He considered again things Samuel Adams had said in the *Dowser* a couple of nights before, about the trial and the soldiers awaiting judgment. Even now, only months removed from bloodshed and tragedy, men like Adams and Hutchinson were more united than they ever would have guessed.

"That's the sort of thing I usually say," he told Sephira. "You're getting sentimental, like me."

Her expression soured. "No I'm not. It's simply a matter of business: If Adams has his rabble in the streets, agitating for 'liberty' and such nonsense, they won't have time to crack houses and pinch the goods you and I are paid to retrieve."

That sounded more like the Sephira he'd known all these years.

"You'll allow Mariz to help me?"

She threw back the rum in her glass. Ethan followed her example but then set his glass on a table. Between the wine he'd had, and the injuries he'd suffered, the rum was clouding his thoughts.

Sephira smirked again, perhaps sensing that he was not his usual, sober self. "Ethan, I could almost take advantage of you."

"No," he said, "you couldn't. And if you tried, you'd have Kannice to deal with, which you don't want."

She laughed, tipping her head back. She had a marvelous laugh—throaty, unbridled. He'd long thought it her most attractive attribute, which was saying something.

"I believe you," she said. "She's fiery, and clever. I can tell. She and I could be friends if not for you poisoning her mind against me."

"I think the beatings did that."

She twitched a shoulder. "Also simply business." She poured herself more rum, didn't offer to fill his glass. "Yes, you can have Mariz for as long as it takes. How much are they paying you? Adams and Hutchinson, I mean."

"Five pounds from Hutchinson. Adams, Warren, and I didn't settle on an amount."

She shook her head, putting him in mind of a disapproving parent. "No wonder you lived for so long in that shabby room above the cooperage. Hutchinson could have offered twice as much, and I expect the Sons of Liberty will plead poverty once you've done their bidding."

"Well, whatever I get, I'll pay you a third. Do you want that in writing?"

"No. You know better than to cross me."

VII

Ethan spoke briefly with Mariz and told Sephira that he would return early in the morning to put their plans in motion. He didn't know where Charlotte Whitcomb was now, but he didn't have any desire to face her again this night. He was tired, sore, and, he had to admit, a little bit drunk.

Sephira, in a moment of uncharacteristic generosity, ordered Nap to transport Ethan to the *Dowser* in her carriage. Ethan accepted the offer, and at Nap's invitation sat with the man atop the box at the front of the vehicle. For a time, they rattled along in silence, though Nap sent glances his way every so often.

"Never thought I'd see the day when you and Miss Pryce drank together," he finally said.

"Neither did I," Ethan said. "Then again, if I'd known how good her rum was, I would have contrived an occasion years ago."

The man's laugh was high-pitched, childlike. Ethan wasn't sure he had ever heard it before.

Nap quieted, eyed him again. "You know it changes nothing. She'll be back after you tomorrow, or the next day. You're rivals before anything else."

"Is that a warning?"

The man shrugged and twitched the reins. "Take it however you want."

They didn't speak again until Nap steered the carriage to a halt in front of the tavern.

Ethan thanked him, eliciting little more than a shift of one shoulder. "You think she's wrong to trust me," Ethan said.

"I think you come to her when you need help, and the rest of the time you show her nothing but disrespect."

"And what of the beatings she's given me? Meted out by you and your friends, by the way. What about all the times she's taken my coin, or my clients? And what about the times she's had me work on her behalf because magick was involved in whatever inquiry she happened to be pursuing? We use each other, Nap. We threaten and we mock and we fight. And every now and then we cooperate. Is that really such a bad thing?"

Nap turned his glare on Ethan. "I'm just saying, don't get used to this, and don't expect the rest of us to treat you like Mariz does. You . . . *conjurers* may stick together, but the rest of us . . . We owe everything we are to Miss Pryce."

"I'll keep that in mind. Good night."

He climbed down off the carriage and Nap snapped the reins and urged the horses on. Once Nap had turned the corner onto Hawkins Street, Ethan let himself into the tavern, locking the door behind him.

The *Dowser* smelled of bay and cream, wood smoke and bread. The evening crowd was long since gone, and Ethan didn't hear Kelf or Kannice in the kitchen. A single candle burned on the bar and embers glowed bright in the hearth, settling loudly, a ribbon of pale gray smoke rising into the flue. He took the candle and used it to navigate the stairs and dark corridor to his and Kannice's bedroom.

He opened and closed the door as quietly as he could, but as he undressed, drawing sharp breaths each time he stretched his belly the wrong way, Kannice stirred.

"It's late," she said, her voice muffled.

"I know," he whispered. "I'm sorry. Go back to sleep."

She rolled over to look at him as he slid into bed beside her. She sniffed, raised herself onto one arm.

"Have you been drinking?"

His face warmed. "I had dram or two of rum, aye."

"Where?"

"Sephira's."

She sat up, fully awake now. "You were drinking with Sephira Pryce?"

"I hadn't planned on it. I went seeking help from Mariz and she . . . She started pouring rum."

"Do you have any idea how worried I've been about you? And there you were drinking rum with . . . I can't believe it."

"In fairness, it was very good rum."

She scowled. "You think this is funny?"

"A little bit, yes. We've spoken of this before, Kannice. You have no cause to be jealous of the woman."

"No, of course not. Except that she's beautiful, and would probably steal you away from me just out of spite."

He took her hand and wouldn't relinquish it when she tried to pull it away. "For her to steal me, I'd have to want to be stolen."

"I know that," she said, her voice softening a little. "But . . . you drank rum with Sephira Pryce."

"Aye. I'm not so drunk that I don't remember." Her frown returned. "I told you, I need help from Mariz. And, as it happened, I needed information from her, as well. About a man to whom she was attracted. She made the rum prerequisite for getting that information."

"I think next time someone asks you to go back to your thieftaking ways, I should forbid it."

He couldn't help it. As soon as he heard her say this, he tensed. He loved the life that they had built together. He was, for the most part, satisfied living and working as a tavern keeper. And he couldn't deny that Charlotte Whitcomb's assault had terrified him. But despite the pain and the fear, he also couldn't deny that he had enjoyed these past few days. His existence had grown . . . not dull, but safe, and a part of him longed for the sort of danger he'd been in since his first encounter with Whitcomb. Perhaps that made him unhinged, but he couldn't help himself.

"I didn't mean that," she said in a small voice.

"I think you did, a little bit at least."

She gathered the folds of their blanket in her fist, let it out, and then gathered it again. "I know better than to think you can give up thieftaking entirely. I've said that since the day you proposed to me, and I've meant it. But seeing you in that bed at Doctor Church's house frightened me so much. And now this. Thieftaking and marriage don't mix very well."

"I know that. And when I married you, I fully expected to give it up. I swore I would and I'll make the same promise now if you want me to. I'll be honest, though. I've missed it. I have some small talent as an investigator. I can help people, and I like that."

"So, are you saying you want to go back to—"

"Not all the time—just now and then. That was the agreement we reached when first we married, and I merely wish to honor it. But a moment ago, when you said what you did—"

"I shouldn't have said it, not even in jest."

Their eyes met, and for a long time neither of them spoke.

"This is who you are," she said, running a finger over his cheek. "I've known that for a long time. And for all these years, life with you has never been boring."

He took her hand again and kissed it.

"But no more drinking with Sephira. *That* I do forbid."

"Fair enough," Ethan said, and blew out the candle.

VIII

He roused himself early, tiptoed downstairs in the dark and cold so that he could change the dressing on his wound and put on his clothes without waking Kannice again.

He left the *Dowsing Rod* through the rear door, in case Lamb and Whitcomb had someone watching the front of the building, and followed a winding route through the South End to Sephira' house. The sky over Boston Harbor had started to lighten from black to a leaden gray and a howling wind flattened the grasses of d'Acosta's pasture, unseasonably warm and scented with rain, though the streets remained dry for now.

Mariz awaited him on Sephira's portico, a slight, shadowy figure. He smoked fragrant leaves from a pipe, the bowl flaring an angry red in the gloaming. At Ethan's approach, he tapped out the tobacco, set the pipe on the stone of the patio, and descended the three stairs to the cobbled path.

"The *senhora* told me to convey her greetings. She does not rise so early in the day."

"So, she told you this last night?"

The man grinned. "Yes."

With that wind whipping around them, they set out for the Neck and the tavern of Janna Windcatcher.

Janna's establishment, *The Fat Spider*, stood on a lonely stretch of road near the town gate. It was a ramshackle building, its roof sagging, its supporting timbers leaning at angles to one another, so that it seemed one of these storm gusts might bring down the whole structure. A sign out front read "T. Windcatcher, Marriage Smith. Love is Magick."

Mariz shook his head at the sign. "She does not fear the sheriff and his watch? Or men of the cloth coming to burn her out?"

"She knows they're all afraid of her, Greenleaf included."

Ethan tried the door but wasn't surprised to find it locked. The hour was extremely early for Janna.

"She's not going to be happy with us."

"Should we return later?" Mariz asked.

Ethan shook his head. He wanted to do this early, when few people were on the street. As it was, he regretted having waited for daybreak.

He knocked, waited, knocked again. At last, he saw candle glow through one of the begrimed windows. The lock clicked and the door opened a crack, revealing Janna, white hair shorn close to her dark scalp. She wore a plain linen gown, and a shawl that she held closed in her fist, the worn wool wrapped tightly around her bony shoulders.

"Kaille," she said with little warmth, drawing out his name. Black eyes flicked to Mariz but settled again on Ethan. "It's awful early t' be knockin'." A West Indian lilt shaded her words.

"I know. We need your help."

"'Course you do. You always need my help." She stared hard at him, lips pressed in a flat line. "You'll buy somethin'?"

"Bread and cheese for both of us."

"All right." She walked away from the door, leaving it open for them. They entered and Ethan closed and locked the door behind him. As always, her tavern smelled of cinnamon and clove, wood smoke and old wine.

"This is about all those spells I been feelin', isn't it?" she called from her kitchen.

"Aye."

"Some been powerful—more than normal, even for you."

"There's a new conjurer in the city."

"Thought as much."

She returned a few moments later, bearing a board loaded with cheeses and a round of bread. She poured Madeira wine into three cups, watered them generously, and set them on the table.

Sitting across from Ethan, she said, "Tell me about this new conjurer."

As he had more than once the previous night, Ethan described his battles with Charlotte Whitcomb, including the attack that nearly killed him. By the time he finished, Janna had reached the same conclusion he and Mariz had: The people of Boston needed to be warded.

"That's high magick she's doin'," Janna said. "Pullin' power like that without killin'? Don't know if I could do it."

High praise indeed. Ethan wasn't sure he had ever heard her admit to any deficiency in her own conjuring abilities.

"But if we can protect people, and beasts—make it impossible for her to enhance her spells in that way—we should be able to defeat her, right?"

"Maybe. Conjurer who can do that might know other ways to strengthen her spells. You say she's young?"

"Very," Ethan said, voice thick.

"And a spy?"

Ethan glanced at Mariz who stared back, candlelight reflected in his spectacles. Sephira probably would have preferred he keep that bit of information to himself. Fatigue had made him careless.

"I think that's possible. She certainly harbors no affection for Adams and his allies, and she's trying to disrupt the trial."

"All right, then. I can help you with the wardin'. We'll use mullein, betony, horehound—like we have before. That'll make the fight easier."

"I don't think you should join us for the fight, Janna."

She glowered. "I don't remember askin' your permission."

He knew better than to argue. Janna walked back behind her bar and gathered the herbs. Ethan and Mariz discussed the exact wording they would use. Ethan wondered aloud if they should wait to cast their warding until they knew when they would confront the woman, but Janna dismissed the idea from her back room.

"No need for that," she called to him. "A good conjurin' will last. We just have to cast it right. We do that this mornin', people ought to be protected for a few days at least."

She emerged from the back room holding three leather pouches, a cloud of fragrant air around her.

"A few days?" Ethan asked. "Then why do I have to ward myself as often as I do?"

"Because you get yourself in too many fights," Janna said.

A snort of laughter from Mariz made her grin.

"It's true, Kaille. You let other spellers pound on your wardin's like that, you better cast them again and again. This is different. From what you said, she ain't attackin' these people. She's trying to draw on them for spells. Our spell will hold. Long enough, at least, for us to drive her off."

Ethan hoped she was right.

They agreed on the wording—*Tegimen pro omnibus ex verbasco et marrubio et betonica evocatum*; Warding all, conjured from mullein, horehound, and betony—and left the *Fat Spider* for the core of the city. They could have cast from the Neck, but they wanted to be certain to reach the greatest possible number of people and beasts.

The sky had brightened and men and women were now abroad in the streets, many of them hurrying in one direction or another, casting anxious glances skyward. The three of them made their way north into the teeth of the wind. Ethan scanned the lanes continuously, expecting at any moment to see the repaired carriage of Charlotte Whitcomb bearing down on them. They halted at the Town House on King Street, on the precise stretch of lane where Preston's men had fired upon the agitators that night back in March. It struck Ethan as an appropriate place to cast their spell.

He watched as people passed by them.

Janna, equally wary, took advantage of a lessening of the flow of people on the street to remove from the pouches several leaves of each herb. She passed the sacks on to Mariz. He took some as well and handed the pouches to Ethan, who gathered what was left in his palm and faced the other two.

When there was no one within hearing distance, he nodded and they recited the spell in unison. Three glowing figures emerged into the silvery light: Uncle Reg, grim, russet like a newly risen moon; an ancient African woman, her expression as forbidding as Janna's, her body a brilliant, luminescent blue; and a young man in Renaissance garb who looked a good deal like Mariz, and gleamed with the warm beige of dried grasses in autumn sun. The spell growled like a wild thing in the stone, in the buildings around them. The very air seemed alive with their magick.

They couldn't know for certain if the casting had worked, but if the strength and effectiveness of the spell could be judged by what Ethan felt, he thought they had done well.

Certainly their conjuring caught the notice of Charlotte Whitcomb. The power of their spell was still fading, when another conjuring ran through the streets. A finding. It slammed into Ethan's legs with staggering force.

"Kaille?" Mariz said.

"She just hit me with a finding spell. Our casting got her attention."

"Do you think she knows what we did?"

Ethan looked a question at Janna.

"Maybe," she said. "Some conjurin's I feel, and I know just what they were. Others . . ." She shrugged. "If our spell worked, it won't matter, and she won't have access to enough power to remove the wardin'."

A fourth glowing figure stepped from the shadows of Pudding Lane. Whitcomb herself, wine-red, as insubstantial as mist: a conjured illusion, a way for the woman to speak with him and see where he was.

"What are you up to, Kaille?" the image demanded, her voice reed-thin, her eyes gleaming like red stars.

"Can't you tell?" he said. "You claim to be so skilled with your magick, I would have thought it would be obvious to you."

"You want to have a care, now especially. You don't want to anger me."

He didn't like the sound of that. "What do you mean?"

"Cast a finding spell. I know where you are. You should know where I am."

Panic rose in his chest. He cut his arm and cast the spell, knowing already what he would find. His magick snaked away through the lanes, only to whip back at him from the north and west. Not far. Just south of the Mill Pond. Usually, he wouldn't have been able to determine a conjurer's location more precisely than that. In this case, however, he could guess exactly: *The Dowsing Rod.*

He said as much to Janna and Mariz.

The illusion of the woman laughed. "Join us."

Ethan looked a question at his friends.

"Do it," Sephira's man said. "We will keep you safe here. You have my word."

Illusion spells were the simplest of magicks, and could often be sourced in fire or water. Seeing and speaking through one's illusion was more demanding. Ethan cut himself. "*Videre per mea imagine ex cruore evocatum.*"

He closed his eyes, felt his consciousness transported across lanes and over buildings until he found himself in Kannice's tavern. Kannice sat in a chair in the middle of the great room, her hands tied behind her and anchored to the chair. Kelf, still in his coat, lay beside the tavern door, bleeding from a raised wound on his temple. Whitcomb stood over Kannice, her forearm bloodied, a knife in her hand. That blood might as well have been a flintlock, full-cocked and aimed at Kannice's heart.

Kannice spotted his illusion and gasped. "Ethan!"

"Not really," the woman said.

"Are you all right?" he asked Kannice.

"She's fine. For now. I think you know that I can kill her with a word. For that matter, I can kill both of them. I can bring down this entire building in a storm of smoke and ember and flame, and you'll never find a trace of either of them. But I would rather not. I have no quarrel with her or the barman. This is between you and me."

Ethan thought the warding he and the others had conjured would protect Kannice and Kelf from spells, but he wasn't willing to risk being wrong. And he knew it couldn't save them if Whitcomb set fire to the building.

"I understand," he said. "What do you want?"

"I want you to send away the other conjurers. You should never have involved them. I should kill the barman simply to teach you a lesson, but I won't. Send them away, and face me alone, as you were meant to."

"Fine. Where and when?"

Her smile didn't reach her eyes. "Long Wharf in an hour. And make sure you send the other two away, Kaille. Immediately. I'll use finding spells to confirm that they're no longer with you. If you try to deceive me, your woman dies."

"I told you I'd do it, and I will. Just be at the wharf."

He started to release the illusion spell.

"Wait."

He let the magick rise again.

"I want to know what the three of you did with your casting."

"Too bad."

"Tell me, or I'll kill them."

"No, you won't. Because you know that if you do, I'll track you down and destroy you. I might die in the process, but I'll take you with me, and there won't be a damn thing you can do about it."

"You sound like a fool."

"And you sound like a spoiled child. I'm giving you what you want: a battle, face to face, just the two of us. The casting—you'll just have to guess."

Whitcomb sidled closer to Kannice, toying with her knife. Ethan was helpless to stop her.

"You'd spend her life for this one secret?"

He didn't want to tell her anything, but he couldn't chance angering her.

"It was a warding," he said. "A powerful one. The three of us cast it together using betony, horehound, and mullein. I thought that if I had others ward me, your spells would be less effective."

Whitcomb had stopped her advance on Kannice. Now she narrowed her eyes. "Why do it there? Why not here in the tavern, or at the home of one of your friends?"

Would his lie convince her?

"We purchased the herbs in the city, and we didn't dare waste even a few minutes taking them somewhere to cast. We had started back to my friend's flat, but stopped here."

"You bought them there? From who?"

"A doctor I know. I won't tell you more than that."

He knew what conclusion she would draw. He hoped the doctor would forgive him.

Satisfaction registered in the vivid eyes. "Of course. Warren. You wear your secrets poorly, Mister Kaille."

He schooled his features. "I've answered your questions. I've agreed to your terms. Now leave the tavern, or I swear you won't survive the morning."

"I'll leave, when I choose to do so. Your threats mean nothing to me. Your magick is no match for mine, no matter how well you're warded. Now, go. Send your friends away and go to the wharf. Don't attempt to deceive me."

Ethan turned the eyes of his illusion spell on Kannice, hoping to God this wouldn't be the last time he saw her alive.

"Go now, Kaille!"

He let the illusion fade. At the last second, just before he vanished, he heard Kannice call his name, but he didn't dare risk going back. Opening his eyes to the morning light of King Street, he swayed momentarily.

"Kaille?" Mariz asked, concern in his voice.

Ethan turned a quick circle, making certain that Whitcomb's conjured illusion was no longer within listening distance.

"She's at the *Dowsing Rod*. She has Kannice tied up and she's hurt Kelf. And if the two of you don't leave me right now, she's going to kill them."

"We're not leaving you."

"Yes, you are," he said rounding on Janna. "In the next minute or two, she's going to cast finding spells to make certain we're not together. You have to leave me. Kannice's life . . ." He broke off to take a steadying breath.

"I don' like this."

"I don't either. But if the spell we cast works, I should be able to defeat her."

"And if it doesn't?" Mariz asked.

"Then having the two of you there won't make any difference."

Neither of them argued the point.

"I need you to go to the *Dowsing Rod*," he went on. "Once you're certain that Whitcomb is gone, go in and see to Kannice and Kelf."

"I can do that," Janna said. "And if you need help with Whitcomb, you know how to find me."

"I do. Both of you."

Mariz gripped his arm for a moment and together he and Janna turned away. Ethan watched them go before striking out for the wharves. As he walked he grappled with his desire to ward himself again. He had told Whitcomb that he'd cast a protection spell with the others, and so any warding he conjured now might raise her suspicions. On the other hand, facing her without a warding in place would be suicide.

Really he had no choice. Turning onto an empty byway, he pushed up his sleeve, cut himself, and cast the spell. Reg appeared again beside him, his footsteps matching Ethan's stride for stride. With his conjuring still humming in the street, another finding spell flowed after him, tugging at his legs like ocean current.

Whitcomb's burgundy illusion fell in step on the other side of him, earning a silent snarl from Reg.

"What was that?"

"What are you talking about?" Ethan said, still walking, staring straight ahead.

"You cast again. Why?"

"It was another warding. Force of habit."

He sensed the glowing figure watching him, as if gauging his expression and manner. He turned and stared back at her, challenging her to disbelieve him.

She flashed a smile and winked out of sight. Ethan and Reg walked on. The smells of fish and tar intensified as they approached the water's edge, and the wind grew even stronger. Ethan walked out onto Long Wharf, the fill of the pier crunching beneath his feet. Even this early, he passed several wharfmen and laborers. Too many. Halfway out, he turned onto Minott's T, the wooden extension that jutted north off the main wharf. It was less crowded than the main part of the wharf, which would help him if the warding hadn't worked. Let her object; she hadn't specified where on the wharf they were to meet.

He walked to the end of the extension, and stared back at the city, watching the entrance to the wharf. Time stretched interminably, each passing minute deepening his apprehension. After more than an hour had dragged by, he started to wonder if she had sent him here to keep him occupied, so that she could carry out another attack on John Adams or one of the other attorneys.

He was just about to leave the wharf and search for her, when a carriage rolled to a stop on the lane fronting the shore. Its driver climbed down from the box; Ethan thought he gripped a pistol in one hand. The door on the near side of the carriage opened and Whitcomb stepped onto the street, elegant in red satin. The driver joined her a moment later, his weapon trained on a large man. Kelf.

Kannice's barman appeared unsteady on his feet, though the blood had been wiped or magicked from his temple. Whitcomb took the pistol from her driver and waved Kelf onto the wharf.

They walked slowly, Kelf's steps uncertain, the conjurer scanning the pier for Ethan. As they reached the "T," Ethan called to her.

She spotted him and forced Kelf in Ethan's direction.

Ethan knew he should have anticipated this. She would be sure to have a source for her spells at hand. He supposed he should be grateful she had chosen Kelf rather than Kannice, but that seemed small consolation. Their warding *had* to work.

"If I'd wanted you on the 'T' I would have said so," the woman called to him as she and Kelf drew close.

"If I'd cared what you wanted, I would have asked." He shifted his gaze. "Kelf, are you all right?"

"Been better," he said, eyes flicking toward the women. "This one gives your kind a bad name."

Whitcomb slammed the butt of her pistol into the side of Kelf's face, opening a new gash and staggering the man. "Keep quiet. And you," she said to Ethan, "you'll speak to me, and me only."

"I have very little to say to you, none of it fit for civil discourse."

She shook her head. "You insist on antagonizing me. Why? We might have been allies, you and I. As we discussed the other day, you've only recently counted yourself a Whig. Adams' cause doesn't mean so much to you. There are opportunities for spellers, here and in London. Come back to the Crown—serve His Majesty once more, as you did in your youth—and I can spare your life."

"You should have thought of this before you tried to kill me."

"You would have relented?"

"No, but you could have spared me this nonsense and wasted less of my time."

"Think of your friend here, Mister Kaille. Continue to provoke me and you not only ensure your own death, you harm him as well."

"Don't worry about me, Ethan," Kelf said, a hand held to the cut on his cheek, his fingers stained crimson.

Whitcomb glowered. Ethan held his tongue, not wishing to subject the barman to any more of her rage.

"Fine, then. Damn you both."

Ethan readied himself, knowing she wouldn't waste time, but would seek to kill with this first casting.

She muttered something he couldn't make out. The red ghost of that odd little girl materialized beside her, and power resonated deep in the water and wood beneath them. The spell struck Ethan in the chest like a hammer blow, driving him onto his heels. But it did no more. His warding held. More important, Kelf appeared to notice none of this, though the blood vanished from his face. He didn't cry out or reel or show any ill effect of her casting.

Whitcomb stared at Ethan and then at the barman.

"Impossible," she said, breathing the word.

She whispered in Latin again, too fast for Ethan to make out. He didn't know what she used to source this conjuring. It occurred to him in that instant that there was much he didn't understand about her magick. She had used life power from others to enhance her spells, but they also had some force of their own. Fueled by what?

He couldn't ponder this further now. Magick groaned through the wharf, another spell fell upon him, nearly buckling his knees. Once more, though, his defenses spared him the full impact of the conjuring. And as before, Kelf looked on without understanding, oblivious to Whitcomb's magick.

"What have you done to me?" She turned the pistol on Ethan.

He bit the inside of his cheek and cast a heat spell sourced in blood. Before she could pull the trigger, she cried out and released the weapon. It dropped to the wood and discharged, the bullet gouging the pier, but hurting no one.

"That spell you cast before," she said, wide-eyed. "What was it?" For the first time since he'd met her, she seemed truly afraid.

"What do you think it was?"

"You've stolen my power somehow."

A mistake of youth, thinking only of herself, assuming the spell had been directed at her. It might never occur to her that they had sought only to protect others. And he didn't correct her.

He threw a conjuring at her—a shatter spell that should have broken her leg, though he knew it wouldn't. She fell back a step, but her wardings were proof against his magick, just as his were against hers. Stalemated.

"We can batter each other with spells until we're both exhausted, making this a test of physical strength—a contest I will win," he added. "Or you can leave now. Get off this wharf, get out of my city."

She didn't answer. Ethan sensed another spell and braced himself. But this one slammed into Kelf, bringing a gasp of pain and driving the man to his knees. That was all, though. He survived her assault.

"No!" She looked from the barman to Ethan. "How did you know to ward him?"

She pushed past Ethan, lifted her petticoats and ran in the direction of the nearest wharfman. Ethan strode after her.

As she drew even with the man, she whirled and cast again. Magick thrummed, and Ethan stumbled at the impact. But this conjuring, too, broke against his warding.

Whitcomb gaped, comprehension coming to her at long last. "All of them," she said. "You warded all of them."

Ethan walked toward her. "That's right."

She sneered. "And now you think you've won."

"I think you have no choice but to end your assaults on Adams and Paine and the Quincys. That's been my concern from the start, my reason for . . ."

Confronted with her laughter, he trailed off.

Something flashed in her hand and, thinking it another weapon, Ethan opened his mouth to shout a warning. But it was a crystal, pale blue, jagged, and as large as her palm.

She raised both arms, holding the stone aloft, and began to chant, not in Latin this time, nor in English. Ethan didn't recognize the tongue. At least not at first. A memory stirred—an encounter he'd had earlier this year with a different sort of conjurer: a young woman who gladly accepted the moniker *witch*.

"That's Gaelic," Kelf whispered. "My Da spoke a bit. Haven't heard it in years."

At first nothing happened, and Ethan wondered if his warding had prevented this incantation from working as well. He should have known better.

The wind grew stronger, pushing so hard at Ethan and Kelf that they had to lean into it. It made Whitcomb's hair dance around her head and shoulders like the asps of Medusa, but otherwise she appeared unaffected.

The surface of the harbor, rough already, surged and fell. Waves broke over the edge of the wharf.

Lightning carved across the gray sky and thunder boomed an immediate response. Rain fell in a sudden torrent, sheets of it blowing across the waterfront and then the city. Men on Long Wharf and others beyond scattered in every direction seeking shelter. The tempest soaked Ethan and Kelf and also Whitcomb, though she gave no indication that she noticed or cared.

Still the gale increased. Foam whitened the tips of the harbor swells, as if they were in the middle of the ocean. Farther out, beyond the North End and past Castle William, where British soldiers had been garrisoned since the King Street shootings, the sky had turned as dark as a bruise. Cloud built upon cloud, like boulders piled in the aftermath of a landslide. That far from shore, the water's surface churned, waves and troughs dancing like demons.

"What have you done?" he called to her over the roar of the storm.

"What I should have long ago. This trial will not happen. You've lost, Kaille. You may live, but you've failed, and your city will burn."

She thrust her crystal toward the sky again, and lightning cleaved the clouds. Thunder shook the pier like the strongest spell. A wave like none Ethan had ever seen on the harbor crashed onto the wharf, its spray dousing him.

Ethan rushed the woman, fighting through the wind and the pain in his bad leg. Reaching her, he grappled for the stone. She cast—how could she while maintaining this tempest?—her spell pounding him, driving him back a pace. He bit his cheek and cast in turn. She tottered, but righted herself.

He grabbed for her again. She lashed out with a booted foot, digging a hard toe into his wounded midsection. Ethan bent and retched.

But he also cast again. A breaking spell, like the one he'd used on her carriage. One of the wooden boards beneath her snapped into pieces. Her foot fell through the hole in the wharf and she stumbled forward. Ethan grabbed at her hands again and ripped the stone from her grasp.

She shrieked her anger. Magick pulsed. The section of wharf on which he stood gave way, and he plunged toward the water. With his free hand, he grabbed for the hem of her petticoats.

Whitcomb screamed again, but couldn't resist his weight. She fell after him. Ethan heard Kelf shout his name. Then he hit the water.

It was warmer than he'd expected, but rough, even under the wharf. The current blasted him into a piling. Whitcomb, struggling to free herself from his grasp, kicked again, her heel catching his jaw.

Ethan released her, tried to swim away.

She surged after him, propelled, he thought, by the storm tide. Her hand closed around his wrist, her grip crushing, as Ethan imagined Kelf's would be. She reached for the crystal.

He balled his fist and swung, hating to strike a woman, but unwilling to surrender to this one.

He struck her nose, and she released him. Blood stained the water and he cast.

She grunted, but did not back away. He swung with the crystal, connected, opening a gash on her cheek.

More blood. He cast again, knowing he couldn't breach her wardings, wanting only to throw her off. *"Pugnus ex cruore evocatus."* A fist spell.

Whitcomb's head snapped to the side. She growled deep in her throat and threw both hands in his direction. Harbor water pummeled him. He hit another piling, his head slamming against wood.

His vision swam. He dipped under, forced himself up again, sputtering. And she was on him, like a wild creature, scrabbling for her crystal.

Good Lord, she was strong!

Ethan tried to fight her off, certain, though he didn't know why, that to relinquish the stone was to cede his life to her. His hand ached from gripping the crystal. Sharp edges gouged his skin. She hammered a fist into the side of his head, forced him under water. Addled, he couldn't throw her off. She prised his fingers loosed one at a time.

Desperate, he loosed his blade from its sheath and drove it into her gut. Her wail spiraled upward, blending with the tumult of the storm, seeming to feed it, to bring harder rain, fiercer wind.

Blood from her wound surrounded them and Ethan cast one last time —the most vicious attack spell he knew. *Falx ex cruore evocata.* A blade spell that would have sliced her in half had she not been warded.

She shuddered at the force of the conjuring, but remained very much alive. Her face had turned ashen, her lips trembled, a faint, frigid blue.

"This isn't over," she said, her voice rough and unsteady.

He steeled himself for another attack. It never came. Instead, she dove under water, and with a sweep of her arms and an undulating kick of her legs, sped away from him.

Ethan stared after her, waiting for her to surface again. She didn't, at least not that he saw. The swells might have hidden her from him. Or she might have drowned. He thought the former more likely.

He still held her crystal. He became aware of Kelf calling for him, sounding truly frightened.

"I'm here!" he hollered back.

"Well, you better get out of that water. There's waves coming like none I've ever seen."

Ethan scanned the water for Whitcomb again. Seeing no sign of her, he swam out from under the wharf and scrambled from the surf.

IX

None alive in the city could recall a storm as powerful as the one that battered Boston that day. Rain fell in opaque sheets, flooding fields and lanes. At times, hailed pelted down on the city. The wind built to such a frenzy that fences and sheds collapsed, roofs blew off houses and shops, chimneys toppled. The surf flowed over the wharves into the streets, reaching King Street and the Town Dock. Nearly a hundred ships at the harbor docks were smashed beyond repair, carriages and chaises were washed away, as were dozens of unfortunate souls.

The storm continued into the evening, the air turning so cold by midnight that a few snowflakes fell in the last throes of the gale.

Ethan and Kelf managed to make it back to the *Dowsing Rod*, and the tavern withstood the worst of the storm, losing only a few clay tiles off the roof, and a shutter from one of the windows.

Ethan spent much of that evening huddled by the hearth in the great room, with Kannice beside him, and Kelf hurrying around the interior of the building, checking for leaks and loose doors and windows. The crystal cluster Ethan had taken from Charlotte Whitcomb rested on a table beside him, reflections of firelight flickering in its depths, tinted green by the blue of the stone.

"It's quite beautiful," Kannice said at one point, as the icy wind keened outside, and blew smoke back into the building through the chimney. "It's hard to believe she could use it to create a storm like this one."

"I don't think she created it," he said, returning to thoughts that had occupied him throughout the day. "She used it, made it stronger. Just like she did with her magick when attacking me. Somehow, she found a way to tie together different magicks, different sources."

Kannice nodded, but said no more. Eventually, Ethan tore his gaze from the crystal to look at her. "I'm sorry. I'm trying to figure all of this out. For when she comes back."

"You're sure she survived?"

Kelf, who had just checked the lock on the front door for the fifth or sixth time, slowed as she asked this, interested in Ethan's answer.

"I'm sure of nothing. But she drew strength from the water. I expect she was able to heal herself."

"I would have preferred that she didn't," the barman said, and retreated to the kitchen.

The next morning, a Sunday, dawned cold, but miraculously clear. Ethan walked through the city streets beneath a sky of deepest azure, a few fluffy clouds soaring past in the lingering wind. Already, men and women were in the streets cleaning up after the storm, piling debris along the streets and repairing damage to homes and businesses. As bad as the damage was, Ethan believed the city would recover quickly.

He found Samuel Adams and Joseph Warren at the *Green Dragon*, a tavern on Union Street, not far from the *Dowser*, that had long been a gathering place for the Sons of Liberty. Josiah Quincy was not with them—according to Adams, he was with John Adams, preparing their defense of Captain Preston and his soldiers. When Ethan asked, Adams assured him that the trial would go on.

"The storm is nothing," he said. "The Court House sustained no damage, and John swears that he and Josiah will be ready on the twenty-fourth. Robert and Samuel say the same." His expression turned guarded. "Unless you come with tidings that would prevent us from moving forward."

"No, sir. Quite the contrary. I believe that the attacks on both pairs of attorneys should be over. As far as I know, the conjurer has left Boston. I don't expect her to return before Wednesday."

"A woman?" Warren asked.

"Yes, sir. An uncommonly powerful conjurer."

"And yet you bested her."

"I was fortunate, yes. And for now, at least, my work on your behalf is complete." He eyed the men expectantly.

"This is most welcome news, Mister Kaille," Adams said, gripping Ethan's hand.

"Yes, sir. It was my pleasure."

"I believe we owe you payment," he said, with a glance at Warren.

The doctor nodded in agreement.

"Unfortunately, most of our assets lie in the eloquence of our members and the influence of those who share our cause. We can pay you a small amount now—say two pounds—and promise the rest at a later date, when we have achieved more of our aims.

Ethan forced a smile. "Of course, sir. I understand. That would be fine." In his mind, though, he could see Sephira shaking her head, amusement and disapproval on her lovely face.

He wished to call on Hutchinson as well, but the mystery the lieutenant governor had asked him to investigate remained unsolved. He returned to the tavern and spent the rest of the day helping Kelf with minor repairs of the building.

The next morning—Monday—he paid a visit to Janna. Somehow the *Fat Spider* had come through the storm in one piece, leaving Ethan more certain than ever that Janna kept the building standing with magick.

Inside, after buying a cup of wine and some roasted fowl, he showed Janna the crystal, described his final battle with Whitcomb, and explained to her the conjurer's role in what had befallen the city.

For a long time after he finished speaking, she sat, dark eyes thoughtful and fixed on the stone.

"If I had to guess," she said, "I'd say she's got conjurer on her daddy's side, and water witch on her mama's. Maybe with a touch of air."

"Water witch," Ethan repeated. It was a phrase he hadn't heard before this year, and still didn't fully comprehend.

"And air," Janna said again. "That's how she raised that wind. It's a different kind of magick. Elemental. It works different from what you and I do. Bigger in a way, but also less exact."

"Then her brother might have it, too, right?"

Janna shook her head. "Probably not. It passes mother to daughter. Sons who have the magick end up sickly. Most don't survive past ten or twelve."

Which meant Francis Lamb, while influential, was probably just a normal man.

"She'll be back, Kaille. If you'd stabbed her on land, you could have killed her. Not in water, though. She's alive somewhere. I guarantee it. Healing, I'd guess. But alive and, with your luck, bent on revenge."

"I'll need help, Janna."

Her mouth twisted sourly. "'Course you will. You always need my help."

Ethan left her a short time later and walked to Sephira's house, where he had a similar, but less precise conversation with Mariz, while Sephira looked on, her mien unreadable. He revealed little about the nature of Whitcomb's magic to either of them, and he kept the crystal hidden in his coat pocket. Janna would be able to help him. And so might Mariz. At some point, in private, he would tell the man more.

Sephira, though, was a different matter. She had been angry with Francis Lamb the night Ethan and she spoke and drank rum, but she had too many ties to representatives of the Crown here in Boston. And he still didn't trust her.

From Summer Street, he strolled back to the *Dowsing Rod*. The moment he entered the building he knew something was wrong. Kannice and Kelf both stood behind the bar, neither of them doing much more than study a lone man sitting at a table near the fire.

Francis Lamb. He wore a dark blue coat, waistcoat, and breeches, and a shirt of white silk. He looked every bit as elegant as he had the first time Ethan encountered him.

Ethan crossed to the bar and removed his coat, folding it over the polished wood.

"Do you know him?" Kannice asked in a whisper.

"I know who he is. His sister was here two days ago. The one with the knife." At that they looked Lamb's way. "How long ago did he arrive?"

"Just a few minutes," Kannice said. Eyeing the man again. "Forgive me for saying this, but he may be the most attractive man I've ever seen."

Ethan chuckled. "I think Sephira is right: You and she have more in common than I realized."

"What?"

"I'll explain later. What is he drinking?"

"Madeira," Kelf said. "The good stuff. Unwatered."

"I'll have some as well."

Kelf poured some into a cup and handed it to him. Ethan strode to the man's table.

"Mister Lamb, how good to see you again."

"Mister Kaille," he said, keeping his seat. He indicated the chair across from his. "Please, sit."

Ethan lowered himself into the chair. "What can I do for you?"

"I thought you and I should be better acquainted. It seems our lives are intertwined. Miss Pryce, Mister Adams, my sister. We have a good many people in common."

"Aye, I suppose we do."

"I understand that until recently, you were a loyalist."

"I was, yes," Ethan said. "I should tell you, Mister Lamb, your sister tried this line of persuasion. It didn't get her far."

"I see." He surveyed the tavern. "This is a humble establishment." His gaze settled on Ethan again. "Don't get me wrong. It's clean. I hear that the food is excellent. And," he added, lifting his cup, "there are few places in Boston that serve Madeira of this quality. But it seems to me that a man of your ability deserves more, would want to give his wife more. I can provide as much. You need never work again."

"We're quite satisfied with the life we have. Now, enough with the flattery and bribery. What is it you want?"

Lamb's huff of laughter was as dry as sand. Firelight danced in his green eyes. "Very well. You have something that belongs to my family. I'd like it back."

"I'm not sure I know to what you're referring."

"Don't play games with me."

Ethan leaned back and sipped his wine. "Perhaps if you told me what it is I'm supposed to have—something about its purpose—I could be of more help. I am a thieftaker after all."

"You don't want me as an enemy, Mister Kaille."

Ethan's turn to laugh "I battled your sister two days ago. I assume we're enemies already. And while your sister has power, I gather you don't. Maybe it's more accurate to say *you* don't want *me* as an enemy."

Lamb's aspect didn't change, nor did he move, except to toy with his cup. "The arrogance of witches," he said. "You think yours is the only flavor of power. I have influence you can't even imagine. I can have this tavern shut down in a matter of days. I can have a noose around your neck before sunset. I can have your mother and your sisters hanged as witches as well, not to mention the African woman and Miss Pryce's Portuguese witch." He drank from his cup, and returned it to the table, his hand steady, his every movement graceful. "You see, power is more than might. Power is nuance, it is subtlety, it is knowing when to threaten and when to keep your mouth shut. You bested my sister this one time, and for that I suppose you deserve a modicum of respect. But I doubt you'll be so fortunate again, and in the meantime, you have a life to live, people you care about, here and in England. Every one of them lies within my reach, just as you do." He opened his hands. "Now, I'll give you one more opportunity: Where is my family's crystal?"

"What does she use it for? What kind of witch is she?"

"I believe that's a conversation you should have with her. If you can keep her from killing you long enough to ask the questions. She doesn't like you very much."

"All the more reason for me to hold on to it. Would you hand a loaded pistol to an enemy?"

"A fair point, but one that betrays your ignorance. Charlotte can use any piece of the same sort of crystal to cast her spells. This piece is no more or less potent than others of a similar quality. It did belong to our grandmother, however. That is my interest in retrieving it. I give you my word."

Ethan wanted to learn more about the crystal, and how Charlotte Whitcomb used it to magnify her power. In truth, though, there was little he could do with it, and he had no doubt that Whitcomb could find another stone of, as Lamb said, similar quality. He also didn't believe Lamb's boasts about his reach were idle. And finally, most important, in all his years as a thieftaker, Ethan had never kept an item for himself because it was worth more than his fee, or because he liked the way it looked, or because he disliked the person to whom it belonged. He had never stolen anything, and he wouldn't start now with this man.

"All right, Mister Lamb. I'll give you the crystal, and I expect in turn that you will leave me, and the people I care about, alone."

"That's up to you. Stay out of affairs that don't concern you, and you have nothing to fear from me." He glanced about again. "You've built a comfortable life for yourself. Ethan Kaille the tavern keeper needn't worry about me troubling him again. Ethan Kaille the thieftaker . . . That's a different matter."

"So you're telling me that I have to return that crystal and also vow not to work in the lanes again?"

"Or join the Sons of Liberty."

"You seem to have mistaken me for someone who's afraid of you." Ethan stood. "Get out."

"What about my crystal?"

Ethan bit the inside of his cheek, and said in his mind, *Discuti ex cruore evocatum*. Magick reverberated through the tavern, Reg appeared, and the chair holding Lamb exploded into fragments and dust, dumping him onto the floor. He landed hard on his back, air leaving him with an *oof*.

"Get out," Ethan said again.

Lamb jumped to his feet and pointed a trembling finger at him. "You shouldn't have done that."

"Do I need to light you on fire? Or shatter the bone in your arm? Your leg? Maybe your neck?"

The man lowered his arm slowly, and darted a look at Kannice and Kelf. With one last hot glare for Ethan, he retrieved his hat from the table and hurried to the door.

"You weren't able to stop the trial," Ethan said, as Lamb reached for the door handle. "What makes you think you can do anything to me?"

"The trial is of little consequence—a minor setback. Nothing more. You're on the losing side of this fight. I gave you a chance to change that. Now it's too late for you."

He set his tricorn on his head and left the tavern.

Ethan walked back to the bar.

"I'm sorry about the chair."

"I'll take it out of your pay," Kannice said with a quick, nervous smile. "What did he say to you?"

"He threatened me. He threatened you and my family and my friends." He stared toward the door. "And he tried to tell me what I can and can't do with my life."

"I think I'll get the broom," Kelf said. He retreated into the kitchen.

Ethan pulled the crystal from the pocket of his coat and set it on the bar.

"What will you do with that now?" Kannice asked.

"Study it. Learn from it." He faced Kannice and took her hand. "This isn't over," he said. "I'm sorry."

"Don't be."

"No, I mean—"

"I know what you mean." She raised his hand to her lips. "You are what you are, Ethan, and I love you no matter what. You didn't go looking for this. It found you, and I encouraged it. Maybe in some small way I had already realized that you need more in your life than the tavern can offer."

"It won't be all the time. I'm still a tavern keeper before I'm a thieftaker, and your husband before anything. But Adams and the Sons are going to need me now more than ever."

She smiled again, with warmth. "So, now you're a patriot *and* a thieftaker."

"I am."

"Well, I was wrong before. The most attractive man I've ever seen is standing right here in front of me." She stood on her toes and kissed his lips. "Now, build me a new chair."

Author's Note

The hurricane that struck Boston on 20 October 1770 was one of the most powerful storms to make land in North America at any time in the Colonial period. It dumped close to two and a half inches of rain on the city in a single day. Its tidal surge reached historic levels, and its winds damaged buildings and vessels alike. The storm killed more than one hundred people.

And yet, though it pounded the city mere days before the oft-delayed trial of Captain Thomas Preston and his soldiers was set to begin, it did not stop the proceedings from going forward.

As to whether the storm's impact was enhanced by the magickal workings of one Charlotte Whitcomb . . . Well, gentle reader, I leave that for you to decide.

— DBJ

Part II

THE CLOUD PRISON

I

Boston, Province of Massachusetts Bay, 24 October 1770

Despite all his years living in Boston, Ethan Kaille could not remember a morning like this one. Undeterred by the previous night's hard frost, and the stiff, cold wind blowing out of the northwest, men and women crowded onto Queen Street in the very heart of the city. Golden light gilded the steeple of the Town House a block away, and the graceful spire of the Old Brick to the south.

The aroma of roasted chestnuts hung over the lane. Vendors hawked them by the half-dozen—two pence. Nearby, a bakery sold small loaves of freshly baked bread. At the corner of Cornhill, an old man played a fiddle, and closer to Treamount, a younger man stood on a wooden crate and railed against the latest outrages perpetrated by Parliament and King George III. At its fringes, the gathering felt almost like a festival.

Most of the throng pressed toward the entrance to the new Court House, which also happened to be home to the city gaol. It stood halfway between the two larger thoroughfares, on the south side of the lane. Here the mood was decidedly more somber, as befitted the occasion.

Today, after delays too numerous to count, the trial of Captain Thomas Preston and his soldiers, the men arrested and held as responsible for the King Street shootings of this past March—the so-called Horrid Massacre— would begin. For a city still in mourning and barely past its trauma, the opening of proceedings marked a welcome milestone. Regardless of political inclination, a good many of Boston's residents hungered for resolution. True, for some this could only come through conviction of the accused; for others acquittal seemed the sole just outcome. Mostly, though, the majority of men and women sought answers.

There were exceptions, of course, people whose political ambitions had them hungering not for answers but for unrest, not for resolution but for renewed violence. For this reason, Ethan had joined the horde seeking entry to the Court House in order to observe the trial.

Generally speaking, the Sons of Liberty, those Whigs who agitated for liberty from the constraints and taxes imposed upon the colonies by the king and his Parliament, hoped the captain and his soldiers would be held to account. But more, they wanted to keep the populace exercised in pursuit of their cause. Samuel Adams, the leader of the Sons in fact if not in title, had told Ethan only days ago that the outcome of the trial did not matter. All parties were innocent, the great man said. And all were guilty. Fault lay with the policies imposed on the province by the Crown. All that mattered was the cause itself.

Individuals on the other side—some called them loyalists, others Tories, and still others by imprecations too rude to be repeated—expected exoneration for the soldiers and their captain. To them, it was clear that the uniformed men had been most foully abused and provoked. The five deaths resulting from the events of that night were regrettable, these persons said, but inevitable given the behavior of the mob gathered outside the Customs House.

If this difference of expectation between Whig and Tory existed in isolation, Ethan would have been content to let the trial run its course in his absence. In recent days, however, perhaps sensing that events conspired against them, a small number of loyalists had taken it upon themselves to attempt, through mischief and intimidation, to disrupt the proceedings. Specifically, a conjurer—Charlotte Whitcomb—had engaged in attacks on the attorneys for both sides. When Ethan attempted to stop her, she turned her considerable powers on him, nearly killing him and then unleashing a storm of unprecedented might. The city was ravaged. More than one hundred Bostonians perished. Still, he managed to drive the woman off. For a time.

The ill-effects of her magick lingered, however. Yesterday, the bells at Boston's various churches and meeting houses had tolled almost continually, marking one funeral procession after another. No doubt the same would be true today, and tomorrow. Grave diggers at the city's burying grounds would be earning their wage and then some.

Ethan would not allow Whitcomb to renew her magickal assault on the people of Boston, or do anything to upset today's proceedings here at the Court House. That was his purpose, and he scanned the lane for the woman, determined that his vigilance not flag.

That his wife, Kannice, had accompanied him this morning to Queen

Street . . . Well, that was not part of his plan.

"How many did you say the trial chamber could accommodate?" she asked him, not for the first time. She stood on her toes, surveying the lane and the wall of humanity between the two of them and the entrance to the building.

"Fifty or sixty," he said. "Standing."

She frowned. "There's more than that many in front of us."

"I told you we wouldn't both get in."

Kannice cast an annoyed glance in his direction. She had dressed for the spectacle, and looked lovely in her best gown—blue satin to match her eyes, with a white stomacher and petticoats. She'd coiled her auburn hair into an elegant bun, and put on the silver locket he gave her the previous Christmas. Ethan, to her chagrin, wore his usual garb: black breeches, a linen shirt that was somewhere between yellow and its original white, a black coat and his tricorn. For him, this was no social affair; it was work.

"They'll let *you* in, won't they?" she asked with some resentment.

"Aye. Hutchinson will see to it. And Adams wants me there, too. I expect this to be the only matter on which they agree today."

"Well, it's not very fair."

He raised an eyebrow, but didn't bother to point out that he could conjure and she couldn't, that he had been hired by both sides within the past week and she had not.

"All right, it's fair. That doesn't mean I like it."

"To be honest, I don't expect it to be very interesting. They'll be selecting the jury today. Hardly earth-shaking."

"I know. But I hear John Adams is quite eloquent. And Josiah Quincy, too."

Patriots both, and yet charged with defending the soldiers. Of the five lawyers, three for the defense, and two for the prosecution, only Samuel Quincy, Josiah's older brother, had loyalist sympathies. Ethan thought this indicative of a larger truth: By and large, the finest minds in Boston sided with the so-called patriots. Once, Ethan had considered himself a Tory, but not since the shootings. He was a Whig now, and devoted to the cause. Kannice approved.

Bells tolled on the Old Brick, and also at King's Chapel and the Meeting House farther south. It was half-past seven.

A burly figure shouldered his way to the Court House entrance. Stephen Greenleaf, the sheriff of Suffolk County. He was tall, hook-nosed, with sharp, pale eyes, and an intimidating scowl, which he directed now at those clustered in the street. Two other men joined him at the doors and at a word from the sheriff opened them. Greenleaf began to admit people to the structure, some individually, others in pairs or small groups. The throng surged forward, people pushing at Ethan and Kannice from all sides. She grabbed his hand.

Within moments—long before Kannice and Ethan even approached the doors—Greenleaf signaled that they were full. Groans went up from the people around them. Kannice sent a pout Ethan's way.

The sheriff searched the mob, and after a few seconds, his gaze locked on Ethan's. Greenleaf gestured impatiently, indicating that Ethan should make his way to the door.

"I have to go," he said.

"Can't you get me in?"

He kissed her forehead. "I can't. You should go home."

The truth was, he didn't want her near the Court House once the trial began. He feared Charlotte Whitcomb's next attempt to disrupt the proceedings, and couldn't so much as guess what her brother, Francis Lamb, might attempt. Lamb wasn't a conjurer, but he wielded influence here and in London. If he chose to send troops into the building, or if he attempted to precipitate another bloody confrontation in the city streets, no one, not even Thomas Hutchinson, would be able to stop him.

"I want to hear all about it," she said. "Every detail."

"By the time I'm done, you'll wish I'd never started. You have my word."

She smirked. "Fine." She kissed him and started away. Ethan watched her go, making certain she navigated the press of people. Once she was clear and able to follow a direct path to Treamount Street, he wove through the crowd to the Court House and climbed the marble stairs to the door.

Greenleaf greeted him with a curt nod and a growled, "Kaille," which was about as warm a greeting as Ethan expected from the man.

"Oi, Sheriff," someone shouted from below. "Why's he allowed in?"

"Because I say so," the sheriff answered. He ushered Ethan inside and followed him, ordering his men to bar the doors. "No one comes in without my approval."

They ascended the broad interior stairway to the building's second floor, and crossed a spacious corridor to the courtroom. A line had formed outside the chamber. Ethan could see that the room was packed, and at least a dozen more spectators waited to get in.

Ethan and the sheriff halted a few paces shy of the line and watched as men and a few women squeezed into the room and situated themselves.

"Have you heard anything of that woman?" Greenleaf asked. "Lamb's sister." *The witch?* Ethan didn't need for him to say it.

"No."

"That's good, I suppose."

"I suppose."

The sheriff's mien darkened. "You're here to observe, Kaille. And to protect us all if necessary. I don't want you working any of your mischief for any other purpose. You understand me?"

"What's the matter, Sheriff? Are you afraid I'll ensorcel your jury?"

"It's not my jury, and you're damn right I am."

"I understand my role here," Ethan said. "My question is this: I know what to do if Charlotte Whitcomb tries to disrupt the proceedings. But what if her brother does? What if he arrives with soldiers from Castle William and orders the court to halt the trial?"

Greenleaf's brow creased. "Hutchinson wants the trial to go forward. And he's the authority here."

"Are you certain of that?"

His frown deepened, but all he could offer was a twitch of his shoulder. "Not entirely." He didn't say more, but led Ethan into the courtroom.

The chamber was large, though filled near to bursting with so many people, it felt cramped. A fire burned bright in the large stone hearth at the front of the room—a decision of questionable wisdom. Already the chamber was far too hot and stank of sweat. Most had removed their coats. Many now shrugged off waistcoats as well.

Before the hearth stood a long table at which sat the five judges, all of them robed, all of them in powdered wigs. In front of the men, the space was divided by wooden barriers: a witness stand, a large square filled with chairs set off for the yet-to-be-selected jury, a pair of tables for the attorneys, and a wooden bar separating the trial's actors from those who had come to watch.

Approximately sixty spectators stood in rows behind that barrier, silent and respectful. Ethan fit himself into a small space by the door where he could monitor those who came and went and also keep an eye on the attorneys. He had expected to see nine uniformed men face charges for the shootings. Instead, only one defendant sat in yet another enclosure adjacent to the table of the attorneys for the defense, John Adams, Robert Auchmuty, and Josiah Quincy.

Ethan had dealings with Captain Thomas Preston two years before in the earliest days of the occupation—an inquiry into the apparent theft of some pearls that led eventually to murders and a magickal battle that Ethan nearly lost. The captain didn't look much different, although the intervening years had salted his hair a bit and deepened the lines in his face. Back in 1768, he had been sunken cheeked and rough looking. His time in command and then prison had served only to accentuate these elements of his appearance. He had a long, straight nose, a strong chin, and well-spaced pale eyes that skipped nervously over the judges, the lawyers, the observers. At one point, his gaze touched Ethan's, but quickly moved on. The captain gave no sign of recognizing him from their earlier encounters.

As Ethan told Kannice out on the street, this day's order of business in the courtroom centered around the selection of a jury. The process was tedious and filled with legal arcana. In the middle of it, another man entered the chamber, seemingly in contravention of the instructions Greenleaf had left with his men downstairs. Not that Ethan thought men of the watch could keep this particular person from doing anything he wanted.

Francis Lamb.

II

Lamb was the newest addition to the Crown's Customs Board, and as such wielded much influence in Boston and throughout the colonies. More than that, though, Ethan had every reason to believe the man a spy who answered directly to the most powerful men in London. He carried himself with supreme confidence and an air of unassailable authority that grated on Ethan's nerves. This day he wore a ditto suit of rich brown. Brown hair swooped dashingly over emerald green eyes and a square, handsome face. He spotted Ethan the moment he entered the courtroom and faltered. He recovered quickly, though, flashed a smile Ethan didn't believe and waded through the mass of people between the door and the defense table until he had positioned himself directly behind Preston and the captain's lawyers.

John Adams marked Lamb's approach, obviously less than pleased by his arrival. The two didn't exchange any greetings.

Ethan turned his attention back to the proceedings, but glanced continually in Lamb's direction. He couldn't quite follow—or even hear—all of the objections to members of the original pool of potential jurors, but before long it became clear that the court had run out of veniremen.

Greenleaf began to the canvass the room for talesmen, landowners who had not served on a jury in the past three years, and quickly gathered a dozen or so who were eligible. Adams and Auchmuty, acting on Preston's behalf, should have been the ones to reject unacceptable jury candidates, but they did and said little. Rather, it was Lamb who consulted with Preston and signaled his disapproval. Before long, they had also cast aside most of the talesmen. The attorneys for the Province—Samuel Quincy and Robert Treat Paine—dismissed one or two others, forcing Greenleaf to continue his search of the room. During this latest orbit of the chamber, the sheriff halted in front of Ethan, his grimace betraying both reluctance and desperation.

"When was the last time you were on a jury, Kaille?"

"It's been some time."

Greenleaf glanced back at Lamb and canted his head in Ethan's direction. Ethan was not at all surprised when Lamb responded with a quick, decisive shake of his head.

"You're fortunate he dislikes you so much," the sheriff said, and moved on.

Ethan eyed Lamb, and didn't look away when the man met his gaze with cool appraisal.

Soon Greenleaf had no choice but to descend to the street and drag in more candidates. While he was gone, Lamb managed to get two more jurors seated, both wealthy, both known loyalists: Phillip Dumaresq and Gilbert Deblois. Adams and Quincy could hardly object. Though Whigs, they were in this courtroom as defenders of Captain Preston. Without a doubt the presence of these two men would redound to their client's benefit. Indeed, so biased were Dumaresq and Deblois, that Ethan hardly believed Samuel Quincy and Robert Paine could allow them to remain on the panel. Paine did appear genuinely distraught, but his rather feeble objections to the seating of the Tories were met with indifference from the Province's judges.

"We lack jurors, Mister Paine," said the acting chief justice, Benjamin Lynde, Jr., his voice quavering. "We can hardly afford to reject men who are both qualified and willing."

"If I may, Your Honor," Paine said in his strong baritone, "the defense has rejected many such men. Why do our objections carry less weight?"

"Because the reputations of Messieurs Dumaresq and Deblois are unimpeachable."

Ethan thought for certain that Paine would persist, but for reasons surpassing understanding, he did not. Muttering to himself, he sat once more, tacitly consenting to the seating of the two men.

It was then—too late by far—that Ethan became aware of a singular absence in the courtroom. One man would have refused to allow such an obvious injustice. Where was Samuel Adams?

Scanning the chamber, Ethan could not find him. He turned back to the attorneys and found John Adams staring at him, consternation pinching his features. He may have been Preston's attorney, but he recognized the impropriety of impaneling these men. He, too, glanced around the court-room before facing Ethan again. Ethan guessed that he had noticed his cousin's absence.

Greenleaf returned with several men in tow, but before this first phase of the trial ended, Lamb managed to place three more loyalists on the jury. They included William Hill, a prominent baker in the Cornhill area who had, during the occupation, made a small fortune supplying the barracks of British regulars with bread, and William Wait Wallis, who was Gilbert Deblois's brother-in-law.

By mid-afternoon, the court had its jury, but it was far from unbiased. Given that only a unanimous panel could convict, Ethan thought it likely that, in all ways that mattered, the trial was over, before any arguments had been rendered.

Samuel Quincy gave an opening statement on behalf of the Crown and then began his questioning of prosecution witnesses. Eight men sat before the court before the end of the day, each of them offering similar versions of events on the night of March the Fifth: Voices from the mob did shout at the soldiers to fire, but Preston could have prevented bloodshed had he acted more responsibly. The last man to testify swore that he heard the captain not only give the order to fire, but also to reload and shoot again.

"I heard him," this man said, staring directly at Preston. "'Damn your bloods,' he says. 'Fire again, and the let the consequence be what it may!'"

Preston gazed straight ahead as the man recounted this, his bearing un-changed. Murmurs rose from among the spectators, but Ethan thought the jury remained unmoved.

After this man stepped down from the stand, Lynde adjourned the court for the day. Spectators began to file out of the chamber, their conver-sations continuing. Ethan remained where he was, watching as the judges and Sheriff Greenleaf tried to decide what to do with the jury, and with the judges themselves. Trials in Boston rarely took more than a single day— probably it had never occurred to Greenleaf or the justices that this one would barely be started by now.

After a few minutes, it grew clear that the jailer would arrange housing for all, and Ethan made his way to the door. As he reached it, Francis Lamb caught his eye, a smug grin tugging at the corners of his mouth. Ethan had no reply. The man had gotten precisely what he wanted. Despite the damaging testimony that ended the session, this day had been a clear victory for those who hoped to see Preston acquitted.

Ethan left the courtroom, wove among the last of the spectators as they descended the stairs, earning a few glowers along the way, and exited the building onto Queen Street. After a moment's consideration, he turned southward and hurried through the tangled lanes of the South End toward Purchase Street and the Adams estate.

Samuel Adams' grand house overlooked the waterfront; Ethan had never been inside, but he assumed the open observatory along the roofline offered a stunning view of Boston Harbor. Once, the house belonged to Adams' father, during whose ownership the property became embroiled in a land bank scandal. Some dozen years ago, newly widowed and beholden to creditors, Samuel almost lost the deed at auction. Only the timely intervention of the provincial courts allowed him to keep his family's home.

Since then, the renown of the house's current resident, the tangled legal history of the property, and the quaint gardens, overgrown and neglected this late in the fall, had made the estate an object of public curiosity. A steady stream of residents visited Purchase Street for the sole purpose of strolling by the structure.

And indeed, as Ethan approached the house on this afternoon, with golden sun angling across its gables, he spied two or three couples walking toward the property. They regarded him with a blend of envy and suspicion when he turned up the garden path and made his way to the front door.

He knocked once, waited, and then knocked again, his trepidation mounting.

He had just decided to leave here and search for Adams elsewhere, perhaps at the *Green Dragon* tavern, when the door opened, revealing Adams in a red waistcoat, white silk shirt, and black breeches. He stared, his head shaking slightly with his usual palsy, and his mien betraying his surprise at Ethan's arrival. To Ethan's relief, though, he saw nothing to suggest that Mister Adams was ill or injured.

"Mister Kaille? What brings you here?"

"Concern for you, sir."

"For me?"

"Yes," Ethan said. "I was surprised not to see you at the Court House today."

Puzzlement greeted this. "Why would I have been at the Court House?"

"For the trial of Captain Preston and his men."

"That's not today. That's not until . . ." He trailed off, his expression clouding. "I would never miss such a thing." He said this last more to himself than to Ethan.

"Sir, are you feeling all right?"

"Yes, of course I am!" he fired back, his mood as changeable as a storm tide. "You're just confounding me with all of these questions is all."

"I'm sorry. That wasn't my intention."

"Well, I didn't say it was. Why can't everyone just leave me be? First Betsy and now you."

"What did Missus Adams—"

"Samuel!"

The cry came from the street. Ethan turned. Adams glared past him. John Adams and Robert Treat Paine strode toward the house, as unlikely a pair as one could hope to find. Adams was short, round, with heavy eyebrows, a weak chin, and round cheeks. Paine, in contrast, was tall, dashing, his aspect more severe than friendly.

The two men made their way up the path to Adams' door, John Adams regarding Ethan critically.

"Did you leave before the court adjourned?"

"No, sir. But the moment it did I made my way here. The truth is, I was in the courtroom for some time before I realized Mister Adams was not in attendance."

"We needed you there today, Samuel," Paine said. "Matters would have turned out better had you joined us."

"Joined you where? What are all of you talking about?"

"Did you do something to him?" John Adams asked Ethan.

"No, sir. You have my word. But I will admit that my thoughts have taken a similar turn."

"By which you mean . . ."

"That I suspect foul play, sir. Someone has acted to . . . to subvert your cousin's memory."

Samuel stared at John and then at Ethan, pale, aghast. "I don't understand."

"Samuel, where's Betsy?" John asked.

"She's inside, baking."

"May we come in?"

"First tell me why."

Adams, Paine, and Ethan shared glances. Ethan saw his own concern mirrored in the faces of his companions.

"You missed the first day of Captain Preston's trial," John said. "And you're behaving . . . oddly. To be honest, I wish Joseph were here to examine you."

Another realization. Ethan's thoughts had been too sluggish this day. Aside from Samuel Adams, Joseph Warren might have been the leading Whig in the city. If one of them was to miss the trial, surely the other would have moved heaven and earth to be there. And yet . . .

"Doctor Warren wasn't there either, was he?" Ethan asked.

John Adams shook his head. "He had a patient who couldn't wait. An emergency, I'm afraid. Completely unexpected. There was nothing he could do."

Of course there wasn't. For now, Ethan kept the thought to himself, and he resolved to do so until he knew more about this mysterious patient the doctor had seen. He suspected, though, that Warren's emergency and Samuel Adams' sudden and uncharacteristic lapse in memory were related, and that both were brought on by spells of some sort.

III

"The trial wasn't today," Samuel Adams said, but he sounded less certain than he had, and more like a man trying to convince himself. "It couldn't have been."

"Would I ever lie to you?" John asked, their eyes locked.

Samuel gazed back for several seconds until at last he grasped his cousin's shoulder. "No. No, of course you wouldn't. But then how could this have happened? You know me, John. I would never forget something as important as this. It's not my way."

"Which is why I want to speak with Betsy."

"Yes, of course." He rubbed his brow, confusion clouding his gaze. "Come in, all of you."

He led them into the house, which was modestly appointed, and in some disarray, with books and sheafs of parchment piled everywhere. It smelled of cinnamon and nutmeg and freshly baked dough. Adams called for his wife and, while they waited for her, cleared several volumes from some chairs and a sofa so that all could sit.

Elizabeth Adams—Betsy—was Samuel's second wife and at least a dozen years his junior. She had a pleasant open face and wheaten hair. Wearing an apron over a pale rose gown, she greeted all of their guests with smiles and John with a brief embrace and a kiss on the cheek.

Samuel indicated Ethan with an open hand. "I'm not certain you've met Mister Kaille—"

"I have," she said. "He came to see you as the occupation began."

"I'm flattered that you remember, Missus Adams."

She faced her husband. "What's so important that you've interrupted my baking? I can't let the dough alone for too long, you know."

"He summoned you at my request," John said, his tone sobering her. "We have a few questions for you, and will try not to keep you long."

"Of course." She gathered her petticoats and sat in a chair near the hearth. The rest of them took their seats.

"I'm not quite sure how to begin," John said.

Ethan leaned forward. "If I may, sir. Mister Adams mentioned to me that you had . . . questioned him earlier, and that perhaps he had responded impatiently."

Samuel's cheeks colored. Betsy raised an eyebrow and regarded him with good-natured rebuke.

"Indeed he did. I asked why he wasn't at the Court House, and he assured me that the trial wasn't to begin today."

"I was so certain," Adams said, his voice low.

"You were equally certain yesterday evening, when you informed me that you would be gone for most of today to observe the proceedings."

"So yesterday, he knew," Ethan said.

"That's right. And by this morning he had forgotten. I've been worried, but I didn't know what to do, and in every other way he's been quite himself."

"So his memory is otherwise intact?"

"As far as I can tell. I simply assumed that the pressures upon him took a toll, and that in short order he would be entirely well again." She bestowed another smile upon each of them. "I believe your arrival has hastened his recovery, and for that I thank you all."

"I take it then," Samuel said with asperity, "that the rest of you are done speaking of me as if I'm not in the room?"

Betsy stood. "I have dough that requires my ministrations." She stooped and kissed Samuel's cheek. "Be gracious with your guests, my dear.

There is Madeira on the sideboard."

Some of the impatience drained from his bearing. "Yes, all right."

She left them. Samuel poured out four cups of wine and returned to his chair. Ethan thought Samuel would ask his cousin for details of the day's events, but he addressed Ethan first.

"What was done to me, Mister Kaille? Clearly this is not normal for me —forgetting momentous occasions, in particular those that relate to our struggle for liberty. Have I been magicked in some way?"

"I believe it's possible, sir, though I have to tell you that this conjuring, however it was done, is well beyond my abilities. I couldn't cast any spell that would cause a man to forget one occasion to the exclusion of all others."

"I find that alarming. Granted, you're the only conjurer I know, but our interactions over the years have given me a healthy respect for your abilities. If this is beyond you, I fear for all of us."

"Aye, sir. Tell me, did you have any unusual encounters yesterday?"

Adams weighed the question. "None that I remember. One admirer bought me a cup of Madeira yesterday afternoon, but I'm blessed to say that sort of thing happens to me with some regularity."

John Adams glanced at Ethan, an eyebrow raised in speculation. Samuel paled.

"You don't believe . . ."

"It's possible, sir," Ethan said. "A tonic of some sort could have been slipped into the wine, allowing a conjurer to bend your memories at some later time. Again, I wouldn't know how to do this, but that doesn't mean it can't be done."

"God save us." Samuel turned to his cousin. "Joseph wasn't there either?"

"He couldn't be. Someone required his services, and he had no choice but to attend to them."

Ethan wanted to ask John Adams for more details pertaining to Doctor Warren's patient, but he held his tongue for now, allowing John to describe for Samuel what transpired in the courtroom.

The more his cousin told him, the darker his expression grew. When John named the chosen jurors, Samuel looked positively apoplectic.

"Deblois? Hill? *Dumaresq?* Robert, how could you let this happen?"

Paine shifted on the sofa, discomfited. "I raised objections. Of course, I did. I tried everything I could. But the judges seemed determined to let Preston have his way."

Ethan and John Adams shared a quick glance, and Ethan guessed the other man was thinking the same thing he was. A better attorney would have prevailed upon the court to reject at least some of these men. But neither of them gainsaid Paine.

"Well, this is a disaster," Samuel said, gaze lowered. "It's bad enough that they've separated the cases. Preston will be exonerated, and all blame will fall upon his men. This trial was supposed to expose the criminality of colonial rule and the corruption inherent in all the Crown has done. And instead, it will declare a few men irresponsible rogues and leave the matter at that."

He eyed his cousin. "What will you do, John? Proving Preston's innocence endangers his soldiers, doesn't it? The best hope for Wemms, Kilroy, and the rest is that the jury finds Preston gave the order to fire, a verdict this jury is unlikely to reach. Which means the men will be found guilty."

"I really can't discuss it, Samuel. That's between my clients and me. Not to mention the fact that their prosecutor is sitting across from me."

Samuel cast a quick look at Paine. "Of course. Forgive me." To Ethan, he said, "Do you have any idea who might have done this to me?"

"I have to guess it was the same woman who conjured last week's storm."

Whatever she had done to Adams hadn't erased that memory. He blanched again at Ethan's mention of the tempest. "What can you tell us about her?"

"She is the half-sister of Francis Lamb."

"Lamb was there today," John Adams said, as if just remembering. "I think he offered more counsel to Preston than I did."

"In that case, Robert, I owe you an apology," Samuel said. "If the judges saw him there, they wouldn't have heeded any objections to seating those jurors. Even I would have been helpless to prevent it."

"You'll be there tomorrow?" Paine asked.

"I give you my word. And if by some chance I'm not, send someone for me. Send Mister Kaille." To Ethan he added, "And you make sure I get there, even if you have to drag me by the collar."

"Yes, sir."

Ethan, Paine, and John Adams left the house a short time later and started back toward Cornhill. Both lawyers spoke of having to prepare for the opening of arguments in the morning. Ethan had a different purpose in mind.

"Can you tell me more about this patient who visited Doctor Warren?"

he asked John Adams.

"I'm afraid I can't. All I know is that he had no choice but to . . ." He broke off, realization widening his gaze. "You believe that was a ruse? A distraction to keep him from the Court House?"

"What is this?" Paine asked.

Annoyance flickered in Adams' features.

"Mister Kaille believes Joseph was kept from the Court House not by a true emergency, but rather by an act of deception."

"And you agree?"

"Think about it, sir," Ethan said, answering for Adams. "Mister Adams —Samuel Adams—forgets to attend, and on the same day, Doctor Warren is presented with a medical crisis that keeps him from attending. One or the other *could* happen, but both? On a single morning? That strikes me as too much of a coincidence."

Paine held a hand to his mouth, a curiously meek gesture from such a formidable man. "Oh. Oh, dear."

"I intend to speak with him," Ethan said. "Unless one of you believes I shouldn't."

"By all means, do," Adams said. "Thank you, Mister Kaille."

They walked on in silence until reaching Queen Street and the Court House. There Ethan bid good night to both men and followed Brattles Street up to Hanover, and that thoroughfare to a modest house on the north side of the street.

Nearing the door, he faltered, halted. The last time he trod this path, he carried Diver over his shoulder. His friend had been shot by one of Preston's soldiers, his shoulder bloodied and shattered. Together, he and Warren saved Diver's life, but at the cost of his friend's left arm.

Ethan took a breath, exhaled, allowing the dark recollections of that deadly night to wash over him and recede. Before he could take another step toward the house, the door opened and Joseph Warren stepped out onto his front stoop. He was young, tall, with dark, expressive eyes and short hair that he powdered. He wore a dark blue waist coat over a white linen shirt and matching blue breeches, his sleeves were folded back to reveal muscled forearms.

"Have you decided yet whether or not to knock?" he asked, crooking a grin.

"I would have gotten to it eventually. I was recalling the last time I came to your house."

Warren's smile slipped. "I remember as well. How could any of us forget? Is your friend well?"

"Well enough, I suppose. His wound has healed without issue, thanks in no small part to your ministrations. But he still . . . struggles to come to grips with the loss of his arm. There's a darkness in him now that frightens me."

"Give him time, Mister Kaille. I've seen many such injuries and it always takes longer than we hope. For you and me, and most others in this city, events have moved beyond the shootings. For your friend, they have not. Seven months is nothing in cases like this one. Be patient, be his friend. That is all you can do."

"Aye, sir. Thank you."

Warren half-turned toward his door, tipping his head. "Would you care to come in? I assume you didn't walk all this way to talk about your friend's injury."

Ethan took a step in the direction of the house, but faltered again as he imagined sitting on the doctor's sofa. The sofa on which he and Warren had placed Diver that night.

"Better yet," the doctor said, "allow me to retrieve my coat. We can walk."

"Again, sir, my thanks."

Warren retreated into the house and called to his wife. Beyond her name, Ethan couldn't make out what he said, but a few seconds later he emerged again, closed the door behind him and joined Ethan on the path, adjusting his coat.

They stepped onto Hanover Street, and at Warren's suggestion set out toward Copp's Hill.

"Do you bring tidings from the Court House?" the doctor asked.

"I can give you some sense of what happened, though I warn you: I'm no lawyer."

"Well, thank goodness for that."

They both laughed. Warren had an easy, self-assured manner. Ethan could see why, despite his youth, he was spoken of as a leader of the patriot cause.

"Before we speak of the trial itself, though," Ethan said, "I wonder if you can tell me why you weren't there today."

The doctor frowned. "I meant to be, of course, but I'm a physician before all else and—"

"I understand that, sir. I cast no aspersions. But I have reason to wonder if you weren't kept away on pretense."

Warren halted. "Pretense! No, that's not . . ." He paled, his gaze straying in the direction of the waterfront. "Dear God."

"Can you tell me what happened?"

"A moment ago I would have sworn I could. Now . . ." They resumed their walk, Warren tight-lipped and pensive. The harbor breeze smelled of fish and ship's tar. Gulls cried overhead, and an eagle circled over the shoreline to the east. "I had every intention of being there. I was on my way out the door when word came in the form of a message carried by a lad who couldn't have been more than ten or eleven years old. He carried tidings of the one thing a physician in Boston fears above all others." His eyed flicked toward Ethan. "Smallpox."

Ethan had to resist the urge to back away from the man.

"You needn't be alarmed," Warren went on, sounding bitter. "The missive I received directed me to a ship moored at Wentworth's Wharf. On board I found three men who appeared to be afflicted. They were fevered, their faces and bodies were covered with what I took to be pustules. And so I spent much of my day doing what protocol demands. I sent word through the safest channels possible to the Selectmen, letting them know that a ship had docked in the city carrying men who might be infected. I sent a second message to Elizabeth, informing her that I expected to stay at the Pest House for a fortnight, and asking her to bring herbs that I would need to treat the men.

"All of this took time. I wanted to be at the Court House, but when smallpox is a possibility . . . Well, all other considerations become secondary."

"Of course."

"It occurred to me, even as I took all necessary precautions, that this is an odd time of year for smallpox to come to our shores. Usually, it's an affliction of spring and summer. But this vessel had been in warmer climes and . . ." He shrugged. "One doesn't trifle with a possible outbreak."

"Where are these men now?" Ethan asked. "Still on their ship?"

"I expect so, not that it matters. Late in the day, their fevers abruptly vanished, and their skin cleared. I was relieved, of course, but also perplexed. I couldn't explain it. I assumed they experienced a shared reaction —in the form of hives—to something they ate or encountered at their last port of call. As advanced as medicine is today, there remains so much we don't know about the body and its various afflictions." They turned onto Princes Street, and Warren pulled his coat tighter. "Whatever the cause of their particular illness, it appeared to have run its course, so I left them, telling their captain to call for me again if they relapsed.

"I have the sense, though, that you are about to tell me there was never any danger of that. They were never ill at all, were they?"

"I wouldn't go that far, sir. Nor would I necessarily hold these men responsible for any deception that kept you from the Court House. For all we know, they were as blameless as you."

"Indeed. I think, Mister Kaille, you should tell me what happened today at the trial."

"Yes, sir. I should begin by telling you what was done to Mister Adams."

"Samuel?"

Ethan nodded and proceeded to tell him about Adams' failure to attend the proceedings and the state in which Ethan found him when he visited the estate on Purchase Street. By the time he had finished, Warren was eyeing him coldly.

"Each time I encounter magick, I am struck by its capacity for evil, be it simple falsehood or more insidious harm. I hope you'll forgive me for saying so, but I consider those with . . . talents such as yours to be a scourge."

"You've seen me heal, sir."

Warren's mouth twitched and he turned his head to stare up the lane. "Yes, I have. I also consider myself a good judge of men's hearts. I don't believe you would ever use the powers you possess with malign purpose. Forgive me for what I said."

"You needn't apologize."

"You're generous." The doctor huffed a sigh. "So neither Samuel nor I was in the courtroom today. At this point, I'm almost afraid to hear the balance of your tidings. I take it loyalists took advantage of our absence."

Ethan told him the rest, naming the jurors Francis Lamb managed to seat. Warren reached the same conclusion his colleagues had.

"We've already lost. And Preston's men may well be doomed."

"Yes, sir."

"You say Samuel is well now, that he suffered no lasting effects from whatever was done to him?"

"I believe that to be the case. I would prefer that you examined him and pronounced him fit."

"Yes, all right. I'll go to him this evening. And what will you do next, Mister Kaille?"

Ethan heard a challenge in the question. "I'll find the person or people responsible for this mischief, sir. And I'll do everything in my power to keep them from inflicting more damage. You should know, however, that if magick was behind Mister Adams' forgetfulness and whatever illness manifested in those men you saw today, I have little hope of being able to help you and your colleagues. I'm an accomplished conjurer, but I couldn't have done either of those things. I haven't the knowledge or the skill."

"That isn't exactly what I had hoped to hear."

"No, sir, I don't imagine."

They turned at the next corner and were soon headed back toward Hanover Street. The sky was darkening—Ethan had thought to be back home long before now. Upon reaching Warren's house, he bid good evening to the doctor and continued on to Sudbury Street and the *Dowsing Rod*, Kannice's tavern.

She would have corrected him. They were married; the tavern belonged to them both. But he would forever consider it hers, which, in part, may have been why he had been so eager of late to return to thieftaking. The truth was, he still struggled with the adjustment to life as a tavern keeper. He was, in his heart, a creature of the lanes. Kannice and he both knew it.

Upon entering the tavern, Ethan was beset by familiar smells and sounds: bay and cooking fish, stale ale and fresh bread, laughter and the clink of spoons on bowls and an incomprehensible din of blended conversations. Kannice stood at the counter with her barman, Kelf Fingarin, both of them ladling stew into bowls and laughing with their many patrons. Ethan had arrived at the very height of the evening rush.

Kannice spotted him and her cheeks warmed. He hurried behind the bar and began to help them, taking over the ladling from Kelf so that the barman could fill tankards with ale, pour cups of Madeira, and make rum flips. A half hour or more passed before the demand for food and drink slackened enough to allow Kannice and Ethan a word to each other.

"I'm sorry to be so late," he said.

Her smile conveyed so much: indulgence, impatience, love, a touch of resentment, and, most of all, resignation.

"The trial adjourned some time ago." She gestured at the crowd. "They told me as much."

"Did they tell you what happened?"

"Most of them don't seem to know. It sounds as though they had trouble filling the jury."

"Aye, they did. And the jurors they selected are just the men Francis Lamb and Thomas Preston wanted. At least five of them are avowed loyalists."

She gaped, the look in her eyes turning flinty. "How could Adams allow that?"

Speaking quietly so that only she could hear, he explained what had happened to Adams and Warren.

"Well," she said when he was done, "at least now I know why you were so late. And, I'd wager, why you'll be heading out into the streets again before the evening's done."

"I need to speak with Janna."

"As long as you don't need to drink rum with Sephira Pryce, we're fine."

He grinned, kissed her. "No, I don't plan to drink anything with Sephira."

They hadn't much time to say more. Additional patrons entered the tavern, and soon Ethan, Kannice, and Kelf were scrambling to keep up with the demand for suppers and drinks. Ethan didn't leave for Janna's tavern until this second surge had spent itself. Then he made quick work of a bowl of chowder and some bread, and slipped out the door.

Stars shone in a sky only dimly lit by the crescent moon, which hung low to the west. The wind had died down, but the air remained cold and tinged with the scent of chimney smoke. Ethan walked to Marlborough Street, and followed the thoroughfare out past the South Meeting House, the pasture, and Rowe's Field. He had walked a good deal this day and his bad leg ached, worsening his usual limp. A dog barked to the east, and a chaise rattled past before turning onto Sheafe's Lane. Otherwise, Ethan saw no one, heard no one. Usually he didn't mind such solitude, even at night. After his recent confrontations with Charlotte Whitcomb, however, he found himself growing wary. More than once, an imagined footfall behind him made him glance over his shoulder at the empty street. It was with some relief that he reached Janna's tavern, the *Fat Spider*.

The *Spider* stood within sight of the Town Gate at the end of Boston's Neck. The building leaned heavily to one side, its ancient roof sagging, its wood worn almost to silver by years of rain and sun and wind.

Ethan stepped inside, and was met with smells of cinnamon, wood smoke, and some sort of savory stew that made his mouth water. He'd eaten little this day, and that one bowl of chowder at the *Dowser* had hardly sated his appetite. He crossed to the bar, sat, and set a shilling on the counter, all under the hawklike gaze of the tavern's diminutive proprietor, Tarijanna Windcatcher.

Janna hailed from West Indies. Her skin was dark, her hair snowy and shorn close to her scalp. He had never known her to be particularly friendly or welcoming. But she liked Ethan as much as he liked her. At least he was reasonably certain she did.

She knew more about magick than anyone he had ever met, and though she complained that he came to her for information far too often, she usually warmed quickly to the subject of spellmaking and different kinds of conjuring power.

"Your woman kick you out?" she asked, eyeing the coin he'd set on the polished wood of her bar.

"No, I'm just hungry, and whatever you have cooking smells wonderful."

The corners of her mouth edged upward. She had always been susceptible to flattery. "Ale, too?"

"Please."

"And questions, right? You don't ever come here without those."

"You know me too well, Janna."

Her expression soured, though only a little. He was buying, which usually loosened her tongue. She took the silver, and shuffled into her kitchen, returning moments later with a bowl of dark, piping stew.

"New recipe," she said. "Tell me how you like it."

As he tasted it, she walked out from behind the bar to a table near the hearth, where her only other customers, three men in work clothes, sat talking.

She refilled their bowls and tankards before stepping back to the bar. By then, Ethan had emptied his bowl. The stew tasted of nutmeg and other spices he couldn't name. It was remarkable—sweet and salty both, and so spicy it made his eyes water.

She peered into his bowl and smiled, exposing sharp, yellowed teeth. "You like it."

"I do."

"Well, good. Now, what do you want?"

Ethan scraped out the last of his stew, set the bowl aside, and drank half his ale to extinguish the fire burning his tongue. Janna chuckled.

"Last week, after the storm, you told me you thought Charlotte Whitcomb might be a water witch. I need to know more about . . . about witches." It felt odd to say this. He had spent much of his adult life denying that conjuring and witchcraft were the same thing, telling people, essentially, that witches were the stuff of nightmare and lore. Now he pursued witches himself. "Ideally, I'd like to speak with one, if you happen know of any who live in the area."

Her entire bearing turned guarded, and she gave a slow shake of her head. "Witches I know, they don't like answerin' questions about what they do, or how they do it, or pretty much anythin' else."

"But you do know some, don't you?"

Her chin dipped fractionally.

"Are they here in Boston?"

"There's one. An earth witch, with access to air and fire. Not in Boston, but close enough."

"Can you arrange an introduction? Please, Janna. I wouldn't ask for a favor like this if it wasn't important."

"You tell me more first. I want t' know what this witch of yours has done. Then I'll decide."

"You know what she's done. You were going to help me fight her, until I had to send you and Mariz away."

Janna shook her head. "When we talked about her that night, you talked about conjurin's and such. You didn't say anythin' about witches until she called up that storm. So I'm askin', what else has she done?"

She refilled Ethan's tankard, set it in front of him, and sat once more. He described for her the day's events, studying her reactions with care as he spoke. She didn't appear surprised by anything he said, but neither did she roll her eyes or dismiss any elements of his tale.

When he finished, she said, "Sounds like you hurt her last week. Those are weak attacks. I'd also guess that she's recoverin' from her wounds somewhere inland, away from the harbor and the river. Memory hexes and disease? Those are things an air witch would do."

"You said she'd need to be part air witch to raise the storm."

"I remember. And now I'm sayin' her air magick has some kick to it, too. Those attacks—they're not strong, and they don' take a lot out of her. But they're precise. This woman isn't foolin' around."

Ethan pondered this, staring into his ale. He knew too little about every aspect of this. He was beyond his depth.

"Adams all right?" she asked. "I like him."

"I think he's fine. Doctor Warren planned to check on him this evening."

She sat motionless for several moments, eyes alight with candle flame and hearth fire.

"You'd have t' walk," she finally said. "A carriage would scare her off. It's six miles or so, maybe a little more. Can you do that? With your bad leg an' all?"

"I can walk that far, yes."

She pursed her lips and narrowed her gaze. "Been a while since I made the journey. Tryin' to remember the way. You'd take the Lower Road, through Dorchester and then the Lower Way down toward the Milton Bridge. But if you reach the river you went too far. There's a mud road off to the left, just past the fifth or sixth milestone. It's the only one that goes left, so it won't matter which stone; if it's not one, it's the other. Take that, and about three hundred paces in, you'll come to a shack on the left. That's her place."

"What's her name?"

"Amanda. Amanda Oakroot."

He frowned at the name.

"She was a slave. Got her freedom, moved out on the land, and re-named herself. Oakroot is as much her name as Windcatcher is mine. You follow?"

"Of course."

"You'll wanna take her something. An offering."

"You mean, like a gift?"

"Sure, like a gift. A bottle of something should work. Always has for me. She don't like people. She don't like men especially. And white men . . . Well, I'll write something for you. A note sayin' who you are and that I know you. You can give it to her. Chances are that will work." Janna stood and started back into a small room off her kitchen.

"She'll talk to me, answer my questions?" Ethan asked.

Janna paused, peered back at him. "Well, I don't know about that. But with the note, she probably won't kill you."

IV

Fearing additional assaults on other Sons of Liberty, on the lawyers arguing both sides of the trial, perhaps even on the judges, Ethan put off his journey to the home of Amanda Oakroot for at least another day or two. Rather, he returned to the Court House early the next morning, expecting to have to wade through another mass of people. He needn't have bothered.

Enough men waited outside the building's doors to fill the courtroom with spectators, but the lane fronting the building was largely empty, the carnival atmosphere of the day before completely absent. Ethan waited with the others and entered the Court House under the watchful eye of Sheriff Greenleaf and the men of the watch. Greenleaf said nothing to him, but their eyes met as Ethan walked past. The sheriff acknowledged him with the most subtle of nods.

Samuel Adams and Joseph Warren arrived shortly after the proceedings began, and squeezed into an empty spot not far from where Ethan stood. They, too, spotted and acknowledged him, but they kept to themselves and spoke in hushed tones. Others among the spectators took note of their presence, but maintained a respectful distance from the most famous of Boston's patriots. Not long after the Sons of Liberty entered the chamber, Francis Lamb arrived. He ignored them, and Ethan, and took his place directly behind Preston.

The proceedings this day were even more wearisome than they'd been the day before. The prosecution called more than a dozen witnesses, but few of them added much to what had been said the previous day, and at least two of them seemed to contradict some of the more damaging early testimony. Late in the day, having questioned the last of his witnesses, Samuel Quincy offered a few closing remarks, none of them memorable or forceful enough to sway Preston's supporters among the jurymen. Warren and Samuel Adams could not conceal their dismay at the prosecution's performance. At one point, Ethan thought Samuel would rush the table shared by Quincy and Paine, toss the two lawyers aside, and assume control of the case himself.

Ethan understood their frustration, but he also sympathized with Quincy and Robert Treat Paine. In the days immediately before Ethan's confrontation with Charlotte Whitcomb and the resulting magick-driven storm, both men had been subjected to terrifying conjured attacks. Terrifying for them at least. Ethan had grown accustomed to such spellmaking, and to much worse. But for two men of letters, whose lives had been shaped by simple logic and what they thought of as the reasoned contours of the law, the intrusion upon their lives of magickal perils and threatening castings had to have been unnerving to say the least.

All of this should have occurred to him the day before, as he passed judgment on Paine's weak objections to the seating of the loyalist jurors. He had been all too willing to assume that the man was simply a mediocre lawyer. Only today, seeing similar timidity in Quincy's arguments, did Ethan connect their poor work to the attacks of the previous week.

After Quincy's summation, Ethan hoped the judges would call an end to the day's testimony. Instead, they invited John Adams to make his opening statement and call his first witnesses. And so the arguments and questioning dragged on until daylight started to fade and many among the jury and spectators struggled to keep themselves awake. Francis Lamb might have been the only person in the room who remained genuinely engaged throughout the afternoon. He seemed to enjoy himself—far too much for Ethan's tastes.

When at last the court adjourned, Ethan approached Adams and Warren, keeping an eye on Lamb as he did.

Adams greeted him with a grimace and a shake of his head. "Hardly an inspiring performance, wouldn't you agree, Mister Kaille?"

"I'm afraid I would, sir."

"I'm glad you were here. I felt safer knowing we were under your protection."

"Actually, sir, I would like to speak with you about that. I don't pretend to know what our enemies may try next, but I don't believe their future attacks will be aimed at this court."

"You don't?"

"No, sir. They have what they want here. Preston is sure to be acquitted. Even if the jury were unbiased, I fear Messieurs Paine and Quincy have been intimidated by last week's assaults. Their pursuit of a conviction has been . . . lackluster at best, and after all they've been through, I can hardly blame them."

"What, then, do you suggest?"

"I have information about someone who may be able to help us with our larger battle. I intend to speak with her as soon as possible. But that would mean absenting myself from tomorrow's proceedings. I'll go only with your permission—I've pledged to work on your behalf. I believe, though, that approaching this person would be a much better use of my time."

Adams looked to Warren, who lifted a shoulder.

"Yes, all right," Adams said. "I fear you're right about this trial. It is a lost cause. Go and speak with this person, and let us know what you learn."

"Thank you, sir."

Ethan shook hands with both men, donned his tricorn, and shambled out of the chamber, hungry, exhausted, eager for a meal and an ale, and an evening with Kannice at the *Dowsing Rod*. Upon his arrival, though, he had no choice but to help Kannice and Kelf with the swelling crowd in the great room. Kannice looked an apology his way, but there was nothing either of them could have done.

Normally, he wouldn't have begrudged the labor. After the day he'd had, however . . . Ethan liked being a tavern keeper well enough, and he still enjoyed thieftaking. He was too old to do both at the same time.

A brief lull in the demand for this night's stew—a rich chowder flavored with bay and sweet cream, and filled with oysters and potatoes—allowed Ethan to bolt down two bowls and savor a tankard of his favorite Kent pale ale. Then it was back to work, although not for long.

He had thrown more wood on the fire and taken the first step back in the direction of the bar, when he spotted a familiar figure standing just inside the doorway. Ethan froze. The man caught sight of him, the skin around his mouth tightening, the look in his dark eyes conveying so much —affection and resentment, memory and loss, longing and bitterness and, above all, fear.

He was tall and lean. Unruly black curls shone with candle light, still untouched by gray. His face, which once had been soft, unlined, filled with mischief and hope, had grown harder in recent months. The angles of his features were so sharp now they could have drawn blood. He wore a dark coat with bright brass buttons. The left sleeve, empty, had been pinned in place.

Diver Jervis.

Between his attendance at the trial and his recent conversation at the home of Joseph Warren, Ethan had thought of his old friend a great deal in recent days. And he had relived again and again that horrid, frigid night on King Street. Still, Ethan hadn't expected to see Diver here. And he certainly hadn't thought to see him alone, without Deborah Crane, Diver's beautiful betrothed.

Ethan crossed to him, eager and cautious.

"It's good to see you, Diver."

"Ethan." Diver's gaze darted away, scanned the tavern, settled on Ethan's face, only to slide away a second time.

"How have you been?"

Diver shrugged. "Doesn't matter right now. Something's happened."

A chill ran through Ethan's body. "Where's Deborah? Why isn't she with you?"

Diver met his glance again, held it this time. "Like I said, something's happened. A woman came to our flat. At least I thought it was a woman. She said she had taken Deborah somewhere—she wouldn't say where. But she said I was to find you and bring you to the waterfront; you would know where exactly—that's what she told me. And then . . ." He twitched his shoulder. "Then she vanished, like she'd never been there at all. I assume you know who she is."

"I think I do." He started to ask Diver to describe the woman, but decided the middle of the great room wasn't the place. He gestured for Diver to follow and led him around the bar and into the kitchen. Once they were alone, he asked, "What did she look like?"

"Pretty enough—light hair and green eyes. Not as tall as Deborah, and slight—wisp of a thing. Younger than me. Close to Deborah's age."

"Don't be fooled by her stature, or her age."

"So you do know her." A statement, tinged with anger.

"I do. I'm sorry you and Deborah have gotten caught up in this."

"Not the first time your fights have spilled over into our lives."

Ethan stiffened. "This isn't just my fight. This woman and her brother are enemies of Samuel Adams and the Sons of Liberty. That's how I got drawn into it in the first place."

Diver dropped his gaze and after some hesitation, nodded. "I take it this woman is a conjurer?"

"She is, and more than that. I won't lie to you: She's as dangerous as anyone to enter this city in some time. She's not insane like Nate Ramsey was, but she's every bit as powerful."

"And she went after Deborah because . . ."

"She wants to hurt me. More than that, she wants to control me, and she knows that threatening you and Deborah will earn her my attention. She knows that I'd do anything to keep both of you safe." He said this last pointedly.

Diver still wouldn't look at him. "Is she right? Do you know where to go?"

"Aye. She and I last saw each other on Minott's T. I assume she wants me there."

"All right, then. I'm coming with you."

Diver said this as if he expected a fight, and not long ago Ethan would have given him one. Taking anyone who couldn't conjure into a magickal fight was madness. Diver would be in peril, and Ethan would be at increased risk, since he would have to keep both of them safe. But he knew better than to think his friend would stay behind, and after all Diver had been through, and given all that was at stake this night, Ethan couldn't refuse him.

"I'd welcome your help," was all he said.

Diver blinked, as if unprepared for such easy acquiescence.

They started back into the great room, but found the doorway blocked by Kannice.

"I thought I'd seen Derrey," she said, voice bright.

Another change. Not so long ago, Kannice had considered Diver a ne'er-do-well. On more than one occasion, she had threatened to ban him from the *Dowser*. Only his friendship with Ethan stopped her, and she had made it clear that she thought Diver abused that friendship at every opportunity. Since the shooting, though, she had shown Diver far more kindness. She was fond of Deborah, and Ethan believed she thought better of Diver for having brought the young woman into their lives.

"Good evening, Kannice," Diver said, his voice low.

Her smile vanished. "What's happened?"

Ethan explained as succinctly as he could.

"And so you're going to find her," Kannice said. "Both of you."

"We're going to try."

Kannice eyed Diver, then Ethan. "Is that smart? Forgive me for asking, Derrey, but this woman has already flooded half of Boston with her magick. What's to keep her from killing all three of you?"

"What's she talking about?" Diver asked.

"I'll explain on the way to the waterfront." He faced Kannice again. "If she wanted me dead, and if she believed she could kill me, she would have come at me directly. She wants something else, and she's using Diver and Deborah to get it from me. They're in danger because of me. Again. What would you have me do?"

She frowned and gave a slow shake of her head. "I'd have you be careful. For once."

Ethan kissed her. "I'm always careful," he said. "I'm just . . . unlucky."

He checked to make certain he had both of his blades before crossing to the door with Diver, pulling on his coat and tricorn, and slipping out into the night.

He and Diver followed Sudbury to Queen, turning to walk past the Court House, saying nothing for the first several moments. This route would take them right past the Town House along King Street. They would walk by the very spot where Diver was shot. Ethan wondered if his friend realized this. He should have known.

"Let's go by the dock," Diver said, turning north onto Cornhill without waiting for Ethan to agree.

Ethan followed.

"Tell me more about this woman," his friend said, voice flat. "What did

Kannice mean about flooding Boston?"

"The woman's name is Charlotte Whitcomb, and she's not just a conjurer, she's also a witch."

Diver regarded him sidelong. "A witch? You've always said witches aren't real. There's only conjurers."

"I know. In the last few months I've learned that's not the case. There are witches. They have a form of elemental magick I don't quite understand, and they can be incredibly powerful. This one summoned the storm that struck the city last week."

"That was magick?"

"Aye."

"And you've gotten Deborah caught up in your fight with this woman?"

Ethan halted, as did his friend.

"This isn't my fault, Diver."

"No? How does she even know about us? How did she know to take Deborah?"

Ethan threw his hands wide. "I have no idea! I hadn't met her before last week, when she nearly killed me. The first time we spoke, she knew who I was, where I came from, what I'd done in my life, who I cared about. She knew about Kannice, my sisters, my parents, and, yes, about you. She threatened me by threatening all the people who matter most to me in this world. I didn't mean to endanger any of you."

Diver stared off at the Town Dock and then at Faneuil Hall, which loomed before them, a shadow in the faint light of the setting moon.

"I know that," he said after some time. "I'm sorry."

He started walking again, and Ethan hurried to catch up with him.

"If she hurts Deborah, I'll kill her myself," Diver said with quiet intensity. "I swear to God I will."

They passed Peter Faneuil's grand structure and turned onto Merchant's Row, which would take them back to King Street, east of the Customs House, where the shootings occurred. Diver pulled a pistol from his pocket. Ethan assumed it was loaded, and, with revulsion at the workings of his own mind, found himself wondering how one would load and prime a flintlock with only one arm. He thrust the thought away.

"That's not going to do you any good," he said. "Not against someone with power like hers."

Diver sent a glare his way. He didn't return the weapon to his coat.

They reached Long Wharf a short time later. Diver stepped onto the pier, but Ethan stopped him with a word. He drew his knife, cut his fore-arm and whispered, "*Tegimen nobis ambobus ex cruore evocatum.*"

The spell hummed in the street and the hulking warehouses around them. Uncle Reg's russet glow brightened the lane, though Diver couldn't see him. The blood disappeared from Ethan's arm, and the warding settled over Ethan's shoulders like a mantle. He assumed it covered Diver, too.

"What was that? What did you do?"

"I warded us both. It may not work against witchcraft, but it should protect us from her conjured spells."

Ethan motioned for them to walk on. Diver fell in step beside him, the pistol still in his hand.

"I've missed you, Diver," Ethan said, his voice low. "I hope you know that."

His friend dipped his chin, but said nothing. Ethan didn't press the matter.

At the edge of Minott's "T," they turned onto the wood extension, their steps echoing too loudly. Ethan slowed, spying a pair of figures at the end of the pier. One of them stood upright. The other . . . The other floated be-side her, as if suspended by an invisible hand.

"Damn," Ethan muttered.

Diver swore, walked more quickly.

Ethan growled his name, but the man didn't slow. Ethan hobbled after him.

"What have you done to her, you fucking whore?"

"Diver, no!"

Too late.

Her spell seemed to shake the wharf. A spectral figure in glowing bur-gundy flashed into view beside her. And Diver flew off his feet and crashed down onto the quay. His pistol bounced, discharged. The report echoed. Smoke rose into the briny air and dissolved. The bullet scarred the wood, but didn't hit anyone.

"Manners, Mister Jervis," Charlotte Whitcomb said, her voice even. "You don't want to anger me."

Ethan helped Diver to his feet.

"Are you all right?"

"I'm fine," Diver said, his wince belying the words.

The two of them edged closer to the woman. Whitcomb looked much as Ethan recalled from their recent encounters, though her face might have been slightly more pinched—possibly the result of the injuries he had dealt her when they fought. His gaze, though, was drawn to Deborah.

She lay in the air, arms at her sides, her hair a scarlet halo around her head. Her eyes were closed, her face at ease. Ethan didn't believe she was in pain. On the other hand, he couldn't be certain that she was even alive. An ill-defined cloud, like vapored breath on a cold night, surrounded her, as if holding her aloft.

"What have you done to her?" Diver demanded, his face contorted by terror and hate and thwarted love, his every breath shuddering through him.

"She's quite well, I promise you."

"*You, promise*," Diver repeated with contempt.

"Diver."

"I've warned you once," she said. "Don't insult me a third time."

Ethan stepped in front of Diver, blocking his friend, though whether to keep her from attacking him, or him from doing something stupid, he couldn't say.

"What is it you want?" he asked. "Why have you taken her?"

"Why won't you attack her?" Diver demanded of Ethan. "You have magick! Use it!"

"He doesn't attack me because he knows better," Whitcomb said. "No spell he might cast can defeat my wardings. And if he were to wound or kill me, he knows the woman would perish."

During Ethan's earlier confrontations with Whitcomb, she had drawn power for her spells from people around her. She couldn't use Diver in that way, because Ethan had warded him. He thought it possible, though, that she could use Deborah as a source for her magick. What if he warded her, as well?

He bit down on the inside of his mouth, blood salting his tongue, and cast a warding intended to protect her. Reg returned and the spell rumbled. Whitcomb's glare snapped his way.

But when the magick of his conjuring met that vaporous cocoon around Deborah, it flared like oil in flame. Ethan had to shield his eyes, and when he could see again, Whitcomb was grinning.

"A warding, I assume, to deny me fuel for my conjurings. Clever. But I don't suppose I have to tell you your spell failed." Her aspect hardened, chilled. "Don't do it again. You don't want to make me conjure. You should understand that, Kaille."

"Good Lord."

"What is she talking about?" Diver asked.

"I draw life from her every time I cast," Whitcomb said with relish. "That temper tantrum of yours when first you arrived—that would have cost her several months. Do try to be more careful."

"Ethan?"

Ethan held up a hand, silencing his friend. "I'll ask you again: What is it you want with us, with her?"

"It's simple, really. I need something done, and I want one of you to do it. I gather that both of you would bear any cost to keep this lovely young woman alive, yes?" She didn't wait for their reply. "And so with her life in the balance, I believe I can convince you to help me."

Ethan didn't want to ask. Anything he or Diver could do for her that she didn't see fit to do herself, would be illegal or immoral or inhuman.

This once, Diver knew enough to told his tongue.

"Neither of you is even curious."

"Neither of us is going to do anything for you. Now let her go."

Whitcomb's smile, illuminated by the burgundy gleam of her ghost, made her look ghoulish. "I think one or the other of you will do whatever I ask. Mister Jervis here would do anything to save his love, and you, Mister Kaille, would do anything to keep your friend from harm. Now, both of you count yourselves among the Sons of Liberty, isn't that right?"

They didn't answer.

"I can hurt her, you know. She can remain under this glamour as if asleep, or I can subject her to torment the like of which she has never experienced. Which would you prefer?"

"Yes," Ethan said, his voice like a garrote. "We both support the cause of liberty. What of it?"

"As I say, I need one of you to do something for me. I need you to kill Samuel Adams."

V

It took Ethan a few seconds to find his voice. "You must be mad. Neither of us would ever do such a thing."

"Not even if I promise you that this woman will die if Adams isn't dead by midnight Saturday?"

"Not even if you threaten to burn all of Boston to the ground."

She kept her eyes on Diver. "But you're wrong, Mister Kaille. Look at your young friend. Already he is thinking of ways he might carry out my demands."

Ethan turned and had to suppress a shudder. She was right. Diver stared not at her, but at the now-empty flintlock in his hand. The rage so evident in his features moments before had given way to an expression that struck Ethan as speculative, thoughtful, but still dark. As if even now he was plotting how to maneuver himself close enough to Adams to do the deed.

"Diver," Ethan said softly.

His friend started, cast an abashed glance at Ethan, his face reddening.

"It's not going to come to that. We are not going to kill Samuel Adams."

Diver appeared shaken and ashamed.

"You still don't understand, do you, Kaille? Perhaps this will help." She spun, both hands raised, and spoke to the moonlight in a tongue Ethan didn't understand. He gathered, from something Kelf said during their confrontation with Whitcomb the day of the storm, that the words were Gaelic.

There could be no mistaking their effect, though. Deborah soared out over the harbor, higher and higher, farther and farther from the pier.

"*Deborah!*" Diver's voice spiraled into the night, anguished, utterly forlorn.

Still she flew from them, and as she did, the vapor around her thickened, grew opaque, until it resembled other low clouds scudding over the harbor. Ethan could only stare after it, awed and pained. Her "cloud" even shifted with the others, though somehow it seemed to circle back to its original spot again and again.

"Bring her back," Diver pleaded, tears coursing down his cheeks.

"I won't. Now listen to me, both of you. You will do this thing I demand of you, or I will release my casting and she will fall into the harbor, still unconscious. If the fall does not kill her, she will drown. If you hurt me, I will let her fall. If somehow you manage to kill me, she will fall. If you anger or disappoint me in any way . . ." She completed the thought with a vague gesture. "I believe you understand."

"The instant you let her fall, you're dead. I've shown that I can best you. I'll do it again," Ethan said.

"No, you won't. My mistake before was fighting you as a conjurer. I will admit that you proved more resourceful than I reckoned you would be. I won't make that error again. You can't hope to overmaster my witchcraft; you barely comprehend it. Any spell you direct at me will fail, just as your warding of the girl did a moment ago."

Ethan hazarded a glance at Diver. He still watched that cloud, fresh tears falling. Ethan didn't think he would ever look away.

"I am leaving now," Whitcomb said. "You have until the Sabbath."

She stepped past them, and Ethan had no choice but to let her go. The truth was, he couldn't risk an attack on the woman. Even if he could overcome her protective castings, and even if Deborah survived a fall from that height, he had no way of reaching Diver's love before she succumbed to the chill waters of the harbor.

He watched Whitcomb go, her lilac perfume hanging in the air around them.

"Diver—"

"What do we do, Ethan? What do we do?"

"There's nothing we can do tonight."

The younger man rounded on him. Ethan had to resist an impulse to back away.

"Listen to me: Deborah is as safe as she can be, for the next couple of days, at least."

"We don't even know if she's alive!"

"Yes, we do. *Listen to me*," he said again. He grabbed Diver's arm to keep him from turning toward the harbor. "Listen! Whitcomb couldn't have used Deborah to fuel that spell if she weren't still alive. For now, she's all right in there. That may be the only thing the woman said that's true. We have two full days to figure out how to free her."

Of all the things Ethan had said, that one penetrated Diver's fear and despair. He drew a long breath, blew it out. "Aye, all right. How do we start?"

"You'll come with me back to the *Dowser*. You're sleeping there tonight."

"I don't—"

"Don't argue with me. I want to know where you are. I want to know you're safe." *And that you won't do anything foolish or dangerous.* "In the morning, I'll be headed to Milton to speak with a witch, someone Janna knows. She'll help us."

"I'll come with you."

"No, you won't. You can't. Janna says she'll barely tolerate a visit from me. Two of us . . ." He shook his head. "Please trust me, Diver. You once did. I'm asking you to do so again."

A reluctant nod.

Ethan still gripped his friend's arm, and now he steered him off the wharf and back into the shadowed lanes of the South End.

The moment they entered the *Dowsing Rod*, Kannice strode out from behind the bar.

"What's happened? Where's Deborah?"

Diver turned to Ethan, tears filling his eyes again.

"I'll explain everything," Ethan said. "First, though, I need you to make up a room for Diver. He's staying with us for the next few days."

She heard enough in his tone to know not to argue or ask more questions.

"Of course," was all she said, before hurrying up the tavern stairs.

Kelf and Ethan led Diver to a table, and the barman brought Diver a bowl of chowder and an ale. Diver protested feebly that he didn't want anything, but Ethan handed him a spoon, and he began to eat, more out of habit than hunger. Ethan remained with him, watching, saying nothing, scouring his brain for ideas. He didn't know enough—not about Charlotte Whitcomb's powers, not about his own.

Within less than a quarter hour, Kannice descended the stairway and caught Ethan's eye. Diver had finished much of his chowder and all of his ale.

"Come along," Ethan said, leading him to the stairway and up to the second floor.

Kannice had left the door to his room open. It was much like the others they had for rent—clean, sparsely furnished, but comfortable.

Ethan had Diver sit on the pallet and removed his boots.

"I'm not tired, Ethan. I want to know what we're going to do."

"I know." He bit the inside of his cheek again. *Dormite, ex cruore evocatum.*

Reg gleamed beside him, his glowing eyes on Diver, expectant.

"We should—"

The young man said no more, but fell onto his side, fast asleep. Ethan arranged him on the bed and covered him with a blanket. He extinguished the candle beside the pallet and left the room, confident that Diver would sleep through the night.

Reg remained with him.

"It was for his own good. He has to sleep, and he won't without a little push."

The ghost said no more than he usually did.

A few patrons still sat at tables throughout the great room. Kannice circled through the room, checking ales and picking up empty bowls. When she returned to the bar, Ethan explained in whispers what had happened at the wharf.

"How did you get him to stay up there?"

Ethan's cheeks burned.

"Ethan!"

"It's just a sleep spell. But I had to do something. He's mad with fear and grief and rage. I'm afraid of what he might do. I believe he would be willing to kill Adams to get her back. I know I would to save you."

She took his hand.

"What will you do?"

"I'll cast another sleep spell in the morning, and then I'll go to speak with Janna's friend—the witch in Milton. If I can learn something from her, maybe I can free Deborah and fight Whitcomb."

"You truly believe this woman would kill her?"

"Aye. Only one thing would stop her. She needs to believe that if Deborah is hurt or killed, I'll be able to do the same to her."

VI

Ethan set out for the home of Amanda Oakroot early the following morning. He had slept poorly, pursued from dream to dream by witches shrouded in a gray mist. He was just as happy to rise at first light.

The day dawned gray and cold, with a gusting wind and a smattering of raindrops. Bundled in his coat, his tricorn pulled down low to shield his face, Ethan walked the length of the city, passing Janna's tavern before leaving Boston through the Town Gate and following the causeway across the Roxbury mud flats. The water was high, and ducks and geese gathered in noisy clusters. He paused halfway across to stare out at the harbor. It took him several moments, but eventually he spotted what he believed to be Deborah's cloud. The sky shifted endlessly, roiled by that hard wind, but always that one cloud wound up back in place. It had to be her.

Watching the sky, he cursed his own weakness, his inability to overcome Whitcomb's magick. He walked on, quickening his pace.

Once on the far side of the causeway, Ethan took the Lower Road, as Janna instructed. His leg already bothered him, but there was little he could do about that. His thoughts returned again and again to Diver and Deborah. Before leaving the *Dowser* this morning, he had cast another sleep spell on his friend, over Kannice's objections. He didn't like spelling his friend, but he didn't trust Diver not to endanger himself and Deborah. Besides, Diver would benefit from the rest, and be more clear-headed when Ethan returned and woke him.

Kannice had packed him some food, and he nibbled on a round of bread as he walked. When he finished it, he pulled from his coat pocket an item he had reclaimed from the back of his wardrobe prior to leaving: the pale blue stone he took from Charlotte Whitcomb during their battle on the day of the storm.

It was heavy, jagged, unrefined. Individual shards of translucent crystal jutted in all directions, each a different size, although they resembled one another in form. Ethan didn't understand how Whitcomb used this stone, but even he, untutored in the ways of witchcraft, sensed its power. He hoped Amanda Oakroot would be able to tell him more about it.

Aside from a few quick showers, the rain held off as he walked, and he made decent time, reaching the mud road Janna had described before midday.

He turned down the track, searching for Amanda's small house. As he limped past copses and bogs, he drew his knife, pushed up his sleeve, and cut himself.

"*Tegimen ex cruore evocatum.*"

His spell thrummed in the earth and his spectral guide emerged from the murky light, russet and luminous like a blood moon. Ethan was far enough from Boston that he didn't worry about Charlotte Whitcomb sensing is spell. He did wonder, though, if an earth witch could feel his sort of conjuring.

He spotted a shack ahead of him and on the left, and sheathed his blade, lest she view the weapon as a threat.

The house looked barely large enough to hold even one person. It was little more than a shingled box, with a crooked door, an off-kilter, black metal chimney that belched smoke into the cold air, and a single pane window on the side facing the direction from which Ethan approached. It was set on stone blocks that lifted it perhaps a foot off the mud.

As he neared the structure, the door burst open, and a woman stepped out onto the path. She was lighter-skinned than Janna, with hair as white and wispy as dandelion seeds. Her stained, brown linen gown draped loosely over a frame that appeared square and solid. She carried a musket, and she planted her feet in the dirt and leveled it at Ethan's chest.

"Who the hell are you?"

Ethan held his hands up for her to see. "My name's Ethan Kaille. I'm a thieftaker and conjurer from—"

"I know that. Don't you think I felt your spell?"

Well, that was one question answered.

"What are you doing on my land, my road?"

"I came looking for you. Janna Windcatcher told me how to find you."

She raised her head so she no longer had him sighted with the musket, though he was certain that if she pulled the trigger she would still hit him.

"You know Janna?"

"Aye. I carry a missive from her in my pocket, and a bottle of Madeira. Both for you."

"The wine from her?"

He shook his head. "That's from me. A gift."

She scowled. "Why would a white man from the city want to give me a gift?"

"Because I need help with a water witch, and I don't know enough about your powers to fight her on my own."

"And why do you think I would take your side?"

He considered answering with a quip about that bottle of Madeira, but he sensed she wasn't in a mood for humor.

"Well, I hoped the note from Janna—"

"That only gets you so far, Boston."

"This woman is a loyalist, newly arrived from London."

She sighted him again with her weapon. "You're not helping your cause. British didn't make me a slave. Colonists did that. And I've never been raped by a woman. Now I'm done talking, and I think you'd better leave."

He eyed the house, noticing something he had missed earlier. A patch of new wood shingles on the roof. He took a chance.

"Was your house damaged by the storm?"

"What the hell business is that of yours?"

"The witch I need help with—she conjured that storm right before my eyes. Turned it from wind and rain to a gale unlike anything Boston has seen for almost a century."

She straightened again, skepticism in her glare. "A witch made that storm?"

"Aye, she did."

"Why should I believe you?"

"You don't have to. Read Janna's letter. Drink a cup of wine with me and listen to my story. After that, you can help me or not, as you see fit.

Either way you can keep the bottle."

"You're that desperate for my help?"

"I am if you're as strong as Janna says. Then again, I suppose she could be wrong about you."

She sneered. "Don't try that crap with me. In addition to being stronger than you, I'm also smarter. You can't bend me to your will like that."

She lowered the musket and strode back to the door. "Come on, then," she said. "I'm thirsty."

He removed his tricorn and followed her into the house, which smelled strongly of smoke and was tidier and more cozy than he ever would have thought possible from outside. An iron stove radiated warmth from the far corner, its chimney following a crooked course to the ceiling. A bed lined one wall, a table and two chairs rested beside that lone window. A small larder behind the table held what looked like ample stores of foodstuff, and neatly stacked wood near the stove promised warmth for days to come.

"This is a nice place."

She rounded on him. "You mocking me?"

He didn't flinch. "I wouldn't. I was being sincere."

Amanda's eyes narrowed again. She took the wine from him and jerked her chin at one of the chairs. "Sit down."

Ethan did as she instructed. She poured wine into two cups and watered both generously. Joining him at the table, she drank a bit and set down her cup. "Let me see that letter."

He dug into his coat pocket and produced Janna's missive, which was folded twice over.

She took it from him, considered it, eyed him again. "You read this?"

Ethan shook his head. "It wasn't addressed to me."

Frowning, she opened the note and read. Twice, her gaze flicked to him. When she finished, she folded it again, set it down, and drank the rest of her wine.

"She calls you a friend. Janna doesn't use that word lightly. She also says you work with Samuel Adams."

"That's right."

"Drink your wine."

He drank. She reclaimed the bottle and a pitcher of water. Upon returning to the table, she filled their cups again.

"How'd you get that limp?" she asked.

Ethan had lifted his cup, but he returned it to the table without taking a sip. "Did Janna tell you to ask me that?"

She didn't answer.

"I was involved in a mutiny, court-martialed, and sent to labor for four-teen years on a sugar plantation in Barbados. While I was there, a fellow prisoner cut my foot with a cane knife—an accident." He shrugged. "I got gangrene. They had to amputate half my foot to save my leg. And my life I suppose."

"Don't they usually hang mutineers?"

"Usually. I was fortunate."

This earned him a raised eyebrow.

"I realized I'd made an error, that the first mate we put in power was worse by far than the captain. I switched sides. So at my court-martial, the captain argued for leniency."

"Fourteen years is a long time."

"How long were you a slave?"

A wry smile touched her lips, and her face was transformed, softened, turned friendly instead of fearsome. "Longer than that," she said.

He begrudged every minute it took him to win this woman's trust. He sensed, though, that she wouldn't be rushed, that to make the attempt would be to forfeit any chance at securing her help.

"What else is in that letter?" he asked.

"She says you're a decent conjurer. Lazy, though. You could be a real power if you put your mind to learning."

A chuff of laughter ran through him. "I suppose she's right."

"That why you need help from me?"

"No. This isn't laziness, it's ignorance. I know a good deal about con-juring, and Janna's taught me a lot. But I find myself opposed now by a witch. A water witch to be exact, with a touch of air magick. And I know nothing about witchcraft."

"This is the one who conjured the storm?"

"Yes, and more." He told her what had been done to Samuel Adams and about the deception directed at Joseph Warren. Finally, he described what Whitcomb had done to Deborah.

She responded much as Janna had to what he said about the Sons of Liberty, noting that such spells required powerful air magick. But when he spoke of the cloud in which Whitcomb had snared Deborah, she grew pen-sive.

"That's some dark spellwork," she said. "And difficult. Tell you the truth, I'm not sure I could do it."

"It's worse than that," Ethan said. "In addition to having witch magick, she's also a conjurer. A powerful one."

Amanda sat back. "Well, damn. That's something different."

"Will a conjured warding work against a witch spell?"

"I don't know," she said. "Guess you'll have to ward yourself and see the next time you meet her."

"You could help me."

She shook her head. "I'm not ready to do that."

He wanted to ask her why, but he could imagine her response. She had at least as much in common with Charlotte Whitcomb as she did with Ethan. Perhaps more. On those occasions when Ethan encountered other conjurers who sought to do harm in Boston—Nate Ramsey, the daughters of Caleb Osborne, Peter Darrow—Sheriff Greenleaf had accused Ethan of having divided loyalties. Was he more devoted to the city, or to others of his kind? And though Ethan had chosen the safety of Boston on each occasion, it had, at times, pained him to pit himself against other conjurers.

"This woman the witch has ensnared," he said, "she's done nothing to deserve this fate. She's an innocent."

"I'm not sure there's any such thing."

The chill in her voice as she said this made Ethan falter. "Well, she's as close as anyone could come. She should never have been involved in this matter. She certainly shouldn't die for it."

"I'm sorry for her, and for her people. But I can't help."

"Fair enough," Ethan said, after a tense pause. "Can I ask you this: If you wanted to protect yourself from a hostile water witch, what would you do?"

She canted her head. "There are protections that work across all the elements. Herbs, stones, even certain metals. Herbs are universal—they feed on fire in the form of sunlight. They feed on air, water, earth. Any witch can use any herb. Stones, metals—they're different. Each has its own affinity. You can ask Janna about that."

"I can do better than that," he said. He produced from within his coat the crystal he carried.

Amanda's eyes widened. He held it out to her and she took it from him, handling it as if it were fragile, or perhaps too hot to hold.

"How did you get this?" She didn't take her eyes off the stone.

"I managed to take if from the woman when we fought. I assume she's replaced it, but I would like to know what sort of power the stone conveys."

She scrutinized the stone for another few seconds before setting it on

the table, standing, and crossing to her bed. There, from a small drawer in
her night table, she drew a stone of her own. It was a single crystal, more
rounded than the spars bristling from Whitcomb's stone, opaque and deep
green. She held it for him to see, but didn't offer to let him hold it.

"What is that?"

"It's called tourmaline." She returned to her chair. "Some people call it
Venus stone or Turkish stone. It's an earth crystal. I use it to amplify my
magick, much the way your friend would have used that." She lifted her
chin in the direction of the blue crystal. Ethan didn't bother correcting her
description of Whitcomb.

"How does that work? Amplifying?"

She shrugged. "I draw power from the earth. This makes doing so easier, allows me clearer control over that power. The closest comparison I
can offer is to using a glass lens to concentrate sunlight so that it burns.
The stone isn't a source for her power. In the strictest sense it doesn't even
make her more powerful. It makes her power more effective and more effi-
cient. Does that make sense?"

It did. "So without her stone, she can still cast spells."

"Yes. They won't be as precise, but they'll work."

"Is there anyway I can use the stone against her?"

She sat back, considering her own stone and the one Ethan held. At last
she met his gaze. "Honestly, I don't know. It's never even occurred to me
to wonder." She toyed with Whitcomb's crystal again. "Unless you, too, are
a water witch, I'm not sure I see how having this stone would help you—
beyond the obvious that is. Her magick will be less exact because she does-
n't have it."

"She can simply replace the stone, though, can't she?"

Amanda handed the crystal cluster back to him. "It's not so easy as that.
It takes years to . . . we call it training a stone. It is true that another crystal
of this quality will help her cast, just as another piece of tourmaline would
be of use to me. But given the choice between this stone that I know, that
I've worked with and grown accustomed to, and even the finest specimen
in the grandest collection in the world, I would always choose this one."

Interesting. Francis Lamb had lied to Ethan the last time they spoke,
when he tried to browbeat Ethan into surrendering the crystal. This came
as no surprise, of course. The man would have said anything to retrieve the
item, and that much Ethan knew. But in this case, his lies could have been
intended to mask a fundamental principle of witch magick.

"Thank you," Ethan said. "That's helpful."

He considered asking her once more to help him in his imminent battle with Charlotte Whitcomb. In the end, he chose not to, thinking it wisest not to push her in this regard. He didn't relish the thought of making this walk again before Saturday night, but he would do whatever was necessary to win her cooperation. And that meant gaining her trust with patience. He drank the rest of his wine and stood. "I won't bother you further."

She said nothing, and remained where she was. Ethan stepped to the door and put on his hat.

"Good day, Miss Oakroot."

He left and started back up the path toward the Lower Road. Before he had taken ten steps, he heard her door open.

"Wait a minute."

Ethan turned. She stood in the middle of the road, vapor from her breath billowing in the cold. She had left the musket inside.

"This an act?"

"What?"

"Are you pretending to be respectful and all, but thinking the whole time that I'm nothing but an ignorant Negro, someone you can fool into helping you? Because I'm not. I'm educated—book smart and taught by life. I've seen enough shit to be wary of men like you."

"With all respect, Miss Oakroot, you don't know me well enough to say what kind of man I am. I don't believe you're ignorant, and I didn't come here to trick you into doing anything you don't want to do. I need help. My friend needs help. I've asked for it. I hope that you'll consider teaching me what you know about witch magick, but I don't expect I can force you to do that today. And with this young woman in peril, I can't linger here waiting for you to make up your mind to help me."

"Ward yourself," she said.

"I did before I reached your house. You felt it, remember?"

"And you don't think a second warding would help you?"

She didn't wait for his reply. Her lips moved, but Ethan couldn't make out what she said. Her spell hit him like a chaise moving at speed, he flew back, hit the ground, tumbled head-over-heels at least twice, and wound up dazed, lying on his belly in the mud.

"Looks like your wardings don't work against earth magick," Amanda said.

Ethan pushed himself up to his knees. "What was that spell supposed to do?"

"Exactly what it did. If I'd wanted to do worse, I don't think your conjurings could have stopped me."

He struggled to his feet, swayed, but managed to walk back to where she waited, poorly concealed amusement brightening her face.

"I don't believe that," he said. "Janna always tells me a conjurer can accomplish just about anything with the right incantation and source for the spell. I don't think this is any different."

"You want to try again?"

"Not even a little."

He chanced a grin, and she answered with a laugh that was deep and musical. It shook her entire frame and exposed straight, white teeth with a small gap between the middle two.

"I'll talk to Janna," Ethan said. "Together, we may be able to come up with a warding that will work. May I come back in the next day or two? Talk to you again? Maybe let you pound on me with another spell?"

"I suppose."

"Thank you." He turned once more, but then paused and glanced back at her. "My spells worked against the water witch. It may be that you can't ward yourself against my attacks any more than I can ward myself against yours."

"Maybe. We can test that, too. So long as your spells don't hurt like mine do."

He smiled again, and started back toward Boston.

"Bring more wine," she said.

Ethan raised a hand in farewell.

VII

By the time Ethan reached Boston, most of the day was gone. His bad leg ached, as did his back, neck, shoulders, and chest from the impact of Amanda's attack. He wanted to go straight to the *Dowsing Rod* to see Kannice and check on Diver, to eat some chowder and bread and drink an ale. First, however, he checked the harbor sky again. Deborah's prison of vapor remained much as it had been. This came as both a relief and a horror.

Once inside the Town Gate, he made his way to the *Green Dragon*, the usual meeting place for the Sons of Liberty. He found Joseph Warren there, and, after searching the room for a few seconds, spotted Samuel Adams, who appeared grim but in good health. Another relief.

"What happened today?" Ethan asked Warren.

The doctor answered with a head shake. "More witnesses for the defense. John is a very good lawyer. He and Auchmuty both. Their questions led these men exactly where they needed to go." He glanced about the room and leaned closer to Ethan. "Would that Robert and Samuel could have accomplished as much with their witnesses," he said, dropping his voice. He straightened. "In any case, after today, I fear even an honest jury would vote to acquit. Preston has little cause for worry."

"And there have been no further incidents directed at you or Mister Adams?"

"No, nothing like that."

"I'm glad to hear it," Ethan said, exhaling the words. "In that case, I should be going."

"If I may say so, Mister Kaille, you don't look well. Have you slept?"

"I've tried, and will again tonight. Thank you for your concern, doctor."

He left the tavern and walked the short distance to the *Dowser*. Familiar smells greeted him—baked bread, bay, musty ale, pipe smoke. Diver spoke with Kannice at the bar. He turned at a word from her, glowered at Ethan. For a man who had probably slept the entire day, he didn't look well either. His cheeks and eyes were puffy, his hair tousled.

Ethan stepped to the bar, kissed Kannice and faced his friend, prepared to be upbraided.

"What did you do to me?" Diver demanded.

"I put you to sleep."

"For an entire day?"

"Aye. I thought it best."

"*You* thought—" Diver leveled a finger at him. He was speaking loudly now, drawing glances from around the room. "That is not—"

"In the kitchen," Ethan said. He didn't wait for a reply, but stalked into the back of the tavern, forcing Diver to follow. He waited for the sound of Diver's footfall behind him before whirling. Diver started to a halt, eyes widening.

"Yes, I put you to sleep, Diver. Because last night you were ready to kill Samuel Adams to save Deborah, and I can't allow you to do that. I spent most of the entire day walking to and from Milton, where I spoke with a witch, a woman Janna knows, who might be able to help us defeat Whitcomb and her water magick. And I couldn't afford to worry about you doing something reckless."

Diver didn't answer at first, nor did he throw a punch, which Ethan half expected.

"What did you learn?" he asked.

Ethan rubbed his chest, which still throbbed from Amanda's attack. "That my wardings don't work against witchcraft."

Diver frowned.

"I intend to go back tomorrow, if I have to. She spoke of herbs and stones that could help us. I know we need more from her than that," he added quickly, seeing the doubt in Diver's expression deepen by the moment. "I haven't yet figured out how to win her trust. But I've only just begun. I won't stop until Deborah is safe. You have to believe me."

"I do," Diver said. "And you have to believe in turn that I'm not the foolhardy cove I used to be. I've changed. I'm wiser now—because of Deborah mostly. Last night was . . . I love her more than anything, Ethan. And I admit that last night my thoughts went places that frightened me. I promise you, though, I can be of help to you, and I can control myself. I want Deborah back—of course I do. And I also want to be a free man when she's safe. Me being in gaol for the rest of my days is not exactly the life she and I have planned."

"No," Ethan said. "I don't imagine it is. All right, I won't put you to sleep again. You have my word."

Diver swallowed, his cheeks paling. "Have you . . . did you see her? The cloud, I mean?"

"I did. She's still just where she was last night. I take that as evidence that she remains safe and healthy."

His friend nodded, as if wanting nothing more than to believe this. "All right. Then what do we do now?" He didn't wait for Ethan's reply. "Sephira has a conjurer, doesn't she? Couldn't he help us?"

"I've gone to Sephira for help too often recently. I don't want to be beholden to her. And she has ties to Whitcomb's brother. I'm not sure—"

"Whitcomb has a brother?" Diver asked, his gaze sharpening.

"A customs man: Francis Lamb. Some think he may be a spy for the Crown. He's dangerous, too, in his own way."

"I'd wager she cares about him," Diver said, as if he hadn't heard. "Maybe not as much as I care about Deborah, but close."

"Diver."

"I'm just saying—she's using Deborah to control us. It could be helpful to have some leverage ourselves."

Ethan shook his head. "If we do anything to Lamb, she's liable to kill Deborah. Not to mention what Greenleaf would do to us. There are other ways, less dangerous ways."

"Right," Diver said, sounding disappointed. "You're probably right. You know more about these things than I do." The words were convincing enough, but he wouldn't quite meet Ethan's gaze.

Ethan studied his friend. "You know," he said, "you were right about Sephira's man. We do need help, but not from him. Come with me to talk to Janna."

"Janna?" He grew diffident in an entirely different way. "I don't know, Ethan. Maybe you should talk to her on your own; I don't think she likes me very much."

"Janna doesn't like anyone very much. And after we tell her what Whitcomb has done with her magick, she'll probably have questions for you about Deborah."

This last was a lie. Ethan couldn't imagine Janna would need to know anything about Deborah. Diver's betrothed was a victim in this, no more and no less. Whitcomb could have done the same thing to Kannice or Kelf or Diver himself. But Ethan wanted to keep his friend occupied.

Diver didn't know enough about conjuring to question Ethan in this regard, and with a little more coaxing, he agreed to walk with him out to the *Fat Spider*.

They left the kitchen, only to be confronted by Kannice, hands on hips, who refused to let either of them leave without first eating some supper. Ethan had to admit that he was ravenous. So was Diver.

They ate, drank their ales, and were out the door with the last vestiges of daylight still glowing on the western horizon.

As they walked out to the Neck, Diver kept his eyes on the harbor and the clouds above it.

"I can see her," he murmured as they passed Rowe's Field.

Ethan looked that way. "Aye. See? Still safe."

"Hardly."

Ethan cringed at what he'd said. "You're right. Forgive me. Not safe, but at least still there, where we know she's alive and waiting for us to help her."

They continued on in silence.

As they neared the *Spider*, Diver slowed. His eyes drawn again to the cloud. "I used to envy you," he said. "I wanted to be a conjurer. I wanted to have access to the kind of power I've seen you wield. After . . . after I was shot, that changed. I wanted nothing to do with magick." He slanted a quick peek at Ethan. "I wanted nothing to do with you. Now, though, I feel useless. And I wonder if having the ability to cast would make me feel different, better."

"I feel pretty helpless right now, too. For what that's worth."

Ethan stepped to Janna's door and pushed it open. Diver followed him inside.

"You see?" he heard Janna say. "I told you he'd show up. He always does when he needs help."

Ethan halted just inside the door. Janna stood behind her bar. And across from her, stood Amanda Oakroot, a coat still wrapped around her shoulders and trailing to the floor, light from the hearth and candles warming her face.

"Who's that?" Diver whispered.

"The witch I talked to today." He motioned for Diver to follow and crossed to the bar. "I didn't expect to see you again so soon."

"No, I don't imagine you did." Amanda tipped her head in Diver's direction, suspicion tightening the muscles around her mouth. "Who is this?"

"The betrothed of the young woman I told you about."

Her expression loosened slightly. "I'm sorry," she said to Diver.

"You didn' tell me about the woman," Janna said to Ethan, an accusation in her tone.

"It hadn't happened yet, or I would have."

"I was thinking about it after you left," Amanda said. "That kind of witchcraft—holding someone above ground, or water—like that: It would take a lot power all the time. She can't afford to rest. And it would also keep her from being able to cast other spells. Maybe not entirely, but for the most part."

"So she'd be vulnerable," Diver said.

Amanda looked him up and down. "You a conjurer, too?"

"No," he said, his face turning crimson.

"Derrey Jervis, this is Amanda Oakroot."

Diver put on a brittle smile. "Nice to meet you."

"Umm hmmm," she said, still appraising him.

"So you had this thought about Charlotte Whitcomb's magick, and you decided to walk six miles to tell me about it?" Ethan asked.

"I also needed more wine."

Ethan raised an eyebrow.

She rubbed a finger over a rough spot on Janna's bar. "You're working for Samuel Adams, and you're a friend of Janna's. After you left I got to thinking that there were only a very few things that could get me to help a white man do anything. But friendship and liberty—well, those are two of them."

"Thank you," Ethan said. "I'm grateful."

"Can we return to what she was saying a minute ago?" Diver asked, making no effort to mask his impatience. "About this woman using all her power to keep Deborah in that cloud?"

Amanda held up both hands and shook her head. "I said that was a possibility. That's all. I don't know enough about this woman or her power to be certain of anything."

"Neither do I," Ethan said "She may be more vulnerable right now. It makes sense that she would be. But as long as Deborah is suspended so high above the harbor, we can't risk hurting her. And we also have to remember that she's a conjurer as well as a witch. Whatever she's done to Deborah shouldn't have any effect on her ability to cast blood spells."

"Then what can we do?" Diver asked.

"We're going to work that out," Ethan said, looking his friend in the eye. "But you have to give us a little time, and you have to trust us, trust me."

Diver nodded, lips pressed in a thin line. He stepped away from the bar to the hearth where he stared at the flames. Ethan watched him for a moment before turning his attention back to Janna and Amanda.

"You shouldn't have brought him here," Janna said, eyeing Diver, her voice low.

"I was afraid he would do something rash. He's been through too much over the last year. If he loses Deborah I don't know what he'll do."

"How did he lose his arm?" Amanda asked.

"He was on King Street the night of the shootings."

She winced.

"Can you free Deborah?" Ethan asked. "Do you have the power to disrupt another witch's spell?"

"I don't know. She's a water witch. Mine is earth magick. We both have air magick, but if she's using clouds and suspending this woman over water . . . Well, that's beyond my reach."

"But if you were both water witches, you could?"

"Even then, my power to undo her spell would be limited."

"It's like conjurin' that way," Janna said. "One conjurer can't just come along and reverse everythin' another one does."

Ethan and Amanda returned to their earlier conversation about wardings, and whether witch magick could protect her from a conjured attack. They experimented: Amanda guarded herself with witchcraft and Ethan threw an itching spell at her. Almost instantly she began to twitch and scratch.

"Make it stop, Kaille!"

He did, though even after he reversed the conjuring, she continued to fidget and rub at imagined bites from invisible insects.

"That was a nasty spell," she said. "Don't do that again."

Ethan promised he wouldn't. Janna could barely hide her amusement.

Knowing that one sort of magick couldn't block spells cast with the other affirmed for Ethan something he had been thinking since his visit to Amanda's home.

"You and I need to face Whitcomb together," he told her. "That's our best chance of defeating her. I would ward you from her conjurings, and you would protect me from her witchcraft."

"That's all well and good, but she's still going to be protected from both of us. How do we defeat her without angering her so much that she kills your friend's woman first?"

Ethan glanced over at Diver, who sat before the fire. He gave no indication of having heard what she said.

He pulled out Whitcomb's crystal again and set it on the bar. Amanda eyed it and then him.

"We've discussed this. She needs that stone, and so keeping it from her helps us. But we can't use it. I'm not a water witch, and you're no witch at all."

"Let me see that," Janna said, reaching for the crystal. She stopped her hand, poised over the stone, looking a question at Ethan.

He motioned for her to pick it up.

As she studied the crystal, Ethan turned his attention back to Amanda. "Isn't it enough that this stone has . . . how did you say it? An affinity for her magick?"

"That's not quite the way I meant it."

"I realize that. But her magick and this stone are linked, aren't they?"

"Yes, but—"

"So it might be possible to turn the stone into some sort of . . . of trap that would capture her spells."

She shook her head. "I've never heard of anything like that."

"That don't matter," Janna said, still gazing into the depths of the stone.

Amanda frowned. "Forgive me, Janna, but you're not a witch, either, and I'm telling you—"

"I know what you're tellin' me," she said, glaring. "You ain't thought of it so you don't think it can be done. In a lot o' ways, the two of you are just the same. 'Cept this one time, Kaille's thinkin' like a conjurer instead of like some magick-less fool. You shouldn't be discouragin' him; you should be tryin' to help."

"But I don't know how!"

"So that means it can't be done? I thought you were smarter than that."

Amanda glowered back at her. Ethan would have quailed to be on the receiving end of such a look from either woman. He half expected them to start throwing spells at each other. But Amanda didn't argue the point further. She regarded the crystal again, seeming to ponder what Janna had said.

"Ethan, I'm going to leave."

Ethan turned. Diver stood before him, struggling to set his coat in place. Ethan reached to help him, but his friend flinched away.

"I can do it."

Ethan let his hand drop to his side. "Where are you going?" he asked after an awkward moment.

"Home. I'm tired. I shouldn't be, I know. After all the sleep you forced on me, I should be able to stay awake for days. But all I want to do is sleep until this is over."

"You know better than to . . ." Ethan was going to warn him away from going after Francis Lamb, but stopped himself. If the idea hadn't occurred to him, Ethan didn't want to put it in his head. And if that was his intention, he would probably lie about it. ". . . than to do anything foolish, right?"

"Aye," he said, holding Ethan's gaze. "I'm no conjurer. I'm definitely not a witch. The woman is beyond me. To be honest, if I could save Deborah without relying on you, I would. But I don't have that choice."

"All right, then. Go home. I'll come and speak with you tomorrow. Perhaps by then, we'll have some idea of how to defeat her."

Diver murmured "Good night" to the others, and left the tavern. After watching him go, Ethan turned his attention back to Janna and Amanda.

"You trust him?" Janna asked.

"Aye. A year or two ago, I wouldn't have. He's . . ." He had intended to say that his friend had matured. And he had. After the shooting, though, he had withdrawn, become harder, sadder.

"I'll be back," he said. "Keep that crystal safe. Please." He wouldn't have left something so valuable with most people. Janna he trusted. He grabbed his coat and threw it on. Reaching the door, he slowed, eased out into the night. Diver walked in the middle of Orange Street, his boot heels clicking, the moon casting his dim shadow across cobblestones and wispy grass.

Ethan felt foolish, and guilty. His friend wouldn't lie to him. That's what he told himself. Even as he formed the thought, though, Diver glanced back toward the tavern, no doubt wanting to know if he was followed. Ethan pressed himself to Janna's door. His friend faced forward again and walked on.

Ethan slipped his knife from its sheath, cut his forearm and whispered, "*Velamentum ex cruore evocatum.*" Magick purred in the ground and wood, Reg appeared, russet and avid, and the concealment spell settled over him like a mist, rendering him unseeable. Ethan set out after Diver, placing his feet with care.

They followed the thoroughfare as it became Newbury Street, and then Marlborough. At Milk Street, Diver turned east, the first in a series of turns that led to the *Apple Tree*, a rundown tavern on Lindal's Lane. Diver entered. Ethan raced to the entrance, but couldn't squeeze inside before the door shut. He would reveal himself if he entered—someone was bound to notice if the door opened and closed for no reason. After a moment's hesitation, he cut himself and cast again.

"*Audiam, ex cruore evocatum.*"

With the thrum of the listening spell, a cacophony of conversations assailed him. At first, he couldn't make sense of any of them, and he despaired of learning why Diver had come here.

But then he heard someone greet his friend.

"Long time, Diver."

"Will."

"An ale?"

"Please."

"I was sorry to hear about . . . well, about what happened to ya."

Silence stretched between them.

"Is Isaac here?" Diver asked in time.

"In back. His usual spot."

"Thank you."

Ethan continued to listen with the spell he'd cast, but for several minutes he couldn't make out Diver's voice amid all the others he heard, and he feared he had lost track of his friend. Still straining to hear, he entered an alley on the west side of the tavern and eased toward the back of the building.

"Well, look who's back. Devren Jervis. I thought you'd had enough of our kind, found the straight and narrow."

Ethan froze, waited.

"It's good to see you, Isaac." Diver's voice sounded strong, as if he were just on the other side of the wall beside him.

"Is it?"

"Actually, no. I can think of twenty places I'd rather be than here treating with you."

The other man's laughter sounded a shade too boisterous. "Now that I believe. Sit down. What are you drinking?"

"I just started this ale. I don't need another. My thanks, though."

"Business, then. What are you after?"

"Information about a man."

"And what are you offering?"

"That depends upon how good the information is, doesn't it?"

More laughter. "I like this new Diver," the man said. "He's not afraid, he doesn't peddle shit and call it pudding. Of course, some might wonder if he oughtn't to show a little more respect. Coming into a man's establishment, insulting him, and then demanding knowledge and giving stubs in return—that could be seen as provocation. Don't you think?"

"I'm offering more than stubs."

"Not that I hear."

"I have coin," Diver said. "I'll pay you for what you tell me, but shouldn't I at least have an idea of what I'm paying for before I assign a price to it?"

A pause, and then, "I suppose. Who is it you're asking about?"

"A Customs man. I think he's new in the city. His name is Francis Lamb."

Ethan cursed himself for mentioning Lamb in the first place. Given the circumstances, given Diver's helpless terror at what had been done to Deborah, and his fury at Charlotte Whitcomb, he should have known better than to speak of Lamb within his friend's hearing.

"I've heard of him," said the man in the bar. "What is it you want to know?"

"Where does he live? Who lives with him? When is he most likely to be home?"

"You ask a lot."

Diver didn't reply.

"I can tell you where he lives. I make it my business to know as much. The rest . . . That would take some time."

"Then it's a good thing I didn't offer you too much coin when I walked in."

The man said nothing.

"So, his address?"

"He lives on Charles Street, about halfway up Copp's Hill, north side of the lane. It's a grand marble house with a portico—four pillars. The house isn't his—it belongs to another Customs man who sailed for England shortly after Lamb arrived in Boston. The furnishings and all—they belong to this other man: Joseph Pomeroy. So if you're wanting to pinch from Lamb himself, you'll need to dive for his purse rather than break the house."

Ethan thought he heard the ring of coins.

"Here you go, Isaac. That and my thanks."

"That's . . . Well, that's generous of you, Diver. I suppose I owe you an apology from before."

"It's all right. But you didn't see me tonight. We didn't talk. I haven't been in here . . . for longer than you can remember."

"The times being what they are, I barely remember anything any more. It's a miracle this place stays open."

"That's what I was hoping to hear. Good night."

"Good night."

Ethan limped back to the front of the tavern, wanting to track Diver to Lamb's house, assuming his friend intended to go there immediately. Maybe he should have been angry, but he couldn't find it within himself to be anything but sympathetic. He wanted Diver to trust him. He certainly didn't want the lad getting himself in trouble with Greenleaf or anyone else. But when Ethan asked himself what he would do if Kannice hung in a vaporous cloud over the harbor, he had to concede that he would trust no one but himself. He wouldn't care about the law, he wouldn't care about friendship, he wouldn't leave anything to trust. He would tear the city to pieces if he had to. How could he fault Diver for feeling the same?

He slowed at the corner of the byway and Lindal's Lane, watching the tavern entrance. After a few minutes, he wondered if Diver had stopped to speak with someone else. He didn't hear his friend's voice inside the building, but neither had he seen him leave. Could Diver have gotten out before Ethan reached the lane?

He waited a few moments more. At the scrape of footsteps, he whirled, ducked back into shadow before remembering that his concealment spell remained in place. A man he didn't know walked past him and entered the

Apple Tree. Ethan followed him, slipping inside before the door closed.

The place was as shabby within as it appeared from the street. Pipe smoke hazed the air, barely masking the stink of sweat, old ale, and stale wine. Ethan remained by the door, but he surveyed the room, seeing no sign of Diver. Too late, he realized the tavern must have a door in the rear. Perhaps Diver anticipated that Ethan would follow him. Or maybe he was just better at this sort of intrigue than Ethan had credited.

He opened the door and left, ignoring the exclamations of surprise from those nearest the entrance. Once on the street, he hobbled as quickly as he could manage toward the North End. Diver had too much of a head start on him, and he would cover the distance faster. Ethan had to hope that his friend wouldn't do anything irrevocable before he arrived.

When he reached Copp's Hill he started up the north side of Charles Street, searching for a house that matched Isaac's description. In truth, all the houses in this part of the city tended to be grand, and several of them had porticos. As the man had promised, though, about halfway to the top of the incline, stood a house with four columns. A lamp burned in one of the downstairs windows. Ethan scanned the street for Diver, but saw no one.

He eased to the lit window and peered into the house. Lamb sat in a large upholstered chair beside an enormous hearth, engrossed in a book, spectacles perched on the end of his nose, a richly embroidered robe tied around him. From all Ethan could see, he assumed the man was in fine health and in no danger.

Which was more than Ethan could say for himself.

"I know you're there, Kaille."

Ethan turned slowly, making not a sound. Charlotte Whitcomb stood on the portico, wearing a robe much like her brother's. Her hair was unbound, gentle whorls falling nearly to her waist.

"Show yourself. Don't force me to find you with a conjuring, or my witch magick."

Her gaze wandered over the front of the house. She sensed him, but couldn't place him precisely. Not that this mattered; an attack spell would still find him. Maybe he simply took comfort in knowing there were some limits to her power. He pulled his knife free; with the murmur of steel sliding clear of leather, her gaze snapped to his location, avid and self-satisfied.

Ethan cut himself, whispered the spell to remove his concealment. She glanced at Reg, even as the spell sang in the ground and the marble. He drew blood a second time and as quickly warded himself.

"A futile gesture," she said, "but I understand the impulse. Now, what are you doing here?"

He stepped from the garden bed in which he stood and approached the portico. "I'm not sure you would believe me."

"Leave that to me. I want an answer."

"I came because I feared for your brother."

She straightened, her brow creasing. "You feared for him . . . Your friend. Mister Jervis."

"That's right. I can't control him. Not even fear for Deborah can do that. If something happens to your brother, it will be on your head."

"Then why did you come?"

"I know what kind of villain you are. I'm afraid you would follow through on your threat regardless of what you've done to Diver."

Even as he spoke the words, something occurred to him, something he should have realized immediately upon seeing her.

"But, I see now that, for tonight at least, my concern for Mister Lamb was unfounded. With your permission, I'll be going."

"And if I forbid it?"

"We'll do battle right here. And unless you intend to use your brother as a source for your spells, you're liable to lose."

"In a duel of conjurings maybe, but you forget—"

"I forget nothing. We're some distance from the harbor, and while you have air magick, I don't believe it's as strong as your water magick. Plus, you lack your crystal. Even if you've located a replacement, you have less control than you'd like." He fixed a smile on his face. "I've been educating myself. How have I done?"

She glowered. "Go, Mister Kaille, while you can. Don't approach this house again. And I would suggest you do everything in your power to keep your friend away, too. It would be a shame if his unbridled passions cost the poor girl her life."

He had no desire to do battle this night. He wanted to find Diver. "Good night, Miss Whitcomb."

Ethan walked away from the house, the spot between his shoulder blades itching, waiting to be struck by some conjuring—fire, or a blade spell. None came. Before long he was beyond her reach.

He made his way to Diver and Deborah's flat on Pudding Lane, but found it darkened. After a few moment's hesitation, he chose to wait for his friend. He sat on the steps leading up to the room. In time he grew cold. He stood and stomped his feet. Eventually he resorted to pacing. Bells rang from the city churches, and then, sometime later, pealed again. Still Diver didn't show up. Ethan considered going back to Lamb's house, though Whitcomb didn't need his help to keep Diver at bay. Chances were she would kill the man at the first opportunity.

Exhausted as he was, he also considered heading back to the *Dowser* and going to sleep. He had made up his mind to do so, when he heard the uneven click of boot heels on stone. Diver turned the nearest corner, a flask in his hand.

Ethan summoned a light, and his friend staggered to a halt.

"Ethan! What are you . . . What's happened?"

"Nothing has happened, Diver. Except that you lied to me. What exactly do you intend to do to Francis Lamb?"

Diver blinked, swayed, his expression turning stony. "Did you follow me?"

"For a time, yes. I lost you after you left the *Apple Tree*. Where did you go?"

"None of your damn business. Now get out of here."

"No."

Diver threw his flask to the ground. Glass shattered, red wine spread over the cobbles like blood. "Go, damn you!" He reached into his pocket, fumbled a bit, but then withdrew his flintlock.

"Are you going to shoot me, Diver?"

"I should, shouldn't I? I figure I owe you that much!"

The words hammered Ethan like a smith's sledge, stealing his breath. He had suspected for a long time that Diver blamed him for the loss of his arm. It was one thing to think this, though. It was another entirely to hear his friend say as much. Even if he was far gone with drink.

Diver raised the weapon until it was aimed at Ethan's heart and he held it there for several seconds, his hand shaking slightly, though not enough to make him miss if he chose to fire. He exhaled, sagged, let his pistol hand drop, only to take another sharp breath, and level the weapon at Ethan again. For a second time, he let his hand fall. Tears streaked his face.

For his part, Ethan stood like a statue. He didn't know if Diver's flintlock was loaded; he doubted it was. In a way, it didn't matter. If Diver pulled the trigger—even if the weapon didn't fire—it would kill their friendship.

He had bitten down on the inside of his mouth when Diver first produced the weapon, drawing blood. He could have used magick to disarm his friend. In the past, he had shattered blades, used heat spells to make enemies drop their pistols, or even wounded the assailants themselves. He didn't want to do any of that tonight; not unless he sensed that he had no other choice. This confrontation had been building for months. Ending it with a conjuring would only delay what was inevitable. Either Diver had come to hate him enough to kill or he hadn't. The next few seconds would tell.

The lad started to raise his weapon a third time, but it almost seemed the pistol had grown leaden. He couldn't aim it again. Sobs shook his body.

And then, abruptly, he could raise it after all. Not to shoot Ethan, but to press the barrel to his own temple.

Ethan leapt forward to wrest the flintlock from Diver's hand. Whether or not the weapon was empty, he didn't want Diver squeezing the trigger with it leveled so. It would only make it easier for him to contemplate self-murder another night, when Ethan wasn't there to stop him.

Diver fought him for the pistol, but not for long, and not with all his strength. Ethan ripped it from his hand, and Diver sank to the street, crying still. He hid his face, his entire form quaking, his gasps echoing in the lane.

Ethan pocketed the weapon, then sat beside him and put an arm around his shoulders. Diver stiffened at his first touch before falling against him.

They sat thus for a long time. Diver's sobbing subsided gradually, until at last he simply breathed, his chest heaving.

"I'm sorry, Ethan," he said, his voice thick.

"For what?"

"Everything. The things I've said to you. The things I've done. All the times I've stayed away from you when what I really wanted was just to be your friend again."

"You never stopped being my friend. And I never stopped being yours. What happened . . . There isn't a day that passes without me wondering if I could have spared you all of this. I'm the one who should be asking forgiveness.

"I think it's time, though, that we both stop worrying about who's to blame for what. I miss you, Diver. I miss buying you ales."

His friend gave a small laugh. "Aye, all right."

"But I'm telling you this now. If you ever turn a weapon on yourself again, I'll crush it with magick and never speak to you again."

Diver sat up straighter and looked Ethan in the eye.

"I've done it before—held a pistol like that, I mean. I've thought of . . . well, you know. Deborah has no idea. She would . . ."

"She'd never forgive you. And neither would I. You have love in your life now. I have some sense of what you've lost, of what you believe you've lost. But you have her and that makes life worth living. You have to promise me, Diver."

He swallowed, gave a reluctant nod.

"Say it."

"I promise. I won't take my own life."

"And you won't get yourself killed doing something stupid."

"Well, now you're asking an awful lot." The wry, crooked grin that touched his friend's face in that moment was as familiar to Ethan as his own name, and as welcome as the first day of spring.

"Promise to do your best, and I'll be satisfied."

"Done."

Ethan stood, held out a hand, and pulled Diver to his feet. "Good. Because now we have to get Deborah back."

Diver sobered. "Do you have any idea how to do that?"

"Well, we have to find her first."

"Find her? But she's—"

Seeing Ethan shake his head, Diver fell silent.

"I'm sure the cloud is still there," Ethan said, "but I don't think Deborah is in it. Not anymore. I saw Charlotte Whitcomb a short while ago. And she didn't look at all like a woman struggling to maintain a magickal spell."

VIII

"Do you think she let Deborah fall?" Diver asked, his voice rising.

"I don't."

"You can't be sure, though."

"I choose to believe she didn't. She wants Adams dead. She wants one of us to do it and to take the blame. I assume she wants to make it seem that the patriot cause is riven with conflict and competing ambitions. The only way she can accomplish that is to return Deborah to her former life when all of this is over. If something were to happen to Deborah, it would undo all her planning."

"I suppose that makes sense. But then where is she?"

"She might be at Lamb's house. Or they might be holding her elsewhere, perhaps at the Customs House. Wherever she is, I have to believe she's safer than she would be in that cloud over the harbor. So we can rest easy tonight, and resume our search first thing in the morning."

Diver narrowed his gaze. "Are you trying to fool me? Is this all some elaborate ruse to get me to sleep?"

"If I was that eager for you to sleep, I'd just cast another spell."

Diver frowned.

"Think about it," Ethan said. "You heard what Amanda said tonight at Janna's: Maintaining that cloud, and keeping Deborah inside it, suspended above the water, would demand a tremendous amount of power. I think Whitcomb was depending on our ignorance of witchcraft. She magicked Deborah into the cloud that first night, but I doubt she left her there for more than an hour or two. Why would she? She scared us—which was what she wanted—and she gave us no reason to doubt that she could do what she threatened. To be honest, I'm furious with myself for not realizing this sooner. I may not have much experience with witchery, but I've been conjuring for decades. I know that magick never comes without a cost."

"We should find her now," Diver said. "We should end this."

"It's not enough to end it. We want to end it well, with Deborah safe and Whitcomb defeated. That will take some planning, and it will require that both of us be at our best. I need rest and so do you."

Ethan feared Diver would argue more, and when he didn't, Ethan's suspicions stirred again.

But Diver promised to heed his advice this time, and Ethan had no choice but to trust him. After watching his friend enter the flat, he made his way back to the *Dowsing Rod*.

Kannice had waited up for him, and over a shared cup of wine, he related to her all that had happened that evening. Long after he finished, she remained silent, her gaze fixed on their entwined fingers.

"I honestly don't know which shocks me more: that he thought of killing you, or that he thought of killing himself."

"What matters is, he did neither."

"You're more generous than I would be."

"He couldn't bring himself to fire at me. The greater danger by far was that he would harm himself. I'm just glad he didn't."

She stood, still holding his hand, and tugged him toward the stairway. "You look like you're half asleep already. Come to bed."

"Aye."

He followed her. As they reached the first stair, though, Kannice halted and faced him again.

"Did you ever learn if the weapon was loaded?"

Ethan shook his head. "No. And I don't care to find out."

He slept soundly—a mercy—and woke early. Kannice insisted that he eat a small breakfast before leaving the tavern, but he still was out the door just as the sun vaulted the eastern horizon. He went first to the law office of John Adams, where he found Mister Adams, Robert Auchmuty, and Josiah Quincy preparing for the day's proceedings. As Doctor Warren had the evening before, Adams assured Ethan that the trial was now progressing smoothly, and that the irregularities of the first day had not repeated themselves since.

"I wish Robert and Samuel would present their case with more vigor," Adams said, speaking of Mister Paine and Josiah Quincy's older brother, "but that is out of my hands. All we three can hope to do is defend Captain Preston to the best of our ability."

Adams added that, as far as he was concerned, Ethan did not need to attend court this day. That suited Ethan. Even if Deborah no longer hovered over the chill harbor waters, she remained in danger. And Whitcomb's deadline loomed.

From Adams' office, Ethan hurried to Diver and Deborah's flat, which was close by. To his dismay, he found it empty and locked. Peering in through a window, he saw that the bed linens were tangled. Perhaps Diver had slept after all. But Ethan had no idea where to look for his friend. Or rather, he did, and his certainty filled him with dread.

He set out for the North End, heading up Pudding Lane to King Street, so that he could walk past the Customs House—the other place where Deborah might be kept.

As he neared the King Street corner, he heard someone whisper his name. He spun, reaching for his blade, only to see Diver emerge from a hiding place behind a pile of wooden pallets.

The lad grinned. "Scared you, did I?"

"Aye, a little bit. What are you doing?"

"Watching the Customs House, of course. I thought about what you said last night—how Deborah was probably in one of two places. I didn't think going to Copp's Hill would be smart. I'd stand out there like a beggar on Beacon Street. But here, so close to our home . . . I figured I could watch for anything suspicious and report back to you later, either to say she isn't here, or to guess that maybe she is."

Excitement shone in his dark eyes as he said this last: a glimpse of the old Diver.

"And?" Ethan asked.

"I'm not certain what it means, but I did see a man enter the building just past dawn. A younger man. Dashing, well-dressed. Nothing like your brother-in-law."

Ethen chuckled. Geoffrey Brower, husband to Ethan's sister, Bett, was also with the Customs Board. He was supercilious and moneyed, but no one would ever have called him dashing.

"That sounds like Lamb."

"I hoped you would say that. He carried a small bundle, and again, I can't say for certain, but I thought it could be the right size for a helping of food."

Ethan turned back to the street and stared at the brick building across the way. "Are you all right this close to King Street?" he asked, not looking at his friend.

"Better than I have been recently. Deborah has been saying that I can't avoid it forever, and she's right isn't she? She says maybe it's time I started thinking about this as the place where I survived the shooting, rather than the place where I lost my arm."

Ethan did look at him then. Diver stared back at him, jaw set.

"She's a wise woman, and you're a wise man for marrying her." He turned back to the street. "I also think you've done a good bit of reconnoitering here. It sounds like she could well be in that building."

"The only problem is," Diver said, "I haven't seen the woman—Whitcomb. I don't think we should do anything until we know where she is, and what she's been up to this morning."

Ethan looked his way again. "I must be in the grips of some sort of magickal delirium, because I thought I just heard Devren Jervis counsel patience."

Diver's face reddened. "Don't tell anyone."

"You should return to the hiding place you were using when I arrived. Watch for Whitcomb. If she enters the building, I would take that as proof that Deborah is there. If not, it might behoove us to set watch on the house."

"All right. What are you going to do?"

"I want to speak with Janna and Amanda again. I left them somewhat abruptly last night."

He said no more than this, and Diver didn't pursue the matter. Ethan sensed a true thaw in their friendship, and he was glad of it.

He cut through the South End, navigated to Orange Street, and soon stood at Janna's door. It was early—it seemed he had come to her early with some frequency of late. She can't have liked that. But it didn't keep him from knocking.

The door opened far sooner than he expected, revealing Janna in her usual linen gown, that same old shawl drawn about her bony shoulders.

"Figured it was you." She turned and walked back to her bar, leaving it to Ethan to close the door and follow. "You followed your friend last night?" she asked over her shoulder.

"Aye. He managed to stay out of trouble without my help."

Janna eyed him as he leaned on the bar. "Not sure I believe that. Tea? Bread?"

"No, thank you. And it's the truth. He found out where Whitcomb's brother lives, but he didn't go near the house." Of course, he didn't mention their confrontation, or the flintlock. "Where's Amanda?"

Mischief lit Janna's face. "She's out back, tryin' to find a use for the stone you left. Don't know if she's had any success, but she sure is determined." She leaned closer to him. "I think I got under her skin a little."

Ethan widened his eyes. "You?"

Janna's laughter followed Ethan through the kitchen of the *Fat Spider* and out the back door.

He had never ventured to this part of Janna's property. There wasn't much to it—mostly tall, thin grasses and beyond them the sour mud and brackish waters of the Roxbury flats. A harrier hovered over the grasses on the far side, and geese flocked noisily in the waters along the causeway.

Amanda stood with her back to Ethan, completely still, her arms raised. She made not a sound, at least not at first.

As he watched her, she lowered her arms and turned. Her frown would have done Janna proud.

"This is your fault," she said.

"I choose to blame Charlotte Whitcomb, but I can see why you'd feel differently."

If anything, her scowl deepened. Ethan joined her where she stood. The crystal rested on a piece of worn, twisted wood about five paces in front of her, short of the mud's edge.

"Have you learned anything?"

"That earth magick can't do much to a stone with a water affinity." She walked to the stone, picked it up, and faced him. "I can't think of a way to make it capture her magick, as you suggested last night. I don't have that kind of power. Maybe if this was an earth stone, or if I had water as a secondary magick. But this is like talking to a stone in English when it only knows French."

Ethan chuckled at the comparison. As he continued to think about it, though, an idea came to him.

"So then maybe the problem isn't the language as much as the complexity of the words you're trying to speak to it."

She cocked an eyebrow. "Interesting. Go on."

He lifted a shoulder. "What if you didn't try to teach it something new, but instead convinced it to stop doing what it usually does?"

"I don't follow."

"Just make it so the stone doesn't work with her magick. Make it entirely . . . how would you say it?" He thought for a moment. "Inert! That's the word."

"You want me to kill the stone."

"Is that the term you use? It sounds right."

"Why bother? As long as we have it, she can't use it anyway."

"But she wants it. Her brother came to me not very long ago and demanded that I return it. He claimed it was a family heirloom, but even if that was true, I expect it was secondary to his true motive. He needs her to cast on his behalf, and to do that she needs the crystal. So maybe we can arrange a trade. She gets her stone, and we get Deborah."

"Except that the stone would be useless to her."

"I'm hoping she won't notice that until after the exchange is complete."

Amanda appeared skeptical. "What if she's not willing to bargain? The stone has value—no doubt. But she may have begun to train a new crystal. And having the woman gives her a good deal of leverage. Maybe too much to give up for so little."

"Surely, it's worth making the attempt."

"It may be."

He refused to let her skepticism dampen his enthusiasm for the idea. "If you can do this to the stone, I'll approach her and try to bargain for Deborah's release. And failing that, I'll precipitate a conflict of some sort, allow her to take the stone from me, and retreat as if defeated. The next time she and I meet—and I'll be certain to confront her again before this day is out—she'll use the crystal as she has before." He grinned. "But if you're successful, it won't work, and that will give us the advantage we need to defeat her."

Amanda appeared to weigh this. "That could work, but she's already weakened. That magick she's maintaining has to be tiring her."

Ethan told her of his interaction with Whitcomb the previous night, and his guess that she had moved Deborah from that cloud to somewhere safer.

"You did suggest that she would be visibly fatigued from maintaining that spell."

"A casting like that? Without her crystal? She should barely be able to walk."

"Then I'm more certain than ever: She must have removed Deborah from the cloud."

"All right, then," Amanda said. "Let's see if I can kill her stone."

She pulled her own stone from her pocket. In the light of day it seemed more alive than it had the night before in Janna's tavern. Green crystals sparked in the sunlight, and parts of the stone shifted and changed color as she moved it, like oil shining on water.

She returned Whitcomb's crystal to the piece of driftwood, and set her own crystal beside it, so that the two stones touched. Then she backed away and motioned for Ethan to do the same.

She raised her hands again, though not so high as when first he saw her, so that her palms were open toward the stones.

The words she spoke meant nothing to Ethan, but he felt their potency, as if they were Latin and she were a conjurer. The air around them felt charged, like in a lightning storm, and her stone glowed with such intensity that even the sunlight couldn't mask its brilliance.

Amanda remained as she was for several minutes, her crystal gleaming that entire time. Wind rustled the grasses around them and the geese kept up their clamor, but after her initial incantation, Amanda made not a sound. Ethan didn't dare move or speak.

Just as Ethan began to wonder if there was any more to her spell than this, the light emanating from her stone flared, forcing him to shield his eyes. He thought he also glimpsed a flash of pale blue, but he couldn't be certain. When the light had faded, both stones looked as they had before Amanda initiated her spell.

And yet, all was not as it had been. The stones no longer touched, but instead rested about two inches apart on that piece of wood. And between them, the wood itself had been scorched black, the burn mark spreading from the tip of Amanda's stone, and ending in a jagged line that matched exactly the form of Whitcomb's crystal.

Amanda lowered her hands. Sweat glazed her face, and her breath sounded ragged. She edged toward the stones, as if expecting them to bolt, or to attack. Ethan followed.

"Did it work?"

"I have no idea," she said. "I've never done this before."

It was Ethan's turn to frown.

She opened her hands, a defensive gesture. "It's true," she said. "I'm sorry. I think the spell did what I asked of it. It looks like it did, but we won't really know until she tries to use the stone for a spell."

"That's quite a risk I'll be taking."

"We'll be taking it together."

"Thank you," he said with a brief smile. "Will she have felt your spell?"

"Probably, but she won't know what it did. Not unless she has earth magick, too. And if she does, we're doomed, so it won't matter."

Ethan reached for the blue crystal, but stopped himself before he touched it. "Is it safe for me to pick up?"

"It should be."

He took hold of it, was surprised to find it cool to the touch. He hefted it; it felt no lighter or heavier than it had before, and it bore no marks from its ordeal. In all ways, it looked as it had.

He pocketed the stone and turned to leave.

"Thank you for what you've done."

"You might want to wait on that until we know it worked."

"I appreciate the attempt no matter what. I'll be back later and we can plan our next maneuvers."

He returned to the tavern and bid Janna farewell before following the lanes back to Cornhill where he'd left Diver. His friend was still in hiding on Pudding Lane. At Ethan's approach, he emerged from his place of concealment and stretched his legs.

"Have you seen her? Whitcomb, I mean."

Diver shook his head. "Only other Customs men, including Geoffrey Brower. I think maybe I was wrong. She's not there." He faltered. "Are you certain she's not still in that cloud, Ethan? I mean I know it takes a lot to keep her there, but you've mentioned a few times how strong this woman is. Couldn't you be wrong about this?"

"Possibly. I don't think I am, but I'm sure of nothing. Stay here a while longer. I need to go to Lamb's house and speak with Whitcomb."

Diver gaped. "You need to what?"

Ethan explained what Amanda had done to the crystal, and his plans for his coming encounter with the water witch.

"So you're going to offer her this crystal in exchange for Deborah."

"Aye."

"And if she refuses, you're simply going to let her have it."

"She'll think that she bested me before taking it. But aye, that's what I have in mind."

"And you don't even know if the witch's spell made the stone useless. You're just hoping."

"It's a better plan than you're making it sound."

"I'm sure," Diver said, sounding anything but certain. "Are all your plans like this? Is this how you prepare for fights with Sephira?"

Ethan frowned. "Some of my plans are better than this," he admitted. "Some are worse."

"I don't suppose I can come with you."

"It's best that you don't. If this becomes a battle of conjurings, I don't want to have to worry about keeping you safe, too. I'm sorry."

Diver mumbled his acquiescence, but clearly didn't like being left behind any more than he did the rest of Ethan's idea.

Ethan left his friend there and walked on to Copp's Hill, pausing in a byway to cut himself and cast a warding, and then continuing with caution to the marble house. Well before he reached the pathway to the front door, he spotted Charlotte Whitcomb on the portico. This came as no surprise; he knew his protective conjuring would warn her of his approach.

"You can't seem to stay away from me, Mister Kaille. Should I be flattered?"

"Hardly. I come to negotiate Deborah Crane's release."

She smirked, leaned back against one of the columns. Once again, he noted that she did not appear to be under any sort of magickal strain. If she still held Deborah in that vapor above the harbor, she was stronger than any magickal being he had encountered.

"There is no negotiation," she said. "I set you a task—you and your friend. When that task is complete, I shall free her, and not before. And if you fail to do what I've demanded before midnight, she will die."

"So you've said. But I carry something that I know you want. Perhaps we can trade. Deborah's life for a piece of treasure. No matter what happens, you and I will do battle again. I expect you would prefer to have this bauble the next time you face me."

Her gaze sharpened and she straightened. "You have my crystal."

"Possibly. Wouldn't that be worth something? Deborah Crane is no one to you. And with your stone, you can accomplish much, perhaps even complete the task you've given us."

"This is a ruse. Why would you offer me such a boon? Surely this girl—"

"The young woman is the love of my closest friend. I've known Diver for twenty-five years. I've been part of the patriot cause for one. Which do you think matters to me more?"

She shook her head. "But still, Adams is . . . he's everything to your cause. Giving him to me in this way—"

Ethan's laughter silenced her. "I'm not giving him to you. You think quite highly of yourself, don't you? I've defeated you before, and when I did, you still possessed the stone. I took it from you. I can do so again. But you want it back, just as I want Deborah."

Her face had paled except for the blazing of her cheeks, and she looked like she wanted nothing more than to flay the skin from his bones.

"You dare to mock me?"

He gazed back at her, his mien placid. "Deborah for the stone. Or shall I just keep it. Maybe I can find a water witch who would value it as highly as you do."

"Your arrogance will be your undoing, Mister Kaille."

"It wouldn't be the first time."

"You cannot have the girl. You're fortunate I don't kill her for your effrontery."

He hadn't really expected her to agree to the exchange. Which meant he needed to provoke an attack and survive it, while convincing her that he was wounded and beaten enough that he would relinquish the crystal without intending to.

"So you don't want this," he said, removing the crystal from his coat pocket and holding it up for her to see. He turned it so that it caught the sunlight and cast a taunting smile her way. "Your brother made it seem that you and your family treasure this crystal above all your other belongings. But perhaps he exaggerated."

"He didn't. We do treasure the stone, but I can't tell from here whether that is ours or an imitation. For all I know, it's an illusion. I felt you conjure before you arrived. I assumed you warded yourself, but maybe you sought instead to deceive me."

"It's your stone, Miss Whitcomb. I assure you."

"I want to see. Bring it closer."

"I think not."

"You're afraid," she said with relish.

"One last chance. The stone for the woman."

She shook her head, confident now. "No."

Ethan shrugged and turned. "Very well." He started away, knowing that he opened himself to an assault.

He had taken all of three steps when he felt her magick tremble in the cobblestones. The spell hit him an instant later, and he sprawled onto the street. He couldn't tell what sort of conjuring she'd thrown at him. It didn't matter; his warding protected him from the worst of the casting. He held fast to the crystal. For now.

He surged to his feet, drew his blade, and slashed at his forearm. His attack—a fire spell—left her reeling, but largely unhurt. At some point she had warded herself.

They both cut themselves and cast. Each staggered under the force of the other's spell. They were evenly matched as conjurers. If Ethan's plan failed, and the crystal still allowed her to access the full potential of her witch power, he might never defeat her.

Ethan cast again, less quickly than he would have had he been fighting in earnest, and so her next spell hit him before he had finished his incantation. His fist spell didn't land as forcefully as it could have. And already, she was casting again.

She hit him with three conjurings in quick succession, and this time when he fell, he did let go of the stone. Not because he meant to, but because her volleys of magick had left him addled. He scrambled for the stone, but another spell hammered him. He barely maintained his grip on his knife.

He cast once more, knocking her back a step. He got to his feet and limped away, leaving the crystal in the middle of Charles Street.

One more spell crashed into him as he retreated, but he kept his feet and hurried on, glad to be away, hoping with all his heart that Amanda Oakroot's spell had rendered the crystal useless.

IX

Ethan returned to Pudding Lane and told Diver to end his vigil.

"I believe Deborah is at the house," he said. "Charlotte Whitcomb wouldn't trust her brother to guard her alone."

"Then we should go get her."

"We will. Amanda and I need to prepare. But I promise you, we'll win her freedom tonight, or die in the attempt."

He convinced his friend to accompany him back to the *Dowsing Rod*.

There, they took time to enjoy a midday meal and an ale. Diver bore dark rings under his eyes, his face more drawn than usual. Ethan wondered if he had slept at all the night before. When they finished eating, Ethan informed Kannice that they intended to return to Janna's tavern to ready themselves for their fight with Whitcomb. She didn't have to voice her concern. Her expression spoke volumes. She put her arms around Diver, a rare display of affection toward the young man, and then kissed Ethan.

"Have a care. The last time you faced her, you nearly destroyed the city."

They shared wan smiles.

Ethan and Diver crossed to the door, but it opened before they reached it, revealing Samuel Adams and Joseph Warren.

The two men halted and cut off their conversation upon spotting Ethan. Both regarded him with disapproval.

"I thought we had an arrangement, Mister Kaille," Adams said, his usual palsy seeming more pronounced than usual. "You were to attend the trial and prevent any further mischief."

"Aye, sir, we did have such an arrangement. We still do. Forgive me. I spoke to Mister John Adams, and he gave me leave to absent myself from the courtroom. But my agreement was with you. I should have directed my request accordingly.

"Indeed you should have."

"Has something happened, sir?"

"Robert is not well. There is some question as to whether he will be able to begin his closing statement today."

"Do you know what ails him?" Ethan asked Warren.

The doctor shook his head. "He speaks of feeling unwell, but can't tell me more."

"And you suspect magick."

"It strikes me as too much of a coincidence to be anything else," Adams said. "You were supposed to protect him, and instead you're off doing God-knows-what."

"He's trying to save the life of the woman I love," Diver said with heat. "And save you in the process." When Adams turned a glare his way, Diver flinched slightly and added, "Sir."

"What is he talking about?" Adams asked Ethan.

Ethan indicated the nearest table with an open hand. Adams' mouth twisted with displeasure, but he and Warren sat, as did Ethan and Diver.

As quickly as he could, Ethan told the two men what had been done to Deborah, and why.

"This woman wants you to kill me?"

"Aye, sir."

"I take it you don't intend to," Warren said wryly.

"Not presently."

"This is hardly a joking matter," Adams said. "This woman—the witch. She is the same one who has been troubling us since before the trial began, the one who you suggested brought the recent storm down on our city. Is that right?"

"It is, sir."

"And why would a woman of such power go to such lengths to turn the two of you into assassins? Why not just kill me herself and be done with it?"

"Samuel," Warren said, his brow creasing, "surely you don't need them to explain. It should be apparent. Already many believe our cause to be riven by conflict and ambition, and peopled with the lowest sort of rabble. Your murder at the hands of patriots would confirm the worst for those who oppose us, and even those who have yet to choose sides in this struggle."

Adams sat back, obviously moved by the power of Warren's logic. "Is that what you believe, Mister Kaille?"

"Aye. Doctor Warren has summed up my thoughts quite precisely."

"I see. So what will you do?"

"We intend to win Miss Crane's freedom and, I hope, drive this woman from our city for good." He glanced at the doctor before going on. "But you should understand, sir, that your life is likely to be in danger from this time forward. Men and women of influence, here and in London, fear you and the changes you seek."

"I'm not sure why."

"Samuel—"

Adams raised a hand, silencing Warren. "The cause of liberty stands on the brink of collapse. In the next few days, Captain Preston will be acquitted. I fear his soldiers will be as well, if and when their trial commences. Throughout the colonies, non-importation agreements are failing. There is talk of British regulars returning to Boston before long. We are perilously close to losing all that we desire. This seems an odd time to try to have me killed."

"Not really," Warren said. "I hate to put it so baldly, but your death at this juncture could well end the movement for good. Your enemies see that our cause is wounded. They seek to exploit an opportunity."

"Again, I agree with Doctor Warren," Ethan told him. "Now, more than at any time since we first met, you need protection, and I am happy to provide it. Today, that means fighting Francis Lamb's sister. Tomorrow it may mean facing down Lamb and his allies on the Customs Board."

Adams said nothing for a few seconds, his head and hands trembling slightly. "I see. I fear I owe you an apology, Mister Kaille. And also you, Mister . . ."

"Jervis, sir." Diver extended his hand, which Adams gripped.

He shook hands with Warren in turn.

"You appear to have healed well, Mister Jervis," the doctor said. "I'm glad of it."

Diver's face went white, as if only now did he remember that it was Warren who had amputated his wounded arm.

"Aye, sir. I believe I owe you my gratitude."

"I wish I could have done more. Mister Kaille is the one who saved your life. That was a grim night. No one knows it better than you."

Diver offered a quick nod, his gaze dropping.

Warren promised that he and others among the Sons of Liberty would keep Adams under guard while Ethan and Diver saw to their other tasks. Ethan assured the men in turn that he would devote himself to Adams' protection once he was certain of Deborah's safety.

Warren and Adams left. Ethan and Diver set out for Janna's tavern.

Amanda and Janna received them with impatience. Janna demanded to know why Ethan had kept them waiting for so long when they were doing him a favor. However, when they learned that Ethan and Diver had been speaking with Adams and Warren, they relented. Indeed, Amanda had questions for them—about what they discussed, what Adams said at every turn of their conversation, and whether Ethan thought it possible that he would have occasion to introduce her to the man.

"I'd be happy to. And I'm sure he'll be delighted to meet you. Both of you," he added with a glance at Janna.

"Good then," Amanda said. "What about the witch? I assume she was-n't willing to bargain away your friend's woman."

"No, but she has her stone back, and I assume she'll rely on it when we confront her."

"We should do that as far from the Harbor and the river as we can. She and I will both have access to air magick, and I can draw on earth magick even at the shoreline. But she'll be weaker, the farther we are from bodies of water."

"Her house, then," Ethan said. "We can try to draw her deeper into the city, but I doubt it will work. She's as canny as she is powerful. Our advantage is that she won't want to leave Deborah unguarded."

"Provided we're right about where Deborah is," Diver said.

"Aye. That's why I want you out on the harbor. I don't think she's in that cloud, but if I'm wrong, and if we manage to defeat Whitcomb, Deborah will fall into those waters. I want you there in a dory to save her."

"If this is just an excuse to keep me out of the way—"

"It's not, although I'll admit that's a happy consequence."

Janna gave a snort of laughter.

Diver eyed her sidelong before turning back to Ethan. "If you ward me, I can help you in a fight. I can shoot. I can . . . I can distract Whitcomb if I have to. You don't have to send me out into the harbor."

"All you say is true. I know you're good in a scrape, and if that was our only concern, I would welcome you with us."

"You just said—"

"It was a poor joke, and I apologize. The truth is, everything we think we know about Charlotte Whitcomb could be wrong. She could have access to earth power, in addition to water and air. Her crystal could still be as potent as ever. And yes, she might still have Deborah in that cloud. We just don't know. And I don't want to defeat her only to learn that Deborah drowned because we assumed we knew more than we did. I know you don't want that either."

His friend had blanched. "No, of course not."

"Can you borrow a dory from someone?"

"Aye. I know just the person."

"Good. Janna, you and I will attack Whitcomb with spells, just as we would any other conjurer. If Amanda can keep her witch magick from destroying us, we should be able to defeat her."

"That's fine," Janna said. "Can we go now? I have food to cook before the evenin' rush."

Ethan could only laugh. "Aye, we can go now."

They warded themselves and one another, until Ethan thought they must have glowed with magick. With their protections in place, they left the *Fat Spider*, pausing as Janna locked the door, and then headed toward the city. At Essex Street, Diver left them, angling toward the waterfront. The small cloud conjured by Charlotte Whitcomb still floated over the choppy waters of the harbor. Ethan knew of no spell that could tell him if Deborah still lay within.

"Do you really think there's a chance she's up there?" Amanda asked him, after Diver's departure. "Or were you just sending your friend away?"

"I'm certain of nothing," he said, his voice low. "And if Deborah were to drown, I would never forgive myself."

Amanda didn't ask more than that, and they continued on up Orange and Newbury Streets. They made an odd company: two African women—one of them renowned in the city as a "marriage smith" and suspected witch, the other unknown to all—and a white man with a pronounced limp, known to be a convicted mutineer, and also rumored to be a witch. They were bound to attract notice.

So Ethan wasn't entirely surprised when, at the bend in Marlborough Street near the Old Brick Church, they found their progress blocked by none other than Stephen Greenleaf, sheriff of Suffolk County, and two men of the watch.

"What's this about, Kaille?" the sheriff asked. He considered Amanda, and sent a wary glance in Janna's direction. "Where are you headed, and who is this woman?"

Janna glared back at him. "We don't have time for this."

"I'll have answers, Windcatcher, or it's to the gaol with all three of you."

Janna cackled. "As if there's a gaol in this province that could hold us."

Greenleaf shifted his stance, appearing uncomfortable. "Well?" he said, addressing Ethan again.

"This is Amanda Oakroot, Sheriff. She's a friend from outside the city. And the three of us are on our way to the home of Charlotte Whitcomb, who has taken captive a young woman we know. We intend to win this woman's freedom."

"Taken her captive? Why wasn't I informed?"

"Because she magicked that woman into a wisp of cloud," Janna said. "What do you suppose you could do about that?"

"Magicked?"

"Tha's right."

"So this woman is a witch?"

"I've told you as much before," Ethan said.

"And offered no proof."

Janna bristled. "Didn' you hear me when I said she magicked a woman up into a cloud? How do you suppose she does that without bein' a witch?"

"You saw her do this?"

"Kaille did."

Ethan would have preferred that Janna leave it to him to treat with Greenleaf. She delighted in baiting the man, which, under present circumstances, would only make matters worse.

Greenleaf looked a question Ethan's way. "Is this true?"

"I don't know exactly what I saw," Ethan said. "One moment she was there, the next she wasn't. I suppose it had to be magick."

"See that?" Janna said. "Nothin' you could have done."

"Still, I should have been informed."

"She threatened to kill our friend if we did anything other than carry out her demands," Ethan said. "Had we told you, and had she learned of this, Deborah would have died." This was close enough to the truth for Ethan's conscience. Whitcomb had no fear of Stephen Greenleaf, but she would have objected had he and Diver attempted to include the sheriff and the watch in their affairs.

"You said you have it in mind to win your friend's freedom. How do you intend to do that?"

"You shouldn't ask questions you don't want answers to," Janna said. "Now, get out of our way."

On another day, Ethan would have tried to temper Janna's disdain for the sheriff. On this day, though, maybe her approach would serve them best. He kept his mouth shut, hoping Greenleaf's fear of Janna and her magick would convince him to back down.

"Charlotte Whitcomb is the sister of a Crown representative, a man whose reputation is above reproach. I would suggest that you turn around and stay far away from her home."

"And the woman she abducted?" Ethan asked.

"I have only your word on that. And as the two of you are known to have caused all kinds of mischief in our city, and are said to be of questionable moral fiber, I'm inclined to doubt the truth of anything you say." He pulled his flintlock from his belt, and full-cocked the hammer. "Now, go home."

His men produced their weapons.

"We don't have time for this," Janna growled again.

"I can handle the sheriff," Ethan said. "Janna, the man on the left. Amanda?"

He glanced at her, saw that she cradled her stone in the curl of her fingers.

"The one on the right," Amanda whispered.

Ethan drew on the grass growing beside the lane and muttered, *"Conflare ex gramine evocatum."* A heat spell.

Janna, it seemed, used the same magick. Almost simultaneously, the sheriff and one of the men beside him cried out and let their weapons fall to the street.

A sprig of maple emerged from the barrel of the third man's pistol, twisting like a vine and producing two leaves, which quickly turned a brilliant shade of red.

"Why, Sheriff!" Ethan said, stooping to retrieve the pistols. "Are you all right?"

"You!" Greenleaf pointed at them with a shaking hand. "You did this. You're witches! All three of you!"

"You saw us do something? Did we wave our hands about like demons? Did we call down lightning or fire?"

"You know damn well what you did!"

Ethan stepped forward until he was directly in front of the man.

"I don't know what you're talking about. I do know, though, that if you truly believe what you're saying, you should have a care about interfering with us any further. A friend of ours is in danger from the same woman who magicked that storm into the harbor some nights back. We mean to free her. If you want to help, you can. Otherwise, stay out of our way."

"I'll see you hanged, Kaille."

"You've said as much for years now," Ethan whispered, "and you haven't yet. I don't think you will. As Janna is fond of saying, there isn't a rope that can hold me. And if you tried, you might learn for certain that I am exactly what you think I am, with abilities you can't imagine even in your darkest dreams."

Greenleaf said nothing. Ethan had forsworn such direct threats for all the years he and the sheriff had been acquainted. The man didn't seem to know how to respond to them now.

Ethan smirked and shouldered past him. Janna and Amanda followed.

"What about our weapons?"

"I'll return them to you when all of this is over. And that other one—" He lifted his chin in the direction of the man with the maple sapling in his pistol—"I'd give it water and plenty of sunshine."

Janna was still laughing as they made their way through Cornhill.

X

Sun angled across the crest of Copp's Hill, painting houses and bare tree limbs in shades of gold. Ethan, Janna, and Amanda paused at the corner of

North and Charles Streets, and Ethan faced the waterfront, trying to spot Diver on the harbor swells. He thought he saw an oared boat beneath that magicked cloud, but he couldn't be certain. He had to trust in his friend's love for Deborah.

They started up the incline, Ethan expecting an attack with each stride. Janna breathed hard as they climbed, but her pace didn't flag. Amanda had long since gone silent, her gaze unfocused, as if turned inward. He didn't dare interrupt her reverie.

As they drew close to the house, a wind rose. At first Ethan thought it natural, a gust typical of this time of year.

It continued to build, though, bending trees, rattling the shutters on homes they passed.

"This is magick," Amanda said, confirming his fears, drawing his gaze and Janna's.

"Could she do this without her crystal?"

"Yes. This is air magick, and it doesn't take much precision to raise a wind. That crystal is attuned to water magick."

"Can you stop the wind?" Janna asked, the corners of her shawl gathered tight in her fist.

"I can, but then she'll know you have a witch with you. Do you want that?" This last she asked of Ethan.

"Never mind," Janna said.

They walked on, leaning into the gale.

"You brought friends."

They halted, squinted through the wind. Whitcomb stood in the middle of the lane, a blade in one hand, the pale blue crystal in the other. She hadn't raised her voice to make herself heard.

"You shouldn't have done that. I can kill the girl any time I choose. I've told you as much."

Ethan didn't want to believe her, but even with the wind blowing dust into his eyes, he observed changes in her. She looked paler than she had earlier in the day, and thin streaks of sweat lined her face.

"Kaille," Amanda said softly.

"I know."

Had she returned Deborah to the cloud when she sensed their proximity to the house? It made sense that she would. Why keep Deborah in the cloud the entire time, when all that mattered was putting her there at the start of this conflict and having her there at its end? If this was the case, it suggested—but did not prove—that the spell Amanda cast on her crystal

had failed. The first time Whitcomb whisked Deborah into the cloud, she
did so without her stone. She could have again. Surely, though, she would
have noticed if the crystal behaved strangely. With all this uncertainty,
Ethan was glad he had insisted that Diver go out on the water.

"What of Adams?" Whitcomb asked. "All I have heard suggests he still
lives."

"That's right."

"Then you should not be here. I made my demands quite clear, and you
still have until midnight tonight—"

"You could give me another week, or a hundred days, or a thousand,
and I still wouldn't do what you demanded of us. Neither would Diver.
You've failed, and now you're going to return Deborah Crane to us, or we'll
destroy you."

She glanced about, appearing unconcerned with Ethan's threat. "Where
is your young friend?" Realization raised her brows. "Ah, of course. On the
harbor, no doubt, waiting to rescue his love. You disappoint me, Mister
Kaille."

Whitcomb raised the hand holding her crystal and whispered in Gaelic.
Ethan spun to gaze out over the harbor. Deborah's cloud drifted closer to
the city. He couldn't judge precisely where it stopped, but he could guess.

"There. Now she is over the shoreline. If she falls, she will be dashed
on a wharf or a warehouse or a cobblestone lane."

Ethan faced her again, feeling helpless. Whitcomb looked even worse
than she had when they reached her. Sweat ran down her face and darkened
the collar of her gown. Her hands shook. But she grinned, pleased with herself.

"What will your friend do now? What will you do?"

He could imagine Diver's desperation as he rowed toward land, hoping
to place himself near enough to save his love. He didn't know how he
would face the young man if all their planning ended in Deborah's death.

"You knew, didn't you? You knew she was in the house. That's why
you've come. But more than that, you didn't think I would be able to put
her back. You didn't think I would be able to do any of this, did you?" She
studied the crystal. "What did you do to it?" She cast an appraising eye at
Ethan and Janna before her gaze came to rest on Amanda.

"You're a witch. Your magick is nothing like theirs, and not quite like
mine, either. Air? Earth?" She must have seen some change in Amanda's
expression. "An earth witch. How charming. You tried to kill my stone?"

"Kaille?" Amanda said again, her voice low but rising.

"I'll deal with him in a moment. First I want to know about you, my dear. An African witch. Fascinating. You live here in Boston? Does the sheriff know of you? I'd be happy to arrange an introduction."

"Your fight is with me, Miss Whitcomb. Leave her alone."

"You're right. My fight is with you. And I'll do more than leave her alone. I needn't tell you the different ways in which you have violated our agreement. But you still have until midnight to carry out my orders. I'll grant you one last reprieve. Go now, and you might still save the poor girl."

Ethan held the edge of his knife to his forearm. "No," he said.

"You would condemn the girl to death?"

"She was going to die anyway. Do you think I trusted you to release her?" He shook his head. "It doesn't matter that now she's over solid earth rather than water." He hoped with all his heart that Amanda was listening to every word. "You were going to kill her regardless."

"That's not true."

"Isn't it? You said yourself, earlier today, that Adams is all. His cause is all."

"And you told me that the girl mattered more to you. Twenty-five years of friendship with Mister Jervis, you said, versus only one in service to this fight for 'liberty.'"

"I lied. I want to save them both—Deborah and Adams. But failing that, how should I choose one woman over the future of the colonies?"

"I believe Mister Jervis would have something to say about that." She sounded less sure of herself. Her skin had turned pasty, sweat dampened her hair and more of her gown.

"He won't have the chance. If she dies, I'll tell him there was nothing to be done. You let her fall before we could kill you. But kill you we will." He bared his teeth. "Look at you. You're on death's doorstep. You're sweating like an overtaxed plow horse. I've seen cadavers with more color in their cheeks. You can't hold her in that cloud for much longer. *That* is why you would grant us this one last chance. To save yourself." Another shake of his head. "I won't allow it. You can set her down and live. Or you can let her fall. And the moment you do, the moment your weakness and exhaustion become too much for you, the three of us will crush you."

"You're lying. You care about her too much."

"I suppose we'll find out soon enough. I don't believe you can hold out more than a few more minutes."

She regarded each of them again. Ethan didn't know if she could use her witchcraft for another spell while maintaining the magick that imprisoned Deborah. He didn't doubt that she could conjure.

He saw fear in her eyes, hoped she wouldn't see the same in his.

"Well? What will you do, Miss Whitcomb? Will you let her fall to earth or live to face me another day? You can't do both."

She retreated a pace. Ethan dragged his blade across his forearm. Blood welled from the wound.

"Not another step," he said.

She hesitated, her gaze flicking to his arm.

He didn't dare risk a glance at Amanda, though he wanted to. Janna, on the other side of him, had drawn blood, too. They might as well have had flintlocks aimed at Whitcomb.

A noise from Amanda—a sudden release of breath—drew the witch's stare.

Amanda raised both arms. "Now, Kaille!"

Ethan cast fire again. He didn't know what spell Janna used. Reg glowed next to him. Janna's spectral guide, an ancient woman illuminated in deepest blue, appeared just beside her.

Their conjurings hit Whitcomb in quick succession. She grunted, lurched back and to the side like a drunkard.

Amanda gave an inarticulate cry—exertion, fatigue, hope, terror. Ethan thought he heard a scream from the harbor shore. He hoped he was wrong.

Whitcomb still gripped her crystal and her knife, and she made use of both of them. She slashed at that hand holding the stone and almost in the same motion raised the crystal over her head. She whispered in Latin, then shifted to Gaelic.

Her ghost—a young girl—glared at Ethan, and grinned with satisfaction when he fell back under the force of Whitcomb's conjuring.

His wardings held. Or he assumed they did. Her spell didn't kill him. Her witchery crackled in the air around them. Wind again, and lightning from a black cloud that marred an otherwise indigo sky.

The first bolt struck a sycamore tree near where Ethan and his companions stood. Bark and smoking bits of wood pelted down on them. A huge branch split from the trunk and crashed to the street, its offshoots barely missing Janna.

Ethan cut himself again and cast. While Whitcomb staggered under the impact of that spell, he conjured a third time and a fourth. Janna did the same. Their magick roared in the lane, as if some huge beast had awakened beneath the city. One last spell from Janna pounded Whitcomb to the ground. She lay in a heap, whimpering, but unable to fight back.

Janna glanced his way, her lips pressed in a taut line. Ethan knew what she would say before she spoke.

"I say we finish her," Janna said.

Before Ethan could object or agree—and in that instant he honestly couldn't have said which he intended to do—he heard someone shout his name from behind them.

All three of them turned. Even Whitcomb managed to raise her head.

"Damn," Janna muttered.

Ethan had to agree.

Stephen Greenleaf strode toward them, followed by those same two men of the watch. None of them brandished pistols, not that they needed to. The scene before them spoke for itself.

"What is this?" Greenleaf asked as he reached them, winded from his climb. He lifted his chin in Whitcomb's direction. "Who is that?"

"Charlotte Whitcomb," Ethan said.

"The woman you told me about. And what have you done to her?"

"Nothing. We had words. She didn't look well when we began to argue and she grew worse the longer we went on. At last, she collapsed. I was just about to attend to her when you arrived."

"That might be the most blatant lie you've ever told me," the sheriff said. "And that's saying something. Minutes ago, you as much as admitted that you intended to harm her."

"I said a lot of things. I told you to stay out of our way, and yet here you are."

Greenleaf wet his lips. "Yes, well, it's my job."

That, of all things, reached him. Ethan allowed himself a small smile. "Aye, it is." He reached into his pocket and produced the weapons he had taken from the sheriff and his man.

He wouldn't kill Charlotte Whitcomb this day. That much was clear to him. He hoped Deborah was free and safe. If she wasn't, he would be back before midnight. But right now, he saw no alternative.

"You should see to her then," he said. "I believe she requires a doctor's care."

"Kaille," Janna said, a warning in her tone.

"We should go, Janna, Amanda. Our quarrel with Miss Whitcomb is over, at least for now."

His gaze met Whitcomb's. She was still pale, and too weary, it seemed, to do more than glower.

"You killed her, you know," she said. "Your friend. You made her fall, not I."

Fear clawed at Ethan's heart, but he kept his voice level as he said, "We'll see. Until next time, Miss Whitcomb."

Ethan started down Charles Street toward the waterfront, flanked by Janna and Amanda. He tried not to hurry, lest he raise Greenleaf's suspicions. But it was all he could do not to run.

Janna started to say something, but Ethan stopped her with a raised hand.

"Not yet, please," he said, breathing the words.

Once they were out of sight of the sheriff, he slanted a glance at her. "All right. You can berate me now."

"Why would you let her live? You know you're going to have to kill her eventually. You could have ended it today."

"With the sheriff watching?"

She huffed and dismissed this with a wave of her hand. "He wouldn't have known any better."

"I'm not sure I agree." To Amanda, he said, "Were you able to do anything?"

"I hope so," she said. "I hope so."

They hurried to the shoreline and followed its contour past one wharf after another, trying to find the spot where Deborah had fallen. After going south some distance, they doubled back, passed Charles Street, and continued on toward Thornton's Shipyard.

As they walked by the North Battery, Ethan halted, swaying, pressure building in his chest. In the distance, on a small crescent of white sand, near a beached dory, one figure sat in the sand. A second lay still, head in the lap of the first. Ethan broke into a hobbled run.

Diver looked up at his approach. Tears streaked his cheeks. He stroked Deborah's red hair with one hand.

"Diver . . ."

"I can't explain it," his friend said, the words choked. "She should be dead. I saw her fall, and I was too far away to do anything. It was so far, from so high. And she fell so fast, until she didn't. At the end, it was like something caught her, eased her to the ground. The hand of God. That's how it seemed." He swiped at a tear before stroking Deborah's hair again. "How is she not dead?" he asked, more of himself than of Ethan.

Ethan faced Amanda, tears blurring his vision. "Thank you."

"You know," she said, "I didn't need that second hint. I heard you the first time, and was already well into my casting. All you did was annoy me."

He laughed through a sob, gripped both her shoulders, and kissed her cheek. She scowled for about two seconds before a smile broke through. "You're welcome," she said.

Ethan joined Diver. Deborah looked to be in good health. Her cheeks were pink. Her chest rose and fell in a peaceful rhythm. She showed no sign of injury; she could have been sleeping.

"She hasn't opened her eyes yet, or said anything," Diver told him. "But I think she's all right."

"Of course I am," she murmured. "I just like you touching my hair that way, and was afraid you would stop."

She opened her eyes, squinted against the late afternoon sun. Ethan had never seen his friend look so happy.

"What happened to me, Derrey? What are we doing here?"

"I'll explain it all," he said. "Or all that I can. I'll probably need Ethan's help before I'm done."

They helped Deborah to her feet and supported her on the long walk back to the *Dowsing Rod*.

XI

As soon as they reached the tavern, Ethan sent for Doctor Warren. The physician arrived within a quarter hour, examined Deborah in one of the rooms upstairs, and declared her in good health.

"She needs food and then rest. I expect she'll be perfectly well within a few days."

He was certainly right about the food. Kannice and Kelf served supper to Diver, Deborah, Ethan, Janna, and Amanda, and no one ate more than Diver's betrothed. Long after the others were sated, she continued to dip pieces of bread into her chowder, all the while apologizing for her "unseemly appetite."

When, after some time, she'd had enough, and had thanked all of them for their efforts on her behalf, Diver took her home. Janna and Amanda left for the *Fat Spider*, the witch promising to stay in Boston for at least day.

The usual crowd remained in the *Dowser* for another hour or two, as they would most any night. When the last of them had gone and Ethan, Kelf, and Kannice had finished cleaning up, Kelf departed, and Ethan and Kannice retired to their bedroom with a flask of Madeira.

For a long time, in the flickering light of a single candle, they spoke not a word. After, their limbs entwined beneath a tangle of blankets and bed linens, Ethan told her of all that had happened over the past several days.

"They truly want Mister Adams dead?"

"That surprises you?"

Kannice propped herself up on an elbow. "It does, yes. I know we have our disputes with Parliament and the king. But assassination . . . That's not . . ." She stopped herself, appearing amused, though the creases in her forehead remained. "I was going to say that's not very British, but I suppose I sound terribly naïve."

"Guy Fawkes would say so." He traced the curve of her shoulder with the edge of his finger. "Adams has been calling for a complete separation from England for two years now, since the occupation began. And just after the shootings, it seemed he was on the verge of getting his way, but not since. Doctor Warren said earlier today that killing Adams now might end the cause for good. I'm sure that's what Charlotte Whitcomb, and Francis Lamb, and their British masters think."

"But not Ethan Kaille?"

She asked this teasingly, but Ethan remained grim.

"No, not me. I think his death in that way would be the match to the fuse. I believe Boston would descend into chaos, and fire and bloodshed would spread from here to Georgia."

Her mirth faded. "Actually, that sounds about right."

"I've told Mister Adams that I intend to keep him safe. I know that's not really thieftaking—not in any form I've ever seen. And I don't guess that you approve. But to my mind, keeping him safe is synonymous with keeping you safe, and Kelf, and Diver and Deborah. The time for separation is coming, but it's not here yet, and if agents of the Crown force a crisis, everything we hold dear will be imperiled. I can't allow that."

Kannice leaned forward and kissed him on the lips. "No," she said. "I don't believe you can."

She lowered her head to his chest, her arm draped over him. And they watched the shadows in their room flicker and shift until they both fell into an uneasy slumber.

Author's Note

On the morning of 24 October 1770, the trial of Captain Thomas Preston began in Boston's Court House, much as described in these pages. Up until that morning, it had been assumed that Preston and the eight soldiers also charged with murder for the 5 March 1770 shootings on King Street (called by Samuel Adams the "Horrid Massacre") would stand trial together. The separation of the two trials would prove beneficial to Captain Preston in particular.

The selection of jurymen for the Preston's trial took place that first day, and did, in fact, place several loyalists on the panel, all but guaranteeing Preston's acquittal. The government's lawyers proved remarkably inept at preventing this. And Samuel Adams, who might have been bold enough to raise objections from the gallery, was inexplicably absent from the court that morning. As to whether this was because of Charlotte Whitcomb's magickal interference . . . Well, we shall never know for certain . . .

[In describing the details of court proceedings, I have relied largely on two books: Hiller B. Zobel's *The Boston Massacre* (W.W. Norton &Company, 1970); and Richard Archer's *As If An Enemy's Country* (Oxford University Press, 2010).]

— DBJ

Part III
THE ADAMS GAMBIT

I

Boston, Province of Massachusetts Bay, 29 October 1770

This should have been a day of anticipation, of justice realized. Only five days before, the trial of Captain Thomas Preston, the senior officer present that horrible March night on King Street when British regulars fired into a mob of protesters, opened with all the fanfare of a festival. Hundreds of Bostonians had crowded Queen Street in front of the Court House, hoping to be seated in the courtroom so that they might watch the captain answer for his crimes.

On this day, with closing arguments expected, and a verdict looming, Ethan Kaille didn't believe that anyone would be pressing for a spot in the courtroom. So late in the process, with the jury filled with loyalists, and the prosecuting attorneys exposed as incompetents, the trial's outcome was no longer in doubt. Preston would be acquitted, if not today, then tomorrow.

A relatively short time ago—no more than two years—Ethan probably would have rejoiced at such a verdict, seeing in Preston a loyal officer of the British Empire, and in those targeted by his soldiers the sort of lawless rabble who deserved the hand fate had dealt them. Not today. Not after the occupation of his city, the shooting in his streets, the near death of his friend Diver Jervis.

He knew better than anyone what had caused the shootings, since dubbed the "Horrid Massacre." His own magickal battle with a crazed conjurer named Nate Ramsey had contributed to rising tensions in the city for days beforehand. Ramsey's spells provoked the mob and the regulars; it was a miracle Preston's men held off for as long as they did. And yet, Ethan couldn't help but hold the captain and his men responsible, at least in part. They shouldn't have been on King Street in the first place. They should never have confronted that horde with their weapons loaded and their bayonets fixed. Ramsay poisoned the city with his spells, but he wouldn't have accomplished so much without the complicity of soldier and citizen alike.

Ethan departed the *Dowsing Rod* for the Court House early in the morning, under a dark gray sky and a cold rain: a perfect reflection of his mood. Kannice had offered him eggs and coffee before he left. He accepted only the latter, earning a disapproving scowl from his loving wife.

He had little interest in observing this last day of proceedings, which, he assumed, would be as tedious as the previous ones had been. He went because Samuel Adams would be in attendance, and Ethan had pledged himself to keep the great man safe. Agents of the Crown—including a powerful conjurer who also possessed witch powers that Ethan scarcely understood—sought to do Adams harm.

Huddled in his woolen coat and tricorn, Ethan gave a grim smirk at the delicacy of his own thoughts. "Harm," hardly did justice to their dark ambitions. They wanted the man dead. Ethan would, if necessary, die keeping him alive.

A few dozen men loitered in the lane outside the Court House, but the street was not as crowded as it had been that sunny morning when the trial commenced. As usual, Stephen Greenleaf, sheriff of Suffolk County, stood at the doorway, pale eyes alight with the gray of morning above his hooked nose and square jaw. Two men of the watch stood with him.

Ethan considered approaching the sheriff and seeking early entry to the building, but thought better of it. His most recent interaction with Greenleaf, only two days before, had not gone well. He doubted the sheriff would be inclined to grant him any boons. Better to wait for Samuel Adams and Doctor Joseph Warren, who would doubtless be along before the doors opened at half-past seven.

Greenleaf continued to survey the street. When his gaze met Ethan's, he paused, his lip curling. An instant later, he looked away, confirming Ethan's intuition.

"Mister Kaille!"

Ethan turned. Joseph Warren, tall, dark-eyed, dashing, wove among the other onlookers, leading Samuel Adams. Both men wore capes, Adams' blue, Warren's red. Adams was almost a full hand shorter, his hair grayer, his face more careworn. His head and hands shook with the mild palsy that had plagued him for all the time he and Ethan had been acquainted.

"My protector," he said, greeting Ethan with a handshake and good humor.

"Let's hope my presence proves an unnecessary precaution, sir."

Warren cast an anxious glance at the men nearest them. "Amen to that."

As word of Adams' arrival spread, people converged on them from all sides, until Ethan found himself beset by men seeking to shake the man's hand or engage him in conversation. Warren appeared alarmed, Adams faintly amused. Ethan didn't wish to overreact, but neither did he want to be caught unawares, lest someone attempt to injure Adams or worse.

"Please step back," he said, instilling his voice with as much authority as he could muster.

Most ignored him.

Adams' gripped hand after hand, bobbing his head in greeting and maintaining what seemed to be a genuine smile. Warren, a formidable presence, did his best to control the mob, but he shared more than one concerned look with Ethan.

"It's all right, Mister Kaille," Adams said, even as he acknowledged still more of his admirers. "One grows accustomed to such attention after a time."

"No," Warren said, "one really doesn't."

Adams laughed.

Ethan and the good doctor were saved by the peal of church bells marking the half hour. Greenleaf opened the Court House doors, and Adams started in that direction, drawing the crowd with him: liberty's pied piper.

As they reached the door, Greenleaf planted himself in Ethan's way.

"I don't think there's room for you in there, Kaille. You should wait out here."

"Do you plan to keep out Mister Adams and Doctor Warren? Shall we ask the rest of these men how they would feel about that?"

Greenleaf's expression curdled. Ethan was certain that if he could exclude these prominent Sons of Liberty, he would. Already, though, others within hearing had halted to await his response to Ethan's question. The vast majority of them regarded the sheriff with open hostility.

"No," the sheriff said, the word wrung from him. "They're free to enter."

"Mister Kaille is my guest, Sheriff," Adams said. "Where I go, he goes."

With more and more people lining up behind Ethan and the others, that settled matters. Greenleaf waved them inside, sending one last filthy glare Ethan's way.

"The sheriff doesn't like you very much," Warren said, as they ascended the stairs to the second floor.

"No, he doesn't," Adams said, before Ethan could answer. "I take that as one more reason to trust and respect our thieftaking friend."

They entered the courtroom and, thanks to the deference of those who had preceded them into the chamber, found a spot up front, directly behind the wooden barrier separating spectators from attorneys, jurors, and judges. Despite the surety that Preston would be found innocent, a sense of expectation had belatedly settled over the spectators. One way or another, this would be a momentous day in the city's history.

The door through which Ethan and his companions had entered the chamber opened again, and a familiar figure strode in: Francis Lamb, dressed impeccably in blue silk, brown hair dipping roguishly over a smooth brow and striking green eyes. He slipped through the gathered spectators like mercury over stone, making his way to his usual spot just behind the box where the defendant would stand. Settling himself there, he scanned the crowd. Seeing Ethan with the Sons of Liberty, he twitched his lips into a cold smile and faced forward again.

Moments later, Captain Preston entered through a different doorway, accompanied by his attorneys—John Adams, Robert Auchmuty, and Josiah Quincy—and followed by the attorneys for the Crown, Robert Treat Paine and Samuel Quincy, Josiah's elder brother.

Soon after that, the jurors stepped into the courtroom and took their places in the panel's box. The judges filed in last, with a rustle of silk and wool. As those who had taken seats rose, the men in black arranged themselves on the bench.

When all was ready, Benjamin Lynde, Jr., interim chief justice of the provincial court, who had presided over these proceedings from the start, recognized Mister Paine and indicated that he should begin his closing statement.

If looks and manner could predetermine ability, Robert Treat Paine would have been a fine lawyer indeed. He was handsome, distinguished, imposing, with a mane of dark hair and a deep, powerful voice.

Sadly, these were the only qualities that recommended him as an advocate for the Crown's prosecution of Captain Preston. On Saturday, Ethan had been told, Mister Paine asked to delay his closing remarks because he felt ill, a development that raised Ethan's suspicions and fears. Now, as he began his statement, Ethan wondered if he had recovered at all, or if he, in fact, suffered not from any malady or magickal spell, but rather from a mortal lack of passion. His argument, delivered in a mumbled monotone, sought to undermine some witnesses and boost others. But his delivery, which had jurors and judges leaning forward in their chairs, as if straining to hear, was anything but convincing.

Most among those watching from the rear of the chamber frowned at this display. Except Francis Lamb, of course.

"This is a disaster," Warren whispered.

Adams didn't bother to respond. His scowl spoke volumes.

"I thought he had a reputation as an accomplished attorney," Ethan said, also keeping his voice low.

Warren dipped his chin. "As did I. I believe we were misinformed."

"He had a difficult task," Adams said, apparently bowing to the inevitable. "He had a poor case, and in John he faced a worthy opponent. They have opposed each other before, and I always had the impression from John that Robert bested him as often as not. I believe my dear cousin took great satisfaction in thrashing him this time."

When Paine completed his statement, such as it was, the judges gave the jurors their instructions. This, too, proved tedious, as each justice, beginning with Edmund Trowbridge, the least senior member of the court, had the opportunity to address the panel. Trowbridge went into tremendous detail, as comprehensive in his instructions as many in the chamber had hoped Paine and Quincy would have been with their prosecution.

"You must remember above all else," he said, at the conclusion of his discourse, "'whoso sheddeth man's blood, by man shall his blood be shed' is a general rule, but not an absolute one. It has many exceptions to it."

Trowbridge provided so much information to the jurors that the judges who followed him had relatively little to add. Not surprisingly, this failed to keep the others from talking anyway. In all, the judges addressed the panel for most of the afternoon—upwards of four hours—before bidding the jurors to retire and seek their verdict.

By the time Ethan, Adams, Warren, and the rest of the spectators shuffled out of the Court House, it was past five o'clock. Rain still fell, light but cold, and the sky had started to darken.

As they walked down the stairway within the building, Ethan glanced back repeatedly, keeping an eye on Francis Lamb. He watched as the man emerged from the Court House behind them and made his way through the crowd toward Cornhill and the North End. Ethan didn't expect Lamb himself to make an attempt on Adams' life, but he preferred to know where the customs man was at all times, in case he gave something away with his behavior.

"Mister Kaille!"

Ethan turned back to Adams and Warren, who, he realized, had been speaking to him for some time.

"I'm sorry. I was distracted."

"Clearly," Adams said, patting his arm. "I was saying that I have no desire to stand in this rain any longer than I must. I am going to walk home. I assume we won't have to wait terribly long for a verdict. So shall we plan to meet here in the morning?"

"No, sir. I'm going to accompany you to your house. Once you're safely inside, I'll take my leave."

"That hardly seems necessary," Adams said.

At the same time, Warren said, "Thank you, Mister Kaille. I was going to insist on just that."

Adams frowned. "You're ganging up on me."

"I'm fulfilling a commitment, sir. In the hope of someday being paid."

He grinned, and Adams laughed.

"Very well, I will accept your company for the walk home." To Warren, he said, "Good night, Joseph."

"Samuel, Mister Kaille."

Ethan and Adams set out through the lanes of the South End toward Adams' Purchase Street estate. At first, they said little. The scents of brine and fish and wood smoke blanketed the city, comfortable and familiar. Ethan looked forward to returning to the *Dowsing Rod*, even if that meant clearing tables and carrying tureens of chowder from the kitchen to the bar.

"How do you suppose they might try to do it?" Adams asked, breaking a lengthy silence.

"I'm sorry, sir?"

"I'm asking—this is all very odd for me—how do you think they will try to have me killed?"

"I honestly wouldn't know, sir. And it may be that after Miss Whitcomb's failed attempt to coerce Diver and me into making the attempt, they have given up on this particular ambition. I just feel we can't assume as much. That would be foolhardy."

"I agree, of course. I'm merely curious. A dark curiosity, I'll admit. But can you blame me?"

"I understand completely, sir. But if I may, I have some experience with this sort of thing. You can't let morbid fears or expectations consume your every waking moment. You should enjoy your time with your wife, you should work as you always do, you should sleep and eat and live. I'll do all that I can to keep you safe, as will Doctor Warren, I'm sure. And Mister John Adams, and Mister Quincy, and all who consider you a friend."

"You're kind, Mister Kaille. I'm grateful to you. But do you truly expect me to live as I would normally? Do you think I can be in my home without worrying about Betsy's safety as well as my own?"

"As to that, I believe you'll be most safe in your home. Any attempt on your person would be a political act, an attempt to make your demise a spectacle. Charlotte Whitcomb wanted Diver or me to do the deed, I believe, because she wanted to expose weaknesses in the cause of liberty. She wanted it to seem that your movement is rife with dissent and disunion, that your followers are animals who just crave blood. Killing you in your sleep, or at your dining table—that reflects poorly on your attackers, rather than on you."

Adams eyed him sidelong. "That makes a disturbing amount of sense. I find it slightly alarming that your mind understands such matters so well." He gave another wry grin. "I also think I'm glad I didn't know all of this earlier today when greeting well-wishers on Queen Street."

"Yes, sir."

They had come within sight of Adams' home, and they covered the remaining distance wordlessly. Ethan accompanied Adams up the path to his front door. There he scanned the gardens, the lane, the adjacent houses. He couldn't see all in the gloaming and the rain, but he felt confident that Adams would be safe for this night.

Adams proffered a hand, which Ethan gripped. "Thank you, Mister Kaille, for your vigilance and our . . . illuminating conversation."

"It's my pleasure, sir. Would you like me to fetch you from here in the morning? We can walk together to the Court House."

He expected Adams to demur. The man surprised him. "I would find that reassuring. Again, thank you."

Adams let himself into the house and shut the door. Once Ethan heard the lock thrown, he walked back to the lane and set out for home. He headed north on Atkinson Street, a different route from the one he and Adams had followed. Before he reached the corner of Milk Street, a figure appeared before him.

He halted, reached for his blade, cursing his carelessness.

"Ethan Kaille," said Charlotte Whitcomb, a cruel smile on her lovely face. "I'm so very pleased to see you again."

II

Ethan freed his knife, shoved his sleeve up, and sliced his forearm. As blood welled, he whispered a warding spell. Magick hummed in the cobblestones and Uncle Reg, his spectral guide, flashed into view beside him, bright russet in the failing light.

Charlotte Whitcomb hadn't moved, although as he cut himself a second time, she did chuckle and shake her head.

"You truly are a fool, aren't you? If I wanted you dead, you would be dead. If I intended to attack you, I would have prevented you from warding yourself, or even drawing your blade. Do you really think me so addled and weak that I would squander such an opportunity had I meant to use it?"

"So what do you want?" Even as he asked the question, he swept the lane with a quick glance. She had never involved others in their conflict, but he had bested her twice, and he expected her to alter her tactics.

"Rest assured, I'm quite alone. As I recall, you are the one who brought strangers into our encounters, not I."

She wore a black cape over a gown of green silk, the high collar of her wrap framing her graceful neck. She had pinned her hair into a tight coil, and she carried a black parasol of oiled silk, fringed in lace.

"I seek only to talk. For tonight."

He hesitated, staring into shadows once more.

"Now, you're just being rude," she said, her mien hardening. "I've told you I intend you no harm. You've warded yourself. And the streets are quite empty. I'm not likely to find anyone who I could use for a spell, am I?"

In their earliest confrontations, she had drawn magick from unsuspecting innocents around them, bolstering her spells beyond his capacity to protect himself against them. Only by placing a warding on all of Boston's citizenry had he thwarted this tactic. But that didn't mean he had rendered her harmless. She was a woman of many dark talents.

"It's raining," he said, "and you're a water witch."

Another smile exposed perfect, sharp teeth. "A chance you'll simply have to take."

Still he kept his distance, until she rolled her eyes and cut the air with her hand in an impatient gesture.

"Very well. I give you my word, sworn on the life of my king, George III, that I intend you no harm on this night. My purpose is only to speak with you."

Ethan could hardly refuse her after that. He walked to her, halting close enough that he could smell her lilac perfume. Reg trailed him, drawing her notice.

"He looks like you," she said, green eyes reflecting the specter's glow. "I don't believe that either of you has ever smiled."

"He has," Ethan said, his voice flat.

She smirked, eyes dancing. "A jest. How unexpected." She struck out toward the waterfront. Ethan fell in step beside her. "I take it Mister Adams is safely in his home. Did you tuck him in before you left?"

"You make yourself a fool when you mock a man like him."

She eyed him before facing forward again. "Perhaps you're right," she said. "That was childish of me."

He didn't bother to hide his surprise.

"You are sworn to his protection?"

"I am," he said. "As you are sworn to his destruction."

"Not necessarily. All things are negotiable."

He was almost afraid to ask. "And what would you demand of me this time? Shall I poison Doctor Warren, or tear down the Town House, or simply accompany you to the *Green Dragon* so that you can cast a spell on all the Sons of Liberty at once?"

"More jests. You're in a jovial mood, I see."

"Hardly. I'm trying to figure out what you want, so that I can go home and rest. I've had a long day."

"Yes, I heard about today's proceedings. It sounded dreadfully boring. I'm glad I wasn't there. The fact is, though, we both know that Captain Preston will be acquitted come morning. That has to come as quite a blow to Mister Adams and his friends."

"I believe they expected such a result."

"Since the selection of the jury, of course. But not before then. Their movement is dying. *Your* movement, I should say. Non-importation agreements are failing throughout the colonies. Merchants here cling to theirs, but in the absence of cooperation from New York, Philadelphia, Charleston, and elsewhere, Boston's stubbornness means nothing."

He couldn't argue. Adams had said much the same thing to Ethan and Warren only a few days before.

"So you're ready to declare victory," Ethan said. "All your ill-intent toward Adams has been rendered unnecessary."

"Oh, I wouldn't say that. Adams may be the Crown's most dangerous adversary in all of North America. Him, Mister Dickinson in Pennsylvania, Mister Henry in Virginia."

"In that case, I would know what it is you want of me, so that I can refuse you and get on with my evening."

She hooked her arm around his and drew him closer, so that they walked as lovers would. "You amuse me, Mister Kaille. That, as much as anything, is why you continue to live."

Ethan extracted his arm from her grasp, thinking that she had far too much in common with his lovely, dangerous rival in thieftaking, Sephira Pryce.

"I continue to live because I choose to, and because your attempts on my life have failed. Now what do you want?"

She halted, and he did the same. "Fine," she said without a trace of humor. "I want Adams dead. That hasn't changed. I know better than to leave the task to you. Indeed, I prefer that you continue as his guardian, so that your failure will be known to all. I have placed a bounty on his head. One hundred pounds—enough to tempt even the most devoted of his followers."

"Why tell me this?"

"Because I believe you will be helpless to stop me no matter how well-informed you are."

He couldn't deny that the very notion of a bounty alarmed him. And one hundred pounds . . . "His admirers, the men who share his commitment to the patriot cause, wouldn't harm him for ten times that amount." He strove to sound confident, to keep his fears hidden.

"I agree most wouldn't, fools that they are. But all it takes is one. Besides, my bounty isn't intended for the Sons of Liberty."

His blood chilled. "Then who? Loyalists in Boston may hate Adams, but—"

"Not just Boston," she said. "Word of this bounty has been sent to every town and city in every colony in North America. And the missive was phrased in such a way that it will attract the notice of conjurers. 'Adams is protected by forces of extraordinary power,' I wrote. 'Similar force will be required to overcome those who ward him.' Not particularly subtle, I know. But none who can't conjure will make sense of it. The powerless can be so dull-witted about such things, don't you agree?"

In truth, he did. That, however, was secondary. If Whitcomb was right, conjurers and witches from up and down the seaboard would be descending on Boston, all with one purpose in mind: to kill Samuel Adams. He would need help from Janna Windcatcher—the dour tavern owner and self-proclaimed "marriage smith" who lived on Boston's Neck—and also from Amanda Oakroot—the earth witch who had helped him save Deborah Crane. He could also call on Gaspar Mariz, but Mariz worked for

Sephira, and she hated Adams as much as she loved gold. Mariz might well be one of those Ethan had to fight off in order to keep Adams safe.

"I've silenced you," Whitcomb said, clasping her hands together. "How delightful."

"You're mad," he said, breathing the words.

"Am I? I think this is quite brilliant, if you must know."

"You're going to turn all of Boston into a magickal battleground."

"And why would I mind that?"

He didn't bother to answer, but instead pivoted away from her and headed toward the *Dowsing Rod*. He needed to develop a strategy that would enable him to meet this latest challenge.

"You haven't much time," she called after him, sounding gleeful. "I sent my missive days ago, even before you rescued that lovely young woman from my cloud. The first conjurers should be arriving in the city any day now."

Damn. After faltering mid-step, he hurried on, eager to be beyond hearing of her threats and taunts.

He walked quickly, his limp growing more pronounced with each step, pain radiating up his leg and into his groin and gut. Reg kept pace with him, dour as always, glowing eyes marking Ethan's every step.

"Can you sense other conjurers in the city?" Ethan asked.

His specter hesitated, nodded.

"Janna, Mariz, that horrible woman. Any others?"

He shook his head, made a small uncertain gesture with one luminous hand.

"Not yet," Ethan said, interpreting.

This drew a second nod.

At least he had a little time to prepare. "Thank you," he said. "*Dimitto te.*"

At this release, Reg faded, leaving Ethan to walk alone in the deepening night. With rain continuing to fall, and the night growing chill, he had the lanes mostly to himself. He peered over his shoulder once or twice, checking that Charlotte Whitcomb hadn't followed him. Not that she needed to. If this latest gambit worked, she could accomplish all she sought without having to do anything more than pay out a small fortune in coin.

Even before he entered the *Dowsing Rod*, he smelled baking bread and—unusual for Kannice—roasting fowl. A din of earnest conversation greeted him as he stepped inside. Kannice stood at the bar, her cheeks flushed, auburn hair pulled back from her face save for a few wisps that flew free. She piled fowl, slices of bread, and what he assumed was squash onto one plate after another. Catching sight of Ethan, she gave a playful roll of her eyes and returned to her task.

He hurried behind the bar and tied on an apron.

"Fowl?"

Kannice shrugged, kissed him. "I was tired of chowders." She canted her head at the line of people waiting for food. "They don't seem to mind. Where have you been?"

He eyed that line in turn and answered with a small shake of his head. "I'll tell you later."

"I don't like that sound of that at all."

"No, I don't imagine."

Kelf Fingarin, Kannice's enormous barman, emerged from the kitchen bearing a laden platter.

"'Bout time, Ethan" he said. "We've been holding 'em off with chairs and knives, haven't we, Kannice?"

Ethan chuckled, plucked a piece of meat from the platter, and popped it in his mouth, drawing a fearsome scowl from the barman.

The evening unfolded much as usual in the tavern. A new wave of customers arrived shortly after Ethan did, and another came in an hour or two later. As Ethan, Kannice, and Kelf served food and drink to these patrons, the door to the tavern opened and a man Ethan didn't know stepped inside.

"He's been acquitted," he said, raising his voice over the noise in the tavern. "Preston's been found not guilty. The court will convene at eight o'clock tomorrow morning to make it all official."

A thick silence blanketed the great room, and every person stared at the messenger, no doubt wondering if he had more to say.

After a moment, though, he simply turned and let himself out of the building.

Still no one spoke, until Tom Langer, one of Kannice's regulars, said, "Well, I suppose that was predictable."

It was as if his words freed every tongue in the tavern. Abruptly, all Kannice's patrons were shouting to be heard. Ethan could make out little of what said, though he did hear some talk of seeking other avenues of retribution against Captain Preston.

"If anyone can find a way, it's Mister Adams," someone else called.

Langer raised his tankard. "Long live Samuel Adams!"

"Hear, hear!"

The loudest conversations quieted slowly, and soon men and women were asking again for more food and drink. Ethan went on serving, but his mood had darkened. No one could have been less surprised by the verdict than he. He had been in the courtroom, had heard Adams and Warren lament the poor performance of the Crown's lawyers. He knew this was coming. Yet he couldn't help the twisting feeling in his gut, like he had swallowed a snake. The soldiers would probably be acquitted, too. The king's men would get away with murder five times over, and there was nothing any of them could do about it.

Worse, he sensed that the people around him didn't care very much. True, the tidings disrupted their merriment for a few moments, and some discussions of the trial continued around the room. Tom Langer and his friends looked angry, as did those gathered around other tables. For the most part, though, the *Dowser*'s customers appeared resigned to the idea that Preston and his men would go free. Ethan wanted to scream at them. Instead, he returned to the kitchen to fetch more bread. Was he any more virtuous than the rest?

In time, the tavern cleared out. The three of them cleaned up and Kelf left for the night. Kannice locked the door and returned to the bar, where Ethan wiped down the wood.

"I'm going to have a little brandy," she said. "Would you like some?"

"Please."

She filled two small glasses and set one near where Ethan worked. She stood with hers on the other side of the bar, watching him.

"You're going to make me ask?" she said after a few seconds.

He stopped working, slung his polishing cloth over his shoulder, and sipped the brandy. The good stuff.

"I walked Adams to his home after the trial ended. I knew what the verdict would be. But on my way here, I was accosted by Charlotte Whitcomb." Her eyes widened in alarm, and he raised a hand to forestall her questions. "I'm fine. She didn't even try to harm me. She doesn't have to." He told her about the bounty, about Whitcomb's expectation that the reward and the wording of the message would bring an army of conjurers to Boston.

"A hundred pounds," Kannice said, sounding dumbfounded. "That seems excessive, doesn't it? For one man's life? I don't know that I've ever seen so much in one place."

"It's a treasure to us. For King George's exchequer it's nothing, one more expense in the ledger. Considering the value of the colonies and the peril they see in letting Adams continue his work here, I'm sure it makes sense to them."

"I've no doubt it does. Don't tell Tom Langer. He'll become a loyalist overnight."

They both smiled, but weakly, and only for an instant.

"Half that much would bring some awful men to Boston. The full hundred . . . Before long, every miscreant and villain in the colonies will be skulking through our streets. And speaking of," she went on, gesturing so forcefully that she slopped a few drops of brandy out of her glass, "expect Sephira Pryce to be first in line. Her and that conjurer of hers."

"Mariz. I was thinking of asking him for help."

Kannice eyed him as if he were insane. Maybe he was.

"Janna will help you. She always does. As for Mariz, I know he's a friend, but he still works for that woman. She'll have him on a short leash in this matter. Mark my words."

"I'm certain you're right. But I have to try anyway. Given what's coming, I can't stand alone."

"No, I don't suppose you can."

They sipped their brandy, both watching the fire. Ethan sensed that Kannice wanted to say more, but was holding back. And he didn't press her. Since all this latest intrigue began, with a visit from Samuel Adams a fortnight ago, and magickal assaults on Mister Paine and John Adams, Kannice had struggled to reconcile her wish that Ethan should be happy with her desire for him to put thieftaking in his past once and for all. It didn't help, he knew, that she had pushed him to involve himself in this matter in the first place. She had wanted him to work for the Sons of Liberty, for Samuel Adams in particular, and had made as much clear to him that first night. He assumed she now regretted having done so.

"Are you enjoying it?" she asked, her thoughts having wandered down the same path as his. She regarded him through her lashes. "I believe you are."

"'Enjoying' isn't the right word. I didn't enjoy seeing Deborah swept up into that cloud. I didn't enjoy being gutted by Charlotte Whitcomb's magickal knife or pounded by her other spells."

"Well, I would hope not."

He tried without success to conceal a small grin. "That said, I do find the intrigue of the lanes . . . invigorating."

She lifted an eyebrow. "Invigorating, is it?"

"A little bit, yes."

"You're mad." The tone was playful, but the words carried some conviction.

"In my defense, I know that I am."

"That's not a very good defense."

He sobered. "No, it's not. And I understand that you would rather I hated it and wanted nothing more to do with any of this. I promised when I married you that I would give up thieftaking."

"You tried to promise that. I didn't let you, not entirely. Besides, this isn't quite the same thing. You're not thieftaking, you're working for Samuel Adams. You're part of his cause, fighting for liberty. I can hardly fault you for that."

"So you don't mind?"

"Not so much that you can't make it up to me." She took his hand. "Why don't you finish your brandy, and then you can show me just how invigorating this new life of yours is."

"Or, we could bring the glasses and bottle up with us."

This proved to be one of his better ideas.

III

Ethan slept later than he planned and had to hobble at speed across the city in order to reach Samuel Adams' door at the appointed time. As it was, when he arrived, he had sweated through his shirt. His bad leg ached.

Seeing him in such a state, Adams asked after his health, sounding genuinely concerned.

"I slept too late, sir, and had to hurry here. I don't move as well as I once did."

"None of us do, Mister Kaille. None of us do."

They walked together toward the Court House, chatting about trifles, enjoying the morning. The previous day's rain had given way to blue skies and a brisk wind off the harbor. The air smelled of the sea, clean and bracing. It was almost easy to forget that assassins bore down on the city even now.

Ethan said nothing to Adams of his encounter with Charlotte Whitcomb. The man could do little to protect himself from those who would be coming for him. That was Ethan's task. Better to allow him to savor this morning before facing the harsh reality of Captain Preston's acquittal.

The throng on Queen Street outside the Court House was larger than

Monday's, but more subdued. Word of the expected verdict had spread through much of the city. Ethan doubted that any of those gathered here remained in suspense.

Shortly after Ethan and Adams arrived, Sheriff Greenleaf ascended the steps of the building, unlocked the door, and began admitting spectators. This time, he barely acknowledged either Ethan or Adams. He looked smug and pleased with himself, though what he'd had to do with today's result, Ethan couldn't say.

As they filed through the building to the stairway, Ethan heard someone calling to Mister Adams. Joseph Warren slipped through the crowd until he reached them, and the three of them proceeded to the second floor together.

As they had the day before, spectators filled the back section of the courtroom and waited as Preston, the attorneys, jurors, and judges took their places.

Justice Lynde asked the jury for its verdict. Not guilty. The reaction among those in attendance was muted. Moments later, the acting chief justice told Preston that he was free to go and gaveled the proceedings to an end. Ethan noticed that Francis Lamb hadn't bothered to attend this last formality. Perhaps he feared a more violent response from the spectators. More likely, he was confident enough in the outcome that he had set to work on his next scheme for subjugating the province.

Within minutes, they were leaving the courtroom again, shambling along with the others.

"Not so long ago, I was saying an acquittal didn't matter," Adams muttered. Ethan could barely hear him. Warren leaned closer. "I was ready to believe that Thomas Hutchinson feared an acquittal more than I did, that any verdict of value would condemn not Preston and his men, but King George himself." He glanced Ethan's way. "I believe I said as much to you, didn't I?"

"Aye, sir."

"Did you believe me?"

"I wanted to."

A faint smile fluttered across his face and was gone. "A good answer, that. Yes, I wanted to. We all did. The truth is, I feel as though I have been kicked in the head. I remember all you told me about that terrible night, about the malign influence of the conjurer you battled. And still, deep in my heart, I hoped for a conviction. It's not that I've changed my mind about the culpability of the king or Parliament. But the thought of Thomas

Preston walking free, of his soldiers facing no consequences . . ." He shook his head. "This is a dark day for Boston."

"We still have some recourse," Warren said. "I spoke of this with Robert last night. There are civil actions we might take against the captain. There is even something called 'appeal of felony,' which would allow—"

"I'm familiar with it," Adams said, sounding disgusted. "You can't really believe that a challenge of physical combat has any place in the laws of a civilized nation."

Warren shrugged, clearly abashed. "No, not really. Others were speaking of it at the *Dragon*. I thought I should mention it."

Adams shook his head. "We have no choice but to live with this disappointment and fight on. And I have to remind myself yet again that I was right in my original formulation. This is not Preston's crime, or that of his men. It was a crime of authority, of power, of the corruption buried deep in the soul of this empire. That is what we're fighting. That is what we shall defeat before long."

Ethan could think of no worthy reply. This, he understood, was what Whitcomb and her ilk feared: the simple eloquence and passion of this man. If someone managed to kill him in the next few days it would only be because they had already killed Ethan.

"Where will you go from here, sir?" Ethan asked as they exited the building onto Queen Street.

"The *Green Dragon*, I think. Joseph, will you join me?"

"I have patients to see today, but I'll walk you there. He'll be safe, Mister Kaille."

Maybe for today. "Thank you, sir. Mister Adams, I can come by to accompany you home later. When would be convenient for you?"

"Anytime at all. Let us say, in the afternoon. Three o'clock?"

"Perfect, sir. Thank you."

Ethan doffed his tricorn and left the two of them there. After a moment's pause, he started in the direction of Sephira Pryce's home on Summer Street. He would have preferred to delay, to visit with Janna and secure her help in guarding Adams from those who would soon be descending upon the city. He had every confidence, though, that she would stand with him, that together they would convince Amanda Oakroot to do the same. He was far less certain about Mariz, not only because he worked for the so-called Empress of the South End, who had long expressed loyalist sentiments, but also because he didn't know what the man himself thought of Adams, of the fight for liberty, of the Crown.

Ethan walked by the pasture, the sweet scent of hay and the lowing of cows a counterpoint to the sour mud of the flats and the rattle of carriage wheels on cobblestone.

Ethan would need to choose his words with care while in Sephira's home. He knew better than to think that she would leave him and Mariz to speak privately, and he doubted that even she, though canny and subtle of mind, would catch the hidden meanings of Charlotte Whitcomb's missive. As he neared the house, a grand marble structure with a pleasing garden and imposing portico, he spotted two of Sephira's toughs standing out front. He thought one must be Afton, a behemoth of a man with lank hair and a homely face. Or it could have been Gordon, who was just as big and no more attractive. The second man—smaller, wiry, dark-haired—was Nap. Aside from Mariz, Nap might have been Ethan's favorite among Sephira's men. Which was somewhat like having hives and choosing one pustule as the most dear.

Nap was as dangerous as his larger colleagues, but more clever and possessed of a sense of humor. He and Ethan despised each other—he could envision them fighting to the death at some point—but Ethan did respect the man, which counted for something.

Both toughs—the first *was* Afton—had spotted him by now. Ethan raised a hand in greeting. Neither responded in kind. The last time he had spoken with Nap, Sephira's man had made clear that he resented Ethan's overtures to his benefactress. He thought Ethan attempted to take advantage of her willingness to help him at times, while otherwise showing her nothing but disrespect. No doubt he saw Ethan's arrival this morning as further evidence of his self-interest.

Ethan followed the stone pathway to the stairs leading to the portico, but halted there.

"Is she in?"

Nap had been leaning insouciantly against a column. He straightened now. "Are you looking for Miss Pryce, or Mariz?"

"I suppose eventually I'd like to speak with both of them. But of course I'll seek Sephira's permission first."

"I'll see if Miss Pryce is receiving visitors."

Nap entered the house, leaving Ethan and Afton to eye each other.

A gust of wind rustled the bare branches of nearby trees, and a flock of crows soared overhead.

The door opened again and Nap waved him inside. "This way."

He spoke with such venom, Ethan faltered before following.

The tough led Ethan through the foyer and common room into the dining room, where Sephira, in her usual raiment—silk shirt, black breeches, and a snug, embroidered waistcoat—sat drinking tea and reading what had to be the previous week's issue of the *Evening Post*, the leading Tory paper in the city. Her hair was piled atop her head in silken black coils, a few stray curls twisting along the side of her neck.

She glanced up as he entered, blue eyes meeting his ever so briefly. She shifted her gaze to Nap, dismissed him with a flick of her eyes. After he left, she turned her attention back to the paper.

"I'm glad you're here, Ethan. You've saved me from having to read this nonsense for a third time." She smiled. "There: You've only just arrived and already I've paid you a compliment. You're more interesting than last week's news."

"I'm flattered."

A servant entered.

"Tea?" Sephira asked. "Eggs? Toast and Jam?"

"Just tea, thank you."

She gestured to the servant, who returned to the kitchen. Sephira motioned a second time, this time at the chair adjacent to hers. Ethan sat.

"I take it you've come from the Court House."

"Aye."

"It's over, then?"

"Acquittal."

"Naturally."

She was baiting him, he knew. He refused to engage her on the merits of the charges, or the guilt or innocence of Thomas Preston.

"I've come—"

"I know why you've come."

He stared, wondering how much to give away, how much to trust in this assertion. "Do you?"

"One hundred pounds is a considerable sum, even for me. And I can't imagine you like the idea of assassins descending on our city to kill one of our own luminaries. I don't like it either."

He sat back. Before he could answer, the servant returned with a cup and teapot. He thanked her, watched her leave the room.

"So you've seen the missive Miss Whitcomb sent." At Sephira's nod, he asked, "And did you share it with your men?"

"I did. Mariz seems to believe that her invitation was meant for more than just common thugs and cutthroats. He tells me there was a message embedded in her wording—something about magick and the fact that the successful assassin would have to get past . . . well, you."

Perhaps this conversation would prove easier than he had anticipated.

"I read it the same way."

"I assume, then, that you would like to dragoon Mariz into helping you. Again."

"With your permission, of course."

In that moment, her mien—smug, entertained, but also displeased—reminded him of Charlotte Whitcomb. They really were so much alike.

"Nap says you take advantage of me."

"Aye, he's told me as much. I've reminded him of the beatings, the times I've worked on your behalf to resolve inquiries involving conjurers, the coin you've taken from me. I gather he doesn't care about any of that."

"It's not that he doesn't care, but rather that he believes you provoke me, and have since the day you declared yourself my rival."

Ethan said nothing, but held her gaze. This conversation could only take them onto dangerous ground.

"I will summon Mariz," she said, with indulgence, "but I want to be very clear about one thing, Ethan. My objection is to the invitation itself. I don't want miscreants entering my city to engage in this sort of mischief. And I don't want that one hundred pounds going to outsiders. You and Mariz shall keep any conjurers who come here from doing harm. In the end, though, I intend to make that one hundred pounds mine."

"What?"

She sipped her tea, eyeing him over the rim of her cup as she did. "As I said, that's a lot of money, even for me. Too much to turn down. And as you have been so fond of pointing out, I am no friend of 'liberty' or Samuel Adams. As far as I am concerned, he is an agitator. Nothing more or less. Boston would be better off without him."

"I'm sworn to protect him."

"Yes, I know. You and I are rivals in this, as in all things. Our interests dovetail to a point, but then they diverge. To be honest, I welcome the competition. I've missed you. Thieftaking is so much more entertaining when I have you to best. And while this is not exactly thieftaking, it's close enough."

"So I'm to work with Mariz until he chooses to put a knife in my back?"

"You're the one who wants his help. You know he works for me, and yet you 'borrow' him repeatedly. Is it any wonder that Nap mistrusts you?"

She ran a finger absently over the embroidery of her table cloth. "Mariz is like any creature of the lanes. You can trust him until you can't anymore. It's up to you to figure out when that inflection point arrives. Or you can leave now, without speaking with him, without accepting his aid. You'll still have to face him eventually, but you won't have to worry about judging his motives. He'll be an enemy from the start."

She watched him, expectant.

Ethan considered his options. He preferred to work with Mariz if he could, but he didn't relish the prospect of having to watch over his shoulder whenever they were together. Then again, he had faith in the strength of his friendship with the conjurer. Kannice would have told him he placed too much faith in it.

"I would like his help," he said at last.

"Of course you would. A word of caution, Ethan: You and Mariz have formed a bond. I understand that. But I pay the man, and he understands that he lives by my forbearance. His loyalty will always be to me."

"I appreciate the warning."

"Good. It's nice to have you back in the game. May the best woman win."

Nap appeared in the entryway to the dining room. "Mister Lamb is here, Miss Pryce."

Ethan sent a sharp glance her way. When last they conversed, Sephira had spoken of her relationship with Francis Lamb as being over, and a disappointment to her.

She regarded him, her expression sly. "Thank you, Nap. Show him in please. And fetch Mariz for Ethan. They need to speak, witch to witch."

Nap smirked, left them.

"You'll have to excuse me now," Sephira said. "I have a prior engagement."

"I thought you and Lamb had parted ways after a misunderstanding."

"You sound jealous."

He kept silent.

"He and I have much in common. With the trial reaching such a satisfactory conclusion, and non-importation failing throughout the colonies, I find that our interests have converged again. It's possible I was too quick to speak of misunderstandings." She smiled as Lamb sauntered into the room. "But don't worry, Ethan. You're still my favorite enemy."

Ethan could only laugh. He stood and inclined his head slightly in Lamb's direction. "Mister Lamb."

"Mister Kaille. I hope I'm not interrupting."

"Not at all. Miss Pryce and I have concluded our business. I need only to speak with one of her associates."

"He's waiting for you outside," Nap said.

"In that case, Sephira, thank you for your hospitality."

He left them, walking with Nap through the house to the front door.

"You prefer Lamb to me?" Ethan asked under his breath.

"No, I don't. Lamb is a pig. I'd just as soon have both of you banned from the house. But I don't have that sort of power."

He opened the door and motioned Ethan out.

Mariz awaited him on the portico. Afton hovered close by.

"Let us walk, Kaille," the conjurer said, his Portuguese accent shading the words.

They set off down the path to Summer Street and turned westward toward the Common.

Mariz chewed on a pipe as they walked, emitting billows of fragrant smoke from time to time.

"You know why I asked to speak with you?"

"I assume it is because of the notice sent through the colonies of an opportunity for assassins. Magickal ones."

"That's right."

"You will have spoken with the *senhora* of this, so I will not bother to warn you of the obvious."

"You mean, that you'll turn on me eventually so that you can kill Adams yourself?"

Mariz shook his head, issued another cloud of smoke. "I have no interest in killing Samuel Adams. And if I were to, I believe Nap or one of the others would slit my throat."

Ethan gaped.

"You cannot be as surprised as you look, my friend. I have told you before that they are suspicious of me. I am a foreigner. I am a conjurer. And I am willing to work with you, which adds to their doubts about me."

"I'm sorry."

He dismissed the apology with a flick of his hand. "I have also told you before that I value our friendship. Your apology is unnecessary. I meant only to explain why I will not kill Adams myself. The *senhora* has promised extra coin to the man who succeeds in this. She will claim much of the one hundred pounds for herself. But each man in her employ will get a share if one of us kills the man, and the man who actually does this will receive the most of all. The others would not be pleased if I was that man."

"But that doesn't mean you'll help me keep Adams alive."

They had entered the Common, and Mariz paused now to knock his pipe against a tree trunk, eliminating the ash. He pocketed it and they walked on.

"As with all matters concerning you and the *senhora*, there is no easy answer to this. I will help you protect Adams from outsiders. But when Nap or Afton or Gordon or one of the others makes his attempt on the man's life, you will be on your own. You will have no help from me. None. You are my friend, but she pays me, and I have seen enough, done enough, that I do not believe she can afford to release me from her service. She will kill me first."

Ethan had no reply. They walked for a time in silence, neither of them in any apparent hurry to end their conversation.

"What do you think of Adams?" Ethan asked eventually.

Mariz lifted a shoulder. "He is an interesting figure, for the colonies. Europe is filled with men like him, and many who are far more visionary. But for this place, I suppose he is bold."

"You don't hate him as Sephira does."

"I do not believe she hates him. As usual, Kaille, your hostility toward the *senhora* leads you to exaggerate her flaws. She sees Adams as inconvenient, as disruptive. She has a business, one she values above all else." He glanced Ethan's way. "I will not debate with you the legitimacy of her priorities. At least not today. I merely point out that she sees Adams as an impediment to her advancement rather than as an object of hatred. And no one knows better than you how ruthless she can be in removing such impediments."

They left the common, starting back down West Street toward the South End. As usual, Ethan couldn't fault Mariz's reasoning.

"Very well," he said. "So how do we keep other conjurers from entering the city?"

"I do not know. I would suggest that more will arrive by ship than by road, but I could be wrong."

"No, I don't believe you are. I'm prepared to keep watch on the wharves, but even with Janna's help in that regard, we can't keep out everyone who attempts to enter the city."

"I agree. A spell then—something that will alert us to the arrival of any who possess magick."

"Aye, that would be best. I don't know the wording."

"Nor do I," Mariz said. "Perhaps Miss Windcatcher will?"

Ethan felt certain she would.

As they navigated back to Sephira's house, his thoughts returned to the dilemma Mariz faced—a dilemma for both of them.

"I know better than to think you can warn me of steps Nap and the others have taken or intend to take," Ethan said. "But I'm relieved to know I won't have to fight you."

Mariz stopped, eyeing Ethan and shaking his head slowly. "I am afraid you have misunderstood, my friend. You may have to fight me. When I said that you would have no help from me when combatting Nap and Afton and the others, I should have been clearer. They will expect me to keep you . . . occupied. They may well demand that I attack you with magick so that you are unable to defend Adams. And the *senhora* will demand this as well. We are both allies and adversaries in this fight. And I will not be able to tell you where the boundary lies. It is even possible that in my capacity as your friend—no matter how well-meaning I may be—I will be acting at the behest of the *senhora*. I am sad to say that, with regard to this matter of Adams, you can never trust me fully. *Never.*"

Something in the tone of his voice . . . Ethan narrowed his eyes. Mariz stared back at him, his features pinching in the slightest wince.

"Damn!"

Ethan whirled away from him, limping at speed back toward Cornhill. After a few steps, he broke into an awkward run. He feared that he was too late, that before the first outsider reached the city he had allowed Adams to be killed.

IV

As Ethan approached Hanover Street, he slipped into a byway, cut himself, and cast a concealment spell. The spell echoed in the stone of the lane and brought with it the glowing form of Uncle Reg, ghostly pale in the late morning light. In days to come, he would need to be wary of casting in this way. Other conjurers would sense his magick. Today, though, he cared only about Sephira's men, and he had left their lone speller back by Rowe's Field.

Once the concealment spell had rendered him unseeable, he continued onto Hanover in the direction of Union Street. He doubted that Nap and the others would be so daring as to enter the *Green Dragon* tavern itself. In which case, they would lie in wait for Adams on the street and make their attempt on his life when he was in the open and most vulnerable.

He also assumed that their assault would be insidious. Sephira's toughs were known in Boston. Her status as a Boston luminary—Empress of the South End—brought them some small renown, too.

A carriage accident, then. Two of them, maybe headed in opposite directions. Something unforeseeable and blameless.

Near the corner of Cold Lane, he caught sight of Nap. In a chaise, as he had thought. Ethan would have bet money that one of the giants—Afton or Gordon—waited somewhere along the same thoroughfare, also in a vehicle. The incident would have to be coordinated with precision, but he didn't doubt that Sephira's men had the requisite skills and malevolence to make it work.

He didn't yet bother searching out the other carriage. He would begin by doing what was necessary to Nap's. First, though, he continued on to the tavern itself.

The *Green Dragon* stood on the west side of Union Street, an unremarkable two story brick building with a steep roof. Its only notable feature—from which it derived its name—was the cast-iron dragon perched above its main entrance, its wings raised, its mouth open in a roar, a tongue of fire twisting from the maw. The ground floor and second level of the building were owned by the Freemasons. The tavern itself, which for years had been a favored gathering place of the Sons of Liberty, occupied the cellar.

Walking with care so that his steps wouldn't be heard, Ethan took a position beside the doorway. There he waited until he was alone on the lane. Only then did he enter the building and descend the stairway to the tavern.

So early in the day, the tavern was mostly empty. A few drank at the bar, and one trio of gentlemen sat around a table by the hearth. The door to the back room stood ajar, and low conversation emanated from that chamber. Ethan crossed to the door, unseen, his steps covered by noise from the men around him.

Peering into the chamber, he spotted Adams sitting with a number of men. Doctor Benjamin Church, lanky, with deep-set eyes and a strong nose, sat to Adams' left, and Josiah Quincy, youthful, his eyes slightly crossed, had taken the chair across from Adams. The other men seated with him Ethan did not recognize.

What mattered, was that Adams was alive and, for the moment, safely surrounded by allies.

Ethan saw no way to enter the back chamber without drawing attention to himself. Instead, he returned to the street and crept toward Nap's chaise.

Sephira's man still sat atop the box, appearing bored and idle, as might the driver for a rich patron. Ethan could see, though, that he remained watchful. For all Ethan knew, Nap anticipated his arrival and interference.

Easing closer to the vehicle, Ethan drew his knife and dragged it over his forearm

"*Incide ex cruore evocatum*," he whispered. Slice conjured from blood. He directed his magick at the bellyband of the lone horse.

He saw the leather shift, watched Nap for any indication that he had noticed. But Sephira's tough kept his attention on the lanes. Ethan dragged the knife across his forearm and cast the spell a second time, aiming it this time at the horse's leather collar.

The animal stirred at the rumble of the spell, tossing its head and nickering.

Nap eyed the horse. Ethan held his breath. Once more, he could see where the leather had separated. After a few seconds, Nap went back to scanning Hanover Street. Satisfied that he had done enough to disrupt Nap's part of the scheme, Ethan turned and walked eastward.

He spotted the second vehicle after crossing the Mill Creek into the North End, as he approached Back Street. Gordon sat on the box of one of Sephira's full carriages.

Ethan watched him, trying to decide what magick to use in this case. He assumed Nap would figure out quickly enough who had sabotaged his chaise, but still, just in case he didn't, Ethan thought it unwise to use the same conjuring here. As he pondered his options, another carriage clattered in their direction, coming from the west as Ethan had, bearing down on Gordon's vehicle.

Ethan cut himself, waited until this carriage was even with Gordon's, and cast when the noise from the horses and wheels would be at its worst for Sephira's tough.

"*Frange ex cruore evocatum.*" A breaking spell, aimed at the rim of one of the rear wheels. It wouldn't be immediately noticeable, as a shatter spell would have been, but it would weaken the wood enough to stop the carriage as soon as Gordon tried to move.

The brute didn't react to the spell at all, and neither did his horses. Pleased with himself, Ethan headed back toward the *Green Dragon*, scanning shadowed alleys and minor lanes until he caught sight of the third man, Afton, hidden between two buildings not far from the *Dragon*.

He would provide the signal for the others, letting them know how to time their attack on Adams.

Believing he understood what Sephira's toughs had in mind, Ethan returned to the Freemason building and waited at the bottom of the stairway.

After perhaps a half an hour, the door to the rear room opened, and Adams emerged, flanked by Quincy and Doctor Church. Adams pulled on a red woolen cape. Quincy and Church also donned capes, both dark blue, and all three men put on tricorns.

Ethan ascended the stairs about halfway, aware that his concealment spell remained in place and that none could see him.

The three men started up the stairs, Church in the lead, Adams between his two friends. It seemed all the Sons of Liberty were taking to heart the threats against their leader.

"Gentlemen," Ethan said, pitching his voice so that his words reached only them.

Church halted, his gaze flitting wildly up and down the stairway, alarm robbing his cheeks of color.

"Who's there?"

"A friend, doctor. You have my word."

"Mister Kaille?" Adams said, searching the staircase as Church had. "Is that you?"

"It is, sir. Forgive me for startling you. I have my reasons for keeping myself concealed. I believe there was to be an attempt on Mister Adams' life this very day, only a short distance from here, on Hanover Street. I now believe it is safe for you to leave the *Dragon*, but I will be accompanying you in my present state, just to be sure."

Young Mister Quincy grinned up in Ethan's direction. "I must say, Mister Kaille, each time I meet you something rather exciting happens. I am beginning to think having a conjurer about could be quite entertaining."

"I'm not really interested in being entertained," Church said. "Not with magick or assassins or invisible men. Forgive me, Mister Kaille."

"I quite understand, sir." Ethan climbed the steps. "If you'll continue to the street, gentlemen, and follow the usual route to Mister Adams' home, I believe we should be fine."

Church's consternation appeared to deepen. Quincy flashed another smile. And Adams, seeming unaffected, led them after Ethan—or at least the sound of his footsteps—up the stairs and onto Union Street.

As soon as the three Sons of Liberty emerged from the building, Afton left his place of concealment and hurried down to the corner of Hanover and Union Streets. Ethan lost sight of him there, but he assumed that the man alerted his colleagues to Adams' approach.

Ethan sidled closer to Benjamin Church.

"Doctor." The man started and huffed a breath.

"Is this really necessary, Mister Kaille?"

"I believe it is, sir. Please listen carefully. I would like you to stay close to Messieurs Adams and Quincy. I would like the three of you to reach Hanover Street together. When you do, I want you to keep to this side of the thoroughfare. Do not attempt to cross until I tell you it's safe. Do you understand?"

"Not really," the man said, his tone sour. "But I will do as you ask."

"Thank you, sir."

On they walked. Ethan kept a few paces ahead of them, and so reached Hanover Street first.

Afton had managed to catch the attention of both Nap and Gordon. They were intent upon him, both having taken up the reins of their carriages, both awaiting a signal. Afton glanced back at Adams, Quincy, and Church, who were only a few paces short of the corner.

When they were no more than five paces away, Afton removed his hat and then scuttled away. The signal.

Nap snapped the reins and the mount ahead of him surged forward. The collar and bellyband gave way, of course, and the horse pulled free of the chaise. But not of the reins, to which Nap held tight. The vehicle didn't budge. Nap was pulled from the box. He flopped onto the street and was smart enough to release the reins before the horse could drag him far. He pushed himself to his knees, a frightful expression on his face. People around him pointed and laughed. The horse halted perhaps twenty yards away.

Ethan turned in time to see the rear wheel of Gordon's carriage collapse into a heap of broken wood. The carriage tipped back to the right, nearly unseating Sephira's man. The horses strained against their harnesses, but appeared none the worse for the ordeal.

"You can go ahead, sir," Ethan said to Church. "Take Mister Adams home. Quickly, please."

The men started away.

"I know you're here, Kaille!" Nap shouted, looking around.

Adams faltered mid-step.

"Please keep moving, sir," Ethan said quietly. "Act as though you're paying no attention, as though you don't recognize my name."

To his credit, Adams recovered immediately, gave an almost imperceptible nod, and walked on, chin raised.

Sephira's men made no attempt to follow. Both were too concerned with the state of their vehicles. Nap still swept the street with his gaze, no doubt searching for Ethan.

For his part, Ethan resisted the urge to taunt the man, instead taking the opportunity to steal away, back to the *Dowsing Rod*. Before he reached the tavern, he veered into a byway and removed his concealment spell.

He entered the *Dowser* through the rear door, finding Kelf in the kitchen.

"Ethan! Didn't expect to see you here so early."

"I don't imagine. Do me a favor, Kelf: If anyone asks, I've been here for hours—most of the morning and through early afternoon."

Before the barman could answer, Kannice walked in. Seeing him, she stopped, quirked a smile.

"I was just telling, Kelf: As far as the rest of the world is concerned, I've been here since before midday, fixing a few items in the kitchen."

She sobered. "I see. And where have you really been?"

"Making mischief on Hanover Street, and saving Samuel Adams' life."

"Well," Kelf said, "boring as that sounds, I can see where you'd want people to think you was here." He left the kitchen muttering to himself and shaking his head.

Kannice stared after him, only facing Ethan again when he was gone. "Are you in danger?"

"Sephira's men will be angry, but no, I don't think I'm in any real danger. I just prefer to keep them off balance."

She had no time to respond. Voices echoed loudly from the great room. Someone said, "Where is he?" And then, "Kaille!"

"No danger, eh?"

"I suppose I could be wrong about that."

He unsheathed his knife, pushed up his sleeve, and stepped out of the kitchen to the bar. Kannice followed. He would have liked to tell her to remain in the kitchen, but he knew she wouldn't listen.

Nap, Afton, and Gordon stood just inside the door. Nap's breeches were torn at the knee, exposing a bloody scrape. Ethan hoped it hurt.

"What can I do for you?" Ethan asked, stepping out from behind the bar.

Kelf had positioned himself near Afton. The two men eyed each other, one taking the measure of the other. Kelf was as big as Sephira's man, and though Ethan had never seen him fight, he assumed the barman knew how to defend himself. Still, Afton was a killer. They all were.

Nap still glared at Ethan. He held a pistol loosely in his right hand. He hadn't raised it, yet, but it was full-cocked.

"You should put that away, Nap," Ethan said, indicating the weapon with a lift of his chin. "You don't want to get hurt."

"I'm already hurt. And I think you're responsible. For what happened to me *and* what happened to Gordon."

"And what would that be?"

He raised his pistol hand, leveling the barrel of his weapon at Ethan's heart. "I swear to God, Kaille."

Ethan cast without pause—a fire spell, fueled by the blood from Nap's knee. The pistol butt burst into flame. Nap cried out and dropped the weapon. It bounced without discharging, settled at Ethan's feet. He kicked it away and at the same time cut his forearm. Blood welled from the wound. Kannice made a small sound behind him, but said not a word.

"That was the blood from your scrape. Imagine what I can do with the blood on my arm. You'd be a torch before you could take more than a step toward me."

Nap's glower dipped to Ethan's arm, then found his eyes again.

"One day, you won't have your blade, you won't have your friends, and you won't see me coming. And that's the day I'll repay you for what you cost us this afternoon." He glanced at the other two toughs. "Come on."

"You might want to consider, Nap, that with conjurers descending on Boston from every direction, it's not safe for the non-magickal to be plotting against Samuel Adams."

"And how did you know we were doing that?"

"A fortunate guess. Nothing like a one hundred pound bounty to give men purpose."

The toughs strode toward the door.

Ethan spoke Nap's name, stopping them. He used a bar rag to smother the flames on the man's pistol. Then he lifted the weapon, the cloth rapped around the charred butt, shook out the powder and bullet and tossed it to Nap. Sephira's man caught it against his chest. He sent one more filthy look Ethan's way and led the others out of the building.

"I was wrong," Kelf said, eyeing the door. "This place isn't so boring after all."

V

Ethan waited an hour before leaving the tavern. He didn't bother to conceal himself, but he carried two blades and he summoned Uncle Reg so that the specter walked with him, as watchful as Ethan, ready at a moment's notice to help him conjure.

They walked out past the pastures and Sephira's home on Summer Street, to the Neck and Janna's dilapidated tavern, the *Fat Spider*.

Janna greeted Ethan with her usual iciness, even after he bought an ale and some food. She warmed, though, when he explained why he had come. Janna liked Samuel Adams. So did Amanda Oakroot, the witch Ethan had met through Janna. As he told Janna, he would need help from them both to keep the man safe.

"I can cast a warnin' spell," Janna told Ethan when he asked, her voice low, her sharp gaze on the four patrons eating in the glow of her hearth. "You'll want one on the waterfront and another on the gate."

"And that will allow you to sense when conjurers enter the city?"

She grinned. "Everyone will sense it. It'll set off a caterwaul that people'll hear from the Neck to the North End, from the wharves to Beacon Hill. I can't keep them out, but we'll know when they arrive and where they enter the city."

"I like that idea," he said. "Do you think Amanda can do something similar to guard against witches?"

"I'd guess so. You'll have to ask her."

Of course. "Aye. That's where I'm headed next."

Her eyes widened. "You're walking to Milton and back today? This late?"

"I don't see that I have a choice."

"All right, then. I'll set my spells as soon as I can. They'll scream like the devil when you come back into the city, but there's nothin' to be done about that."

"Thank you, Janna."

He stood, reclaimed his hat from the table, and turned away.

"Kaille."

He stopped, regarded her.

"This can't go on. Not for you, not for me, not for Amanda. This woman, Whitcomb—you have to put an end to this. To her, if necessary. I know you don't like that sort o' thing, but this is too much. You hear me? Finish it."

He faltered, dipped his chin, and left her.

Ethan exited the city by way of the Town Gate at the end of the Neck, crossing the Roxbury Flats on the causeway. An eagle circled over the brackish water, wings splayed, white head and tail shining in the afternoon sun.

The walk to Milton would take the balance of the day. He wouldn't be back in the city until well after evening's fall. But this journey couldn't wait. He didn't know how many witches were on their way to Boston. Probably only a few. Even one, though, could be enough to cost Adams his life. Ethan's powers, while formidable against any conjurer, would have no effect against a witch. He needed Amanda's help. Kannice might have wanted him to hire a carriage for this journey. She certainly wouldn't have begrudged the expense to save him such a long walk. But he didn't want to draw attention to his errand, or to Amanda's home, by arriving there in a chaise. He expected Amanda would feel the same.

As he walked the Lower Road toward Dorchester, Ethan considered Janna's parting words. Less than two weeks had passed since he first clashed with Charlotte Whitcomb, although it felt to him like their feud had consumed months of his life. She had nearly killed him more than once. She had imprisoned Diver's love, Deborah Crane, in a cloud that hovered high above Boston Harbor. She had done her best to harass and intimidate the attorneys arguing before the Provincial Court in the matter of Thomas Preston and the March shootings. She had subjected Boston to a storm of rain and wind and surf that killed more than one hundred men, women, and children. And now she placed the entire city in peril yet again.

Janna was right: Ethan almost never sought to kill those he opposed. He had wanted Nate Ramsey dead by the end, and his encounters with others had ended similarly. But more often than not, if there was any way at all he could spare a life, that was what he did.

Did Charlotte Whitcomb deserve his mercy?

His immediate impulse was to say that she did not. But it was one thing to think this, and entirely another to take her life. He had killed in war, he had killed in personal combat, he had killed with firearms, with blades, with magick. And every death he caused took a toll. He hated and feared Ramsey more than he had any man before or since, and yet even that killing haunted him, justified though it had been. The truth was, he couldn't imagine taking Whitcomb's life, and he would have been ashamed to admit why to Janna. He had never taken the life of a woman, and he couldn't bring himself to start now.

He was still contemplating this as he turned off the main road onto the narrow country track that led to Amanda Oakroot's house. His leg ached, and he dreaded the walk back to Boston.

The last time he had come to speak with the earth witch—also the first time—he had warded himself as he walked down this road, inadvertently alerting her to his approach. He no longer felt the need to protect himself in that way, but he didn't wish to surprise her.

As he walked, he plucked from a low branch a few stubborn maple leaves, their autumn color well past its brightest. Using the leaves, he called Uncle Reg to his side, the summons humming in the earth as any spell would.

A few moments later, as he came within sight of her small house, she stood on the top step of the low stairway leading to her door, hands on her hips, the afternoon breeze stirring her white hair.

"You've come a long way. Again."

"Aye, that I have."

"Did you bring me another flask of wine?"

Ethan's gait faltered at this. He should have, he knew. In his hurry to see her, he had forgotten.

She frowned. "I'll take that as a no."

"I forgot. I'm sorry."

Amanda shrugged. "You're here now. Might as well come in." She stepped back into the house, leaving the door open.

Ethan entered behind her and shut the door. The house was warm within, and as tidy as he remembered from his first visit. It smelled of wood smoke and a sweet burning herb he couldn't name.

"What's Whitcomb done now?" Amanda asked. She poured water into a kettle and set it on her iron stove. "I assume you want tea."

"Thank you, yes." Ethan rubbed his hands together and held them above the stove. "To answer your question, she has placed a one hundred pound bounty on the head of Samuel Adams and invited every assassin in the colonies—magickal and non-magickal—to come claim it."

Amanda had retrieved two cups and saucers from a shelf and set them on her table. At this, though, she turned to look his way. "That I hadn't expected."

"Janna will help me with the conjurers who come seeking that reward, but we're helpless against witches. And I know you like Samuel Adams."

"I do. So you want me to return to Boston tonight?"

"Whenever you can. Sooner would be better."

"And this time, when you fight Whitcomb, will you finish her?"

Ethan narrowed his gaze. "Have you been talking to Janna?"

She crossed to her larder, where she took a tea box from a shelf and spooned leaves into each cup.

"Amanda?"

She sighed. "It's possible she sent an image of herself here and told me you were coming."

"So, you knew what Whitcomb had done."

Amanda rounded on him. "Look, I'm willing to help you, even though it means leaving my home for a city I don't like very much. But you need to answer Janna's question. We can't keep fighting this woman. I can't leave home every time she finds a new way to threaten Adams and the Sons of Liberty. She wouldn't hesitate to kill Adams, or Warren, or, for that matter, you or me or Janna. She very nearly killed your friend's betrothed—I still can't say how I managed to keep her alive. The point is, she doesn't deserve your mercy."

"It has nothing to do with mercy," Ethan said. "You and Janna seem to think that I'm protecting her life. I'm not. I'm protecting myself from killing."

She started to reply, but appeared to think better of whatever she had intended to say. In the end, she merely shook her head. For several minutes, neither of them spoke. When the kettle steamed, she poured water into each of the cups. She carried them to her small table and sat, waving Ethan over. He joined her, stirring his tea absently, still silent.

"You've killed before," she said at length, eyes on her cup.

"Too many times. I was in the English navy before I was a prisoner, during the War of the Austrian Succession. And I've faced my share of enemies in the years since."

Amanda sipped her tea, but seemed at a loss for words. Ethan drank from his cup. Mostly, though, he was impatient to strike out for Boston, to be home with Kannice.

He stood, reached for his hat. "I'll consider what you've said. You and Janna both."

She nodded.

"But if I can find some other way, I will."

"All right," she said. "I'll come to the city tomorrow and set a protective hedge at all the entry points. You won't have to fight any witches. At least not aside from Whitcomb herself."

"Thank you." He walked to the door, but halted there and faced her. "You know, I could have reached out to you with magick the way Janna did. I didn't have to walk this far."

"Then why did you?"

"Because I'm asking you to make the journey to Boston, and I thought that if I was going to make such a request of you, I should be willing to demand the same of myself."

"Some would call that a waste," she said. "Of time, of energy."

He opened a hand, acknowledging this. "I know. But that's the way I am. I can't help myself, and at this point in my life, I can't change. I'm not sure I would want to if I could."

Ethan opened the door, put on his hat.

"Kaille."

He checked himself, faced her.

"I said *some* would call that a waste. I'm not one of them. Thank you for walking all this way. I'll see you soon."

They shared a smile and Ethan let himself out of the house.

VI

Night fell long before he reached the Roxbury Flats. His leg throbbed, and he was famished. His journey home, however, gave him time to ponder further Janna's demand. He would have preferred simply to drive Whitcomb from Boston and the province, but that only made her someone else's problem. She would continue to foment trouble, to attack patriots and undermine the cause of liberty. He needed to rob her of her influence and, if possible, her power. Failing that, as Janna insisted, he would have to kill her.

That led him to Francis Lamb. Naturally, the customs man would not tolerate Ethan harming her, even if she was only his half-sister and even if she brought her fate on herself. Defeating one of them meant defeating both, which struck Ethan as both a problem and an opportunity.

As Ethan passed through the Town Gate at the north end of the Roxbury Causeway, an unearthly wail pierced the night, seeming to rise from the very ground on which Ethan walked.

The watchman at the gate started violently.

"What in God's name is that?"

"Wolves, I think," Ethan said, walking away.

"Wolves? In the city?"

"Or catamounts."

"Catamounts?" the man called after him. "You think they're in Boston itself?"

"It's possible." He kept his face forward so the man wouldn't see how amused he was, and he silently thanked Janna for the spell she had cast. He assumed she had extended her wardings to the waterfront.

The *Dowsing Rod* was still crowded when he arrived there. Kannice greeted him at the bar with a kiss and a bowl of fish chowder. Kelf filled a tankard with the Kent pale that Ethan preferred.

Ethan offered to get to work, but Kannice assured him that she and Kelf had matters well in hand. "It's not been so crowded tonight. Where were you?"

"Milton."

"You walked to Milton? Again?"

"I had my reasons."

"How's your leg?"

"About as you'd expect."

She scowled.

The door to the tavern opened, and a young man with a musket stepped inside. "The sheriff says there's wolves in the city. A pack of them. He's organizing a hunt. Two shillings per head to those that fire a killing shot. We're meeting at the King's Chapel Burying Ground in a quarter hour."

He left and conversations erupted all around the tavern. Before long, at least twenty men had exited the tavern.

Ethan shook his head as he watched them go.

"What's the matter with you?" Kelf asked. "Wolves are no trifle, you know."

"There are no wolves," Ethan said. "They're chasing noise and nothing more. But if they're not careful, some poor dog is going to be shot tonight."

"How do you know there's no wolves?"

Ethan cast a look around the tavern at the crowd that remained. "I'll explain later."

He finished eating and set to work on the platters and tableware in the kitchen that needed cleaning. When all was done, and Kelf had left for the night, Ethan and Kannice retired to their room. Ethan was sore and exhausted. Within seconds of lying down, he was nearly asleep.

"What was that about wolves?" Kannice asked, undressing in the light of a single candle.

Ethan told her of Janna's spell and explained why he had gone to see Amanda Oakroot. He also told her about his conversation with Mariz earlier in the day. Weary as he was, his words seemed to come from a great distance, and he wasn't entirely certain how clear he made himself.

Kannice kissed his brow and he woke slightly.

"Did any of what I said make sense?"

"Some. You can tell me again in the morning."

She blew out the candle and Ethan fell into a deep slumber.

He woke some time later—it was still dark—to a yowl similar to the one he'd heard on the Neck. He thought this one came from the waterfront, and for some minutes he lay in bed, wide awake, his heart pounding.

A conjurer had entered the city. At least one. And this, he knew, was but the beginning. He closed his eyes again, skeptical of his ability to fall back asleep. Somehow he did, only to be awakened by yet another magickal shriek. This one came early in the morning—daylight shone around the edges of their window.

He glanced at Kannice and found her awake and watching him.

"I suppose that wasn't a wolf, either."

"Good morning." At her raised eyebrow, he said, "No, that wasn't a wolf. Or a catamount. Or a ghost. It was Janna's spell. Another conjurer has entered the city."

Ethan swung himself out of bed and reached for his clothes.

"Well, in that case, I think I know what you're doing today."

He had been buttoning his shirt, but he paused now. "Do you need me here?"

"No," she said with some regret. "Are you going to be fighting these conjurers?"

"Honestly, Kannice, I don't know. I hope not. But they paid to get here, and they came hoping to earn a hundred pounds. I don't expect persuading them to leave Boston of their own volition will be easy."

She thinned her lips, looking away.

"I'm sorry," he said. "I'm just . . . There's not much I can say that's going to make you happy about this. These conjurers are descending on the city, all of them hoping to kill Samuel Adams. Someone has to do something about that."

"Maybe they'll do you a favor and attack one another."

He faltered again, this time while reaching for his boots. For several moments all he could do was stare at her.

"Ethan?"

"That's precisely what they'll do," he said. "You're brilliant."

She grinned. "Am I?"

"Well, you're smarter than I am."

She answered with a mock frown. "That is hardly the same thing."

Ethan sat on the bed again and pulled on a boot. "You're right: They will attack one another. Each wants to be the successful assassin, which means all of them will be in a rush to reach Adams and kill him quickly. But it may also mean that each will do all he can to stop the others. That may be our one advantage."

"'Our advantage,'" Kannice repeated. "Do you expect Mariz will help you?"

He shook his head. "I was thinking of Janna. I'm not sure I want Mariz's help. I can't trust him in this. Even yesterday, as he was warning me not to rely too much on his good faith, he was distracting me so that his friends could try to ambush Adams."

Ethan finished dressing, leaned over to kiss her brow, and crossed to the door.

"Show your face every now and then today," she said, her voice falsely bright. "Just to let me know you're alive."

"Aye, I'll do that."

He left her, let himself out of the tavern, and hurried to Purchase Street and the Adams estate. It was another cool, crisp day, the sky above Boston a deep, cloudless blue. He took a moment to pull some grass from beside the road and used it to cast an illusion spell. Most spells of this sort could be fueled with water, or even the vapor in the air around him. But he needed to place this illusion in Janna's tavern on the far side of the city, and he had to make that illusion speak aloud.

Standing still with his eyes closed, he projected the image of himself into the *Fat Spider* and called Janna's name. In his mind, he could see the dark interior of Janna's tavern, the banked hearth still smoking slightly, hints of daylight peeking through shuttered windows and locked doors.

He had to call for Janna several times before he heard footsteps on her stairway and saw her descend to the great room carrying a candle.

"Kaille," she said. "How did you—" She stopped herself and scrutinized the illusion he had conjured, edging closer to it. "Where are you?" she asked, her tone changing to one of concern.

"I'm on my way to Adams' house. You would have heard your conjurer warning during the night."

Janna shook her head. "I hear nothin' durin' the night. I sleep. I heard one in the evenin' when I was still open. It came from the gate and I just assumed it was you, comin' back from Amanda."

"It was. Greenleaf mistook the sound for wolves and organized a hunt."

She laughed. "You're makin' that up."

"No, I'm not."

Her laughter redoubled until she was wiping tears from the corners of her eyes. "Oh, my. That's just about the best thing I've heard. That'll improve my mood for the whole day."

"Well, don't be too amused. Two more conjurers entered the city during the night. We need to protect Adams, without delay."

"All right, I'll be there."

"Thank you, Janna."

He started to let the illusion fade.

"Kaille."

Ethan poured more magick into the spell, strengthening the image, and improving his ability to see and hear her.

"When you say Greenleaf organized a hunt . . ."

"He offered a bounty for every 'wolf' found and shot, and he mustered men from taverns and their homes."

She was still laughing when he released the magick of his spell.

Ethan hurried on to the Adams estate, only slowing to survey the lanes as he came within sight of the house. He hadn't felt any conjurings yet this morning, but that didn't mean there couldn't be a speller lurking in the vicinity, cloaked in a concealment casting.

Not knowing if Adams and his family were even awake yet, he didn't approach the door. He merely took position outside and, after warding himself, placed a second warding on the house. Uncle Reg watched him, shimmering in the morning light.

"Stay with me," Ethan said. The ghost nodded, and together they watched for would-be assassins.

He had been there for perhaps a quarter of an hour when he heard the door open.

"Mister Kaille? Is that you?"

Ethan turned. Samuel Adams stood in his doorway wearing black breeches, a white shirt, and a red waistcoat.

"Good morning, sir."

"What are you doing? You look like a sentry."

"You answer your own question, sir."

"Well, come in and have a spot of tea and something to eat."

He had no chance to explain why he couldn't do that. Magick surged through the lane, tickling the soles of his feet, setting him on edge. Someone had conjured, and not from any great distance.

"Please get back inside, sir," he said, searching Purchase Street and the abutting lanes for whoever had cast the spell. "Lock your door."

"I don't really think—"

Ethan wheeled. "Sir, I've just felt a conjuring. Someone is coming for you. Close and lock your door, now!"

Adams' eyes went wide. He shut the door. Ethan assumed he threw the lock. An instant later, Ethan spotted him at one of the windows, where he peered out at the street.

Ethan drew his knife, pushed up his sleeve, and cut his arm. He didn't yet see anyone. Again, he wondered if whoever was coming had concealed himself.

"*Aufer carmen, ex cruore evocatum.*" Remove spell, conjured from blood.

His conjuring murmured in the ground and a man materialized no more than thirty paces from where Ethan stood.

Ethan slashed at his forearm and cast a sleep spell. The man, who was of medium height and build, with dark hair and a pallid complexion, shuddered at the impact, but he didn't fall asleep, and a moment later he renewed his advance. He cast in turn, his conjuring slamming into Ethan with the force of a mule's kick. The ghost that winked into view beside him was pale yellow, the color of sand.

Ethan kept his feet, fired back three spells—shattering, fist, and fire—in quick succession.

The other conjurer staggered. When the third spell hit him, he dropped his blade. Ethan strode toward him, cutting himself and casting yet again—another fire spell. The man had reached for his knife, and now he reeled. By the time he recovered his balance, Ethan was on him.

Ethan hammered a fist into the man's gut, and another high on his cheek. The conjurer lashed out with a kick, catching Ethan in the knee of his bad leg. He fell back, managed not to topple to the street. But his retreat allowed the man to seize his knife and conjure again. This spell didn't defeat Ethan's warding, but it knocked Ethan down.

The conjurer cut himself again, but the conjuring Ethan felt in the cobblestones didn't wipe the blood from his arm. Instead, it sent the man sprawling. Ethan leapt to his feet and pounced. Two blows to the man's chin left him addled. Ethan took his knife and laid the edge of it against the conjurer's jaw.

Looking up, he flashed a smile at Janna, who sauntered to him, holding a pouch of fragrant herbs. Ethan recognized the smells of mullein, horehound, betony, and lavender.

"Thank you."

"Never mind that. What are we goin' to do with him?"

Ethan gave her a quick wink. "I was going to cut his throat. You don't think I should?"

"No!" the conjurer said.

This close to the man, Ethan noticed what he had missed before: the conjurer was young—not more than twenty. He was breathing hard, sweating. Exertion, to be sure, but also fear.

"Where are you from?"

When the man didn't answer, Ethan pressed the blade against his neck. "You come to our city, try to kill our friend, attack me with your magick. If you think I won't slit your throat ear to ear, you're a fool. Now, where are you from?"

"New York. White Plains."

"And you arrived last night?"

"First thing this morning."

"And you'll be leaving this afternoon."

Silence met this. Again, Ethan increased the pressure. Tiny beads of blood appeared along the edge of the blade.

"Y-yes! This afternoon. The first ship I can find."

Footsteps beyond Janna made her turn and Ethan look up. Mariz slowed to a walk a few steps shy of them, his knife in hand. Seeing the young man on the ground, he sheathed his blade. His gaze found Ethan's. Both turned away before long.

"You see there are three of us now," Ethan told the New York conjurer. "All of us determined to keep you from hurting Samuel Adams." This much was true, even where Mariz was concerned. "If you show your face here again, if you so much as whisper a word in Latin, we'll see that it's your last. Do you understand?"

The man nodded.

"*Discuti ex cruore evocatum.*" The blood vanished from the man's neck and his blade shattered, the metal chiming like a bell. The young man flinched. Ethan stood, looming over him. "Get up and leave. Don't ever come back."

The man climbed to his feet, tentative, gaze skipping from Ethan to Janna to Mariz and back again. He stumbled away toward the waterfront, peering back at them repeatedly until he turned a corner and was beyond their seeing.

"Do you think he'll really leave?" Janna asked.

"Aye. You don't?"

She hiked a shoulder. "Maybe, maybe not. You're a good man, Kaille. Sometimes I fear you're too good."

"So you've told me." He shifted his gaze to Mariz. "What are you doing here?" he asked, a chill in his voice.

"I felt the spells and feared for you. If you would rather I go, I will."

Janna scowled at them in turn. "No, we need the help, don't we, Kaille?"

Ethan didn't answer.

She narrowed her eyes. "What is this?"

"Ask him."

"He is angry with me, and with reason," Mariz said, as Janna pivoted his way. "The *senhora* is as interested in Charlotte Whitcomb's reward money as one might expect. She has directed me to help defend Adams from outsiders who seek his death, but I am also to help her and her men collect the bounty."

"So do we need to be fightin' you?" Janna demanded, her tone icing over in turn.

"I will not hurt Adams myself. I have explained as much to Kaille already."

"You deceived me," Ethan said, flinging the words at him. "Every minute you took to 'explain' was intended to keep me occupied, to give Sephira's other toughs a chance to kill him."

"Yes," Mariz said. "And I all but told you that I would do such things. I am required to by my position with the *senhora*."

"So you said. I think in this case, we won't be needing your help. You should go."

"That is shortsighted, my friend. You are—"

A howl skirled into the morning air from the waterfront—up in the North End, if Ethan had to guess. Another conjurer entering the city and setting off Janna's spell. The three of them stared in that direction.

"As I was saying," Mariz went on, more pointedly, "you are angry with me, and I understand why. But my offer of aid is sincere, and you will need my magick before this is over."

"Your magick is of no use to us if we can't trust you. Every time we rely on you, I'll be looking for deception, trying to determine how what you're doing could benefit Sephira and the others." Ethan shook his head. "I can't risk being distracted in that way. Go, Mariz."

"Kaille," Janna said, her voice low.

Ethan glared her way, and she glared back, uncowed.

"You really think you and I alone can fight off these outsiders?"

"I don't think we have a choice." He eyed Mariz again. "He's not our ally. Not in this. He's more akin to a spy."

Sephira's man bristled. "That is unfair. I repeated nothing of our conversation to the *senhora*."

"And yet, you still almost managed to get Adams killed. Go. Don't make me say it again."

Mariz lingered for another moment. Ethan thought he might say something more, but he merely turned and walked away, back toward Summer Street.

"I hope that wasn't as foolish as I think it was," Janna said. "That's a powerful conjurer you just sent away."

"I know. And he was more than that. He was also one of the few people in the world I consider a friend."

"Then call him back!"

Ethan shook his head. "I meant what I said. I don't trust him. Not with this. It may not be his fault, but he would betray us, and Adams would die."

"All right. Then what now?"

"Now, I keep Adams safe from the next attack. You heard that wail a few minutes ago. Already, there's another conjurer in the city. You have a tavern to open, and an earth witch to welcome."

"So you're sendin' me away, too?"

"No," he said, his tone softening. "I'll be acting as Adams' bodyguard until this is over—and I can do that because I have no other responsibilities. You do."

"Yeah, all right."

"First, though, come with me."

He gripped her arm gently and led her to Samuel Adams' front door. Mere seconds after his knock, the door opened, revealing Adams himself. He held a full-cocked flintlock.

"I saw you fight that man," he said without a greeting. "That was most impressive."

"I had help, sir. This is Janna Windcatcher. She lives on the Neck and runs a tavern called the *Fat Spider*. She makes excellent stews and fowl. And she's the most accomplished conjurer in all of Boston. Without her, I couldn't have defeated that man. She's as committed to your protection as I am."

Adams smiled at Janna, but she regarded Ethan, thoughtful and, he thought, grateful.

"Miss . . . I'm sorry, what was the last name again?"

"Windcatcher, sir," she said, facing him.

"Yes, forgive me—Miss Windcatcher. It is a pleasure to meet you. Thank you for your protection."

"It's my pleasure. I don' know if Kaille's right about the rest, but I do make fine food. You should come sometime. Bring your missus."

"I just might do that. The *Fat Spider?*"

"That's right."

"Sir," Ethan cut in, "I think we should move your wife and children to another location, and then I should get you to the *Green Dragon*. I believe you'll be safest there."

Adams heaved a breath, but didn't argue. "Yes, all right. I'll gather Betsy and the children." He tipped his head in Janna's direction. "I hope we meet again soon," he said to her, and bustled into the house.

"Thank you," Janna whispered to Ethan when Adams was gone. "That was . . . You didn' have to say all that."

"Every word of it was true."

"I know. But you didn't have to *say* it."

They grinned.

"I don't know if the Sons of Liberty will pay me for protecting Adams, but if they do, I promise to share equally with you and Amanda. That's the least I can do."

"I appreciate that," Janna said. "What should I tell Amanda when she arrives?"

"She knows what to do. She spoke of creating a 'hedge'—a way of protecting the city from witches. After that . . . I don't know. We'll need her to defeat Whitcomb."

"We will at that."

He expected her to return to their previous conversation about killing Whitcomb. She didn't. Instead, she reached out and gripped Ethan's hand for just a second. It might have been the first gesture of true affection she had ever shown him. Then she left, walking back toward the Neck.

VII

Ethan and Adams accompanied Betsy and Adams's two children from his first marriage, Samuel and Hannah, to the home of one of Betsy's close friends. Once Ethan and Adams were on their own again, Ethan shrouded them both in a concealment spell and the two of them followed a round-about route through the city to Union Street and the *Green Dragon* tavern. Ethan spent much of their journey peering over his shoulder, searching lanes for possible enemies, and peeking around corners.

He knew the concealment conjuring rendered such vigilance less necessary, but he couldn't bring himself to eschew these precautions.

Adams still carried his flintlock, though he hid it within a coat pocket. Ethan kept hold of his knife. He silently conveyed to Uncle Reg that he should remain with them. Adams had no idea the specter was there.

As they slipped through throngs of people in Cornhill, invisible and as silent as they could be, Adams looked around wearing an expression of amazement, as if this were his first experience in Boston.

"This is remarkable," he whispered at one point, as they traversed a relatively empty stretch of road. "It's been many, many years since last I could walk the city streets without being accosted even once. I rather like it. I hadn't realized what a burden fame—and infamy—can be." He glanced at Ethan, eyes dancing. "Perhaps you can teach me that particular charm?"

"I would if I could, sir."

They reached the *Green Dragon* without incident, and once they were inside, on the stairway leading down to the tavern, Ethan removed the spell. In the building's cellar, they found Joseph Warren, Benjamin Church, and others Adams counted as friends. Satisfied that Adams would be safe, Ethan left, promising to return for him at the end of the day.

He stopped in at the *Dowsing Rod* as Kannice had requested, and after a quick conversation about the morning's events, made his way to the water-front. Since the wail that interrupted his discourse with Janna and Mariz, no other conjurers had entered the city. He assumed the young man from New York had taken his warnings to heart.

That left two other conjurers in Boston whom he needed to find and deal with.

In a byway across from Wentworth's Wharf, Ethan cut himself and cast a finding spell. The conjuring rumbled in cobblestone and tendrils of magick spread from where he stood, searching out conjurers. The spell revealed to others where he was. He didn't care. He wanted them to know that he pursued them, and he hoped, too, that they would sense each other and recognize that they were rivals.

Within a minute of his casting, his magick snapped back in his direction. Twice. One conjurer was in the South End, near the Battery, not at all far from the Adams home. Ethan congratulated himself on his foresight in moving Adams and his family from the house.

The other conjurer was much closer, on Middle Street as best Ethan could tell, too close to the *Green Dragon* for his peace of mind. He set out in that direction. He still held his knife, though he carried it in such a way— the hilt in hand, the blade concealed within the sleeve of his coat—that none would see. He dismissed Reg for now, lest the glowing figure give Ethan away to the conjurer he stalked.

He approached the thoroughfare slowly, hoping to spot his foe from the safety of an alley. At first, no one caught his eye. He spied no specters, no men brazenly wielding knives and bloody forearms. As he watched those walking the lane, though, one man did catch his eye. His hair was brown but salted generously with gray. His shoulders were broad, and a hint of a paunch gathered beneath his coat and waistcoat. He wore a Monmouth cap and walked the edge of the lane like a man headed somewhere in particular. Except that after walking eastward for a block or so, he turned and headed back in the other direction with that same purposeful gait.

He repeated this pattern two more times, on each occasion walking west almost all the way to the Mill Creek, from which he would have a clear view of the corner of Union Street. If he sought to catch Adams as he left the *Dragon*, this was as good a tactic as any.

Uncertain as to whether this man was a conjurer, Ethan did the one thing he could: He placed a new warding on himself. His magick thrummed like a harp string, and Reg glowed beside him for just an instant before vanishing again at a look from Ethan.

The spell, though, did what he had hoped. At the first touch of that magickal hum—something only a conjurer would notice—the man faltered and glanced about. He resumed his walking a few seconds later, heading eastward and attempting to adopt an air of calm, even as he eased a blade from his belt.

Ethan stepped onto Middle Street and followed the man. As before, the conjurer walked in this direction as far as Beer Lane before halting for a time. Ethan stopped a short distance short of the same corner. When the man resumed his pacing, westward once more, back toward the *Green Dragon*, Ethan waited where he was.

As the conjurer reached him, Ethan grabbed the man with both hands, yanked him into a gap between two buildings, and threw him to the ground.

The stranger sprawled. Ethan gripped his knife, shoved his sleeve out of the way, and cut himself.

"*Pugnus ex cruore evocatus!*"

The fist spell elicited a grunt and kept the man from scrambling back to his feet. But Ethan couldn't tell if whatever wardings he had in place had held. The man pushed at his sleeve, but before he could cast, Ethan shattered the steel of his weapon with a second conjuring.

"Next one breaks your neck," he said.

The stranger glared up at him. "I don't think so. My wardings blocked your first casting. They'll block another."

Ethan advanced on him. "Then I'll thrash you."

"You're welcome to try, ya bloody bastard. But you'll find me tougher than I look, and willing to die for what I think is right."

Ethan slowed. "What you think is right? You believe murdering a great man like Samuel Adams in cold blood is 'right'?"

The man's forehead creased. "No, you believe that."

"No, I don't. I'm trying to keep him alive."

"Well, so am I. That's why I'm here."

Ethan held up both hands. "Let's begin again. My name is Ethan Kaille. I live here in Boston, and I'm tasked with protecting the life of Samuel Adams. You're not from here. You're one of those who came in response to the bounty—one hundred pounds—that's been placed on Adams' life."

The man's posture eased a bit. "That's right to a point, friend. I came because of the bounty, but not to collect. I think it's barbaric, and I'm determined to keep Adams safe, as you claim to be." He started to stand, but stopped himself with a glance at Ethan. "May I?"

Ethan nodded, wary still. This could have been a ruse, though he didn't think it was. And if this man had come for the stated reason, he would be a welcome ally in this fight.

The stranger brushed himself off and then proffered a hand. "Robert Valk, out of Philadelphia."

Ethan gripped the man's hand, calling himself a fool and bracing for an attack. None came. They shook hands and then stood in uncomfortable silence.

"I suppose I owe you an apology," Ethan said.

"Nah, you don't. Anna would tell me—Anna's my wife—she'd say 'Rob, it's your own fault, coming to another speller's city without so much as declaring yourself.' And she'd be right. Especially with that bounty on the offer. I can tell you, we have our own Samuel Adams in Pennsylvania, in a manner of speaking."

"Mister Dickinson."

Any doubts Ethan harbored as to Valk's sincerity vanished in that moment. A smile so broad, a gleam of pride so brilliant, couldn't be feigned.

"That's right," he said, brown eyes shining. "John Dickinson. You've read his *Letters.*"

Dickinson's *Letters from a Farmer in Pennsylvania*, written several years before, had circulated through the colonies and won praise for their clear and eloquent denunciation of the Townshend Acts.

"Only recently," Ethan said. "I've come late to the cause. But I thought them quite compelling."

"That they are," Valk said. "And so I know what it is to protect a man like Adams. If someone put a bounty on Farmer John's head, I'd do all I could to protect him. That's why I'm here."

"And I'm glad you are."

Valk looked Ethan up and down while patting his own paunch. "Between the two of us, we're a little worn around the edges. Are we the only ones protecting him?"

"The only conjurers you mean? No, not exactly."

Valk narrowed his eyes. "That doesn't sound very certain."

"We're not alone, but the other conjurer working with us is older than I am."

"Well, I suppose that's all right, so long as he's got some power."

"Aye, *she* does."

The man raised an eyebrow. "She, then."

A thought came to Ethan, one he should have entertained before now. "You felt my finding spell, didn't you?"

"I did."

"It located a second conjurer as well. In the South End, near Adams' home. We should be looking for him, or watching for his approach, since he'll know where to find us."

"All right, then. Lead the way."

They left the gap in which they had fought and walked along Middle Street toward Union and the *Dragon.* Every few seconds, Valk cast a glance Ethan's way, as if sizing him up. Again Ethan wondered if he had been too quick to trust the man.

After the fourth or fifth time, Ethan glared back. "Is there something on your mind, Mister Valk?"

"I'm wondering how you managed to toss me around as you did. You're not all that younger than I am, and I'm the bigger man. Plus, it seems—forgive me—but it seems you're lame."

"What is your profession, Mister Valk?"

Valk frowned. "What do I . . . I'm a shopkeeper. Wares—tools and such. What difference—"

"Up until recently, I've been a thieftaker. I've worked and lived in the lanes, and I've gotten into a fair number of scrapes. Tossing you around wasn't all that difficult." He grinned, hoping to soften this, though not too much.

"I suppose that would explain it."

They walked on in silence. Upon reaching Union Street, Ethan turned toward the *Green Dragon*. Valk followed. They walked past the building, peering into byways and scrutinizing those on the lane with them. Seeing no one skulking near the tavern or behaving oddly in the street, they returned to the corner of Hanover and paused there.

"What ought we to do now?" Valk asked, still glancing around.

"I'm not exactly certain," Ethan admitted. "I assume the other conjurer my spell found is watching the Adams estate. In which case, we may need to go there. But the truth is, we need more of a plan than we've got right now. I can't simply fight every conjurer who enters the city. We need to drive them away, and I need Janna for that."

"Janna? That's the other speller you're working with?"

"Yes. Janna Windcatcher."

Valk frowned. "What kind of name is that?"

As he asked this, Ethan caught sight of a familiar form walking in their direction. "It's a name she chose for herself," he said absently. "Come with me. Pull out your blade, but don't cut yourself. Not yet. And don't say a word unless I tell you to."

Ethan didn't wait for an answer, but walked toward the man he had seen. Nap. As he approached the tough, he produced his own knife and pushed up his sleeve.

Sephira's man spotted him and slowed. His gaze shifted momentarily to Valk before settling on Ethan again.

"Kaille," he said, drawing out Ethan's name. "You live here now? I never see you anywhere else. Except Miss Pryce's house."

"I could say the same about you. Where are the giants?" In response to Nap's puzzled look, he said, "Afton and Gordon."

"Ah. They're around." He lifted a chin in Valk's direction. "Who's this? Another witch?"

"I'm not a witch!"

Ethan held up a hand, silencing Valk. "He's a friend. And yes, he's a conjurer, too. We're working for Adams. And we're perfectly willing to do whatever we have to—cast any spell we need to—in order to keep him safe."

Nap stilled, like a wolf. "Are you threatening me?"

"Aye. That's just what I'm doing. If you get within a hundred paces of Samuel Adams, I'll set your clothes on fire. Fifty paces, and I'll snap both your legs like they were kindling. Ten paces, and I'll break your neck. Care to test me?"

Ethan thought that was just what the man wanted. No doubt, he carried a new pistol, one Ethan hadn't yet burned. Likely he itched to use it. After a brief, tight silence, though, he shrugged and forced a smile.

"I was just walking. There's no need for threats."

Ethan didn't answer. Nap eyed Valk again and walked on, brushing past Ethan without bumping into him.

"Who was that?" Valk asked.

"It doesn't matter. He's not a conjurer, and so for now at least, he's not the greatest threat to Adams."

Even as he said this, however, he turned to watch the man slip among others on the street until he vanished from sight.

"How good are you with your conjurings?" Ethan asked.

"I'm pretty good," Valk said, sounding confident.

"And would you recognize that man if he came back here?"

"Certainly."

"He often keeps company with two large, muscular toughs—"

"The giants."

"Aye. They're homely, with long, lank hair, and they're truly behemoths. I want you to stay here. If they return—individually or together—I want you to keep them away. With magick; you're no match for them physically. Don't hurt them too badly. You don't want them as mortal enemies. But keep them far from that tavern over there." He pointed at the *Green Dragon*.

"All right. Where are you going?"

"I need to have a word with Thomas Hutchinson."

"*Hutchinson?*"

Again, Ethan was reassured by the vehemence of Valk's response. He packed so much contempt into his repetition of the acting governor's name that Ethan nearly laughed.

"Why would you want to speak with him?"

"Because despite what you've heard about him—all of which is prob-

ably true—he is trying to keep the peace in this city. Presiding over the assassination of Samuel Adams is hardly the legacy he seeks." Valk didn't appear convinced or appeased, but Ethan pressed on. "Remain here. I won't
be long, and then I'll introduce you to Janna."

"Very well."

The Philadelphian stared after Ethan as he walked away, as forlorn as
an abandoned puppy, but Ethan trusted him to remain there and to keep
Sephira's men away from Adams.

The Town House stood only a few blocks from Hanover Street. Ethan
covered the distance as quickly as his bad leg would allow, and soon stood
before the door to Hutchinson's chambers, awaiting admittance.

The acting governor's clerk opened the door and motioned Ethan inside before withdrawing to an adjacent chamber and closing the door.
Ethan removed his hat.

Hutchinson was tall, barrel-chested; his steep forehead, large eyes, and
pale complexion made him look perpetually weary and beleaguered. The
last time Ethan had spoken to the lieutenant governor, Hutchinson had expressed his distrust of Francis Lamb. Ethan hoped his sentiments in this
regard had not changed.

"Mister Kaille," he said without enthusiasm, his attention as much on a
sheaf of papers upon his desk as on Ethan. "It seems whenever I see you
some dire threat menaces our city. What is it this time?"

Directly to the point, then. Very well.

"This time, Your Honor, it is a bounty set upon the life of Samuel
Adams."

Hutchinson paused in his work to gape at Ethan. "Say that again."

"A bounty, sir, on the life of Samuel Adams. One hundred pounds.
And the announcement of this reward has been disseminated throughout
the colonies. Already men are coming to Boston hoping to collect. And
worse, a special appeal has been made to conjurers. The missive claims that
Mister Adams is protected by a conjurer, and therefore the successful assassin will need to wield magick of his own."

Still Hutchinson gawked. "That is most remarkable."

"Aye, sir, it is."

"And is it true that a conjurer protects Adams?"

Ethan toyed with his tricorn. "There may be some merit to the rumors."

Hutchinson's thin smile conveyed so much: satisfaction with his own
cleverness, delight in Ethan's discomfort, disdain for anything magickal.

"Do you have any idea who is offering such a substantial reward?"

"I know exactly who it is, sir: Charlotte Whitcomb. The half-sister of—"

"Francis Lamb. Yes, I am familiar with her now. We've met on a few occasions." His expression had turned grim. After a few moments, he reclaimed the papers he had been studying. "That is unfortunate, but I doubt very much there is anything I can do."

It was Ethan's turn to stare slack-jawed. "How is that possible, sir?"

"I wasn't aware, Mister Kaille, that I am required to explain to the likes of you how I wield my authority."

"When you allow one person under your jurisdiction to buy the murder of another?" Ethan could barely keep his voice from trembling, so great was his rage. "I believe, Mister Hutchinson, that you are required to explain such a thing to *all* who are under your authority!"

"You forget yourself, sir!"

"I forget nothing, Your Honor. Something you should keep in mind. If Samuel Adams is harmed, much less killed, I will hold you personally responsible. And so shall every man and woman in the lanes. I'll see to it. Every miscreant, every cove who makes up the so-called 'rabble' of whom you like to speak with such scorn. If you thought you suffered at the hands of the mob that destroyed your home during the Stamp Tax agitation, imagine their rage should Samuel Adams be killed with your acquiescence."

"You are threatening sedition! I would be within my power to have you imprisoned for speaking to me so."

"As I've recently reminded Mister Greenleaf, sir, you should ask yourself, if all you think you know about me is true, is there a gaol in North America that could hold me?"

Color drained from Hutchinson's cheeks. "I think you should go, Mister Kaille."

Ethan made no move to do so. "You would let him be killed? Truly? Even knowing that you and Adams have been enemies for all these years, I find that difficult to believe, sir. You and I have been at odds before, but I have always thought you a man of honor, someone who seeks only the best for the people of Boston and the province. You must see that Adams' murder would be a spark to dry wood. The city would burn."

The acting governor exhaled and set down his papers once more. "I don't want that. You're correct in that regard. But what I said before is true: In this matter I am helpless to act."

"Because of Francis Lamb's involvement." Ethan offered this as a statement. Hutchinson gazed back at him until, at last, he tucked his chin ever so slightly.

"The last time we met," Ethan went on, "you said certain things about Francis Lamb and your relationship with him. Do you remember?"

"I do."

"And are those things still true?"

Hutchinson faltered. "I'm not in a position—"

"Let me ask it this way: If Francis Lamb were to leave Boston and never return, would you be sad to see him go?"

The lieutenant governor answered with a bark of laughter. "Hardly."

"That is all I need to know, sir." Ethan turned to leave but then faced the man again. "I regret the tone of my earlier remarks."

"As I regret mine, Mister Kaille. You are right about my feelings for the city and the province. I wouldn't want anything to happen that might threaten the current peace. And I much prefer to best my foes in the realms of politics and discourse than with violence and bloodshed."

"I believe that, Your Honor."

As Ethan reached the door, Hutchinson spoke his name forcing him to halt again.

"Do you think you can . . . achieve the outcome you mentioned a moment ago?"

"I don't see that I have much choice, sir. It occurs to me that the bounty placed upon Mister Adams' life lies at the root of all we fear. I can't defeat an army of assassins. But if I can eliminate their incentive, perhaps I won't need to."

"That sounds sensible. If I could help you I would."

Ethan considered this. "It may be that you can. Would you be willing to tell Sheriff Greenleaf that he is to leave me alone until next you and I speak?"

"You desire *carte blanche* in this matter?"

"Aye," Ethan said. "I'm doing battle with cutthroats and conjurers. I may need to bend a law or two, and I don't have the time or inclination to fight on a second front."

"You're serious."

"I am, sir. If you truly desire to help me, this is one way."

Hutchinson weighed the request briefly before nodding more decisively than before. "Very well. I will speak with him later today. You have my word."

"Thank you, sir."

Ethan left the acting governor's chambers, let himself out of the Town

House, and hurried back toward Union Street. He was still more than a block away when he felt the first spell roar in the street.

VIII

Ethan broke into a hobbled run, sliding his knife free and pushing at his sleeve. He slowed as he neared the corner of Hanover and Union Streets, but he saw no sign of Valk, nor of anyone else who appeared to be conjuring.

Walking now, his breath coming in gasps, he turned onto Union Street and approached the *Green Dragon*.

Another spell churned in the cobblestone. He thought it came from behind him. He whirled, retraced his steps.

Two more spells drew him to a byway. He peered in, saw nothing, stepped into shadow and wove past piles of refuse and stacks of old wooden pallets. The alley stank of rotting vegetables and urine.

One more spell rumbled and Ethan heard someone grunt. He pushed by one last mound of rubbish. A young man—tall, solidly built, with red hair and pale features—stood over Valk, who lay on the filthy ground, curled in a ball as if to protect himself from kicks and blows.

Ethan cut himself and cast a spell he had learned from Nate Ramsey. A barrel filled with trash lifted off the cobblestone and soared at the man. At the first touch of magick, he spun toward Ethan. In the next instant, he dove to the ground to avoid the barrel, which crashed into a wall, scattering refuse everywhere.

Ethan cut himself a second time. He cast again: a shatter spell. The force of it knocked the man onto his back. His knife flew from his hand and clattered on stone.

The conjurer scrabbled after the weapon, but Valk grabbed hold of his leg and hauled him back.

Ethan ran to them both. The stranger kicked at Valk with his free foot, catching Ethan's new friend in the temple. Valk released the man, cradled his head with both arms. By now, though, Ethan had reached them. He kicked the stranger in the side, and the man folded in on himself, retching. Ethan retrieved the young man's knife, pocketed it, and with his own blade cut himself again.

Looming over the stranger, blood glistening on his forearm, he said, "Who are you?"

"Who are *you?*" the pup wheezed.

Ethan cast again: a fist spell that shuddered through the man's form. He drew more blood.

"I can do this all day. Now answer the question."

"To hell with you."

His next spell pounded the man as the others had, and for good measure, Ethan kicked him again.

"What does it matter who he is?" Valk demanded, staggering to his feet. "He was after Adams. He attacked me. He would have done the same to you if he'd had a chance."

"So what do you suggest we do? Shall we take him to the sheriff and have him placed in a cell? He'll be imprisoned for all of five minutes. Or do you believe we should execute him?"

Valk stared down at the man, his mouth twisting with distaste. "No," he said after a brief silence, "I don't want to kill him. Or anyone else for that matter."

"Hence my question. His accent is familiar." Ethan squatted beside the man and set the point of his knife at the corner of the man's eye. "I think you're from Providence. Or maybe Newport."

The pup glowered, but didn't deny this.

"In which case you might know the name Ethan Kaille."

Recognition flashed in the lad's eyes. He shot a glance at Valk but quickly focused on Ethan again.

"That's right. I'm Kaille. What you couldn't know is that I've taken to working now and again with Sephira Pryce. And I can tell you she won't be pleased to find you in our city trying to collect a bounty she thinks of as her own."

"That's not what I was doin'!"

Ethan simply watched him and waited.

"You can't tell her. Please. She'll kill me. She won't bat an eye doin' it."

Still he said nothing.

"All right! My name is Ezekiel Oxley."

"Of Providence?"

"Warwick," he said, sounding defeated.

"Close enough. How did you get here?"

"Horse, carriage, a bit on foot. I haven't much money, and so I had to scrape—"

"I don't need your life's history. Do you have a horse here?"

The man shook his head.

"Very well. Here's what you're going to do, Mister Oxley. You're going to walk out of this city through the gate at the end of the Neck, and then you're going to follow the Middle Road to Dedham. There, if you can manage to buy a horse, you're welcome to do so. And if ever I see you in the city again, I will take you directly to Miss Pryce. Do you understand?"

"Aye."

Ethan extended a hand to the pup. Oxley regarded it, looked at Ethan again, and finally gripped it and allowed Ethan to pull him up.

"Can I have my knife back?"

"No. That's the price you pay for coming to my city and threatening the life of Samuel Adams."

The pup scowled, but stalked away. At the mouth of the alley, he paused to stare back at them. "Can you honestly say you aren't tempted at all? A hundred pounds?"

"I can honestly say it," Ethan told him. "When you get to be my age, you'll see that there are more important things than money. We need Adams more than we need coin."

Oxley's frown returned. He was still shaking his head when Ethan lost sight of him.

Ethan faced Valk, who had a bruise on his temple, a bloodied lip, and tears in his clothes at his elbow and knee. "Are you all right?"

"Well enough. What did you learn from Hutchinson?"

"That he would very much like for us to make this problem disappear. Come along. I'd like to be certain Adams is all right."

Valk didn't move. "We're going to meet him? Now?"

"Aye."

"Well, at least allow me to heal myself first. I don't want to him to see me looking like this."

Ethan could only smile.

When Valk had healed his bruises and cuts, the two of them walked to the *Dragon* and descended the stairs to the tavern. The great room was mostly empty, but Ethan heard voices coming from the rear chamber. He made his way to that door, which stood partially ajar, and pushed it open. As he surveyed this room, he felt a wave of cold crash over him. He saw Joseph Warren, Josiah Quincy, and a few other Sons of Liberty, but Adams himself was no longer there.

"I'm surprised to see you here, Mister Kaille," Doctor Warren said, crossing the room to greet him. "Samuel left here a short time ago. A quarter hour, perhaps a little more."

"To go where, sir?" Ethan asked, struggling to keep his voice even.

"Wherever it was you summoned him."

"Wherever I—" He broke off, fear rising in his chest like a storm tide. "I didn't summon him."

Warren blanched. "What?"

"Who said that I did?"

"There was a message," the doctor said, "delivered by a boy who couldn't have been more than ten years old."

"And none of you questioned it? Not even Mister Adams himself?"

"No! There was something in it—some mention of yesterday's adventure and your ability to go unseen. I don't recall the exact wording, but whatever it was convinced Samuel—convinced all of us—that the message was genuine."

"And you didn't see them?" Ethan demanded of Valk.

"No! You heard him: He said a quarter hour ago. By that time I was fighting off the lad from Warwick."

Of course. No wonder Oxley had been so compliant. If that was truly his name. He had accomplished what he sought. He wasn't there to kill Adams, at least not directly. He was a distraction, a ruse aimed squarely at Ethan.

Did Sephira have Adams? Had Nap or Afton or Gordon already killed the man? Or had one of the assassins from outside of Boston learned the identity of Adams' magickal protector?

"Did Mister Adams leave here alone?"

"No," Warren said, seeming to find in this question some cause to hope. "Benjamin—Doctor Church—he said he would accompany Samuel, that he needed to return home anyway."

Ethan took some solace in this as well. "Good. And do you know where they were headed?"

"That I don't. Samuel didn't say, though it seemed that the missive directed him somewhere other than his home."

"If I may," Josiah Quincy said, stepping into their circle. "I had the impression that Benjamin's offer to accompany Samuel came not just from an intention to leave, but also some proximity between his home and where Samuel was headed."

"That could be helpful, sir. The question is, what is near the Church house?"

"Province House isn't far," Warren said, "but I can't imagine a message from even his most trusted allies would have the power to draw Samuel to the governor's mansion."

"No, it must be one of the churches," Quincy said. "Trinity Church is but a stone's throw from Benjamin's home. The Old South is bit farther, but it's a landmark anyone would know."

"This note was purportedly from me," Ethan said. "So it would have to be a place he believes I would frequent. I've never been to Trinity Church, nor have I had occasion to visit the Meeting House." For that matter, it had been years since last Ethan entered any church for the purpose of attending services. But Ethan's sister, Bett, her husband, a customs man named Geoffrey Brower, and their son, George, worshipped at another of the city's revered sanctuaries. Adams might know this, and he also might remember Ethan's association with a young reverend who served in the same church. These ties could have been enough to convince Adams of the authenticity of a message, supposedly from Ethan, arranging a meeting at the church.

"King's Chapel," Ethan said, ending a brief silence. "That's where they've gone.

"You worship at King's Chapel?" Quincy asked, sounding surprised.

Ethan kept himself from laughing. The King's Chapel congregation was filled with loyalists, wealthy ones at that. Moreover, Henry Caner, the rector at King's, would have been appalled at the very idea of an infamous "witch" joining his congregation. Ethan and Caner had known and disliked each other for years, ever since Ethan first befriended Reverend Trevor Pell, who happened to have conjurer blood in his veins. Pell considered Ethan a friend. Caner viewed him as a malign influence on the young preacher.

"No, I don't worship there. But I have ties to the place. I don't know that Mister Adams is aware of them, but it's possible." Certainly Sephira Pryce was. For now, he kept this thought to himself.

He started for the stairway, followed by Valk, Warren, and Quincy. He feared for the doctor and Quincy. For that matter, he also worried about Valk's safety. Sephira's men were ruthless and skilled. On the other hand, having the Sons of Liberty with him might prevent Sephira's men from resorting to violence. Warren and Quincy were well-known throughout the city—as much so as Sephira herself.

Ethan didn't dissuade any of them from coming with him.

They walked the length of Hanover Street to Treamount, and followed that lane to King's Chapel and its famous burying ground. The church itself was a ponderous stone structure that lacked the delicate soaring spires of most of Boston's other sanctuaries. The cemetery, on the north side of the church, was the final resting place for a number of the city's luminaries, including Governor John Winthrop, Mary Chilton, and the Reverend John Cotton, grandfather of famed persecutor of so-called "witches," Cotton Mather.

As they neared the burying ground and chapel, Ethan searched for Adams and Doctor Church. He saw neither of them.

"Wait here," he said to Doctor Warren. "I'm going to check inside."

Without awaiting a reply, Ethan walked the stone path to the chapel entrance, a pair of heavy oak doors. He pulled one open and slipped inside.

The interior of the chapel was as elegant and beautiful as the exterior was homely. Pews of polished wood, many of them boxed and reserved for Boston's finest Tory families, faced a simple but graceful altar and a rounded chancel. Two stories of windows around the entirety of the main sanctuary allowed sunlight to stream in, illuminating gallery and pulpit alike. The place smelled of bay and candle smoke.

At the closing of the door and Ethan's footsteps on the central aisle, a figure at the pulpit turned.

Henry Caner, of course. Ethan would have preferred young Mister Pell, or even the acerbic and forbidding curate, John Troutbeck. Caner would be least disposed to offer assistance.

"Is that Mister Kaille?"

Ethan put on a brave face and continued forward. "It is, Reverend Sir. I'm sorry to disturb you."

"Not at all," Caner said descending from the pulpit. He was a heavy man, with a thick eyebrows and a small, bow-shaped mouth. He wore a traditional black robe and white cravat, and a wig of white curls of a type not worn by most men for at least a decade. "How can I help you?"

"Well, sir, this is going to sound quite odd. But I'm wondering if you have encountered Mister Samuel Adams or Doctor Benjamin Church in the past hour or so."

Caner opened his mouth slightly and eyed Ethan, appearing bemused. "Well, I must say, Mister Kaille, I did not expect that. I don't believe Samuel Adams has ever stepped foot in this chapel. I'm not sure I'd know what to do if he did."

"I thought as much, sir, but I had to ask. Again, please forgive the intrusion."

"No apology is necessary, but now *I* have to ask: Why did you think Adams would come here?"

"I thought he could have been lured here, by the expectation that I would meet him."

"A ruse."

"I'm afraid so."

"Is he in danger?"

"I fear he is, yes. I should probably go and search for him elsewhere."

"What should I do if I see him before you do?" Caner asked. It struck Ethan as a generous question. He had to remind himself that, despite the rector's loyalist leanings, and his fear of conjurers, he had, on more than one occasion, proved himself generous of spirit and truly devoted to the Christian teachings he preached each Sunday.

"Thank you for asking, Reverend Sir. If you see Adams, please give him sanctuary in your chapel and get word to me as soon as possible. I can always be reached at the *Dowsing Rod*, on Sudbury Street."

"Very well. That's exactly what I will do."

Ethan thanked him again and left the church. His companions awaited him in the chapel yard.

"I take it Samuel isn't inside," Warren said, tense and watchful.

"No." Ethan gazed across Treamount, toward the Granary Burying Ground, and, beyond it, the Common and Beacon Hill. Sephira had once attempted to kill Ethan amid the grasses and woods of the Common. Would she do the same to Adams? "This way," he said, leading them in that direction.

They walked determinedly, grim and silent. Valk didn't seem to realize that with Warren and Quincy he was in august company. He carried his knife in hand, and he swept the lanes and grasses with his gaze, fully engrossed in the search for Adams.

As they left the Granary and walked deeper into the Common, Ethan spotted a cluster of people ahead of them, walking in their direction. He further quickened his pace, as did the others. The closer they drew to those he had spotted, the more certain Ethan grew that they had found at least part of their quarry.

Sephira walked arm in arm with none other than Francis Lamb. Ethan couldn't deny that they made a stunning pair: he, tall, lithe, with his dashing swoop of brown hair, and she looking as she always did, her hair down, an amethyst jewel shining at her throat. Nap and Mariz walked ahead of them. Afton and Gordon followed.

Ethan didn't see Adams or Church. In truth, he found it hard to believe that either Sephira or Lamb would have wanted to be anywhere near the actual assassination of the man. Was he dead then? Or being held somewhere?

Nap was the first to recognize Ethan. He said something over his shoulder, alerting Sephira. Ethan slowed so that Warren and Valk could pull abreast of him.

"That's Sephira Pryce," Ethan said to Valk. "She's not a conjurer, but she and her men are dangerous, to say the least. All of them are likely to be armed, and all of them know how to handle blade and flintlock alike. Sephira most of all."

"Who's the fop walking with her?" the conjurer asked.

Warren chuckled at the description. "That is Francis Lamb. A Customs man. I don't believe he is a conjurer either. But he wields a good deal of influence here and in London."

"His sister *is* a conjurer. She is also the source of the bounty that drew you here. Be on your guard." Ethan had time for no more.

"Ethan," Sephira purred, halting a few paces from him. "What a lovely surprise. What brings you to the Common?"

Ethan flicked glances to Nap and Mariz. The former eyed him with open hostility. The latter would barely meet his gaze.

"We're looking for someone. Maybe you can help me."

"I doubt it. But I'm willing to try."

"Splendid. May I speak to you in private for a moment?"

She looked sidelong at Lamb. "I suppose." She detached herself from the customs man and followed Ethan as he walked some distance from the others. Nap watched them like a dog guarding his master, but at Sephira's signal, he remained where he was.

"What do you want?" she demanded when they stopped, all pretense of courtesy gone.

"I want to know where he is."

"Where who is?"

"Adams, of course."

She regarded him as if he were mad. "Samuel Adams?"

"Don't play games with me, Sephira. Not about this."

"Or what?" she fired back, her tone a match for his. She started away, but then halted, whirling back toward him. "Wait. You don't know where Adams is? Do you know if he's alive?"

"That's what I'm trying to find out from you."

"And I have no idea." She said this in a raised voice, and peered back at the others, who stared after them, tense and uncertain. "You have this wrong, Ethan," she went on, more quietly. "If I had him—or rather, if my men did—he'd be dead, and I would have my reward money from Francis's sister. And if by some chance, I hadn't yet collected, do you honestly believe I would be here, strolling along the mall?"

He had to admit, her denial had the ring of truth.

"So you didn't have that message sent to him?"

"I haven't the faintest idea of what you're talking about. Now, may I return to my stroll?"

Ethan had more questions, but, having confronted her, he didn't believe she would be able to answer any of them.

"Yes, of course. I owe you an apology."

"You do," she agreed. "I wonder if Nap isn't right about you. We've grown too familiar with each other, you and I. I sense a lack of respect on your part, just as he does. It may be that I need to put you in your place, as I have in past."

"I think you'll find that harder than you used to," he said. "And if I were you, I wouldn't look to Nap for wisdom."

She gave a sly smile. "Shall I tell him you said so?"

"He hates me enough, Sephira. Let it lie. Please."

"Well, since you asked so nicely . . ."

They walked back toward the others.

"You and Lamb make a handsome pair," Ethan said.

She glanced at him, surprise raising her brows. When he said no more, she faced forward again. "That's all? No stinging coda to your compliment?"

"That's all."

"In that case, I will thank you, and ask you to leave us."

He was more than happy to comply. If Sephira didn't have Adams, who did? And where? He, Valk, and the two Sons of Liberty needed to resume their search. Every lost moment put Adams at greater risk.

They took their leave of Sephira and her orbit of men and headed back toward the lanes of the city. As they came to Common Street, Ethan slowed again.

"No," he whispered. "It couldn't be that easy."

"What was that?" Warren asked, catching up with him.

"This way." Ethan walked on with more certainty. Soon they reached Winter Street, and then Benjamin Church's house. Ethan followed a flagstone path to the door and knocked, peering back at Warren as he did.

"Could it be this simple?" the doctor asked.

Before Ethan could speak, the door opened, revealing Hannah Church, wearing a plain linen gown of pale blue, her light hair up in a bun. Warm air wafted out of the house, smelling of cinnamon and fresh bread.

"Mister Kaille, how nice to see you. Benjamin," she called. "You have more company."

More company.

"Send them in," came the reply. Church sounded in high spirits.

Missus Church stepped back from the door and indicated with an open, delicate hand that they should enter. They filed into the house and to the common room. There to their general relief, and Ethan's embarrassment, they found Church and Samuel Adams seated comfortably before a fire, drinking tea and eating scones.

"There you are," Adams said to Ethan, his hands and head trembling somewhat with his usual palsy. "I received your missive, but Benjamin and I weren't exactly certain where to go."

"Aye, sir. May I see the note you received?"

Adams' face fell. "Yes, of course." He fished in his pockets until he found a small, crumpled scrap of parchment, which he handed to Ethan.

Ethan crossed to the nearest window and smoothed the paper.

Mister Adams,
Please meet me as soon as possible in front of King's Chapel. Tell no one where
you are headed. Come alone.
—Kaille

The hand was a fair approximation of his own, though apparently written in haste. Blotches of ink stained the parchment and one large spot partially obscured his name. This one struck him as intentional, as if the author wasn't certain of the correct spelling.

Warren joined Ethan by the window and Ethan handed him the missive before turning back to Adams.

"Did you know the lad who brought this to you, sir?"

"No, I'd never seen him before. I assumed he was an acquaintance of yours, or perhaps your wife's."

"And how is it that you wound up here, rather than at the chapel?"

"Well, I'm sorry for that, and I hope—"

At Ethan's raised hand, Adams fell silent.

"You needn't apologize for anything, sir. But you should know that I didn't write this message. I knew nothing about it and can only surmise that it was intended as a lure, to remove you from the protection of your friends and lead you into harm."

The man paled as Ethan spoke. "Oh, dear." He eyed Warren and Quincy. "All of you have been concerned for me."

"You could say that," Warren said, his tone dry.

"I'm so terribly sorry." Addressing Ethan again, he said "To answer
your question, We waited in front of the chapel for a few moments, but
then Benjamin suggested we wait here instead. He thought that you would
work out eventually where we had gone."

Ethan watched Doctor Church as Adams said all of this. The doctor
kept his eyes on the fire, his cheeks unnaturally flushed, his jaw tight. He
must have been as disturbed as the others by this ruse that had come so
close to placing their leader in peril. Ethan had to admit, though, that he
sensed as much guilt as trepidation in the man's demeanor. Did he hold
himself responsible for having failed to anticipate the ruse sooner? Or was
there something darker at work?

He didn't like thinking this way. He was new to the cause of Liberty.
Warren, Adams, Quincy, and others had known and worked with Church
for years. Who was Ethan to question the man's motives?

"You were clever to bring him here, Benjamin," Quincy said. "For all
we know, you saved his life."

Warren and Adams voiced their agreement. Church answered with a
tentative smile. He didn't look Ethan's way.

"Well, Mister Adams," Ethan said, pocketing the missive, "we should
return you to your home."

"Do you think so? Betsy and the children aren't there. I'd be alone.
Wouldn't I be safer here?"

Church glanced around the room. Ethan couldn't help but think that he
looked alarmed by the suggestion.

The truth was, Adams raised a valid point. Under any other circumstance, Ethan would have preferred that he remain here. Right now, however, he wasn't certain he trusted Benjamin Church. Yet he didn't feel confident enough in that judgment to mention his suspicions to anyone else.

"I'm reluctant to place Doctor and Missus Church in danger. That was
why—"

"Josiah and I will remain here," Warren said. "I daresay, all of us together can keep Samuel safe. And this will give us the opportunity to speak
of ideas I have for restarting non-importation."

Ethan didn't think it wise to press the matter further. "Very well, sir.
Mister Valk and I will leave you."

"Well, introduce us first, Mister Kaille," Adams said.

He stood and held out a hand to Valk. The conjurer abruptly grew diffident. He gripped Adams' hand, but could barely meet his gaze. Ethan introduced them, referring to Valk as "a friend from Philadelphia."

"A city I've often hoped to visit," Adams said. "I have great admiration for Messieurs Franklin and Dickinson."

"Yes, sir," Valk said with enthusiasm. "Thank you, sir."

They left the house shortly after. Ethan paused outside to place wardings on the house. Valk did the same and then they followed Orange Street toward Janna's tavern.

"Anna won't believe I met him," the conjurer said after a time. "She'll think I'm making it up. She's even more of an admirer than I am. She'll be jealous above all else."

"Janna was as pleased to meet him as you are. Perhaps that will make your introduction easier."

"You don't think she'll like me?" Valk asked.

"Janna doesn't really like anyone. She's prickly, to say the least. She and I are friends, but it's taken years of work."

"I see. Is she rich?"

Ethan laughed. "Hardly. She was once a slave. When she was a girl—"

Valk halted in the middle of the lane. "Wait. She's African?"

Ethan bristled. "That's right. Is that a problem for you?"

The conjurer walked on, falling in step with Ethan. "Well, I suppose not. I just . . . I'm not used to working with their kind."

Their kind.

"Well then maybe you and I should part company here, before we reach her tavern. As I said, Janna is my friend. So is Amanda Oakroot, an earth witch who is helping us. I won't allow you to insult them, or to treat them any differently than you would treat me."

"I don't mean to, Mister Kaille. I was surprised is all."

Ethan wasn't sure he believed this. He watched the man, waiting for him to elaborate.

"All right, maybe it was more than that. In Philadelphia, Africans are still slaves. I thought they were here, too."

"Some are. If Adams has his way, there won't be any slavery in Massachusetts. And I would welcome that development. If liberty is our cause, how can we enslave anyone?"

"I agree with that. We Quakers are no fans of the institution either, and Mister Franklin has spoken of abolishing the trade." He shook his head. "I never should have said what I did. I look forward to meeting her. And to meeting the earth witch."

They walked on, silent, brooding.

"I've never met a witch before," Valk said as they neared the *Fat Spider*.

"I haven't met many. But Charlotte Whitcomb is a water witch. We can't defeat her with conjurings alone. And Amanda has proven herself a powerful ally." He pointed to the rundown building looming on their right. "That's Janna's tavern."

They slowed, halted before her door. Valk eyed the building, doubt clouding his expression. Ethan understood why—the sagging roof and listing supports, the gray, weathered wood and clouded windows. The *Spider* always looked to be one strong gust of wind away from collapse.

"Is it safe?" Valk asked.

"It always has been."

They started forward only to halt again when Valk spotted the sign Janna had posted out front.

"'Marriage Smith.' What does that mean?"

"Janna traffics in love spells and elixirs intended to encourage amorous behavior among the romantically reluctant."

Valk studied the building again. "Boston is a more interesting city than I had anticipated."

Ethan grinned, opened the door, and waved the conjurer inside.

Aromas of spiced fowl and fresh bread greeted them. As always, a few patrons sat around Janna's hearth, but the tavern was far from crowded. Janna wiped the bar, and Amanda Oakroot sat opposite her with a teacup in hand. they looked up as Ethan and Valk entered.

"Who's he?" Janna asked, without so much as a "good day."

Ethan waited to answer until they had crossed to the bar. "This is Robert Valk," he said in a low voice. "He's a conjurer from Philadelphia who came here to protect Adams when he heard of the bounty." Ethan indicated the two women in turn. "This is Tarijanna Windcatcher and Amanda Oakroot."

"It's a pleasure to meet you both."

Neither woman acted particularly impressed.

"You the one who's been conjurin'?" Janna asked. "Magick's been rumblin' my tavern all day long."

"I'm one of them," Valk said. "Kaille conjured some, too. We were fighting a speller who sought to do Adams harm."

Janna looked to Ethan, as if seeking confirmation of this. At his nod, she turned back to Valk. "You hungry?"

"If you're serving whatever it is smells so good, I sure am."

That drew a smile. "You wait right there. Kaille?"

"I'll have some, too, thank you." He placed a shilling on the bar. "For both of us."

Janna retreated to the kitchen. Amanda still studied Valk, her mien conveying little warmth. None of them spoke. Janna returned with two platters of food.

Valk tore into his, but after two bites his face reddened.

"I think I need an ale," he said. "That is some spice!"

Janna chuckled and filled two tankards.

As he and Valk ate, Ethan told Janna and Amanda of the latest attempt on the life of Adams.

"We should be in the streets and not in here," Amanda said, an accusation in her tone, her eyes on Ethan. "Waiting here has been a waste of my time."

"You're right, and I apologize. But I have a thought in this regard. We can't just fight off conjurers and assassins all day. We have to find Whitcomb now and drive her from the city, or at the very least get her to remove the bounty."

"Or just kill her," Janna said, her tone pointed.

Valk pointed a chicken leg in Janna's direction. "I agree with her."

"If you ask me, Kaille," Janna went on, ignoring him, "that note that drew Adams from the *Green Dragon* was from Whitcomb herself. She was trying to get done what she wants done while savin' herself a hundred pounds."

He thought she probably was right.

"If we force her to leave Boston," she said, "she'll only take her mischief somewhere else."

"I know," Ethan said. "I've had the same thought."

"Good! Because she's evil. She's already done too much damage here."

"I agree with that, too."

"Then why not kill her and—"

"Let it be, Janna," Amanda said in a low voice. "He has his reasons, and I understand them."

Ethan expected Janna to grow angry. She didn't. She studied Amanda and then Ethan, but she held her tongue, and, after a moment, refilled Ethan's tankard, though he had barely touched his ale.

For a long time none of them spoke. The only sounds came from Valk, who devoured his food and repeatedly doused the fire on his tongue with ale. Ethan ate more slowly, his thoughts churning. At first, ideas chased themselves around his head, going nowhere. In time, though, the initial elements of a plan took shape. What he had in mind wouldn't solve all their problems. But it might be a start.

"I have an idea."

Ethan looked at Amanda, making no effort to hide his surprise. "I was about to say the same. You first."

Her brow furrowed in concentration. "I've been thinking about this for days, since we rescued your friend from that cloud over the harbor."

Valk's gaze bounced between them, puzzlement twisting his features.

"I'll explain later," Ethan said. "Go on, Amanda."

"Well, I've been wondering why the working I used on Charlotte Whitcomb's crystal didn't kill the stone." To Valk, she said, "Render it unusable, so that it wouldn't concentrate her magick for spells."

He signaled his understanding, and she faced Ethan again. "It's possible that my working did something else, something I didn't intend, something even more useful. It could have given me access to her crystal, so that it's now as responsive to my magick as it is to hers."

Ethan gawked.

She explained what she had in mind, told Ethan she needed him to bring her one item before her working could be completed. What she said drew approving nods from Janna. Mostly.

"The problem with all of this," Amanda said after laying out her plan, "is that I don't know if any of it will work. Her stone *might* respond to my magick. Or it might not. I'm not certain, and I won't be until we face her. It's possible my magick won't do a thing, and Whitcomb will kill us all."

"I think I can guard against that," Ethan said. He went on to describe his ideas, for Whitcomb and Lamb both.

"Isn't it enough to deal with one of them?" Valk asked, when Ethan had finished.

"I don't believe it is. I don't trust either of them, and I don't believe their affection for each other is a match for their ambitions. Obviously we'll do as much as we can with each. Ideally, though, we should trim both of them."

"All right," Janna said. She didn't sound entirely pleased, but she seemed to understand that, for now, the plans he and Amanda had put forward were the best for which they could hope. "Starting with which one?"

"I'll go to Lamb," Ethan said. "You and Mister Valk here should work on conjuring together, simultaneously. You and I have done it before. He's never worked with either of us. And I believe it will take all three of us to overcome Miss Whitcomb's wardings."

"All right. You come back here as soon as you're done with Lamb. Try not to get yourself killed in the process."

IX

He masked himself with a concealment spell before leaving the tavern, and from there walked to Sephira's house, hoping to determine if she had returned from her jaunt with Lamb.

A tough he didn't recognize, burly and red-haired, stood on Sephira's portico, watching the lane, massive arms crossed over an equally massive chest. He gave no indication that he heard Ethan's approach. A carriage waited behind the house, its driver leaning against the box, smoking a pipe and looking bored.

Ethan crept to the house and listened at one of the windows. He heard no voices, saw no one within the house. Assuming that Sephira and Lamb were still together, he retreated to the edge of the yard and waited.

He didn't have to linger long. He heard Sephira's laughter before he saw them. A few seconds later, they strolled into view, in much the same configuration Ethan had seen in the Common. Afton and Gordon walked together, leading them now. Sephira and Lamb followed, trailed by Mariz and Nap, both men watchful, neither of them speaking. Sephira laughed again; Ethan assumed Lamb was relating a story.

They approached the house and Sephira told Mariz to assume sentry duty on the portico.

Mariz said something Ethan couldn't hear and Sephira shrugged and entered the house. The others followed her inside, including Afton and the burly red-head. Once they were gone, Mariz stood alone, his eyes sweeping over the road and coming to rest on a spot not far from where Ethan stood, concealed by his spell.

Sephira's conjurer peered back at the closed door before stepping off the portico and wandering slowly in Ethan's direction. He walked to within perhaps ten yards of Ethan, whose alarm deepened by the moment, and then halted. He removed his pipe and a tobacco pouch from his coat pocket, filled the pipe, and lit it with a conjured flame. His spectral guide— a young man in Renaissance garb—materialized beside him, glowing a warm beige, the color of fall grasses. The specter stared straight at Ethan.

Noticing this, Mariz squinted his way, too. "Kaille?"

Ethan didn't know if his friend had come this close by chance or if somehow he had determined that Ethan was there. He longed to ask. A few days ago, he wouldn't have hesitated to reveal himself to Mariz by answering. Now though . . .

He remained still and said nothing. The specter continued to gaze his way, and Mariz watched his ghost in turn.

"If you are there, I will not reveal you to anyone. You have my word."

Maybe he should have responded. He valued their friendship and wanted it to survive this circumstance. His trust in the man, however, had been shaken by their earlier encounter. Ethan remained still, said not a word. Eventually, the specter faded from view, and a minute or two after that, Mariz wandered back to the house, leaving a fragrant cloud of smoke in his wake.

Ethan stayed where he was, afraid to give himself away with any movement at all. A half hour passed. His bad leg began to cramp simply from standing still. He stretched it slowly, silently, watching Mariz the entire time.

At last, as the sun swung low in the west, gilding clouds over the Roxbury Flats, the house door opened, revealing Sephira and Lamb. They stepped onto the portico and Sephira motioned Mariz inside. He cast one last glance in Ethan's direction, light briefly catching the lenses of his spectacles and making them appear opaque. He entered the house and closed the door.

The unfamiliar carriage emerged from behind the house, the driver steering it onto the lane and halting just where the path to Sephira's door met the street. Ethan started toward the carriage, walking slowly and giving the two draft horses a wide berth, lest they grow restive at his approach. All the while, he watched the pair on the portico.

Lamb took Sephira's hands in his own and said something to her in a voice that forced her to lean closer to him. She replied, eyes shining, a coy smile on her lips. He kissed her cheek and left, his hand holding hers until the last possible moment.

By this time, Ethan had positioned himself at the rear of the carriage, but had not yet touched the vehicle. He marked Lamb's approach, and just as the man opened the door and climbed into the carriage, Ethan climbed onto the back, clinging to the wooden frame with both hands. The vehicle continued to rock slightly as Lamb settled into his seat. An instant later, it lurched forward and started its rattling journey back to the North End.

Ethan held on tightly, his hands soon growing stiff and sore. They rolled through the center of the city and on toward Copp's Hill. The swaying of the vehicle gave Ethan's aching limbs no rest.

Eventually, mercifully, they came to a stop in front of the grand brick home that Lamb and his sister had made their own. As Lamb opened his door to climb out, Ethan jumped off the rear of the carriage.

He drew his blade, cut himself, and removed his concealment spell, following Lamb up the walk to the door. Such spells didn't wear off instantly, and in the twilight Ethan would remain difficult to see for several seconds.

So when Lamb turned at the sound of his steps, he narrowed his eyes, like a man peering into shadowed corners. "Who's there?"

"Ethan Kaille, Mister Lamb."

Lamb straightened and cast a look toward his door. Ethan thought he must be wondering if he could bolt into the house. He gestured with his blade, so that it caught Lamb's eye, and then he set the steel over his arm.

"You don't want to run," he said. "Or more to the point, you don't want me to have to stop you."

The man wet his lips. "What is it you want?"

A spell roared in the cobblestones. Ethan sensed that it came from some distance, and he assumed Janna and Valk were, at last, practicing their simultaneous conjurings.

"For now? Just to talk. Let's take a stroll, you and I. Just in case your sister is home."

Lamb eyed the house again.

"Don't do it, Mister Lamb. I'd hate to have to hurt you, but I will. I'm in no mood for games."

Lamb turned back to him, drawing himself up to his full height. "You give me your word that I will come to no harm?"

"I promise that you will come to no harm *during this conversation.* Beyond that, your well-being is entirely up to you and your sister."

Lamb didn't appear entirely pleased with this reply, but perhaps he realized that it was the best for which he could hope. "Very well."

They set out toward the crest of Copp's Hill. As the walked, Ethan felt another spell, and then a third.

"What is this about?" Lamb demanded, haughty and terse.

"I believe you know."

"I don't. And I thought you said you weren't in the mood for games."

Ethan huffed a dry laugh. "It is about the bounty your sister has placed on the life of Samuel Adams."

"That sounds like a subject you should bring up with her. I know nothing about it."

"I'm bringing it up with you, sir. I want you to understand the possible consequences of what she has done. I have pledged myself to the protection of Mister Adams, and already I have thwarted several attempts on his person. I have every confidence that I can keep him safe. But on the off chance that I fail, you should know that I will have no choice but to avenge his death."

"You're threatening Charlotte?"

"I'm threatening you. If Adams is hurt, you will be hurt. If Adams dies, you will die. I speak not only for myself, but for other conjurers and a witch who have similarly sworn themselves to Adams' service. We will make it our life's work to punish you for whatever happens to Adams."

Lamb's face had gone white, but to his credit, he maintained his air of superiority. "You will find, Mister Kaille, that I don't take kindly to threats."

Ethan said nothing. Instead, he bit down on the inside of his cheek and, tasting blood, said within his mind, *Pugnus ex cruore evocatus.*

A fist spell didn't often penetrate the warding of a conjurer, but Lamb possessed no magick. The spell pounded his gut, stopping him in his tracks and doubling him over. He clutched at his midsection, gasping for breath, his eyes bulging.

Ethan stopped walking and regarded him coolly. Yet another distant conjuring hummed in the lane. "That was one of the weaker spells I know," Ethan said, referring to his attack on Lamb.

"You told me . . . no harm would come to me . . . during this encounter."

"Aye. I lied. Just as you did when you told me you knew nothing about the reward your sister had offered for Adams' death. Come along."

Lamb unfolded stiffly, still breathing hard. His first few steps were halting and awkward.

"I can kill you any number of ways," Ethan said resuming their traverse of the hill. "I won't bother to list them all. Suffice it to say that the others who possess magick are just as capable of bringing you harm as I am. It's possible your sister can keep you safe from one of us, but not all, not forever."

He expected more defiance and false bravado from the customs man. None was forthcoming. Lamb walked gingerly, one hand straying repeatedly to the spot on his gut where Ethan's magickal blow landed. Ethan had to remind himself that this was not a man accustomed to physical confrontation. All the better.

"I take it I've conveyed my message effectively."

Resentment blazed in the man's green eyes. "Do you enjoy brutalizing people?"

Ethan laughed, knowing this would serve only to further wound the man's pride. "You call this brutalizing? Do you know what your sister has done to my friends, my colleagues, and to me personally? This is nothing, sir."

Lamb halted, livid now. "She is my *half*-sister, and I am *not* responsible for her behavior! Facts you are too willing to ignore!"

"The two of you share political leanings, you both worked to undermine the trial of Captain Preston and will no doubt do the same with the trial of his soldiers. Both of you fear and despise Samuel Adams and the Sons of Liberty. And both of you—through wheedling and intimidation—have tried to enlist me in your cause, though you know it to be diametrically opposed to my own. So, you'll have to excuse me, sir, if I struggle to distinguish between the two of you on such matters."

"My point, Mister Kaille, is that I don't control Charlotte. No one does. You speak of me changing her mind about this bounty on Adams as if it's a simple task, and I'm telling you that it's not."

"I couldn't care less if it's simple. My warning to you stands. If Adams is killed, you will die." Ethan twitched his shoulder. "If you value your life, you'll find a way to convince her. And if she values your life, she will allow herself to be convinced."

Ethan started walking again. Lamb hurried to keep up with him.

"It is a crime to threaten an agent of the Crown. I could have you arrested."

"Is it also a crime to offer money to encourage others to commit murder?"

Ethan turned onto Snow Street, heading south back toward the Mill Pond. Lamb followed.

"Charlotte hasn't handled this well," he said at length. "I acknowledge that. And I can certainly try to reason with her."

"Mister Lamb, you seem to be under the misconception that you and I are engaged in a negotiation of some sort. We're not. I have said what I came to say. Call it a threat. Call it an oath. Call it whatever you like. It does not change the essential truth that your fate and that of Samuel Adams are now inextricably linked. So long as Mister Adams is well, you have nothing to fear. But if he suffers even the most superficial of injuries . . . Well, whatever happens to him, will happen to you as well."

"You're not listening to me!" Lamb said, his fists clenched at his sides.

"Not really, no."

That silenced the customs man until they reached the end of the lane at the base of Copp's Hill and veered onto Princes Street. As they did, Ethan caught sight of a formidable figure a block ahead of them. Lamb spotted the man at the same time.

"It would seem that we have at our disposal an arbiter who can help us resolve our dispute," Lamb said with relish. "That is, if you don't flee like a thief in the night at the very sight of him."

Ethan had to concede that he would have preferred to avoid Sheriff Greenleaf. That said, though, he wasn't about to give Lamb the satisfaction of seeing him slink off.

He walked on, chin up. Lamb deflated slightly, but still he waved over his head, trying to catch Greenleaf's attention. Before long, he succeeded. The sheriff altered directions and headed for them. For now at least, he was alone.

As they drew near, Lamb called, "Sheriff Greenleaf, how fortunate we are to have met you. Mister Kaille and I—"

"Good day, Sheriff," Ethan said, talking over Lamb. "I was at the Town House today. I'm so sorry to have missed you."

Greenleaf had shown interest in what Lamb had to say, but Ethan's greeting, intended to remind the sheriff of any orders Hutchinson might have issued, soured his expression.

"Yes," Greenleaf said. "How unfortunate."

Lamb glared at them both. "As I was saying, Mister Kaille and I seem to disagree about what is permissible behavior in your fair city."

"I'm sure you do, sir. Mister Kaille can be disagreeable."

"Just so. And—"

"Unfortunately," the sheriff went on, "Other matters require my attention just now. I will have to hear of your dispute another time."

He tipped his tricorn and walked on, leaving Lamb standing in the middle of the lane, flummoxed.

"What did he mean? What other matters? He is threatening me!" he shouted after Greenleaf. "Aren't you going to do something about that?"

Greenleaf didn't break stride.

"I'm not certain he heard you," Ethan said.

"I'm quite certain he did."

"Actually, you're right. I'm certain he did, too."

Lamb rounded on him. "What have you done?"

"I've beaten you." Ethan walked away.

Lamb remained where he was. Ethan glanced back. The customs man stared after him, open-mouthed.

"Remember, Mister Lamb," Ethan called to him. He held up a hand and crossed his fingers. "Your fate and that of Mister Adams are like this."

"But Charlotte—"

Ethan halted and faced him once more. "Yes, Charlotte. I have much to say to her. Tell her to meet me on the west side of Faneuil Hall tonight at the stroke of eight."

"She won't do it."

"See that she does."

"Do you swear to come alone?"

"Certainly," Ethan said and walked on.

The sun had set, though the western sky still blazed with hues of pink and rust. To the east, the full moon broke the horizon, ovate and orange, brilliant against the velvet sky.

Ethan walked into the South End and to Purchase Street to retrieve for Amanda the item she had requested. Then he returned to the central thoroughfare and continued out along the Neck.

Night had fallen by the time he returned to Janna's tavern. Valk sat in the warmth of the hearth, eating again. Janna and Amanda stood by the bar, across from each other. Otherwise the Fat Spider was empty. Ethan assumed Janna had sent away her usual patrons.

"How did it go?" Amanda asked, as Ethan joined them and gave to the witch what she had asked him to retrieve. Valk left his table and followed Ethan to the bar.

"I believe Lamb knows what we expect of him," Ethan said, "and I'm sure he's frightened. Whether he can make any difference or not . . . that I don't know. How did your conjurings work out?" he asked of Janna.

"Not too bad. Your friend knows his way around a casting. We'll be fine."

"Good. I told Lamb that we would expect his sister at Faneuil Hall at eight o'clock. I would like you three to get there before I do. I don't want her to prepare herself in any way for an assault from three of us. Do you know how to conceal yourself and Mister Valk from a finding spell?"

"Sure, I can do that."

"You'll need to." To Amanda, he said, "Will she be able to sense you?"

"Probably. We'll be on land which gives me a small advantage. Not much though. The waterfront's close there."

"I know. But I don't think she would have agreed to meet elsewhere."

"I'll hide myself. It'll be all right."

"Should we practice spelling together?" Valk asked. "All three of us, I mean."

"I'd rather not. Whitcomb knows now that I want to meet her. She'll sense any spells we cast and could figure out what we have in mind."

"We practiced just the way you and I have done it with Mariz," Janna said. "You'll be able to match us."

"All right. The three of you should go. I told Lamb to direct her to the west side of Faneuil Hall. I'll be there precisely at eight."

Janna and Valk returned to the hearth, where Janna cast a spell that Ethan assumed would hide them from a finding. The building seemed to shake with the force of the conjuring, and Ethan begrudged even this small clue as to what they were planning. He hoped Whitcomb wouldn't glean too much from the one spell, but he knew how canny she was.

Amanda retreated to the back room of the tavern to cloak herself in her own magick. Again, Ethan hoped their precautions would be enough to fool the woman.

At half past seven, Janna led them all to the door and, once they were out on the street, locked the tavern. Janna, Valk, and Amanda headed into the city, intending to turn off of Marlborough Street long before they reached Cornhill, so that they could follow a less direct route to the hall.

Ethan lagged behind them, bathed in the argent glow of the moon, and remained on the main thoroughfare after they turned off. He walked slowly and, as he neared the center of the city, cast a warding spell, in part to catch Whitcomb's attention, and, he hoped, to distract her from the proximity of the others. As the bells on the city churches struck eight, he stepped into Dock Square and approached Peter Faneuil's grand structure.

At the eighth peal of the nearest bell, two figures emerged from the shadows on the north end of the building and approached Ethan. One he recognized as Charlotte Whitcomb. The other was a young man, pale, wide-eyed, but otherwise devoid of expression. Whitcomb gripped his arm and steered him toward Ethan.

Ethan was certain the man had no idea where he was or what Whitcomb had in mind for him. Ethan knew full well. Whitcomb had learned to cast using the lives of innocents to fuel her conjurings. This was how she had overcome Ethan's wardings in their earliest battles. He had prevented

this subsequently by casting wardings over the entirety of Boston's populace, but in his desperation to keep Adams safe, and his hurried preparations for this night's encounter, he had failed to do so again. He cut himself
now and tried to ward the young man, but he doubted he would succeed.

Whitcomb's laughter at the touch of his magick and the appearance of
Uncle Reg confirmed his fears.

"Don't you think I would have anticipated such a spell, Mister Kaille?
Your wardings won't help him. And your spells won't touch me. Now,
what do you want? Why did you call for this meeting?"

He took a chance. "After today's events, I'm eager to put an end to this
matter once and for all."

"Ah, yes. I congratulate you on getting to Adams before I did."

His blood turned cold. "So you *were* responsible for the forged missive
he received today."

"Let us say simply that if I could see to the deed myself, I would save
one hundred pounds. That's not an inconsiderable sum."

Questions swarmed in his mind. Whitcomb gave him no opportunity to
ask any of them.

"I repeat, Mister Kaille, what am I doing here? And who are you to
summon me in this way?"

Fine. His questions could wait. The time had come to tame this woman
once and for all.

"Very well" Ethan said. And raising his voice, he called, "Janna."

Janna, Valk, and Amanda walked out of Shrimpton's Lane, one of the
narrow byways opening onto the square.

"I was led to believe you would be alone," Whitcomb said, regarding
his friends with disdain, though not, he noticed, with much fear.

"Yes, I know. A deception on my part. I don't like to lie, but you and
your brother do so with such frequency that I didn't scruple to keep my
promise. I must say, I find it quite liberating telling you and Mister Lamb
what you wish to hear and then doing whatever I want anyway."

"I demand to know why I'm here."

"Because I intend to convince you to withdraw the bounty you've
placed on Mister Adams."

She laughed at this. "Do you?"

"Aye." He held his blade to his forearm. Janna and Valk did the same.

"You understand," she said, sounding smug, "that my wardings are
proof against three spells just as they are against one."

"I've no doubt. But are they proof against one spell just as they are against three?"

Puzzlement creased her brow.

Before she could ask what he meant, Ethan said, "Now."

He watched Janna to time his movements and incantation with hers, knowing Valk would do the same. The three conjurers cut themselves in unison and recited the spell as one. "*Percussio, ex cruore evocata.*" Their magick roared in the street—it seemed the earth itself were splitting asunder. The casting—a battering spell—hammered Whitcomb, making her head snap to the side as if she had been struck with a club. She released her hold on the young man and fell hard, the side of her head striking cobblestone with a dull thud.

Ethan and his companions stood a moment, Ethan's own amazement at their success mirrored on their faces.

Uncle Reg lingered at Ethan's shoulder, and Janna's spectral guide, an ancient African woman suffused with a brilliant blue glow, hovered at hers. Next to Valk, stood a third ghost: a young woman who glowed a gentle, pale green.

"I've never done anything like that," Valk said, breaking the silence. "That's the most powerful spell I've ever felt, much less conjured."

Janna took a step in Whitcomb's direction. "She fell hard. You think she might be dead?"

Ethan judged from her tone that she would have welcomed this. He walked to the prone woman and squatted beside her. She breathed still. He took her wrist in hand. Her pulse remained steady and strong.

"She'll have a headache when she wakes," he said, dropping her hand. "But beyond that she should be fine." He canted his head in the direction of the young man who had been standing with Whitcomb. "Do you think you can help him?"

"I'll try."

Ethan searched the pockets within Whitcomb's gown until he located the jagged, light blue crystal she used to augment her witchcraft. He also found a small pistol, silver with an ivory butt, that he slipped into his own pocket.

Straightening, he walked back to his companions and handed the crystal to Amanda Oakroot.

"Your turn."

She returned his gaze, grim, thin-lipped. "I don't know if this will work."

He smiled. "So you've told me. Do what you can. Nobody can ask more of you than that."

She nodded and moved off to one of the byways off the square. Ethan and Valk carried Whitcomb to another dark alley. Janna remained with the young man, casting spells intended to free him from Whitcomb's thrall.

Valk and Ethan positioned themselves at the mouth of the alley. Ethan watched the lane where Amanda worked. Valk glanced back at Whitcomb every few seconds.

"Shouldn't we heal her?"

"If you want to, you can. But she came within a hair's breadth of killing me not so long ago. I won't waste my blood on her."

Faint light, in shifting, flickering hues, emanated from where Amanda applied her workings to the crystal. Minutes passed. Bells struck the quarter hour, and then the half. Janna finally succeeded in rousing the young man from his waking stupor. After a short while, he walked off on his own, his first steps unsteady. Janna walked to the mouth of Amanda's alley and positioned herself there.

A moan from behind made Ethan and Valk turn. Charlotte Whitcomb stirred, groaned again, then turned onto her side and emptied her stomach. She tried to sit up, but collapsed onto her back once more. Ethan walked to where she lay and stood over her.

Her eyelids fluttered open and she peered up at him, squinting in the shadows and moonlight. When she recognized him, she closed her eyes again, clearly disgusted.

"What did you do to me?" Her voice was rough, thin.

"We cast as one, and so defeated your wardings. We've freed the man you intended to use to fuel your spells, and we've taken the crystal with which you concentrate your witchcraft. And if I have to put a bullet through your head before the night is out, I'm perfectly willing to do so. I'll even use your pistol."

She looked up at him again, her gaze clearing. Perhaps she heard the resolution in his words. "What do you want?"

"I've told you once."

"The bounty is offered. What do you expect me to do?"

"Withdraw it, and broadcast that withdrawal throughout the colonies as thoroughly as you did the original offer."

"Impossible"

The scrape of a boot on cobblestone made them look to the byway entrance. Amanda and Janna stood in the moonlight, stern, straight-backed. Amanda grasped a crystal in each hand. She met Ethan's glance and held up

Whitcomb's crystal for him to see.

He turned back to Whitcomb. "You had better hope you're wrong."

"What are you talking about?"

Amanda walked to where she lay and held out the crystal to her.

Whitcomb stared at the stone, at Amanda, and at Ethan. She didn't reach for the crystal right away, though he thought she trembled in anticipation of its touch.

"Don't you want it back?" Ethan asked.

"Why would you offer it?" Even as she asked the question, her eyes fixed on the stone.

"Because we don't need it anymore."

"What does that mean?"

He said nothing. Amanda stood motionless, hand extended, the crystal glinting with moon glow on her palm.

At last, as if unable to stand the temptation any longer, Whitcomb snatched the stone from her.

And the instant her fingers closed around it, light erupted from the crystal, purest white, blinding. Ethan shielded his eyes. Whitcomb flinched away, squeezing her eyes shut. Valk and Janna turned away as well. Only Amanda appeared unaffected.

Whitcomb cried out and dropped the crystal, her body spasming, the convulsion radiating up her arm and through her entire form. When it spent itself, the light faded from the stone, which now rested on the street beside her, she stared at her hand. The skin on her fingers was blackened and blistered.

"What did you do?" Tears glistened at the corners of her eyes.

"A working," Amanda said. "The most powerful I've ever attempted."

"What sort—"

"It ties your life to that of Samuel Adams."

Whitcomb's glare snapped to hers. "What?"

Amanda grinned, the first change in her expression Ethan had seen that entire evening. "That's right. Forever more, your fate and his are intertwined. If he falls ill, so will you. If he dies . . . Well, you understand."

"But what if his death is natural? A product of old age?"

"Then yours will be, too: a product of his old age."

"But he must be . . . he must be near to fifty. He's thirty years my senior."

"Yes," Amanda said. "How very sad for you."

Whitcomb studied each of them in turn, horror distorting her handsome face. "I don't believe it," she said at last. "You're lying. Such magick is beyond you."

"Just because it's beyond you, doesn't mean it's beyond me."

"But a working of that kind would require—"

The objection died on her lips. Amanda held something between her thumb and forefinger. A lock of hair, silvered by age and also by the moon. The same lock of hair Ethan had gotten from Adams earlier in the day, at Amanda's request.

"From the head of Samuel Adams," Amanda said. "With that, and with your stone, I had all I needed for the working."

Whitcomb gazed at the hair, unable to look away. Any doubt she had harbored, any hope that might have sustained her, vanished when Amanda produced that tiny tuft of hair.

With a snarl she grabbed for it, but in that same moment light flared again, a flame this time. It was green, the color of the other stone Amanda held: her own tourmaline crystal. This fire consumed the hair in the span of a single heartbeat, leaving nothing but ash and a tiny cloud of smoke, pungent with the stink of burnt hair. Whitcomb's hand hovered before her for a breath before dropping to her side.

"There is nothing you can do to undo this working," Amanda told her. "Even if you find a way to kill me, the magick will endure. So unless you care to sacrifice yourself in pursuit of Adams' life, you had better find a way to call off your assassins."

"And if that isn't enough," Ethan said, "I have told Mister Lamb that I will tie his fate to that of Samuel Adams, by deed if not magick. Are you both willing to die for this folly?"

"But what if it's too late? Already, there are men here who are intent on killing him and collecting the reward."

"Aye. I suppose they'll step over your body when they take the money from your home." Ethan tipped his hat. "Good night, Miss Whitcomb."

Together, he and his friends walked away, leaving her in the alley, in a pool of her own sick.

X

Ethan, with Valk beside him, paid a visit to the Adams house that night, apologizing to Mister and Missus Adams for disturbing them so late in the evening.

He explained as much as he could of what had transpired in Dock Square, although he didn't discuss the particulars of Amanda's working, which he thought might trouble Missus Adams.

"You believe, then, that this matter is settled?" Adams asked.

"I believe it will be soon. Miss Whitcomb and Mister Lamb have every incentive to keep you safe and thus call off the bounty they've set upon your life. I expect they'll spare none of their considerable resources in communicating to all in the colonies that they no longer intend to pay out that reward. I would prefer to continue our arrangement for a few more days, but I believe you'll be safe again before too long."

"Well, thank you, Mister Kaille. I'm most grateful. And when all of this is over, I promise to pay you what you're owed."

"Thank you, sir."

From Purchase Street, Ethan and Valk walked back to the *Dowsing Rod*, where they found Kannice and Kelf serving ales, flips, and chowder, as usual. Ethan ducked into the kitchen, removed his coat and hat, and donned an apron. For the rest of the night, he was a barman rather than a bodyguard. Valk ate and drank with the rest. At the end of the evening, Ethan and Kannice made up a room for their guest.

Ethan and the conjurer parted the next morning. Valk was eager to return to Philadelphia and his Anna. He insisted that Ethan and Kannice come to visit sometime soon.

"I know it's hard to leave a tavern unattended, but a few days of travel and adventure will do you good."

Ethan wasn't entirely convinced, but Kannice promised that they would try to make the journey.

After Valk had taken his leave, Kannice laced her fingers through Ethan's and pulled him into a kiss.

"So, Whitcomb and Lamb have been tamed. Does that mean I finally have my husband back?"

"Almost," Ethan said, knowing that wasn't the answer she wanted to hear.

"Almost?"

"There are a few conversations I must have before I can go back to being a bar hand."

She frowned. "I assume one is with Sephira Pryce."

"Mariz, actually," he said. "But I'm sure Sephira will manage to have her say. To her mind, I've cost her a hundred pounds. She won't be happy with me."

"Well, it wouldn't be morning in Boston if Sephira Pryce wasn't unhappy with you over something."

He kissed her again. "I'll be back as soon as I can be. You have my word."

Ethan left the tavern, stepping into a gray, foggy morning. The air was still and raw, and rich with the smells of the harbor: brine, ship's tar, seaweed. Gulls cried from the waterfront, and a chaise rattled past, ghostlike, the clop of horse hoofs sounding hollow and flat. He raised his collar and walked to the Adams house. He walked with Adams to the *Green Dragon* and left him in the company of several Sons of Liberty. Once he was convinced that the man was safe, he left the tavern and headed out to Summer Street.

When he reached Sephira's house, he found the Empress and her men outside, readying for a journey in the larger of Sephira's two carriages.

Sephira wore a purple cape, clasped at the neck, and a long black skirt that brushed the polished toes of her black boots. Her satin black hair was up in an elegant bun that rested at the nape of her neck.

"Ethan," she said upon spotting him.

Nap and the others, including Mariz, turned to look at him before resuming their preparations. Nap and Afton were securing horses to the front of the vehicle. Gordon sat on the driver's box. Ethan resisted the urge to ask him how the repairs on the rear wheel had gone, or to warn Nap to take extra care with the harnesses. He reached the end of Sephira's drive, but halted there at the edge of her property. He sensed that to trespass this particular morning would be dangerous.

She sauntered to where he waited. "I've just had word that the bounty on Adams has been withdrawn. I can only assume that you're responsible. That's one hundred pounds you've cost me."

"I just told Kannice that you would say as much."

"So you admit it."

"I admit being responsible for Miss Whitcomb's change of heart. I don't concede that you would have collected."

She smirked. "No, I wouldn't expect you to. Have you come to gloat then?" Before he could answer, she said, "No, that's not your way. You've come to speak with Mariz."

The conjurer stood apart from the others, staring at the ground in front of him.

"I would like a word with him, yes."

Her smile this time struck him as genuine, rich with self-satisfaction.

"I'm sure. Good day." She started to pivot away, but stopped herself. "I'm not happy with you, Ethan. Taking a job from me here and there, at a cost of a few pounds—that's one thing. This could have been lucrative. I won't forget that."

"I saved you from yourself, Sephira. You didn't want Adams dead. Not really. Think of what it would have done to this city. Boston would never have been the same, and the comfortable life you enjoy right now would have been lost to you, perhaps forever."

She considered him, weighing his words. "You may well be right. Still, I don't like being bested. Be on your guard." She walked away. As she passed Mariz, she said, "You will rejoin us in the Common."

"Yes, *Senhora*."

Sephira climbed into the carriage, as did Nap and Afton. Gordon snapped the reins and the vehicle stuttered into motion. Ethan watched it go, aware that Mariz had joined him at the edge of the lane.

"She knows we've fallen out, doesn't she?"

"I felt your spell yesterday evening, and made the mistake of saying so in front of her. She asked me why I was not helping you and I told her."

"I assume she was pleased."

Mariz didn't deny it. "I would like to think that 'fallen out' is an exaggeration," he said instead. "I would still consider you a friend, Kaille, and would like you to think the same of me."

"I do," Ethan said. "But I fear that I placed too much faith in our friendship. I expected too much of you, forgot who you work for."

"That may be, yes. My first duty is to the *senhora*. I have told you this before."

"Several times. I should have listened with more care. Our . . . disagreement was my fault, not yours. That's what I came here to say." He extended a hand, which Mariz gripped.

"I am grateful to you, and pleased that I may continue to call you a friend."

Ethan made to leave, but Mariz spoke his name, holding him there.

"As your friend, I should tell you that neither the *senhora* nor her other men are kindly disposed toward you at this time. Nap especially is your mortal enemy. He speaks often of your discourtesy toward the *senhora* and expresses a desire to put you in your place."

This was nothing Ethan hadn't sensed for himself, but hearing it set him on edge. No one would seek the enmity of any of Sephira's men, Nap least of all.

"And what does Sephira say about this?"

"Little. She does not speak ill of you, but neither does she seek to calm Nap's passions. I believe she sees some value in them. And I will confirm what you said earlier: I expect she was pleased by the notion that you and I were on poor terms. We would probably do well to appear less at ease with each other in front of the others."

"All right." Ethan shook his head, staring into the fog in the direction Sephira's carriage had gone. "I thought this would become easier once I stopped thieftaking."

"As we all did," Mariz said. "That may be what troubles the *senhora*. You told her that you are no longer her rival, but little has changed. The two of you are still at odds, and your presence in the lanes seems undiminished."

Ethan responded with a grim smile. "You sound like my wife. Thank you, Mariz. I'll give that some thought."

They walked up Summer Street together, parting with another handshake at Marlborough Street. Mariz continued straight, toward the Common. Ethan turned and made his way out to the Neck and Janna's tavern.

So early in the day, the door to the *Fat Spider* was still locked when Ethan arrived. Amanda let him in and led him to the kitchen, where Janna stirred a vat of dark, fragrant stew. Ethan told them what he had heard from Sephira—that the bounty had been withdrawn—and he thanked them for their help the night before.

"Never mind that," Janna said. "You been paid yet?"

She glanced at Amanda and they both laughed.

"You'll be the first to know when I have been."

"You know," Janna said, "all we did was protect Adams. Whitcomb is still a danger. I warned you she would be if we let her live."

"I know. And I told you I wasn't prepared to kill her. Were you, truly? Would you have murdered her last night?"

Janna stared at him for several seconds before shaking her head. "No," she said, her voice low. "I'm no killer. And I know you're not either. In this instance, I might prefer that you were, but then we wouldn' be friends, would we?"

"Probably not." He turned to Amanda. "Will you be heading home soon?"

She nodded. "Later today. But I'll be around again. I like the city more than I thought I would."

"I'm glad. I can't thank you enough for all you've done these past couple of weeks. I shudder at the thought of what might have happened without you here to help us."

"It was my pleasure. You're welcome in Milton any time."

Ethan shook her hand, bid farewell to Janna, and left the tavern.

As he walked up Orange Street, his thoughts returned to something that had struck him the day before, when Adams went missing and again when he spoke of this with Charlotte Whitcomb. He took a slight detour and stopped in at a house along the way to the center of the city. The person he sought there wasn't at home. He continued on, back to the *Green Dragon*.

Entering the tavern, he saw that Adams was deep in conversation with Warren, and also with William Molineux and the well-respected North End silver smith, Paul Revere.

The man Ethan sought, however, sat alone at a nearby table, sipping from a cup of Madeira. Ethan approached and cleared his throat.

Benjamin Church looked up, surprise registering in the deep-set eyes. "Mister Kaille."

"May I sit, Doctor?"

"Of course." He indicated the chair opposite his own.

Ethan lowered himself into it, checking their surroundings as he did. No one had taken notice of his arrival.

"What can I do for you?" the doctor asked.

Ethan didn't answer. He stared at the man, scrutinizing his face—the hooked nose and weak chin and high cheekbones—wondering if his nondescript aspect and mild demeanor masked the heart of a traitor.

"Mister Kaille?"

"You know that the Sons of Liberty hired me to protect Mister Adams."

Church's brow creased. "Well, yes, of cou—"

"And you may know as well that even if I hadn't been hired, my devotion to the cause of liberty is complete."

"I'm glad to hear it," the doctor said, still sounding puzzled.

"I tell you this because I feel it's important that you realize the depths of my sense of duty to Mister Adams and all he holds dear."

Church set down his cup. "Perhaps you should just come out and say what is on your mind."

"Perhaps you should lower your voice," Ethan said. "For your own sake."

The doctor went still for an instant, then reached for the cup once more, his hand steady. He was composed. Ethan had to give him that.

"I don't believe I understand you."

"I've been trying to make sense of what happened to Mister Adams yesterday. His mysterious departure from the *Dragon*, the forged note, the fact that he wound up at your house. The sequence of events perplexed me. Until last night, when Charlotte Whitcomb said something about it."

Ethan sensed that Church was reluctant to ask. But he did. "And what was that?"

"She congratulated me on finding Mister Adams before she did. It seems she was responsible for the false message he received."

"Why tell me this?"

"Why indeed." Ethan leaned forward, his eyes boring into Church's. "I can't yet prove anything, doctor. But I have been a thieftaker for many years, and I have unraveled more daunting mysteries than this one. I will be watching you, tracking your every move, monitoring your every conversation, doing all I can to uncover the truth. And the moment I can prove what you and I know to be true—that you are guilty of the worst sort of treachery, that you have turned your back on men who consider you a friend and a fellow soldier in a battle for our very freedom—I will expose you for what you are."

He thought the doctor would respond with denials, with a show of outrage and righteous anger. He did none of these things. He stared back at Ethan, lips tight, his face pale save for bright red spots high on his cheeks.

Before either of them could say more, someone called to Church by name.

They both turned, and Samuel Adams, who had been walking their way, halted in mid-stride. "Mister Kaille! I had no idea you had arrived."

"Yes, sir," Ethan said, getting to his feet.

"I suppose you're ready to accompany me home."

"I'm in no rush, sir. Take your time."

"Then you'll let me buy you an ale?"

"It would be my pleasure, sir."

Adams put an arm around his shoulder and steered him toward the bar. Ethan glanced back at Church, but the doctor hadn't moved. He gazed straight ahead, hands resting on the table before him, his expression inscrutable.

XI

Ethan returned to the *Dowsing Rod* late in the day, in time to help Kelf and

Kannice with final preparations for the evening rush. He didn't speak of his confrontation with Church, nor did he intend to. Not with anyone, not yet. Certain though he was of the ugly truth, for now he had no evidence.

When their long night of work ended, Ethan and Kannice retreated to their room and their bed and the gentle comfort of candlelight and quiet passion. After, as she traced his unshaven cheek with a soft finger, Kannice asked him if he was all right.

He took a long time to respond.

"I am," he told her, capturing her hand and kissing it.

"Then why so quiet?"

"People think it's ending," he said. "The first trial is over. The second won't last long. Samuel Adams is lamenting the end of non-importation. He fears the cause of liberty is dying before his eyes."

"And you disagree?"

He turned to her. Her periwinkle eyes shone with candle flame and wisps of auburn hair hung over her smooth brow. She was so lovely. In that moment, he could easily have been convinced to give up the lanes and return to the tranquil life of a bar hand. Sephira Pryce would have been pleased.

"I do," he said. "Adams may fear the movement has stalled, but London and the Crown's agents here in Boston—they're terrified." He thought of Lamb, of Whitcomb, of Church. "They're doing all they can to prove Adams right, and they're failing. They know they are, and soon enough Adams and the others will realize it, too. All's calm just now, but I believe that's an illusion."

"When did you become such an expert in the matters of politics?"

He grinned. "I don't know, but I'm sure it's your fault."

Their amusement faded.

"Are you frightened?" she asked.

"A little, yes. Of the uncertainty, mostly. But I'm also hopeful. Their fear makes them dangerous. It also exposes their weakness."

"I take it this means you'll be doing more work of the sort you've done these past few weeks."

"Aye, I believe it does. If you'll allow it."

She leaned in and kissed his lips. "I will. Naturally. And should you need a place to meet, other than the *Green Dragon* that is, I expect you to use the *Dowser*."

"So you can keep an eye on me?"

"Partly. And partly because having Samuel Adams here is bound to be good for business."

He laughed. She blew out the candle and nestled against him.

"I'd like to think that your magick gives our side an advantage," she said in the darkness. "But I suppose the Crown has conjurers and witches, too, doesn't it?"

"Too many," Ethan said. "And they have allies everywhere. Even in places we wouldn't think to look."

He felt her shift, lift her head.

"That sounds ominous."

"It does, I know."

When he didn't say more, she asked, "That's all? You're not going to explain?"

He should have kept silent. "I believe there's a Crown agent within the Sons of Liberty."

"Do you know who it is?"

"I know nothing for certain."

"But you suspect someone."

Another pause. "Aye," he breathed.

"I see. I won't ask you more. But have a care, Ethan. If this person knows you suspect him, he's likely to come after you."

Ethan knew she was right. He kissed her again, and she lay back against him. He stroked her arm, staring into the darkness, wondering if his ultimatum to Church had been a grave mistake.

Before long, he decided it hadn't. True, he might have placed himself in some peril. But he had also issued a necessary warning. Maybe Church would think twice before acting against the Sons of Liberty again.

Kannice soon fell asleep, her breathing slow and steady. Ethan remained awake, listening to the creaks of the building as it settled, the bark of a distant dog, the low whistle of the cold wind blowing off the harbor.

He had tasted winter in the day's air. The city slumbered for now, and would for a time. It wouldn't take much, though, to wake her again: a thought that inspired both apprehension and hope.

Author's Note

As far as we know, there was no plot against the life of Samuel Adams, magickal or otherwise, in the fall of 1770 or anytime before or after. That said, the conditions that led to my fictional scheme were real enough. By October 1770, non-importation—the agreement among Whig merchants to refuse to import goods made in England—had fallen away in New York and Pennsylvania and was on the verge of doing so in Boston as well. Captain Thomas Preston, the commanding officer of the soldiers who opened fire on the King Street mob on 5 March 1770, was acquitted of all charges. Few expected his soldiers, whose trial would begin in early November, to face any serious punishment. Agitation for liberty did appear to be lessening. Boston was entering a period of relative calm that would last for a couple of years.

The desire for liberty, however, lived on, as did efforts by the Crown and its representatives to make this period of quiescence permanent. We do not know exactly when Doctor Benjamin Church, a member in good standing of the Sons of Liberty, began to spy on his fellow patriots. His treachery was not exposed until 1775, when his infamous correspondences with General Thomas Gage were made public. I have chosen to hint at earlier betrayals, not because I possess historical proof that they took place, but rather because they make for interesting narrative possibilities. I hope you will indulge and enjoy this liberty I have taken with the historical record. I certainly intend to have fun with this new story element in future Thieftaker tales.

— DBJ

About the Author

D.B. Jackson/David B. Coe is an award-winning author of historical fiction, epic fantasy, contemporary fantasy, and the occasional media tie-in. His books have been translated into more than a dozen languages. He has a Masters degree and Ph.D. in U.S. history, which have come in handy as he has written the Thieftaker novels and short stories. He and his family live in the mountains of Appalachia.

Visit him at http://www.dbjackson-author.com and http://www.davidbcoe.com.

CPSIA information can be obtained
at www.ICGtesting.com
Printed in the USA
BVHW031029291121
622769BV00007B/283